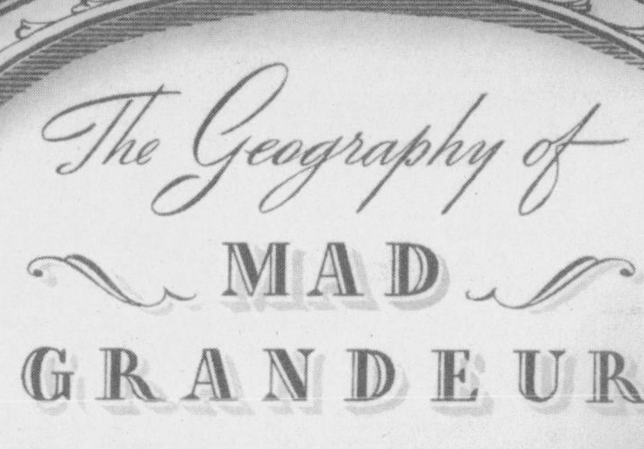
The Geography of
MAD
GRANDEUR
ATHLONE
ROUTE OF MARTYN-LYNCH
....FROM CASTLEBAR TO DUBLIN....
LUCAN
CLONMACNOISE
R. Liffey
DUBLIN
WICKLOW
WICKLOW HEAD
Landing of d'Estournelles
IRISH SEA
WEXFORD
VERNON SISSON, Designer

Books by
OLIVER ST. JOHN GOGARTY

GOING NATIVE
TUMBLING IN THE HAY
I FOLLOW ST. PATRICK
AS I WAS GOING DOWN SACKVILLE STREET
AN OFFERING OF SWANS
POEMS AND PLAYS
WILD APPLES

Mad Grandeur

Mad Grandeur

A NOVEL BY

Oliver St. John Gogarty

J. B. LIPPINCOTT COMPANY

PHILADELPHIA *NEW YORK*

PRINTED IN THE
UNITED STATES OF AMERICA

DEDICATION

My dear Mrs. Comstock,

There is, as you know, in the grounds of your country house at Wyckoff, a large, light brown building which looks like a church without a steeple.

It is lighted on each side near the roof by three windows framed in apple green, and by a long, raised lantern in the roof itself, which gives it from within the appearance of a yacht.

A door of glass on the south side opens on an apple tree, and beyond it to the continuous woods of the Ramapo range of mountains, which from afar girdle twice five miles of paradise with a double wall of translucent blue.

Clear water rises beside it from its roofed-in stony well.

This building is about nineteen yards long from the hall to its manorial fireplace, by which a little window permits one to gaze out upon the far-flung, flawless scene.

Silence stills the sunbright air like dew. This is about the biggest building used for domestic purposes I have ever known. This is where your artist son worked; and this you were kind enough to place at my disposal when he went to join his regiment. Under its timbered roof I have sailed to many lands over many seas, including the Sea of Time.

This tale of the Eighteenth Century I gratefully dedicate to you. If it bring back any of the breadth and liberality of that great period you will realize how appropriate is this little token of my gratitude and homage to yourself.

OLIVER ST. JOHN GOGARTY

Contents

BOOK I

BOOK II

BOOK III

Mad Grandeur

BOOK I

I. THE TOUCHER BRINGS TIDINGS

HYACINTH MARTYN-LYNCH roused himself to fuller consciousness. The bride who had fallen asleep on his arm the night before was gone. He heard a faint rustling. Raising himself on an elbow, he looked across the room. There against a window in the morning glow stood Ninon, brushing her long, sleep-tangled hair. He gazed in admiration at her graceful gestures. How long, he wondered, could he observe her unobserved?

She put by the comb and taking a small lace cap from the dressing table began to adjust it to her crown of hair. She would turn soon and see him watching her. Knowing that this would end his opportunity of taking her by surprise, Hyacinth said:

"That nightgown of yours is perfectly transparent against the window."

"Oh!" Ninon exclaimed, and made a hasty and embarrassed search for a covering. Finding none, she blushed and ran to the bed. "Let me in," she said, turning back the covers with a sweep.

"Oh, Ninon, darling, how cold you are. What have you been doing? How long have you been up?"

"I did not want you to wake up to find me all untidy. You are not to toss my hair again."

It hung down in two long plaits, one on either side, by her simple, almost childish nightgown.

Hyacinth looked at the little cap by which she sought to give herself a matronly air.

"Where did you get that?" he asked. "It looks like something that was chosen for you by your Aunt Penelope. Why must a newly married woman try to be matronly all at once? Twenty lace caps would not make you look old. So you may as well take it off."

"Can't I wear it for my birthday? I'm twenty today. And I got a dozen of those caps of Carrickmacross lace for a wedding present and a birthday present both."

"Penelope?"

"Yes. She chose them."

Ninon cast down her eyes as if she had been found wanting. He hastened to admire the cap of which he had just disapproved. It would never do to make her feel disconsolate on the first morning of her married life.

It would never do to quarrel with anything Aunt Penelope had done. She was the half sister of Colonel Lynch, who had willed Hyacinth his broad acres; her brother was Sir Richard de Vesey. Aunt Penelope had had the care of the two orphan girls, the late Colonel's daughters, Ninon and Mabel. Ninon had married Hyacinth Martyn, cousin and nearest male kin of her father, the Colonel, who had expressed a wish in his will that Martyn should not let the name Lynch die but should add it to his own. So Ninon's husband had become Martyn-Lynch. Hyacinth had yet to accustom himself to the suffix, and his friends continued to call him Martyn.

With her pretty cap on, it was obvious that Ninon did not intend to seek again to be pillowed on Hyacinth's arm, early though it was. He lay and stared at the ceiling, wondering with slight amusement what notions of married life Aunt Penelope had harboured when she took Ninon shopping to buy her trousseau. Aunt Penelope was an "old maid," but not in any disparaging sense of that term, for Aunt Penelope was serenely independent of men.

While Ninon was sitting up in bed, tying the ribbons in the bosom of her nightgown into pretty bows, Martyn-Lynch heard the sound of hooves on the cobbles immediately under his window. He heard a man dismount and he guessed that the silence that ensued was due to the act of tying the horse to the area railings. Soon it was broken by a knocking on the hall-door. There was only one servant in the house, an old retainer named Judy who slept in the basement and acted as caretaker of the town house in Dublin which

Colonel Lynch had left to Martyn with his name. Hyacinth and his bride had welcomed the opportunity of using it for the sake of the sanctuary it afforded after the rounds of entertainment which had preceded their marriage. Here they were resting for a few days before setting out to take over from the builders their new county mansion in County Mayo.

The knocking grew louder.

"Damn the fellow, whoever he is. What can he want at this hour?" Hyacinth took his watch from a bracket at the bed's head. "I would look out of the window if the fool had not wakened the neighbourhood. All eyes are on the house now," he remarked.

Ninon said, "Judy will let him in."

"I will go down and try to get a glimpse of him from the study window," Hyacinth said as he put on his dressing gown. "Judy may not have heard the knocking, and he has not rung the bell."

Ninon pulled the bell rope in the bedroom. Far down in the basement the bell could be heard ringing. Meanwhile Hyacinth descended to the front room. He pulled aside the curtains and the blind and saw a broad-faced, brown-eyed man of middle height and thirty five years of age or a little under.

The man's quick eyes caught the slight movement of the shade. A hand went up to the forehead and off came a hat. Its owner made a profound bow. He could not possibly have seen who it was that had moved the blind, but apparently he was ready for every emergency and elaborately courteous. Hyacinth could see no harm in his visitor and his curiosity was whetted. He waited for Judy to admit the caller, and as he returned to his room, he could hear an argumentative discussion in the hall. He caught the phrase, "A personal and confidential dispatch from Headquarters. Tell Mr. Martyn that or it will be the worse for ye if ye don't."

As Judy gasped, the caller took the opportunity to inform her further:

"And the emissary is Mr. Plant."

When Hyacinth entered the bedroom Ninon asked excitedly:

"Who can it be? And what has happened? Hyacinth, my darling, you are looking very serious. What can it be?"

Hyacinth was thinking hard. Where had he seen that face? And what were the associations that it brought up in his mind? Of course —horses! The race track! Had anything happened to his race horse, Green Glint? If so the news would not be sent to him for no one knew that he was its owner; it was in the name of his friend and kinsman, Denis St. George. Unless the messenger was from Denis himself, he could not have come with tidings of the horse's form.

Judy entered.

"There's a queer betwixt-and-between down in the hall, yer Honour, who says that he has something personal and confidential to tell you. He'll tell it only to yourself and it took him three days to find you and the three days are gone waste already and he must see yourself."

Ninon looked at Hyacinth and then at Judy.

"Put him in the sitting room. You cannot leave him standing in the hall," she said.

"Well, since it's yer own orders, I will," Judy said, and left the room.

As Hyacinth Martyn-Lynch was drawing on his stockings he exclaimed suddenly:

"Darling, I will take my oath that he comes with tidings of the Baronne and the Chevalier. They were to leave Brest in the first week of this month if they could persuade the owner of a fishing boat to take them. Good Heavens! Just imagine, the whole arrangement went out of my head. If they arrived and were not met and smuggled inland, they would be imprisoned and held pending identification from France. No one dares to enter the country without a special permit from the Government."

Ninon was puzzled. She took up the last part of Hyacinth's statement.

"But could they not be identified?" she asked.

"Of course, of course, in time," Martyn answered. "But the boat that brought them would be confiscated. And we cannot send an Irish boat near the coast of France. It is all clear to me now. The man downstairs is Toucher Plant and he is sent here by Tiger Roche."

Getting no answer Hyacinth looked around. His wife stood with her hands clasped against her neck.

"Toucher Plant and Tiger Roche. They must be terrible people."

Hyacinth laughed. "The Tiger may be terrible to the Toucher. That's as it should be. That is how the Toucher is controlled. The Tiger got his alarming appellation from the lower classes—foot-pads and highwaymen whom he harasses, aided by other young bucks enlisted by him in his Society for Aiding Order. Some such society for helping the night watchmen is sorely needed in this unprotected town, where a citizen's life is not safe near the Liberties or in the back streets after nightfall. Oh, there are a lot of less useful people than Tiger Roche."

"How did he know we were here?" Ninon asked after a pause.

"Egad!" Hyacinth said in surprise. "That is rather remarkable. But I suppose that there is little that goes on in this town, even a quiet honeymoon, that Plant, the factotum of the Tiger, does not know."

"I have heard Uncle Richard speak of his French cousin, but I had not heard that the Chevalier was coming to Ireland."

"He is coming to Ireland until things settle down in France and there is a chance of having his estates restored. Your Uncle Richard thought that it would be far wiser for him to come here to Ireland than to attempt to enter England. It would make for less ill-feeling, for one thing, with those ruffians who are in power in Paris."

"But who is la Baronne?"

"La Baronne is the widow of le Baron de Ronquerolles, another French relative of your uncle with whom he was more or less brought up when he was sent as a little boy to France. The lady was left desolate in an out-of-the-way part of the mountainous southwest in a lonely chateau. The peasants murdered her husband only last year when he and she thought that the Terror was over."

"Murdered? Why was he murdered?"

"God alone knows why peasants murder people. But Uncle Richard asked that she be brought over when the Chevalier tried the seas. It seems Uncle Richard has fond memories of her from his days in France, and now that she is widowed, he is particularly anxious for her safety."

"And to think that Uncle Dick never told me a word about it at all!" Ninon seemed put out till Hyacinth said:

"He told me only three weeks ago when he got the information about the probable date of their arrival. 'Got Roche to see this through,' he said. You know how peremptory your uncle can be? And I think that this is Roche's messenger who is waiting. I hope it is he and that there is still time to meet them."

So saying, Hyacinth left his bride and went downstairs to interview the "emissary."

When he entered the room off the hall he could see no Mr. Plant. Either Judy had drawn the curtains of only one window or the Toucher had put them back again.

"Your Honour's servant." The words came from the darkness of the end of the room.

"Why are you standing in the dark over there? Come out into the light, and let me see you. Who are you?"

"I'm the man that cheered yer Honour at yer Honour's wedding. Out of consideration for yer Honour I was hiding my boots." Hyacinth saw that if the condition of the boots were to be accepted as evidence, their wearer had ridden hard and far.

"It's far I have ridden this morning since the break of light," the Toucher said. "Ye'd think that the Rocky Road to Dublin was as smooth as yer hall, the way the old mare took it when she smelt that there was something outrageously important in the air. The news come through this morning that they'll be here this night."

"You are Toucher Plant," Hyacinth said. "I think you told my servant that the news arrived three days ago."

"I had to ascertain that you were not at Martyn Hall nor at Marino nor out with the Earl of Meath, and it took me three days to find your domicile." The Toucher seemed aggrieved.

"You said just now that the news came through this morning." If Martyn-Lynch sought to embarrass the Toucher he failed.

"Aye. So it did. It was here before in rumour but this morning it was confirmed. Confirmed enough to satisfy Mr. Roche. The French Quality is coming in from the sea tonight at Wicklow, he says. The fishermen got wind of it three days ago, them that were leaving Brest at the same time as the Quality was putting out."

"I must say that you choose a nice hour of the morning to waken my house. Has not Sir Richard taken this matter in hand? He knows well that I cannot leave town at this very moment."

"Oh, indeed he does, yer Honour. He's setting out himself. He may be gone to meet them by this, for all I know; but I thought you would like to know. His niece is gone with him to take the lady off the boat."

This was indeed news to Martyn. He would tell Ninon the moment he heard all that the Toucher had to say. Richard had purposely spared him the journey, because he did not want to separate lovers on their honeymoon. So he had taken Ninon's younger sister, Mabs, to meet la Baronne. This did not look as if the attempt to land in the face of coast-guards, patrols and watchers were so difficult as he had been led to think.

"I understood that no one but some Wicklow fishermen was in the secret and allowed to meet those who are landing. How comes it then that Sir Richard can not only go himself but take his niece?"

The Toucher was contrite.

"Yer Honour got me wrong. Excuse me style. It's a bit variegated, as Mr. Roche would say. What I wanted to convey to yer Honour is that it is not advisable for anyone but those that has an excuse like fishermen to approach the coast. No; and for that matter not wise for them that arrives by night to be seen together. We cannot even have saddle horses within five miles of the rock. That's what has brought out Sir Richard: to bring the gentleman back in his chaise and his niece to take the lady to a cottage for a night's sleep till I drives the both of them to town in the morning. It's all well planned by the Tiger—yer Honour's pardon—I mean Mr. Roche. Nothing can go wrong with them plans barring an informer or a calm at sea. And I am of opinion that Mr. Roche is in a position to rule the informer out." A wry smile spread over the broad face of the Toucher.

Martyn asked, "But how can they be met?"

"Only by those concerned. By the fishermen. If they are caught they'd have to be caught in the act of haulin' them up the cliff, and even then who's to know that they haven't saved them from a wreck or that they are escaped prisoners of war? One of the fishermen will take the gentleman to where I shall be in readiness to receive him, which will be a few miles from the road. The cousin—" he checked himself—"the other fisherman will take the lady to the cottage where Sir Richard's niece will be."

"If possible let me understand you," Hyacinth said. "As far as I can judge, the arrangement is that some fishermen whom you know are to bring the émigrés ashore tonight. They are to separate at once. You are to wait until the gentleman is brought to you, so that you may bring him to Sir Richard. Meanwhile, the lady is to be taken to a cottage where Miss Mabel Lynch will meet her and house her for the night. You will drive them to Dublin in the morning. Sir Richard will drive in with the gentleman."

"Yer Honour has it at first offer," Plant exclaimed enthusiastically. "There's one thing that ye haven't got because I hadn't time to reveal it to you. And it's this, yer Honour. Mr. Roche says that it would be no harm if the lady and gentleman were to go as far inland as soon as possible into the country and not to keep knocking about Dublin where there is sure to be talk."

"You may assure Mr. Roche that neither the lady nor the gentleman will be likely to be seen knocking about Dublin. But you have not told me why it was necessary for you to come knocking so early upon my door. That act was hardly ordered by Mr. Roche. Did he send you here?"

The Toucher hung his head. He seemed unduly embarrassed. It was not wise to prevaricate about the Tiger. So the Toucher could only tell a halftruth.

"'Sir Richard will meet the Chevalier,' he says. 'His cousin has just been married,' he says, 'and that is enough to keep him out,' he says. 'But, of course, he will be soon informed,' he says. 'And the sooner the better,' he says. That is what brought me here. Sir Richard has already set out. I thought that if Mr. Roche thought that you should be informed the sooner the better, there was not much time to lose. So I came with the message the minute the boys confirmed it on the coast. I must be getting back as soon as I can. That is what has me in such a hurry. With Sir Richard gone there was no one but yourself."

Hyacinth looked at the strange figure, who stood before him with downcast eyes. He tried to guess what was in the Toucher's mind, and he was not left long in doubt.

"One never knows rightly what emergencies may arise," the Toucher added. "And Sir Richard's gone."

Martyn-Lynch realized the implication.

"So it's money you want?" he asked. "I am quite sure that Sir Richard has made all necessary provision, but I cannot be sure that your requirement may not be genuine. So in order to be on the safe side, how much do you want?"

The Toucher assumed a magnanimous air of devotion to a common cause. He pretended to make a rapid calculation. Then in an impersonal voice, "Five guineas should be ample," he said.

When Ninon came down to breakfast, Hyacinth had all the news with its details for her.

"How exciting!" she exclaimed. "Fancy escaping in a fishing boat out of revolutionary France and running two blockades. I do hope that nothing amiss may happen. Could we not go down to meet them in Wicklow?"

"That is just what we cannot do," Martyn said.

"But Mabs is there, or going there," Ninon said, protesting.

"Our presence near the coast might arouse the suspicion of the already suspicious coast-guards and lead to the discovery and arrest of our visitors as they landed. Let us wait until they arrive here in Dublin. It is quite possible that they may come with us to the country. The farther inland they go, the safer they will be. People from

France are not welcomed to Ireland by the Government, which has just scotched a rebellion attributed to the example of the late Revolution in France."

Ninon said, "But the Government could not be so stupid as to think that a friend of Uncle Richard's like the Chevalier would come over here to foment a revolution. Is he not the victim of one himself?"

"Who are we to set a limit to the stupidity of any government?" Hyacinth replied, and kissed his wife before she could answer.

II. A LANDING FROM FRANCE

TOGETHER THEY LAY chest downward on the top of the Black Rock. The long dark man, the older of the two, was Bill Tyrrell from the little fishing village of Arklow some miles down the coast—Arklow, that still held some of the sailor breed whose eyes took their color from the sea.

They were gazing from the cliff's edge over the water some fifty feet below. Their dark blue jerseys, their sea boots and even their faces were obscured by the night.

Tyrrell's cousin lay beside him. He had chosen his cousin, for this was an enterprise that admitted of no leakage of information; an incautious word might mean discovery and death. These were taciturn men.

A little light burned steadily out at sea. It would have been impossible for ordinary eyes to judge its distance from shore, whether a mile or only a few hundred yards.

The night was dark and calm, the sea still as a mill pond. The tide was at its height. At the foot of the rock the self-erasing water flowed, the same sea that had borne out the glory of Ireland in the fifth century to harass the frayed edge of the Roman Empire. The same sea that had borne St. Patrick as he and his companions sailed northward past the Black Rock after their repulse near Arklow centuries ago. The sea that had borne in the town-founders, the devastating Danes and after them the Norman castle-builders and the English in their turn, to hold, civilize and exploit the land.

The sea was invisible from the cliff. The men could hear its sigh as it subsided slowly in the darkness and rose against the sheer rock.

"I wouldn't say but that it would be about midnight now," Tyrrell's companion remarked after a long look at the steady light.

"Aye," the big man answered.

As he spoke the light went out. "Well done!" he exclaimed, when apparently it almost immediately appeared again. But it was not the same light that reappeared. It was the signal prearranged.

The first light shone from Tyrrell's boat, which was manned by his three sons. It had been fishing all day in full sight of the guards of the coast. At nightfall the fishermen had lit their light and, if any of the coast watchers were observing them, he would be indeed a quick-witted and alert man to discover that the lamp that for a moment went out was not lit again. The light that instantly took its place was the light of a Breton fishing boat.

All day long Tyrrell's sons had cruised in their boat in sight of shore. Few fishermen ventured far out these days for fear of being captured by the French, who had taken many a brave barque and merchant ship and brought them into Havre or Brest as prisoners of war. It was not unusual for a boat to be fishing all day and keeping so near to shore. It would have been unusual if they had not lit the boat's lamp as night fell.

The men on the Black Rock had been anxious, for the fall of the wind might have brought the French boat in late and they dare not linger till the dawn. But with that suddenly obliterated light that had reappeared so quickly, their anxiety was relieved. The boats had met out there on the dark water. One of the boys would board the Breton vessel and pilot her gently to the face of the rock, to fend her off as best he could until the precious freight was landed and taken safely up the rock-hewn stair. Then he too would land, and be helpful in setting the two passengers safely on the invisible shore. He would leave his brothers at their fishing or to anchor without a riding light until the French boat got away.

It had been planned thus because if they had changed vessels and if they were surprised at the landing, the French travellers would be trapped, for they could not get away and back to France in the boat of local men. The bargain had been made with the Bretons to land their passengers under the headland on the Irish coast, where all assistance would be given. The Bretons could make no landing except after dark, for there were three British ships of the line in Dublin Bay, and many frigates continually on the watch for vessels which might bring Frenchmen of another and very different class—Revolutionaries—to Ireland.

Not the least consideration, though one not insisted upon by the Tyrrells, was the consideration of their own safety. They would not be implicated in the action of a foreign boat, whereas if taken with French people in their own boat in perilous times like these, it would be difficult to prove that they were not aiding agents of the Directory to enter the country and to foment a Revolution as bad as that which had but lately bathed France in its best blood. All Frenchmen were suspect in Ireland; it mattered not that these two were victims of Revolution. By the time that was proved, their smugglers would have been hanged.

It was precisely because the two French travellers were of the aristocracy that their identity would be difficult to establish. As aristocrats, they had been obliged to leave France as surreptitiously as they were entering Ireland, with nothing to show that Le Chevalier d'Estournelles had been a Colonel in the Imperial Guard before His Majesty Louis XVI fell a victim to the Insurgents who made the Revolution. He had been at the Court of St. James's but was now an émigré seeking refuge from the spleen of the post-revolutionary remnants of the voracious gang of lawyers who composed the Executive in Paris. Clemente, his travelling companion, was the widow of d'Estournelles' half brother, the only son of his mother by her second marriage. They had been lucky enough to persuade the Breton fishermen to take them out of France. The fishermen, though least affected by the politics of the Republic, had the love of the Chouans for aristocrats.

Once d'Estournelles had acceded to the terms of the fishermen he had, by landing at night, laid himself open to imprisonment for such irregular conduct. If caught, he would probably be left to linger in gaol for days or even weeks before, in these distracted times, he could obtain a hearing at Dublin Castle. And prejudiced as imprisonment would make his case the demand would be enforced for evidence of identification, evidence impossible to obtain from France. The Irish Government had reason to be suspicious of everyone entering Ireland from the continent. Although they had crushed the premature rebellion fomented by the excesses of their soldiery in Wexford, there was much evidence that the country was far from being at ease, and every indication that it would be incited to rise by agents provocateurs who had stolen in from France under various disguises. Might not the Chevalier be a self-styled aristocrat but really an agent of the Directory in Paris? It would take time to discover that he was an aristocrat but if he could enter the country without consulting the Government, very well then, the onus of producing proof of his bona fides lay on him. The Irish Government might not wish to let a possible Philip Egalité escape.

He had taken the only way he could to get out of a country where, though the people were sick of successive revolutions which had placed so many mean and rapacious rascals at the head of affairs, there was no security as yet for an aristocrat with unconfiscated property.

His half brother, Baron de Ronquerolles, whose lands lay far to the south near Grasse by the Mediterranean, had fallen a victim to the local *sans-culottes* who leapt up for a moment like a flame from a fire that was thought to be extinguished. They murdered him, though he had been passed over in the general Revolution, because they coveted his land.

D'Estournelles was not yet proscribed as an émigré. But he and Clemente had relations by blood and marriage with prominent landowners in Ireland. It was to these he was bringing the little widow, and was coming himself to live for a time—at all events until the reaction against the Republic should grow and his estates which had not been as yet confiscated restored in a new order.

And to one of these kinsmen, Sir Richard de Vesey, he owed his safety up to this point on the Irish sea. He would follow whatever plans Sir Richard had devised for him on land.

Tyrrell and his companion were silent as the boat approached the shore. Presently voices came strangely from the sea—just a word or two in muffled tones.

The tall man rose with his arm and shoulder in a noose of rope. On his back a dark lantern was slung.

"Hold hard now. I'll go down," he said.

He disappeared over the cliff's sea face, climbing down rugged little steps so old and weather-worn that they hardly afforded a foothold. Some said that the Danes were the first to cut them; others that smugglers used them to come in unobserved from the sea.

Tyrrell's fingers were as firm as his feet. Down he went, feeling for his foothold at each step, until he came to a little ledge five feet above the tidal mark. It was full tide now and that made it possible for the boat to approach the cliff, for the currents were for the time being stilled.

He stood on the little ledge and turned round to look. It was the French boat, right enough. The men's caps, seen in the ship's light, were enough to tell you that. But to dispel all doubt, there stood the two passengers: the barely discernible figure of a tall, cloaked man standing upright, whose person gave an impression of elegance and strength; and, in the poop, a dainty little figure in cape and hood looking up at him. The binnacle light lit her face, which was fresh and rosy in spite of three and a half days at sea. She had received every assurance that all would be well in kindly Ireland, but it was hard to realize that there could be a welcome behind this black forbidding wall at whose feet dark sea-weed clave and coiled. The immediate business of landing safely in the dark on a cliff ledge of a jealously guarded shore kept her thoughts from retrospection, even from regret, so urgent had all the circumstances about her become.

The tall figure said something in French. The Breton captain replied in dialect as he took a purse.

"There goes the *Grace,*" said the latter, paying a compliment to her courage as the little lady tripped forward to trust herself to the invisible man with the deep friendly voice who spoke from the face of the rocky fastness.

Her companion handed her up as the swell made his action possible. "Courage, Clemente," he said.

La Baronne Clemente Ysabeau de Ronquerolles had reached Ireland in safety. Colonel le Chevalier Constant d'Estournelles took hold of a firm hand that helped him on to an invisible ledge.

A dark lantern opened.

"Welcome, yer Honour," Bill Tyrrell said.

The Chevalier's first impression of the state of the country was reassuring. Here were men who addressed a man's honour. He heard the grinching of the boat hooks on the rock as the Frenchmen pushed out to sea.

"Put this around you, me Lady," he heard a deep voice say.

Bill Tyrrell indicated that Madame de Ronquerolles was to clothe herself in a net. When he opened the lantern he saw her standing holding the net helplessly in her hand. On her face was a look of wonder.

"It's meant for a seat, yer Ladyship. It's the best we could do," he said.

His son put the net about her and Bill Tyrrell brought the ends, which were fitted with loops, together with a line. He left about six feet of the rope free. This he passed round the lady's waist—"Just in case yer Ladyship slips out of the seat." Then, "Hold a minute. I was told to give you these," he said, as he handed two stout gloves to Clemente. "To save yer hands as you're going up. My son will follow you. You need not be afraid."

"Do you understand, Clemente?" d'Estournelles asked.

She nodded her head, as though she could not trust herself to speak.

She was drawn gently upwards into the darkness of the night. On the cliff's summit the party had to divide. Two travellers seen together by the sea's edge late at night would be sure to be accosted either by the coast watchers or the mounted patrol that hourly searched the shore. On the roads there was no hiding a waiting chaise. A secret landing had to be followed by a secret journey. This was beginning now. For want of a little caution it would be foolish to throw away success.

"My son will take the lady to a cottage near Kilruddery," said Tyrrell. "I am to hand yer Honour over to a fellow who is to wait for us at the first bridge on the Arklow road. He was to wait under it and only come out when the patrols pass, or I come. That will give yer Honour an hour."

Down they went to the flat ground from the slanting rock. Clemente was led by young Tyrrell.

"We must part here," Bill Tyrrell announced.

D'Estournelles bowed over Clemente's hand.

"Until we meet tomorrow, *adieu,*" he said.

"If yer Honour will give me yer hand, it will be easier here." D'Estournelles did as requested and he was helped over a wall that fenced the highroad.

"We must cross into the fields and skirt the road for a bit. They often lie in ambush on this road when the tide is in. They are trying to prevent gun-running and the landing of foreign men. They cannot see us in the fields. We are not far from the stream."

After half an hour through the fields, Tyrrell came to a little brook. He guided the visitor along its bank until they came to a wall that looked like the boundary of some estate.

"That's the wall of the road. Toucher Plant, yer guide, should be under the bridge. There's plenty of room to stand beside the water in there." D'Estournelles waited against the boundary wall while Tyrrell felt his way along the river's edge.

The Chevalier thought that he could make out the shape of mountains against a moonless sky. Trees spread above him. What he thought were mountains might be only the gloom of forest trees. He had been in Ireland before, but not in this part of the country. He had taken Mrs. St. George safely out of France a few years ago, during the Terror. The Chevalier bore deep in his heart the frail charm of the Irish lady, Ellice St. George, and looked forward eagerly to seeing her again. Her son, Denis St. George, would be his host now, and Clemente would be entertained at the house of Sir Richard de Vesey.

It was Sir Richard who had caused all the arrangements for their landing to be made. So far all had gone well. He hoped Clemente had not to go as far as this—in a strange land, with a strange fisher lad, in the middle of the night.

Suddenly he heard Tyrrell's deep voice.

"Are you in there, Plant?" it said.

"Whist! Of course I am."

"Well, then, come out of that. The gentleman is here."

"Give me time to sprout and throw a sheltering branch and I'm your man." In the dark it was impossible to see the middle-sized figure who emerged, as it were, from the earth.

"This is the gentleman I was to bring to you once I got him safely ashore," Tyrrell said.

"For the love of God, will ye whist? You could never tell who'd be listening to us in these times with spies and troopers all over the place. What d'ye mean by saying he come ashore? Who's come ashore? Nobody's come ashore. He's been here since he was born. Haven't ye wit enough to see that?" he asked, turning dramatically on Tyrrell, who turned away taciturnly.

"Well, here he is anyway." Turning to d'Estournelles, he said: "This, yer Honour, is Toucher Plant."

"Before you go away, I would like you to take this," d'Estournelles said, proffering a handful of *louis d'or*. But Tyrrell shook his head.

"Anything I or my family can do to help the Quality, you are welcome to. It's better for us not to tarry here. Three men together at night makes an illegal assembly in Ireland and you could be hanged or gaoled for it. I bid yer Honour goodnight!"

"It's like this, yer Honour," the Toucher explained, when Tyrrell had gone. "It's not good for us to be seen near a coast road. We didn't like to risk keeping a pair of empty saddles in waiting—the militia is up to all tricks like that—so we have to walk yerself and her Ladyship to shelter. And I'm not particularly partial to the sea either," he added inconsequently, and sighed.

"What do you mean?" asked d'Estournelles.

"It's like this, yer Honour. If I was to be caught aiding and abetting people escaping from France, it's not the Quality they'd believe I was abetting—though I always mixes with the Quality—but Revolutionaries and bloody cut-throats, and I'd find myself in the forecastle of a man-o'-war like many another poor fellow that was torn away from his peaceful home to serve in His Majesty's fleet, and there's three men-o'-war in Dublin Bay at the present moment and they're not there only to dance with the ladies neither."

"Where are you to take me?" asked d'Estournelles.

"Himself said I was to take you to see Deaf Burke. He has a . . ."

At the unfamiliar name d'Estournelles turned.

"And who is Deaf Burke?"

"And do you mean to tell me you don't know who Deaf Burke is? No. I had forgotten. How could you? But when it comes to the prize-fight with Mr. Dashwood's fancy, take the shirt off your back and lay it on Deaf Burke."

"Does this man know that I propose to visit him at this hour of the night?"

"Know it? And why should he know? Aren't half the gentry who belong to the Hellfire Club interested in Deaf Burke and drinking with his trainer who is training him in this salubrious region?" He waved his arm to include the Wicklow mountains.

D'Estournelles tried to unravel the strange puzzle.

"I presume that I am to go to Dublin in the chaise of one of Sir Richard's friends?"

"Now you have it! That's the idea. Once you get in among the gentry, there's neither soldier nor sailor that can lay a finger on you."

As they trudged along over the fields, d'Estournelles kept wondering why Sir Richard could not have provided a less extraordinary guide. He knew the difficulty of obtaining trustworthy help in these times of distrust, treachery and rebellion, but somehow this fellow Plant seemed to have something unstable about him. Nevertheless he realized too that the manner of his and Clemente's landing committed Sir Richard to secrecy and to the adoption of the greatest precautions.

Suddenly out of the darkness the Toucher whispered, "Whist! Do you hear that?"

"I hear nothing."

"Well, if it is a patrol coming across country—you never can tell where they are—lean on me and pretend to be drunk."

"I assure you that I will do nothing of the kind."

"All right. Every man to his taste, I always say."

They had crossed four or five fields and the night was bright enough now to enable the traveller to see the fences. They crossed one of these by a stile.

"Mebbe you see that?" Plant inquired.

"The lights, you mean?"

Through the trees, a clearing showed four lights in a row.

"That's the training camp of Deaf Burke. That's where the Quality has come to see him, the real gentry, the gallus fearless fellows, with their horses and game-cocks and their pugs. Them is members of the Hellfire Club and that's where they dice, and don't they drink! And such goings on!" He turned up his eyes. "If I had money and thousands of acres I wouldn't object to joining it myself. Not that they are by any means easy going. For half a groat they'd run you through. They are always insulting each other and duelling, till honour is satisfied. That's what 'ud make me feel uncomfortable if I was a member, which I am not. And as for the ladies—aw, don't be talkin'."

D'Estournelles moved away as if the Toucher had given him an over-familiar dig in the ribs. He was beginning to have misgivings of a country that, though it had promised so well at his landing, could yet countenance such fellows as this Plant.

"Going back to horses," the Toucher continued, rapidly changing the subject on realizing that his last remarks met with no response, "there was a member of the Hellfire Club who leapt his horse out of the first story window of his aunt's house in St. Stephen's Green, and it's no small leap—thirty feet at least—to win a wager, which he did and no harm to the horse. Then he went to the Holy Land."

"A pilgrimage after such wantonness?"

"No. He wasn't after any wantonness. He went to play hand-ball ag'in' the walls of Jerusalem, or it might be Jericho. I can't be sure. I'm not much up in Holy Writ. And he won that wager too. Why, there's boys in that Club who would think nothing of laying their houses and their lands on a hand of cards . . ."

"Boys?"

The Toucher was nonplussed. And when he was nonplussed, he laughed.

"Be boys I mean men," he said. "They do be saying," he continued, "that once when a member ran his servant through for disturbing him (he was drinking with the boys—the men, the Members), and he was had up by the Governor of Dublin and sentenced to death by hanging with a silk rope such as they use for the Peerage, his wife cut off the water supply to the city, for she owned the pond and the Governor had to let him off. Them was the days; but everything is going downhill now."

A horse whinnied.

"That's the sound, me lad. That fellow, or twenty others, will be taking you up to Dublin as soon as it is light."

Gravel crunched under their feet.

"Someone's demesne?"

"Aye," said Plant, "the Earl of Meath's."

As they neared the cottage, the sounds of voices and laughter could be heard. It seemed as if the occupants were engaged in some game, as indeed they were. The door opened and dazed d'Estournelles with light.

"Now, before you go in," Plant said, "if you have any foreign gold pieces, it would be well to let me keep them for you. They hang anyone found with French money in their possession, knowing that it has been paid for services against His Majesty, as they call him over here."

D'Estournelles made no reply. They reached the door. A hangdog fellow stopped them, then asked, recognition dawning:

"In the name of God, isn't it Toucher Plant?"

"Is that you, Flash?" Then, "Whist!" the Toucher admonished. "Who's inside?"

"There's Tiger Roche," said Flash. "And there's Mr. Dashwood, Fosdyke and Sir Richard."

"I don't think that we need send for the Tiger. Tell Sir Richard that there's a gentleman here who would like a jaunt to Dublin when it suits him to go home."

As a last admonishment the Toucher warned, with a great show of secrecy:

"Now don't in a moment of forgetfulness throw any French money on the board when they're playing cards. There's some of them who would take it badly and some of them would not. There's no knowing what way the Quality is taking this war. Some wants to fill their houses with French ladies and some would send a Frenchman to the gallows. It seems to me that there's French and French. You'd be surprised. But if you don't want to put it in safe-keeping, keep your money to yourself. Here's your portmanteau and in you go. I'm not in the mood for gambling or I'd go in myself. When you have been under a bridge as long as I have been what you need is a drink."

Flash had greater awe than the Toucher for this obvious aristocrat.

"Whirra, what d'ye mean, talking like that to his Honour?" he whispered to the Toucher. Then addressing the Chevalier with deference he asked:

"If it's yer Honour's pleasure, I would carry your bag."

D'Estournelles' opinion of the country's condition rose again. Here at least, though this might be its last stronghold, was conservatism and appreciation. The Chevalier yielded up his travelling bag and followed the fellow into the cottage.

D'Estournelles was astonished at the sight he saw. The men inside the cottage were so absorbed in their strange sport that they took no notice of the Chevalier's entry, and he was content to stand unobtrusively by the door and watch the extraordinary proceedings. Nine men in coloured coats and long brocade waistcoats and lace ruffs stood with bent heads and arms straight down pillared on their knees. Their golden buckled shoes and lace stockings shone and their silk knee breeches glistened as each in turn took the weight of a tenth gallant who went leap-frogging round the room against time, which Sir Richard took with a brightly dialled watch.

"Go it, Dashwood!" the leaper's backers yelled from the center of the room, as he neared the last human fence. It was a steeplechase confined to owners, now that the horses they owned had run their course for the year.

The jumper came to the end of his "chase." He mopped his brow with a fine handkerchief; a friend handed him the rapier he had discarded for the occasion. From his chair Sir Richard drawled:

"Admirable, Dashwood, truly admirable. I consider eleven seconds demned smart going. Fosdyke made a good effort—his going was a shade speedier even—but he fell on Roche. Dashwood wins."

Dashwood mopped his brow again. He went round the room and shook hands with the different fences which he had taken in full career. He went to the only table in the room and filled himself a glass of brandy.

"What the devil are you whispering about?" Sir Richard de Vesey shouted from his chair.

"I was informing Fosdyke that doing faster time over the course did not constitute him the winner. He failed at the last fence. He still owes me a thousand guineas," Dashwood answered.

"My decision was final," Sir Richard said. "All bets on Dashwood must be paid."

"He bet me nine wenches to a thousand guineas," Fosdyke protested. "I simply ask him to produce the women. Surely it is unlawful to bet with what you do not possess?"

Sir Richard said: "Now let me consider that. In the rules of racing, to bet without money is unlawful, but to bet with women! Damme. In that case it seems to me that it would be more unlawful to have them to bet with. What do you say, Roche?"

The Tiger turned a broad, puzzled face. He was still angry because Fosdyke had caught his foot against the hilt of his sword as he endeavoured to leap over the Tiger's expansive shoulders. Some stones had become detached from the hilt.

"Dashwood is the very man to have them and to keep them in readiness. Eh, Dashwood?"

"I won't pay until he produces them, then," Fosdyke growled.

"Now, Fosdyke, I have ruled on your liability. As for these nine wenches—well, Dashwood?"

Dashwood looked about him. Only grinning pugs, the roughs who surrounded Sir Richard's pugilist, Deaf Burke, could be seen in the corner doorway.

"Is Toucher Plant out there, Flash?" he asked. To the company he explained, "This morning I ordered that droll scoundrel to be here with nine young mountainy women with a nice peaty flavour—something that will hang in their shawls and savour of the soil. Tell the Toucher to appear. I never bet beyond my means."

A general laugh greeted this announcement. Flash left the room. Outside he found the Toucher endeavouring to extract from Dashwood's English servant information about the form of the pugilist, Bert Wallins, Dashwood's fancy, brought over to battle with Deaf Burke.

Flash explained as well as he could the position of things within.

"Yes," the Toucher confessed, "he told me to collect them; but he's only an English landlord and only a honourary member of the Hellfire Club. Besides, I couldn't gather them in Wicklow when Wicklow obeys only the servants of the Earl. Furthermore, I had better and nobler work to do, rescuing one of them French grandees."

"Well, let me tell you," Flash said, "that if your neglect costs Mr. Dashwood a thousand guineas, you—grandees or not—need never appear about the place again."

"You wrong me with my 'neglect.' I passed on the task to Medlicott, the gardener. I wouldn't debase myself. But for all that I'm ashamed of Mr. Dashwood for distrusting me."

Flash's face cleared. His beetling brow became smooth.

"Medlicott is in the greenhouse," he said. "I saw him stoking the stove in the vinery this evening."

Together, with a lantern swinging between them, they ran down the path a few hundred yards long that led to the greenhouse.

Sparks flew from the little chimney of its furnace room. They knocked on the door; there was no answer, but they could hear the sounds of many people coughing within. A girl's voice complained:

"Yerrah, Mr. Medlicott, is it suffocating us ye'll be?"

Flash kicked the door. At length a great stooped gaunt man opened it. Blue peat smoke surrounded him and poured out past him into the night air. He scowled at them with streaming eyes ringed with red.

"What in the name of God are ye doing in there anyway?" Flash asked.

"And what has ye shedding tears?" the Toucher asked innocently.

Angrily the Scots gardener answered.

"May ye roast, Plant, but it's yourself ought to ken. Had I kenned, I'd never have accepted the five sheelings ye gave me the morn."

"What has yer eyes red?" Flash asked.

"And why wouldn't they be red? Have I not been in there for the last half hour, smoking whores for his Lordship?"

Meanwhile, noticing men looking at the door, Sir Richard de Vesey turned on his chair. He rose and approached d'Estournelles. To relieve him from any effort his memory might have to make to recognize a plainly dressed and travel-stained figure, d'Estournelles was about to introduce himself.

"Why, of course. I'd know you anywhere, my dear cousin! What do you think brought me here but to await you? The sight of you delights me. To think that you arrived safely! Now let me see. . . . Before I introduce you to these gentlemen, I must order you a meal. Flash! Bring the Colonel meat and wine. If not, some of your rascally eggs." Again Sir Richard turned. "And Madame la Baronne?" The Chevalier nodded in confirmation of her safe arrival.

"We have all been a little hilarious, as you see," Sir Richard continued. "This is Dashwood, who hails from Woburn, Marlow and Henley in England, and who has had the audacity to match some fellow of his against Deaf Burke. Burke, stand up! This is Roche, Bagshot, Forster, Wentworth, Charlement, Luttrell, Tottenham, Ball-Acton. . . . Let me see. . . . Oh, yes, Fosdyke—and a whole score over there." In an aside to d'Estournelles, Sir Richard explained that Roche had arranged the details of the landing of the two émigrés; then he resumed in his former tone, "Let us come over to the table. Will one of you boys bring a chair?" While the men were exchanging greetings with the Colonel, Flash brought food and set it on the table. Before he seated himself, d'Estournelles had time to express his thanks to Roche, who gruffly belittled the part he had played in arranging the landing.

"Now," said Sir Richard to his guest, "I will not permit any conversation. That is, not till you have finished your meal. Gentlemen respect a traveller's fatigue. And you over there, take his portmanteau to my coach. The best hospitality is to bring him as quickly as possible to my house in the city and a comfortable bed." True to his word, Sir Richard maintained silence while the Colonel dined. Once he had finished eating, Sir Richard rose and said to the company, "You will forgive us, gentlemen, and hold us excused."

The Chevalier's esteem for Ireland rose still higher. There were men with the grand manner still left upon its soil. And that was more than could be said for France. Yet there was not an Irish name among the gentlemen. Were there two races in this land? What had become of the O'Neills and the O'Donnells and the Taafes who could be met on the Continent? One of the O'Donnells was the Duke of Tetuan. Had a new aristocracy taken their place at home? Which race had set the tradition of Irish liberality, hospitality, arrogance and, for the huckster, scorn?

With such thoughts in mind, as he drove away with Sir Richard, he inquired about the antecedents of Tiger Roche, whom he had particularly noticed during the leap-frog contest and in his brief introduction to the merry company just before he had dined. What was Roche's station in society? His manners were not quite those of an aristocrat, though he had an assurance and a distinction of his own.

"Roche?" Sir Richard explained. "Norman originally, as the name shows. I knew something about his mother. She went to live on a small property near Kilkenney. He is said to be a natural son of the Duke of Ormond. I would not like to be too inquisitive. He got into the Club for 'services rendered' to many of its members. He is the best duellist in the country, knows all about the rules. He has no money. A fellow like that cannot descend to trading, so he has nothing to offer but his sword. That he is employing with a band of half-squires like himself in keeping the footpads and other marauders from overwhelming the citizens. They have formed a Society for Aiding Order. The watch in Dublin is quite inadequate. There are outrages and fights every night. Just now we are more or less under military law.

"There are those who think that Roche's armed men are quite as dangerous as the ruffians whom they are determined to exterminate," Sir Richard added with a laugh.

"Nothing but his sword." D'Estournelles repeated Sir Richard's phrase to himself. To how many gentlemen had not that description applied? At the moment it could be said to apply to himself, for he was a gentleman without property. He could not be a trader. A gentleman without property had "nothing but his sword," except what he might win dicing or at the card-tables.

Tired as he was, his mind suddenly warmed to the thought that here in England he had fallen into the reign of Queen Elizabeth rather than that of King George. These gorgeous, gaily clad gentlemen of figure were a remnant lost to all the rest of the world but still surviving here.

"I am afraid that you will consider that the sports of our country are somewhat gross, my friend," Sir Richard said, as if partially reading the other's thoughts.

The Chevalier did not reply for a moment. Then he said:

"I am a little puzzled about the boxer you called Deaf Burke. He did not seem deaf when you ordered him to stand up."

"No. No. Not deaf in that sense. Deaf to punishment. That is why the gentlemen of the Fancy call him Deaf Burke. He is a sturdy pugilist and I hope that he will win for me against Dashwood's champion, a first-rate English fighter called Bert Wallins. Dashwood has laid a thousand guineas with me, and more with men I could name, that his man will defeat anything we can produce in this country. He would not believe in the prowess of Deaf Burke. I warned him that he may have to pay dearly for his doubts. It only made him the more eager. I hate to have my opinion questioned as if I did not know a fighter when I saw one. For two years I have backed Burke. He has never failed me, not once. Saw him go ninety rounds with Jabez Kent and he was no mean English boxer. Burke is in better fettle now than he was then. Wallins will have to be mighty stalwart to stave off Burke when he settles to his fight about the twentieth round or so."

"In France *la boxe* is not a sport enjoyed by gentlemen. I am afraid that I am unable to comment on its status in this country. I saw a fight between boxers in London. It seemed to be a brutal affair, and one that depended more on strength and endurance and brute courage than on skill."

The roll of the coach in this thin morning air sent Sir Richard to sleep. When they reached Dublin he apologized profusely to his almost equally sleepy guest.

"We will pay our respects to la Baronne and to my nieces and my sister in the afternoon. Now it is time that you had some sleep in a bed."

"I speak as an émigré and an exile. It is with the greatest embarrassment that I broach the subject at all; and I would never have permitted myself to do so did I for a moment think that what I have to say could be regarded as a misgiving of mine about the generous hospitality of your country and of yourself, Sir Richard. But as it is a boon I cannot see any way of returning at any certain date . . ."

"Now, now, my dear Constant, is that any way to talk to me, to us? Let us add up the reckoning, if you will. How often have our families entertained one another? How long have I stayed at the d'Estournelles house with your good father? Our kinswomen Mrs. St. George and la Baronne, what do they owe to you, who have risked your life to effect their escape from blood-maddened France? Why, man, you make me talk like a huckster balancing accounts. You will honour us by staying as long in our country as you can tolerate our ways. La Baronne will remain with my family, that is with my sister and her nieces—niece, for Ninon is married now—so long as there is any danger, or even discomfort, in returning. And I pray you particularly to remain here and not in England in order not to prejudice the return of at least part of your estates. Well I know that no Frenchman emigrates if he can help it. Let us make your exile as light as this light-hearted land's welcome can do."

Sir Richard paused and at last said:

"I have this meeting of my man with Dashwood's to attend. I can all the more readily leave you, since you are not anxious to see the match. You will be with my niece and my sister Penelope. Then in a week or so, if you will pardon the delay, I shall start you all out for the west of Ireland, a country that, given a fine day, of course, is, I dare say, as lovely as any in this world—or the next. I am a poor authority on the latter, I must admit," he added with a short laugh. "If any friend of mine could consider himself an émigré in this country I would feel everlastingly disgraced."

III. LA BARONNE IS MADE WELCOME

MEANWHILE LA BARONNE had been guided to one of the new cottages that a wealthy landowner called Tottenham, a gay blade and a Hellfire Club member, was building on his estate. It was so lately built that the thatch was still golden on its roof and on the little dormer that peeped from above the door. Here Clemente was to meet Miss Mabel Lynch, the younger sister of Ninon. Mabel would take her to Dublin and then, after a visit to the city, they would go with Mabel's Aunt Penelope to Lisadill, the family's country estate in the West. There they would be within visiting distance of the Martyn-Lynches' new mansion.

Young Tyrrell knocked and shook the latch. "Are you there, Miss?" No answer. He knocked again; still no answer. This caused him some confusion, which was quickly sensed by his companion, and by no means allayed by what almost immediately followed.

A young girl sprang from beside a bush and clasping la Baronne with a joyous hug, addressed her in French:

"Oh, you are safe? How wonderful! Was your journey marvellous? It must have been. Welcome, welcome to Ireland."

Composing herself, Clemente answered.

"I can talk English, Mademoiselle."

Mabel ceased to caper up and down with joy. Crestfallen at the reception of her well-dictionaried French, she kicked the door of the cottage. This would have surprised Clemente even more than the effusive welcome, could she have been sure in the dark that the sounds of a boot on the door were not made by Tyrrell.

The door was opened by an old woman who must have been hard of hearing.

"Oh, Missy, I thought you were in! Whatever brought you out at this hour of the night?"

"To welcome la Baronne, who has just landed from France."

"There were those who could be trusted to bring her here," the old woman said reprovingly, and muttered to herself, "in the dead of night with all them sojers about, it's a mad young lady entirely." She brought forward a chair which she dusted with her apron and offered to the Baroness. She stirred up the fire and went to lay the table.

"We won't put her at the fire, Nora, till she has seen her room. Oh, it's a lovely little room! Blue and white. Come and see it, Madame." And Mabs led her charge to the little bedroom. Presently her voice was heard shouting:

"Nora, there's no hot water!" Then, as an afterthought: "Nora, don't let Tyrrell away without a drink."

When she entered the little room the Baroness threw herself on her knees beside the bed, buried her face in her arms and burst into the relief of tears. Sobs shook her cloaked form. Mabs stood and looked on in wonderment. At last the little lady ceased to weep. She remained kneeling for a space. She was silent now as one in prayer. After a while she rose and wiped her eyes.

"Forgive me, dear," she said, "but when we met that boat on the black sea after three days and I knew we were safe after searching for hours in the dark, fearing to hail any craft . . . and Constant was anxious too . . . I felt it. . . . Oh, it is good to be safe at last! We could not be sure of anything. No messages could reach you to say that we had started. We had to obey the directions that came to Constant through a priest at Louvain. They were a month old and we could not be sure that you on this side would be able to keep the date. Can you not imagine how good it is to be safe and far away from murder and robbery? And anxious days and awful nights?"

Mabs at last got her to sit by the fire while the supper was prepared. When all was ready, Clemente refused to partake of any food. Her appetite had gone, she declared. Here Nora proved her worth by bringing Madame a glass of sherry. After sipping it, her appetite returned and she was persuaded to take a little food.

"More bacon and eggs for me," said Mabs. "We must make an early start. Only that I may never have another chance of sleeping in a bedroom with such a lovely little dormer, I'd stay with you in your room," she said to la Baronne apologetically.

The Toucher, though he had spent all the night with the associates of the prize ring and the followers of both pugilists, was spick and span and punctual with the chaise. He had it from the steward of the Tottenham estate. A fine cream cob pawed the ground between the lancewood shafts. The Toucher sat newly shaved and clean-cravatted under a new chimneypot hat. Mabs saw him from her dormer. She ran down. La Baronne was up before her.

"There is a strange man at the door," Clemente whispered. Mabs opened the upper half of the door and leaned out.

"Good man, Toucher," she called out and waved a hand.

Gravely the Toucher saluted with his whip. He was now a full-fledged sporting gent. And he would show the lady from France that the Plants knew how to handle the ribbands. It was a pity that Sir Richard and d'Estournelles had a few hours' start. What a thing it would be to overtake Sir Richard's coach on the way to Dublin, with a flourish of his whip in passing. Miss Mabs would be sure to tell her French Ladyship who were inside.

When all was ready for the departure, Mabs, much to Clemente's amazement, sprang up on the front seat and seated herself beside the driver. Madame de Ronquerolles could hardly keep herself from remonstrating with the child over her hoydenish behaviour.

The yellow spokes flashed merrily the minute the sea-mist, which drifted inland to a depth of at least three miles, had lifted and revealed the morning sun. The Toucher flicked the cob ever so lightly with the whip and it increased its pace. The explanation soon appeared. A large coach was coming toward them up Windy Hill. The Toucher straightened his back and kept his bridle hand low with tightened rein. The cob lifted her feet and paced in a way that would be sure to grig the driver of the oncoming coach. He saw one of the occupants look out; then he turned and spoke to Mabs. He was an adept at making conversation, particularly when his intention was to impress others by his apparent familiarity with a superior.

He turned from Mabs and saluted, bringing his whip handle across his face obliquely, then gently inclined his head. This latter action came as a surprise to the coachman of the magnificent equipage, who hardly returned the salute.

While Mabs was asking animated questions as to the identity of the travellers and the Toucher was parrying them as best he could, Clemente, who was astonished at the familiarity of her young companion with a coachman, thought well to intervene.

"Don't you think that you would be better, dear, if you sat by me? It must be cold there on the front seat."

"The Toucher knows everybody," said Mabs.

"The morning air will spoil your complexion if you expose yourself so much," Clemente suggested, hoping that the hint would remind Mabs of a sense of the proprieties.

"I never knew I had a complexion," Mabs answered, turning a broad, merry face with bright colour on the cheek bones and sparkling blue eyes above them, eyes dark enough to look into the sunlight and yet retain their blue. Her mannish driving coat was open at the neck and exposed a long, dazzlingly white throat. This coat and the way she pointed out recognized sights to Plant made the chaise look as if it were being directed by a boy. La Baronne became resigned to this mode of travel, and contented herself with saying:

"At least you should button up your coat, my dear."

"There's a bay for you, your Ladyship," the familiar Plant indicated, as the shoulder of Killiney Hill came nigh.

Solicitude for his French charge may have been partly responsible for a plan he was making—to stop at Blackrock en route—but perhaps the thought of a glass of Guinness's brew was a greater influence. There was a good excuse to halt and livery the cob. He would begin by suggesting it to Miss Mabs.

"We'll be soon on the Rocky Road to Dublin and it's herself would like a drink, I'm thinking."

"No, no," Mabs exclaimed. Though she was tempted by the thought of la Baronne's dismay if they were to halt before some hostel or inn, Aunt Penelope's strict injunctions had to be obeyed: there was to be no delay in bringing la Baronne to Dublin. She was to be ever mindful of the respect due to a guest.

"She's beginning to sweat and by the time . . ." the Toucher continued. Mabs realized that it was to the cob he was alluding when he spoke of "her" liking a drink.

On hearing a slight exclamation of delight from Madame at the sight of mountains which were suddenly revealed between the trees on the left side of the road, the Toucher turned around. He echoed her sentiments, but with somewhat more vigour, perhaps, than she could have long sustained.

"Them's mountains for ye, yer Ladyship! Aye, and rocks on the top of them that no man at the present day could blast with gunpowder let alone lift. Auld Finn MacCool or the auld Druids flung them at each other long ago when they disagreed, mebbe, about ways and means. That red one is called the Two Rock and the other the Three. They say that they were put there to provide the country with a difference. No matter what side you took you'd always be one out, more or less. Make Sir Richard bring ye for a picnic there and never mind the Strawberry Beds! It's either them or the Scalp for real privacy."

When they reached the city Mabs realized that the Toucher was set on making his drive a one-man procession. Instead of driving directly from College Green towards Rutland Square, he turned to the left down Dame Street past Dublin Castle and over Bloody Bridge, then round by Capel Street, past Henrietta Street, where the Quality resided and were mostly to be seen, up Dorset Street past the house in which Brinsley Sheridan was born, and at last via Granby Row to the north of the Square. When he had been recognized and wondered at to his heart's content, he resigned his position of privilege and brought the ladies to Sir Richard's town house.

La Baronne was pleasantly surprised at the grandeur and the

furnishings of the mansion. She made no remark but dropped her eyes when Sir Richard's sister, Penelope, was introduced. She took a seat and admitted that she would like a fire when Penelope rang for a servant.

"What has this niece of mine been doing to you? I hope that she treated you well and did not take you out of your way on some madcap chase, to look at game-cocks or horses. It is distressing enough to have to enter the country by its cliffs at night without being diverted from your destination in the morning. Now at last we can make you comfortable," she added, as the fire began to crackle in the brass-bound grate.

Clemente, realizing that it would seem ungracious to complain of the hardships of her journey, dwelt on the novelty and the surprising beauty of the Irish scene. It bore a strange resemblance to Brittany with gorse in bloom, and she had heard that there were Druidical remains, too, as in Brittany.

"Mabs, come away from that window. How often have I told you that you must not draw attention from the street?" Aunt Penelope ordered, for Mabs was waving both arms at somebody in the street below.

"But it's delightful to see the sun on the house-tops and the hills beyond."

"Quite so," said Aunt Penelope. "But you must be more elegant in your delight."

Outside, St. George could guess why Mabs beat so hasty a retreat from the window.

Turning to her guest, Aunt Penelope said: "You must see Ninon, my recently married niece. The whole house is in disorder since her wedding. That is why so much of the furniture is still against the walls: we had to make room for the guests. Will you excuse me? I think that is she coming in."

When her aunt left the room to look for her sister, Mabs felt that the whole weight of doing the honours of the house had suddenly descended upon herself. Catching la Baronne's eye upon her, she stood up and, crossing to a large mirror which rose from a marble table between the windows, looked at herself in the glass and then invited the Baroness to follow her example.

At seventeen, Mabel was almost too tall for her age, but she was lissome and well-knit, and as lithe and agile as a boy. She had bright, golden hair and a bright complexion that made her look always as if she were bubbling over inwardly with some exciting tale. Her flat bosom and broad, almost square, shoulders accentuated her boyishness, as did the long legs and slim hips.

While Clemente was examining herself in the mirror, Mabs kept moving behind her and regarding her from various angles. At last the Baroness asked her what she was doing.

"I don't think that you look better in it than you do out of it," Mabs volunteered.

The Baroness raised her eyes with a puzzled smile.

"That's the mirror that taught Hyacinth—he's my brother-in-law now, Hyacinth Martyn-Lynch—how to look at Ninon. You see she's not really pretty but she has what I am not supposed to have; and that's why he married her."

The Baroness looked wide-eyed at Mabs.

"You are only a girl. As yet you are hardly grown up. But what is it that you are not supposed to have?"

"Charm," said Mabs and pouted.

"My dear, my dear," the Baroness went on kindly. "Charm is the rarest quality a woman can possess. It is rarer far than beauty. It is a thing in itself, a radiation, an innate gift like genius. None of us can acquire it: we can only simulate it if we are not lucky enough to have been endowed with it at our birth. And even then we ourselves are no judges of it. We can only judge it by the effect of our personality on the opposite sex."

Mabs cogitated for a moment. Then she blushed and said stubbornly: "I don't care whether I have it or not. I won't allow any man to judge me." She flung herself into a chair.

"It is not charming for a girl to cross her legs," the Baroness murmured, then continued in a brighter tone:

"You were telling me about that mirror. Is it possessed of any magical quality? Why should one look better in it than out of it?"

Mabs jumped up at once.

"That's what I have been trying to find out. But I can't see myself from behind when I am looking into it. Hyacinth said that he never realized how lovely Ninon was until he saw her with her head bent down gazing into the mirror. He called her the lady with the heart-shaped face. You see, Ninon's forehead is broad and runs quickly into her hair. Then her eyes are very wide apart. When you look at her from the front you do not notice that she has a long pointed chin which she can bring up bewitchingly when she lifts her head sideways. She was looking down trying to draw when Hyacinth first noticed that she has a rare—no—a kind of beauty which is revealed only to those with eyes to see. At least that is what he said."

The Baroness listened attentively. The description did not fit Mabs. There could be little family resemblance between the sisters, she thought as she looked at Mabs' round button of a chin, with its central dimple.

"What was she trying to draw?" she asked.

Mabs ran to an escritoire and took paper and pencil.

"I'll show you. You take a book and hold it over the paper so that I have to look into the mirror to see my hand. Now I try to copy this square and put in the diagonals from corner to corner correctly. You try and I will watch you from behind."

"But who will hold the book?"

"I forgot that," said Mabs.

"Do not trouble. I can understand how Ninon must have looked to her husband when he saw her in the mirror. The light is kinder in a mirror—sometimes. And it was an unusual attitude for a face. After all, there are not many moments when a lady permits herself to be gazed at unawares. I can well believe that your sister is worthy of all that appreciation."

"But he said a lot more. He said that her soul does not peep through her green-black eyes but glows full-bodied when she looks with her face near to his. Denis St. George never said anything to me as poetical as that."

"Denis St. George?" the Baroness inquired.

"Oh, you will love Denis. He is a great friend of ours and of Hyacinth's. He has property in Galway, and the Chevalier got his mother out of France during the Terror and they took a long time coming here. She is even said to be an old flame of his. Now she is a widow and he is here."

Clemente's look checked the stream of Mabs' narrative.

"My dear, really, really, you must not talk like that. A young lady should exercise the greatest discretion. You have allowed your tongue to run away with you. If you want to be loved you must be discreet."

Voices on the landing put an end to admonition before Mabs could assure the Baroness that she did not want to be loved.

"Clemente, this is Ninon, my niece, the bride of Martyn-Lynch." The Baroness recognized at once the justice of Hyacinth's appreciation.

About middle height, Ninon walked with a gait which added to her charming poise. Her broad, intelligent face, pensive in repose, became animated when her lips parted and she spoke a few melodious words of greeting. Her face, with its olive skin, was indeed heart-shaped. From in front her nose looked straight and even a little broad, but in profile its extreme delicacy was apparent. Seen from the side it looked frail and aquiline. Her mouth was placed exactly between her nose and chin, which was rounded. Her teeth were bright but they overlapped a little, a feature that pouted her lips forward slightly and gave them an inviting charm. Mabs had a great advantage over her sister in her strong, level, flawless teeth.

The light from the high windows caught Ninon full in the eyes as she advanced to greet the Baroness. It could be seen that they were of that indefinite colour called hazel, and had black radiating lines in their golden irises. A bright chevelure grew in curls immediately above her forehead and shone as if she had placed an ornament in front of the rich volume of her dark brown hair. Her waist was so fine that it looked too narrow for her well-rounded limbs. Her bosom was almost as inconspicuous as that of her sister, though she was four years older. When she smiled her great dark eyes, set wide apart, glowed steadfastly.

"Your arrival has relieved us all of so much anxiety," Ninon said to the Baronne. "And the thought of having you with us forever means a new life to us all. Is it not so, Aunt Penelope?"

"So I was saying," Aunt Penelope replied.

Clemente inclined her head. She was thinking that Dublin City was not populous enough to provide an adequate barrier between its citizens and the rusticity by which they were surrounded.

Penelope repeated that she had already told the Baroness how happy she and Mabel would be to have her with them at Lisadill and up in town, of course, twice or even thrice a year.

Madame was confirmed in her opinion about rurality when Ninon rocked from one foot to the other as if the uncertainty of what to say or do were conveyed to her feet.

"Yes," she thought, "I am right: the boulevards and salons of Dublin are not extensive enough to conceal the background of the country and its rural manners." Ninon was soon relieved of any diffidence which the perfect composure of la Baronne awakened, by the arrival of a visitor.

A tall young man, slender and erect, entered the room, and looked about him at the company. His sunburnt face bespoke the athlete and sportsman. His expression was that of one to whom saddle leather is dearer than the leather that binds books. At twenty-three, Denis St. George already had the characteristics of a full-fledged Irish gentleman.

"Ah!" he exclaimed. "She is still here."

Mabs turned, put her hands behind her back and gazed out of the forbidden window. Although she had just spoken warmly of Denis to the Baronne, now that he was here, Mabs pretended not to be interested in his presence.

"Yes," Penelope said, thinking Denis meant la Baronne. "She has had a frightful time: over three days at sea in a fishing boat and a climb in the night up those slippery cliffs. I must say that Mabs brought her to us with all possible dispatch. Didn't you, dear? Oh, I do wish that you would cease to draw attention from the street. Baronne, this is Denis St. George."

St. George turned, and seeing Clemente for the first time, stooped from his height in a bow and took the little hand that the Baroness extended. His blue eyes were fixed on her face.

"You are more than welcome," he said warmly.

Turning to Penelope, Denis asked if Sir Richard had returned with Constant d'Estournelles.

"Yes, but I have forbidden them to appear before dinner. You will meet the Chevalier when we all assemble. Can you have patience until then?"

"I must go to find Hyacinth," he said.

When Denis left, the ladies were alone once more.

"Mabs, dear," Aunt Penelope said, "you look tired. Won't you go upstairs for a rest?" Though spoken mildly, Penelope's words had the effect of a command rather than a request. With a petulant toss of her golden hair, Mabs left the room.

"You must forgive my sister's apparent lack of manners and breeding," Ninon said to Clemente as soon as Mabs had left. "She is at an age where impulse easily overrides good form."

"I understand perfectly," said Clemente with a warm smile, "and I admire her spirit, which as yet is too high and young to be held in check by stale convention. When she grows a little older, that same spirit will be controlled and directed with the grace of full womanhood. But she is still only a girl."

"We are hoping, Baroness," said Aunt Penelope, "that your stay with us will give Mabs an object lesson in the deportment becoming to a lady. She is at a most impressionable age, and is readily influenced by the example of those she admires. Her admiration for you is apparent already, and will surely grow with further association."

"Nothing would please me more," replied Clemente, "than to be able to act as preceptress to your niece."

"You are most gracious," Ninon said, "and I am sure Mabs will benefit enormously by being near you, as we hope she will be in the months to come." Then, feeling that the talk of her sister's lack of discipline cast discredit on herself, Ninon added: "Do you know, I am sure that Denis' presence has a good deal to do with Mabs' behaviour. She is confused and disturbed by her feelings for him, which she is too young to understand. Though she is strongly attracted to the lad, her independent nature makes her resent this attraction. Her confusion over Denis reflects itself in her deportment."

"How true," said Aunt Penelope. "You, Ninon, showed a trace of the same attitude toward Hyacinth. I should not be surprised if Denis and Mabs married one day. They are well suited to one another. Denis has a firm, steadfast quality that would complement Mabs' youthful flightiness."

It was later in the afternoon that Constant was presented to the ladies in the great drawing room. Denis had left them to see Martyn-Lynch. Mabel, after a brief pretense at taking a nap, had rejoined the ladies. They were making tea. Seeing Constant enter, Sir Richard, who in spite of Penelope's directions had preceded him, ordered some sherry for the Chevalier and continued to talk to Madame Clemente and to pay her many a gallant compliment.

Constant was given the warmest of welcomes. Aunt Penelope blushed as brightly as if her cheeks were those of la Baronne, who, now that she was rested, looked cheerful and eager and full of hope in the country that was to be her home. She seemed sweet, dainty, and demure.

Ninon talked of the beauty of the West and of her curiosity to see the new house that was just completed for her and Hyacinth. She reminded Clemente that the new Martyn Hall was not far from Lisadill, Sir Richard's country estate, where Clemente would stay with Mabs and Penelope, and expressed the wish that the three would be frequent visitors to Martyn Hall. Aunt Penelope feared that Lisadill might prove lonely for la Baronne until she was assured that all Clemente wanted was silence and peace.

"But, my dear, you will have time to brood, and brooding will fill your rosy face with pale melancholy."

"Not with you and Mabel to talk to me and tell me your old country's history. We will read all the books in the great library at Lisadill. Mabel, do you hear me, darling—shall we not?"

"Yes, yes," Mabel said hurriedly. "But not *all* the books; some of them are Latin ones and some are in Greek. All the books with pictures of birds and flowers and horses and the hairy men in knee breeches who clench their fists and glare at one another—I love that kind of book."

"Mabs, you must not speak of such savages!" her aunt said reprovingly.

"Uncle keeps one," Mabel answered, alluding to the boxer, Deaf Burke.

When, after a time, the men withdrew, it removed the constraint which might otherwise have affected the ladies' conversation. They fell to talking about a trousseau, for all the clothes with which it would be necessary to furnish the Baroness amounted to little less than a trousseau. And trousseaux were in the air, so to speak. Ninon, who was now worldly-wise, could speak with authority on the best houses where each commodity might be inspected and purchased if approved. Her own trousseau was as yet hardly unpacked.

Aunt Penelope would go with the ladies on their shopping expedition and act as arbiter if consulted. Not that she wanted to have everything held up for her approval. She knew that she must yield to French taste.

Earlier in the day when Clemente, hearing that they planned to go shopping, had held up her little store of money, Aunt Penelope had said: "My dear, you would not deprive us of the privilege of entertaining you. You must keep your money, now that all your supplies are cut off, for your return journey to le Chateau du Moulin. Revolutions cannot go on forever. They do not do that even in Ireland, my dear. And the French people are likely to come to their senses more quickly than the people here. You are not my guest so much as a part of our family. Regard me as your sister and Mabel as your niece.

Money is not indispensable. In Ireland we live on our pride. A short time ago you very graciously offered to act as preceptress to Mabs. That would more than repay us for any hospitality we are able to offer you."

Now that Aunt Penelope had risen, Mabel could not conceal her eagerness to be up and doing. She jumped up and ran across the room to open the door for her aunt.

"Mabs, you really must remember who you are. You must not walk like that. What will Madame Clemente think? You have had an opportunity of seeing what ladylike deportment is, and I hope that you will benefit by la Baronne's example, even if my instructions go unheeded."

"I protest, Aunt; I do not comprehend your meaning."

Aunt Penelope said curtly: "At least you comprehend that you are not a boy."

Mabel's eyes flashed. She opened the door so widely that she could hide herself behind it until they were all out of the room. She closed it gently behind her aunt and her company. Rushing to the window she opened it and, leaning out, whistled to Denis St. George, who was leaving by the hall door.

"Will you take me or not?" she asked.

Denis put his finger to his lips and reëntered the house. Seeing him do so, Mabs left the room and leaning over the banisters applied the front of her waist to them and slid down the stairs.

In the hall she repeated her question.

"How can I do it?" Denis expostulated. "There are so many difficulties in the way. Suppose your aunt were to find out."

"It would then be too late for her to prevent it. I should have seen the fight. There would be no difficulties in the way if I asked Tiger Roche."

"Oh, you must not do that. I will find out what time we start for the scene. I do not know the exact spot. The start will be early and my seat is outside at the back of Sir Richard's coach."

She blew him a kiss and was gone. To Denis, the gesture was ample reward for whatever displeasure he might incur by humouring Mabs' wish to see the fight. Another young man might have thought her a hoyden for having such a wish and acting on it. To Denis, who loved sport above all things, it was part of Mabs' attraction that she too loved action, risk and excitement.

IV. WHAT DEAF BURKE HEARD

THERE IS A dell on the La Touche property near the Glen of the Downs, a few score yards off the highroad, into which coaches could turn and remain unseen. It looks as if it were formed by an old quarry whose sides had long since healed from the scars the pick and blasting powder made. The floor was high and likely to keep firm even under rain. The curved face of the rock made a little natural amphitheatre and the open mouth could be closed by the coaches of those whose men were about to contend. When the coaches were drawn up, the sides of the opening could be roped off and thus prevent those from entering whose presence was not desired at the ringside. From above, of course, the curious might look on; but as the plot was purposely chosen so that it would be out of the reach of interlopers from the city, it offered a most suitable meeting place on neutral ground. Although the Huguenot La Touches were by now an old Dublin family, nobody could say that they favoured fisticuffs. And as both Dashwood and Sir Richard were satisfied with the situation, there was no more to be said.

The men were to meet at noon. Dashwood's black and yellow coach had drawn up early. The space beside it was reserved for Sir Richard's party. Next to it could be seen an ostentatious carriage, deep in the body, which was suspended by great straps on luxurious springs curving in from behind in a high arc. It was the private carriage of Tiger Roche. Two tents pitched under the rock gave shelter to the fighters and their attendants.

The fight was about to begin. It would start as soon as Sir Richard's arrival was announced. A murmur from the beggars and rapscallions on the cliff edge was the inappropriate herald of the baronet's approach.

"What the deuce has delayed him? Gout again?" Dashwood asked. Tottenham could not say. He contented himself with the trite remark that one was better late than never. On the carriage came. That it was pretty well crowded was evident. There were two on the box beside Tulip the driver, and three or four on the seat behind. How many were within, who could say? Bravely the prancing horses came on from Kilmacanogue. You could hear the hoof-falls now. And now they were deadened as they turned into the grass. Cheers from the quarry top greeted the baronet. His hat answered through the window. A lithe figure leapt down from the back of the coach, a strange figure elaborately dressed in a *ventre d'or* waistcoat, cherry-red coat, plush knee breeches—overdressed even for a cynosure of fashion. He put down the step and opened the door for Sir Richard. It was Toucher Plant, whose presence on the coach was due to "services rendered" lately to Sir Richard.

All eyes were on the door. Dr. MacDermot was first man out. Wild huzzas from the quarry top greeted the sporting doctor, who resided near Martyn Hall and was a familiar figure at every sporting event. He raised his broad face and lifted his hat with, "Thank you, lads." Greatly to his amazement the cheers turned to derisive cries, for behind him the Toucher was raising his hat as if to appropriate the applause.

The golden buckle of Sir Richard's shoe appeared. Sir Richard showed a comely leg; he was soon on the ground. Next down came Denis St. George. But his appearance was unnoticed in the turmoil of applause, and no heed was paid the slim figure who remained behind on the coach top.

"Up, Sir Richard!" And the quarry top was ridged and the air filled with greasy caubeens and battered beaver hats. Mr. Plant led Sir Richard respectfully to his ringside seat. He waved the spectators aside contemptuously as he went.

"The Toucher, be all that's holy!" could be heard from an astonished gaping mouth, to whose owner credit was due for recognizing the Toucher in his gorgeous, if somewhat gaudy, disguise.

"Eh," asked Sir Richard, "what is that?"

"We were recognized and applauded by one of the race-goers in the English camp. This, Sir Richard, is your seat."

Up to this Bert Wallins had not been seen by anyone in Sir Richard's entourage—excepting, perhaps, the persuasive Plant, who may have insinuated himself into his company at Raheny, where he trained in the strictest privacy on Lord Charlemount's estate. If one could trust Toucher Plant—and there were many who would before they knew him well—he had beheld Wallins face to face. In a quiet inquisition held by Tiger Roche in the headquarters of the Society for Aiding Order, the Toucher gave this account:

"He's a tall, red-headed huer of a man, wid a pale face and a long reach. He's a cold-blooded huer be all accounts and is coming on fast. Over on the other side he has not been beaten yet. There's something iv the dark horse about him or they wouldn't have him boxing only against English partners."

To which, on consideration, Tiger Roche had replied with a solemn question, accompanied by a persuasive gesture.

"Who are you backing, Plant?"

When a finger and thumb were removed from his throat, the Toucher gasped, "Bert is a boxer, but I'm backing Deaf Burke."

"If you are lying, you know what it means," the Tiger remarked. For a moment it had seemed to the Toucher that the hilt of a sword was the most prominent ornament in the room. He recalled that feeling now as the fight was about to begin.

Before the men took the ring an usher or ring-keeper was sent with a whip among the riffraff on the quarry top to tell them that if there was so much as a shout or a remark out of them during the fight they would be flogged from the field. What good was it taking all these precautions if they were to spoil a fair fight with partisan cries? An objection might be lodged that Bert Wallins could get no fair fight in Ireland if he were harassed by a hostile mob.

This may have accounted in part for the very favourable reception the visitor from England received. Herbert Wallins was twenty-four, and six feet tall. He stood upright with perfectly proportioned limbs. His skin was creamy white, and over his pale face—which was made paler thereby—hung a bell of dark copper-coloured hair, so dark that it went with a pallid rather than a freckled skin. His eyes were of an indefinite yellow hazel. They were deep-set and their thin, clearly defined lids were well protected by their brows. His step was very noticeable when he walked. He used his calves as it seemed unduly, and lifted his heels high. This, though it gave him a springy stride, left no more agility in reserve. He leant against the corner post in silence and appeared not to attend at all to the admonitions of his second. One would think by the way he ignored them that the man was tired or ill. Even the yells of encouragement he did not seem to hear.

"What the devil's the matter with him?" Denis St. George asked MacDermot. The doctor shook his head. Such nonchalance was beyond his experience.

"It's only English reserve," the Toucher volunteered.

As his seconds showed no concern at what appeared an unusual indifference, the Toucher was probably right. An Englishman does not wear his heart on his sleeve. Yet this coldness had a strange, chilling effect.

The pale face turned and said something over the shoulder. A little old fellow with a bashed-in nose looked about him and replied. What the question was no one could guess, and there were many on the spot who lived by guessing. But a mystery was added to the scene and silence ensued as a result. What was on his mind?

Then a second bent down and examined the lacing of his principal's shoes. He knelt and bent a knee as a seat. Wallins sat down. The other shapely white leg was extended. The shoe on it was examined.

Strangely, the air was tense and fears began to form unreasonably for the Irishman.

"Looks a cool character," Sir Richard remarked to St. George.

Whatever anxiety was in the air, the arrival of Deaf Burke gave the audience an opportunity to relieve their bosoms. A part of the hilarious reception he received was due to this release. He stooped under the ropes and walked with leisurely steps across the ring. No one saw him cast an eye at his opponent. He shook hands with Sir Richard, as was customary when a man was your chief backer. He undid his silken sash of Sir Richard's colors, purple and black, and fastened them to his corner's post. Bert Wallins loosed his sash of black and golden stripes and likewise tied it to the post to mark his corner. Burke's hand looked strange. The skin was taut and dry as he extended it. Bert Wallins' hands, now that you came to examine them, were wrinkled too. The hands of both men had been steeping in brine off and on for weeks. Deaf Burke was, for an Irishman, rather reticent. This was not owing to the fact that he had not had a glass of whiskey since Dashwood's challenge was accepted by his patron, but to a certain phlegmatic turn. He spoke seldom. He was a man hard to rouse.

His appearance was remarkable. He stood an inch shorter than his opponent, his shoulders sloped until they were caught up and lifted by his swelling deltoid muscles. His nose was broken. What his face had looked like undisfigured it was impossible to conjecture. It must have been a fine open countenance, for even with a nose so smashed that it went down straight and slanted sideways from the hump of bone between his eyes, he had still a certain blackguardly beauty about him. His brow was broad in comparison to Wallins' but sharp outside the eyes. About the colour of his eyes there could be no doubt. They were of the very dark blue that is found combined with a pure white skin and blue-black hair only in Ireland. The type was a remnant or a sport and to be seen only in the West. The de Burghoes, or Burkes, as they came to be called, were the first of the Norman conquerors to blend with the native Western Irish stock. The result was that they spread and became the most distinctly Irish of the Irish in the land.

Deaf Burke turned and, as a greatcoat was hung loosely on his shoulders by Flash Dunne, his principal second, stood in the corner nearest to Sir Richard and the coaches. The day was one of those sunless, bright gray Irish days, so there had been no tossing for position. There was no sun to dazzle either man's eyes.

The shouts and cheers died down. Their place was taken by ejaculations, followed by little mocking cries. Suddenly all went still.

In the middle of the ring stood Tiger Roche. There was no need to raise his hand for silence.

"Gentlemen and the rest of you," he began, "I have been asked by those seriously concerned to say that no matter how this fight goes it is to be marked by no scenes such as those that followed Burke's victory on this very spot over Jabez Kent. That scene was a disgrace to this country and it was enough to take much of the credit of a fair fight from Burke.

"No matter what way this fight goes there will be no interference either by seconds or supporters.

"It is no use asking you up there to remember that you are Irishmen. I should be sorry if you were. You are a lot of indiscriminate ragamuffins who stand for nothing but disorder and noise. But on the first attempt to interfere either by shout of encouragement or cry of mockery, you will be beaten from the field by the ring-keepers and the first one of you who attempts to return will be shot. I am speaking now as the chief of the Society for Aiding Order." He ceased and produced a small book. He turned over some pages, held it with both hands and continued, "This fight is to be fought after this fashion, under the Broughton Rules, which read:

"One. That a square of a yard be chalked in the middle of the stage; and on every fresh set-to after a fall, or being parted from the rails, each second is to bring his man to the side of the square, and to place him opposite to the other, and till they are fairly set-to at the lines, or the scratch, it shall not be lawful for one to strike the other.

"Two. That in order to prevent any disputes, the time a man lies after a fall, if the second does not bring his man to the side of the square within the space of half a minute, he shall be deemed a beaten man. After the half minute an addition of eight seconds shall be given him to come up to the scratch.

"Three. That in every main battle, no person whatever shall be upon the stage, except the principals and their seconds.

"I remain upon the stage for the present to keep decorum and to assist gentlemen in getting to their places. Everybody is to quit the stage as soon as the champions are stripped, before the set-to.

"Four. No champion to be deemed beaten unless he fails to come up to the scratch within the limited time, or that his own second declares him beaten and throws his sponge into the ring. No second is to be allowed to ask his man's adversary any questions or to advise him to give out.

"Five. That to prevent disputes, in every main battle the principals shall, on coming into the ring, choose from among the gentlemen present two umpires, who shall absolutely decide all disputes that may arise about the battle; and if the two umpires cannot agree, the said umpires to choose a third who is to determine it.

"Six. No person is to hit his adversary when he is down, or seize him by the ham, the breeches or any part below the waist: a man on his knees is to be reckoned down.

"The umpires are already chosen. I am the third in case of an irreconcilable dispute. The ring is twenty-four feet square. Deaf Burke wanted to fight in one six feet square. This was disallowed as being unfair to a man's agility. The rounds are ended when there is a knock-down. There is to be no clinging in the tackles. If a man cannot throw his adversary at the first offer, there is to be no holding to his arms or fists. Every five minutes there will be an interval of two minutes for the services of the seconds or of the doctors if they are needed.

"The fight ends when the sponge comes through the air or a second fails to bring his man up to the scratch.

"So as not to catch the eyes of the fighters if they face in their direction, I will ask those grouped about the coaches to remain still. Bookmakers will be expelled if they discourage either man with their shouts.

"The crowd must quit the ring now, leaving only each man's second to serve him.

"Out you go!" he called, and waved away the ostlers and the string who had followed Wallins in Dashwood's train to Ireland.

"What the devil are you doing there?" Roche asked Plant, who was bending down attired in his parti-coloured costume and endeavouring to impress the assembly by his familiarity with Deaf Burke, who now waited, sitting on his second's knee.

"Burke has for second, Flash Dunne; and the skilled help of Dr. MacDermot," the Tiger added.

A cheer began to grow. But the crowd bethought itself in time.

"Herbert Wallins has for second Seaman Spong and the well-known English horse doctor, George Pratt, a familiar figure at the Curragh."

"There will be no Umpire in the ring." At a sign the seconds stood up as their men rose. "And now, silence. The men are about to strip!"

With surprising agility for so big a man, the Tiger leapt the ropes lightly, and stood beside his coach gazing intently at the ring. It was a fine sight to see the way the fighters loosened their cravats and drew off their shirts. To one person at least, high up on Sir Richard's coach, it brought a blush to behold the naked flesh over the ribs that gleamed, scalloped, and the great serrations of the muscles that come up from the spine to make the armpit deep.

There was a groove down Deaf Burke's back that held a shadow instead of showing the spines of the backbone as Wallins' back did. Deaf Burke gave the onlooker the notion that he was a slower man than Wallins: that if it were to come to a running match Wallins would win. But this was a match not of speed but of manhood, between the very reserves of life that lay deep down in the being of each man.

The light glowed on the rippling arms of Wallins as he handed his silk shirt to his second. They were at the scratch now and were set to.

Wallins took one step forward to meet Burke who was standing at the line. Like a flash his body that was straight became an arch from his lifted right heel to the knuckles of his left hand. As a man strikes a holly tree with the back of an axe and slides the bark aside leaving the shining white exposed, so Bert Wallins' fist at the first blow skinned the forehead of Deaf Burke. The bone stood white for an instant, then little points of blue gathered and covered it with blood.

First blood to Wallins! But Burke kept on. Again the lightning left flashed out. Again Burke took it on his bent brow. It could be seen that Burke moved his head neither to the right nor left to avoid a blow but lowered it a little between the bastions of his shoulders. Again he took a direct blow. But on he came amidst the silence. The men were lonely antagonists in the ring so far as human sympathy was concerned. No help except that which their manhood lent. Bert was hitting hard and rapidly and with great accuracy, but it was to be observed by the old hands who knew Burke that Bert was backing all the time he was hitting. Let him smite away. Burke was not called "Deaf" on account of his hearing.

The blood was in Burke's eyes now. Bert struck with his right, seeing that his left had no power to stop his opponent. To bring up the right he shifted his feet. Was it at the feet and not the face that Burke was gazing? Bert's right foot moved back.

In the middle of the shift a swinging blow struck him on the ribs —the floating ribs that are so hard to break. He toppled over on his left side like a stricken steer. Wallins was grassed. The first knockdown and round one went to Burke. Cheers rang in the hollow of the cliff.

The Tiger advanced to the ropes and raised his hand for silence. A general gasp was all that came from the crowd.

"I wish that he'd protect himself better," Sir Richard said. "I have offered to have him taught boxing. He says it would spoil his nature."

Burke stood back with both his arms depending. He was bent forward and the depth of his chest was somewhat hidden by his stance. From his forehead blood was dripping. He leant forward to let it drip on the ground so as to keep it from dripping into his eyes.

Bert was up at once. Never would it be said of him that he took refuge from his opponent by lying on the ground. His coolness was sinister. Without ostentation he brushed the grass off his knees, leaving only a green stain on his breeches and white stockings. His second led him up to scratch.

He smashed at Burke with undiminished speed. The fist glanced over the imperceptibly dropped head. A dull smack resounded through the quarry's hollow sides. Bert gasped. Over his heart a dark weal began to form. Bert played for breathing space but this was denied him. Like a skater sliding without daring to lift his feet, Deaf Burke, with bleeding face and hair clotted on his forehead, followed grimly. Though he had worked his way in close enough for one of his terrific swinging blows to land, Burke struck straight out somewhat in the way that Wallins did, but he did not aim for the face. He hit Bert in the chest on its strongest part, the middle of the breast bone. It was enough to break a striker's fist. Wallins' ribs were paralyzed. He could not even gasp; breathless he sank forward, but before his open hands could feel the protecting earth he was smashed sideways. He fell and rolled. Another round for Burke.

They were set to again.

Again Burke, taking awful blows on his own face, knocked his rival sideways off his feet. Infuriated, the pug leapt up, only to be grassed with a blow that brought Burke's body round after it like a man swinging a scythe.

Shouts of "Round!" arose from Bert's corner.

This brought the seconds out to bring their men up to scratch. Wallins caught Burke round the waist, leaving Burke's arms free. It was a grave blunder. Burke wrenched his body sideways and got his left elbow on Bert's left shoulder. He raised himself off the ground, to which no wrestler would have essayed to fling him. Bert saw what he thought was his chance. He flung Burke back; but Burke's arm was round his neck and Bert was bent forward from the waist. Flung from behind Burke's back, his right fist flailed the imprisoned face of Wallins until he was forced to desist by the cuts his rival's teeth had made on his knuckles.

When released, Wallins fell flat. He crawled on the ground and collapsed with his face buried in his arms. His second pulled him to his corner by one foot. The bottle-holder took out the plug and poured brandy directly into his clenched mouth through the gap made in his teeth. He spat blood. When he opened his eyes he refused to drink any more. Brought to scratch, he retreated to gain time. Time was not given him, though he milled well on the retreat. Grunting like a boar, with lowered head, Deaf Burke took the blows and went indefatigably on. Suddenly, with a surprising long left, he grassed the Englishman again. The merciless crowd roared, forgetful of the caution.

"Go on, the Deaf 'Un! You have him flat-footed."

The Tiger crossed the outer ring and shook his fist. This restored order but not silence. Still a dull mumble came from the bloodthirsty rabble overhead.

"Surprising, very surprising. I never dreamed he had such a long left," Sir Richard was heard to say.

In his corner they were forcing Bert to drink. He put his finger into his mouth and threw away a loosened tooth. He rose like a man revived. Burke, who was carrying the battle to the Englishman, was evidently set on grassing him until his courage would be gone, and with it the hope of victory against a granite avalanche.

He tried by the very force of his blows to knock Wallins off his feet, for as the crowd had not been slow to see, "he had him flat-footed." All the jauntiness that was in Bert's step had gone. But his heart was undaunted. For every blow dealt by the "Deaf 'Un," Bert lashed at him again. Some of the blows were turned by Burke's shoulder, which he shrugged sideways, now left, now right. Bert was seized about the waist and lifted by one arm high into the air. With the other Burke flung the Englishman over his shoulder and turned to stand over or fall on him when he fell. But he didn't fall. It was Burke who was twisted on his legs, for the Englishman in his flight caught him round the neck and saved himself from a heavy throw.

"Let go!" both seconds called together.

Bert was the livelier in breaking away. Leaping back to get his distance, he brought his right fist sharply against Burke's left eye. It had hardly left its mark when a dark lump began to show. Burke's eye was closing.

The question rose, "Is it round five or six?"

"Six," Roche said, and settled that.

Burke made a mistake. He felt his eye for a second. While his fist was against his face two sickening smashes hit it. Burke reeled; Bert was on him and smote him down. Slowly Burke turned on the ground. Slowly he rose with his hands holding him for a moment on all fours. He rose, and when they had been set to, he swung a bent arm right into the dark target of Bert's bruised ribs. Bert gasped and bent towards the stricken side. Burke missed his head with a swinging blow but in the mêlée flung his opponent on his side.

Round seven went to Burke.

Each second bent a knee and the men sat down on them. With a towel Pratt the Vet fanned Bert Wallins. Dr. MacDermot spoke to Deaf Burke. "Don't mind his pretty face," he admonished. "Do as you are doing and soon he won't be able to breathe. Don't forget, no matter how hurt you are."

"I will not," said Deaf Burke.

"Round eight!" called Tiger Roche.

Rumor said that Bert Wallins was forced by his trainer to run up and down the steps of a lighthouse every day while he was in England. However he came by it, there was no doubting his soundness of wind. He danced away from Deaf Burke. MacDermot, watching, saw him hold his ribs for a moment now and then. Burke was no heavy-footed lout. He could follow. He got his man in a corner; he could smash his head against the post now. But a shattering hail direct into his face kept blinding Burke, who was seeing now with but one eye. He must have kept the doctor's advice in mind even though his temper was sorely tried.

Left and right from his hips he flung blows into Bert's chest, and though his own head was rocked back, he stooped, and as a man with one hand flings a fifty-six-pound weight over his head, he brought up his fist and smashed Bert's jaw-bone. Bert spun and fell and lay turning over and over. At last his second, Seaman Spong, bit his ear. "Lie still until your head clears. You're only in the merry-go-rounds. Ye'll be right again presently."

And right again he was. That great spirit which makes England fight best when most forlorn came to Wallins now. He knelt until his second, looking into his eyes, closely, gave him leave to get to his feet. He vomited before he rose and came up to scratch.

Burke stood back. He had heard of ruses before where a man let on to be weaker than he was to take his rival off his guard. Little he thought of the force of the blows that made Bert's weakness all too genuine.

Though he was strict about the rules he had made against giving either fighter any encouragement by word or cry, the Tiger's remark, overheard by Burke, might have been construed as breaking them. To some grunt of Sir Richard's he said casually:

"When Burke is pleased to fight, we will see a change come over the scene. So far he is but on holiday."

It was undoubtedly encouraging and flattering to the pugilist, who sat in his corner within three yards of Sir Richard, to gather that such a judge as Tiger Roche relied on him. But to the doctor he was saying, "Doctor, both my eyes may soon be closed. That forehead cut has swelled the other eyelid. Lance it for me, Doctor."

"Lance it, no: but I'll keep yer lid open with a stitch." Expertly the doctor lashed eyelid to eyebrow, with what appeared to be housewife thread. The quivering eyelid settled and stayed open.

What the doctor whispered satisfied Deaf Burke. He stood up from his second's knee a moment before his rival took the ring. With his clear fearless eyes Bert Wallins came on, serene save for a mutilated mouth and a lop-sided swollen jaw. He leapt like a tiger and plied his fists a score of times into Burke's wounded face and eyes. He tripped Deaf Burke, threw him back flat with his head against the corner post. But Flash and the doctor had cushioned the post with their hands before he struck it. His head could not have been broken. And yet he lay still as death. His chest was heaving and quiet enough. He was not dead, that was plain; but was he unconscious? Flash turned his head and tried to encourage him with friendly profanities —a ruse as old as the heroic days when Laeg his charioteer reviled Coohoolin.

"God blast you, you bastard, when are ye going to fight? Ye're not even sweatin' yet." There was no response. The gold ornaments of the Tiger's watch could be seen swinging as he counted the time.

Then a strange thing happened. Down from the back of Sir Richard's coach a lithe figure in a long fawn travelling coat leapt and ran to the ring. Over Deaf Burke it bent and said something rapidly, then ducked under the ropes and climbed back again. The effect on the half dead man was magical. He looked at Sir Richard and nodded his battered head.

In his trepidation Sir Richard had only eyes for his supine fancy. Still lying on his back, Deaf Burke coolly wiped his unblinking eye. With his right hand he guarded it, for it had now no protection. The left was too far gone. He rose with a limp. Flash led him to the middle of the ring where Wallins waited. Burke waded after the agile Bert. On that athlete came again. His tactics were repeated. Deaf Burke bore the awful punishment and still held his fist before his one staring eye.

At last they heard it. To Wallins it sounded like the sound a woodsman makes when he tramples sticks down tightly in the fire. The blow had ascended to Bert's right side. It bent his body like a bow. Gasping and stooping sideways, Bert made shift to give way. Burke stalked after him and found him where fists up, he came to a stand to face him. Bert gazed at Burke with unwounded glassy eyes. Burke swung his arm for his head this time, but held it in mid-air. Bert Wallins stood unflinching. What had happened? What made Burke forbear?

Untouched, Bert Wallins fell. He rose only to fall face downwards where he lay, face pillowed on his arms.

His second pulled him by a leg into his corner.

In Burke's corner Dr. MacDermot said: "When I saw that the blood was mixed with foam on his lips, I knew that his ribs were broken. But what did St. George's young friend from the coach say to you when you were stretched?"

Deaf Burke was dumb.

"Well, if you won't tell me, I suppose I am not to know. Christ! There's the sponge in the ring. You have won, you villain of the world! You have won! Let me snip out the stitches."

And the tearful doctor slapped the back of Deaf Burke, who was blind now, for the time being.

"Out of the ring!" the Tiger shouted to those encroaching. He raised his hand:

"I wish to make a proclamation. You will depart quietly and give the gentlemen at least a quarter of an hour to get away from this. After that you can misbehave to your hearts' contentment. Each competitor must have unobstructed room to leave with his own party.

"Deaf Burke has won. . . . A moment. . . . Just now he is blind and needs attention. He offers to come unaided up to scratch. Bert Wallins, though defeated, is not disgraced—far from it. He fought several rounds with a broken jaw-bone. He has three ribs stove in. He cannot breathe without spitting blood. Mr. Dashwood accepts defeat for him.

"I will permit you to applaud from your places, Bert Wallins of England who fought so bravely under such grim handicaps!" But as blinded Burke cautiously measured three paces towards the scratch, holding his hands in front of him, indescribable screams, whistles and wild huzzas hailed him. As he came up to scratch, carrier pigeons were released and flew off, bearing the news of Burke's victory to backers far from the scene. Fully five minutes elapsed before the Tiger got a hearing.

"In recognition of his great fight Sir Richard has given Bert Wallins a purse of fifty guineas. One thing more. You have behaved, for your like, woundily well. So that you may neither choke the ways or run alongside harassing the coaches with your begging, a handful of coins will be thrown into the ring by Mr. Plant here when all the parties are clear away."

"Is there no one else could do it, yer Honor?" a voice asked from the ledge. "I'm going with Sir Richard's party," Plant protested. The Tiger turned to him.

"Do you think for one minute that I will permit you to mount with that Macaroni mixture on Sir Richard's coach? That dress would make the paint look shabby. You will remain here and distribute the money. If the crowd is not content, I will tie one hand behind your back!" So saying, the Tiger entered his coach and followed Sir Richard.

Dashwood's coach was in the way. It had been ordered to remain by its owner so that Wallins might be conveyed to his quarters in greater comfort than could be had in a chaise, though he declared that he could breathe more easily sitting up. Dashwood took Sir Richard's offer of a place. Dashwood's party was distributed amongst those who had space for accommodation.

When they were well out of hearing and out of sight, the Toucher took the ring. "Stand back!" he shouted, as the motley crowd began to descend. "I wish to make a proclamation." The announcement was derided. "I must remove the ropes before I throw the money among ye," he added.

An officious ruffian, anxious to curry favour with the money-carrier, removed the top rope, coiled it and presented it to the Toucher, who intended to sell it foot by foot as a souvenir. But the crowd was close at hand.

In order not to be overwhelmed, the Toucher turned and cast into the ring the handful of various coins which he had been given by the Tiger. It was a pity and a hardship that he could not have counted them first, if only to get an idea of the amount of the Tiger's largesse. Judging by the time the scramble and the ensuing fight lasted, this must have been considerable.

With the rope under his arm, the Toucher followed Flash and the others, who were leading the blinded warrior from the scene of his encounter. As he caught up with Dr. MacDermot, who had given his place to Dashwood in Sir Richard's coach, a messenger crossed the ring coming from the Englishman's tent.

" 'E says as 'ow 'e'd loike to shake hands wiv ye," he said, addressing Burke. Flash repeated the message.

"Lead me to him," said Deaf Burke. "And where is Flash? Flash, give him half the purse, for he's a gallus fighter."

"Don't be an idiot," Flash responded. "Sir Richard has already sent him fifty guineas to make up for the punishment he took. Keep your money; but take my arm and I'll lead you to him."

The doctor, when invited home by Sir Richard, had said, "No, I must attend to Burke. Wallins will need my services too. He has only a horse doctor to attend to him."

So the humane "Johnny Mac" remained to render what help he could to the battered contestants.

"There is one thing that still puzzles me, Burke," he said, as he cut the hair from the wound in Burke's forehead. "What was it that St. George's young friend whispered into your ear when we gave you up for unconscious?"

But on that subject Deaf Burke was dumb again.

It took the Toucher to get it out of him, and by that time Burke was celebrating with Flash, the Bugler and others of the fraternity.

If the doctor repeated the Toucher's account of the story accurately, what Burke revealed had the ring of the incredible. Perhaps that is why the doctor believed it; being incredible, it was all the more possible in Ireland.

"It was Miss Mabel, Sir Richard's niece, yer Honor. 'Get up, Burke,' sez she. 'D'ye want to disgrace me?' she says. 'I have laid my Uncle's coach and four on ye to win and here ye are reposing,' she sez, 'face downwards like a tailor's goose.'" Lapse of memory of the heroic style may have caused the slight discrepancy in the Toucher's version of Burke's position. "'Ye wouldn't have me locked up?' she says. 'Deaf ye are, and blind ye may be,' she says, 'but you've only got to hit him once and both of us is made forever. I wouldn't mind so much if me Uncle knew of the bet; but you know the kind of man he is, he is so woundingly particular.'"

In spite of his reticence, Dashwood took the defeat of his champion like the sportsman that he was. Then he commented:

"Extraordinary fellow, that Roche, eh? Seems to have the crowd well in hand. How does he do it?"

Sir Richard laughed. "More by terror than by popularity," he said.

So merrily the coach trundled home. On its outside seat St. George was instructing Mabs how best to avoid discovery. She might jump down on the opposite side as the coach was coming to the door, make her way to the stables and from them, at a later opportunity, into the house. Aunt Penelope might know where she had not been, but that would be very different from knowing where she had been.

Mabs was lucky. Though she almost ran into her Aunt on the stairs, that lady was in such a state of agitation that she did not notice, or had overlooked her absence.

"Run and find St. George immediately," she said. "And tell him that he is to take horse at once and ride as hard as he can to Galway. His mother is ill: ill with anxiety, the housekeeper writes. There must be no delay. Ninon and Martyn are preparing to set out. They will stop at Attymon House on their way to Martyn Hall. You and I and La Baronne will go on to Lisadill in a day or two, as soon as we shall have made our purchases and our dresses come in from the dressmakers. You missed many lessons in good taste by not shopping with us this afternoon."

BOOK II

V. THE ROAD TO ATHLONE

It was said that Ellice St. George's frequent indisposition was the result of an accident in the hunting field which occurred in the autumn of the year after her adventurous return from France, aided by the Chevalier d'Estournelles. Her maid had informed a confidant here and there that she was "active enough in a way on her feet but she was that proud that she would not be seen limping."

In the mornings she went for a round of the rose garden, which had walls of cut-stone almost ten feet high. On some fine days she sat in the chaise and drove to the town, where the merchants came running from their shops to receive her orders.

On rare occasions she would stop the chaise and condescend to talk to some member of the Galway Blazers on his way from hunting the fox; but the weather rarely admitted of her taking the air. However, when the hunt met at Attymon House, she was to be seen in her chair on the top of the steps, perhaps languid from loss of sleep but always gracious, always exquisite.

Her father had been an American of French extraction who had owned an estate in Virginia; in the hall at Attymon House there was a bold-eyed portrait of him at the Court of Louis Quinze. Her grandfather was born in France. Her Virginian father had brought her up in France where, upon a visit to Paris, she met her sparkling future husband who was travelling through the continent on one of those educational "grand tours" on which some of the Irish landlords relied perhaps too much. Yet to this traffic with France and Italy were due the munificence and good taste that furnished the great mansion houses of the Irish countryside.

On the morning after the birth of her son Denis, her husband was killed in a duel by an officer of the Dublin garrison, after embarrassing the estate to some member of the Hellfire Club in an all-night game of cards. She had no liking for the Hellfire Club. Last winter her son had shot his man before he had been elected to its membership; it was not the duellist who had killed his father but a fellow who in his cups had been heard to say that "on the face of this earth there is no more tiresome sight than the sight of an invalid woman." He may or may not have been aware of the fact that recently the mother of young Denis St. George had become an invalid. But certain members were aware, and just for the sake of trouble interpreted the remark as an insult and as such proposed it to Denis. His position as a guest acted on his mettle. He challenged the member who had made what was perhaps no more than a general remark. The remark was in bad taste and it broke an unwritten rule that women were not to be a theme for conversation or discussion at the card tables of the Hellfire Club.

St. George shot his man and was invited to become a member of a club which set more value on the duel itself than on the justice of the cause in which it was fought. Duels were fought not for justice but for honour, and honour is a touchy thing. The best that could be said for the duel was that it preserved decorum, but in the Hellfire Club it had become almost a form of sport rather than a defence of convention.

Hyacinth envied Denis for the expedition with which he now set out from Sir Richard's town house to join his mother. He simply took horse and departed. He would be at Attymon House in twelve hours. Martyn-Lynch would travel in the great coach with his bride and the Chevalier. And he had to wait until all the luggage was gathered and packed. Who would have thought that so many various things were necessary to the existence of women? His bride's luggage was voluminous enough in all truth, but there were many articles which seemed superfluous until a question about them brought out the fact that they were indispensable to the furnishing of a boudoir.

"Let the child have her way," Aunt Penelope said. "This is no time to grudge her her little fancies." So the cases were piled up on the coach, enough to invite all the highwaymen between Dublin and Ballinasloe.

The question of conveying the Chevalier arose. His presence was not particularly noticeable in the city. Those whom he had already met asked no questions, simply because it did not occur to them that there was any irregularity about his status. They accepted him as some sort of relative of Sir Richard. But it was another thing altogether to convey him across a disaffected and dragooned country where everyone was suspect under military law. Martyn, prone as ever to exaggerate difficulties and given to over-cautiousness in surmounting them, thought that the Chevalier should make the journey as he had made it from France, in disguise. But how to propose it without giving him offence? How could he ask a guest to hide himself, now that he had reached what he considered to be his destination? This had all the appearances of an insurmountable difficulty, but like most of Martyn's forebodings it solved itself.

It solved itself in two ways. First, the Chevalier had little luggage. The clothes he had travelled in were still disguise enough. He carried no uniform in his baggage. And Aunt Penelope had already explained the situation to the Chevalier, who had accepted it with a laugh. He was to travel on the box seat of the coach beside Feeney, the family coachman; and, if accosted, to talk nothing but Italian. Aunt Penelope did not go on to explain to the Chevalier that that language would pass him off as one of the many Italian craftsmen and cooks who were in a colony in the city and whose skill was in continuous demand throughout the country wherever there was a mansion being built or staffed. The Chevalier did not ask why he must be Italian. He knew that to speak French at the moment would bring upon him the obstinate suspicion of the officer, English or Hessian, who might be in charge of the district through which he would pass. He knew that he could not speak English and pose as a servant. His accent would betray him. He therefore accepted Italian as the least suspicious of the foreign languages.

At last all was ready for the long road. Aunt Penelope, wearing a dress with panels of cream and black, which gave her the appearance of one of those lady doctors of Salerno, came out upon the steps to see the party off. Feeney raised his whip. Timsey, his son, rode postillion. Ninon and Hyacinth waved goodbye from the carriage window. As they started off, Mabs threw them a huge bunch of flowers from an upper window of the house, which Hyacinth caught as he leaned out of the carriage. Mabs and Clemente would remain with Aunt Penelope for a few days, and then all three would go on to Lisadill.

The town smelt of turf-smoke in the morning air. The lesser houses had a blue plume above their roofs. The tall four-story mansions sent up a darker reek. The well-to-do burned coal. Pigs scuttled from under the leaders' feet as the coach went its way. Angry cries recorded the protests of the swineherds.

The bridge was blocked. Early as it was, this was always the way on a market day in the big town. Carts piled high with vegetables coming in from Crumlin, Kilmainham, Rathmines and the southern farmsteads closed the thoroughfare. No one made as if to give way to the carriage folk. You might think by the leisurely time they took that the surly boors obstructed the coach on purpose. There was only room for a cart or a carriage at a time. Feeney would take no risk of having his emblazoned panels scratched.

At last Timsey whipped up. They were over. Past the House of Parliament they went, past the great western front of Trinity College, the gates of which were opening to admit milkmen, to the right past Daly's coffee house, on to the end of Dame Street, and up Cork Hill. Splendidly they stepped it past Christ's Church, and so along the top of the ridge, south of the river Liffey on which Dublin stands, called Thomas Street.

As they cantered up towards Gallows Green the way was blocked again, this time impassably. Forty or fifty dragoons closed the road. They sat erect, sabres on shoulders, with the rumps of their horses turned towards the coach. They were enclosing a dense, dark-clothed crowd. Something was going on. Contending cries, groans, curses and cheers arose. Suddenly the crowd ran hither and thither. Stout ruffians jostled each other as in a game. The coach was completely held up.

Martyn grew impatient. He pulled down a window and with his head out shouted to Feeney to ask the cause of the delay. Feeney was gazing fascinated at a scaffolding between ladders on which a pair of masked men were at work.

"Are they hanging anyone, Feeney?"

"They've hung him, Sir."

"Well, then, what are the crowd doing?"

"It seems they're playing football with his head." It was true. As soon as the rebel had been executed and beheaded, after being drawn and quartered in accordance with the law, the executioners threw his head down into the street and immediately a yelling crowd kicked it to and fro. There was no sympathy for this rebel. He had proved to be an informer who had turned "King's Evidence" and betrayed his comrades in an attempt to save his neck. True, he had been promised a partial pardon, but whether for reasons of public policy or because the Military Governor had a contempt for informers, the Royal clemency was withheld and now the rebel's head rolled between the spurning feet of rival factions, a sad witness to the fatuity of trying to be on two sides at once or of trusting lawyers' promises.

The ghastly head rolled out from under the horses. Martyn saw the poor smitten face of the weak-hearted wretch who had the courage neither to go forward nor to hold his peace. He saw the small reddish side-whiskers on the flat-sided head. The man might have been a member of the lower middle classes, a scrivener perhaps (for it was among the semi-literate in the city that the seeds of rebellion were kept smouldering) who like many before him had tried to make the best of both sides. Now sympathizers with those he had attempted to betray were kicking his head over to the ranks of the Orange loyalists, who hated a rebel. They had kicked it back and it had rolled temporarily from the field. Lest Ninon see the gruesome thing, Martyn closed the window and drew down the blind. Moreover, it was dangerous for an aristocrat to be seen by men so roused.

An ensign, seeing the coach delayed, detached a company of dragoons who, riding on each side and now and then striking with the flat of their sabres, cleared a way through the fetid ranks of the populace. Soon they were clear and the coach rolled on between the clanking files of horses. As they turned north at Kilmainham, Martyn left the coach and thanked the officer. The latter judged Martyn to be a personage of some importance, and drew a card from his vest to write out a permit for him, explaining that it was a precaution against possible delay from the pickets posted across the country at the junctions of all the mail roads. Everyone, the officer said, must have a permit to travel ten miles from his address. Without such a permit he would be liable to arrest and detention in a guard-house until his bona fides were established. Martyn thanked him and placed the paper in the pocket of his waistcoat. He entered the coach and the journey was resumed.

"I hope that the Chevalier did not take my description of him amiss if he heard it," Martyn said. "It was necessary to satisfy the officer before we could proceed."

Ninon nodded her head and said that the sooner Sir Richard put the Chevalier's position on a more satisfactory basis with those in authority, the happier it would be for all. As things were, the Chevalier was in an anomalous position. His very disguise was a danger. If it were penetrated by any of the soldiery he might be shot and Martyn and herself arrested for complicity in harbouring a Frenchman who had entered the country surreptitiously. La Baronne, being a woman, was not similarly placed. Would it not have been advisable, Ninon asked, to remain in the city until the position of the Chevalier was established?

"Impossible," Hyacinth said hastily. "It would have resulted in an inquiry, and then those who were responsible for his entry would be thrown into prison. Better wait until the manner of the Chevalier's entry had become more dim in memory; leave the matter to the healing hand of time."

"I'd rather you left it to Uncle Richard. He could have got it in a few weeks."

"How could you expect me, darling, to delay one minute from

ushering you into your new house? Even if you could have waited, it would be impossible to keep Mrs. St. George waiting for a sight of her hero, the Chevalier."

So they travelled on down the long hill bordering the Liffey on the south as it descended from the ridge of Dublin. The river was one long tranquil reach at this stage, where the village of Chapelizod nestled under the braes of the Phoenix Park—Chapelizod, Seapul Isoud in the Irish, which means the chapel of Iseult of Ireland.

Sir Richard's country seat was on the right. You could see its chimneys from the hill that led down into sheltered Lucan village. They were smoking. Lucan House was always ready. It was about an hour's drive from the city, and there was no knowing when Sir Richard would take a whim and drive out with a host of friends to sleep, and to wake in the silent morning air away from the cries of the town.

Leixlip, Maynooth, where the ducal Castle of Leinster stood in ruin, replaced by a lordlier house nearby, and Kilcock were passed, and the canal was crossed a mile beyond the village. Then came the long straight by the dark water mill that led to Kinnegad. It was but twelve miles to Mullingar and then they would be only an hour or two from Lord Longford's seat of Packenham Hall. He had urged them to break their journey for the night at his house. Had they passed by even without this specific invitation, he would have been offended. It was never necessary to announce your coming to a place like Packenham Hall.

Evening was in the trees of the long drive that wound through grassy mounds to the house. Lights were beginning to show. His Lordship had been informed of the approach of his friends. He stood in the yellow light of the open door.

"Damn my blood, but it is good to see you," he said.

Early the next morning, as Ninon was stepping into the coach, she drew back. A large wicker cage occupied her seat. She turned to his Lordship, who was framed by the ample door.

"Oh, yes! A gamecock. That's all it is. I owe a cock to St. George. Like Socrates, what? Not a deodand exactly; so don't sacrifiçe it unduly. Will you be so very kind as to carry it along? Perhaps it will retrieve St. George's fortunes in the main."

At the first jerk of the traces the cock crew. A cheery cry answered from the hall door. Away the great carriage went. South first and then west it would go on the straight road to Athlone, where the river Shannon slices off one third of the country with its long flat arc like a scimitar.

The Chevalier was on the box seat beside Feeney. There was sure to be a search of all save official carriages crossing the Shannon into the wild regions of the West—the wild regions where you might say anything that came into your head, as the catch had it:

West of the Shannon may be said
Whatever comes into your head;
But you may do, and chance your luck,
Whatever you like west of the Suck.

Dragoons galloped past on their way to the city. But they were only a detached party skirmishing in front of a larger body which was on its way with a wagon-load of prisoners. Here and there they would leave the high road to search any copse that might shelter a rescuing party of rebels in ambush. Presently the coach met a strong company of dragoons trotting with drawn sabres beside a long military wagon in which dejected countrymen lay or stood. Those who were wounded could not be seen. They were hidden in the straw which a kind officer permitted to be supplied to them to ease the pain of broken limbs as the wagon jolted along.

In order to avoid the discomfort of stopping for a meal at an inn, they had been provided with food and wine by the thoughtfulness of Lord Longford. Ninon opened a basket and took out a parcel of meat between two slices of bread. This was a dish called after the infamous gambler John Montague, the third Earl of Sandwich, who sat at play for twenty-four hours with no other meal but slices of beef put up for convenience between two slices of bread. A sandwich.

All was going merrily. They were making good time. Moate was already behind them. They were on the straight but undulating road directly to Athlone. No molestation so far.

"Don't let us congratulate ourselves on it," Hyacinth advised, when Ninon expressed satisfaction at the going.

Suddenly the day darkened. They were under a long drive of beeches which met overhead. "We are only a mile or so from Athlone," Hyacinth said.

After a slight rise the trees grew scantier. Rows of hovels hemmed the long, wandering, muddy street. To the left the silver spread of the river shone clean and expansive in contrast to the foul and narrow street.

At the opening space before the bridge, two large wooden guardhouses had been hastily erected. From these, on either side, a score of soldiers emerged and drew a cordon across the way.

At a signal the coach drew up. A tall fellow in a sergeant's uniform approached the window.

"Vill you dismount, pliss," he ordered.

"Don't move, dear," Martyn said as he leaped down on the roadway. He left no time for the step to be put down. "See here, Sergeant, I am Martyn-Lynch. I am well known in Connaught. I am neither a rebel nor a comforter of rebels, and therefore I resent this delay."

"Pliss," the Hessian sergeant repeated. His men began to take the baggage down from the top of the coach. Three or four men drove back a crowd of half-clothed idlers and boys who had gathered with eager faces to catch a glimpse of the contents of the portmanteaux of the great. Ninon's trunk was the first to be unstrapped.

"Where the devil is your officer?" Martyn demanded hotly.

"Pliss?" The sergeant repeated, smiled and shook his head. Thereupon Martyn flung aside the soldiers who were delving in his wife's effects. Promptly half a dozen men gathered round him and he was held. In vain he struggled to shake off his captors. Ninon tried to attract his attention, and leaning from the window called to him in French. She was alarmed lest the Chevalier's identity be discovered in the course of the search.

A young officer approached. Seeing the struggle and the lady leaning from the coach, he came up to the group.

"Officer," Martyn called to him, "will you not call off these ruffians? My name is Martyn-Lynch and I resent this outrage on my freedom."

The young officer spoke to the Hessian sergeant who saluted but made no other sign of compliance.

The officer admitted to Martyn that the Hessian troops were independent to the extent that they were answerable only to officers of their own.

"Tell you what I'll do, Mr. Lynch. I'll run up to the barracks and try to get the Hessian officer out. I am afraid that he will hardly make an exception in your case. Orders to search all equipages except those of the military command are in force."

By this time all the baggage was lying on the road. A box of China and knick-knacks was being prised open.

"If your ruffians break any of my property I shall return to report you to Dublin Castle this very day," Martyn said.

"Pliss," the sergeant repeated soothingly. From the interior of the coach a loud cock-crow shrilled. The faces of the soldiers, Hessian or Brunswick, remained impassive but cheers hailed the call of the fighting bird when the quick-witted crowd realized what the crowing implied. At once they took the side of Martyn, who, though an aristocrat and evidently a landlord, was a sportsman who carried his own cocks on his coach.

The little officer returned.

"I cannot move the Hessian. The arrogance of these foreigners is enough to make us detested by the people who see no difference between us. He says, however, that if you are bona fide you have only to produce your passepartout and the sergeant will permit you to proceed."

"Damme. I had clean forgotten it." Martyn fumbled in his pockets and produced the piece of paper that the officer in Dublin had provided.

The Englishman glanced at it and nodded to the sergeant who took the sheet. He was about to put it away without reading it, when Martyn demanded that it be given back.

"How am I to know that there will not be another posse of these oafs at Ballinasloe and that I shall not again be subjected to indignity?"

As he pocketed the sheet the handles of his pistols came into view. The sergeant made as if to take them. Martyn swung himself into the coach. This sudden action and his indignation caused the sergeant to forget the most important of his orders: to collect all firearms. Obviously Martyn, who made no attempt to conceal his personal pistols, was no skulking rebel.

When the last of the luggage was replaced the cordon divided. The soldiers released the horses and the coach crossed the river and moved slowly through the "Irishtown" of Athlone and resumed the open high road.

As the carriage slowed to face the little hill that gave on the open country, Ninon burst out laughing. Her husband looked at her in amazement.

"The diversion you created saved the Chevalier," she explained. "They never thought of ordering him to come down from the box; and he has far more to risk and to lose than either of us." And true it was. The Chevalier had sat through the scene with folded arms and an aplomb that evidently only a well-trained valet or a foreign artisan to whom the whole affair was a puzzle, could possess. It was apparent that he was one of the household, and he passed through the guard as little molested as Feeney, or Timsey the postillion, or Red Dander, the fighting cock in his sheltering cage.

VI. A GREEN BOUGH IN THE CHIMNEY

ON A GENTLE eminence rising from the lake stood the great house, newly built, set like a great gem in the semi-circle of a ring of trees. Martyn Hall would be seen less starkly when the trees, planted in a curved line from either side, began to grow. The house was built of the blue-gray stone which has made Ireland famous the world over for the stamina of its houses. It was on the part of the estate that Hyacinth had owned before he had inherited the additional acres from Ninon's father, Colonel Lynch. Martyn's old house on the property, near the present site, had been torn down to make way for the new Martyn Hall. The glass in its windows, which had just been fitted, was still dull from the glaziers' handling, but soon the polished panes would flash back the sun from the southwest.

Unlike most Irish mansions, which faced north, this house stood facing the southwest, towards the lake and the faintly drawn line of the thin, blue, distant hills. The decision to depart from the custom of the architects and to turn the house, as it were, round-about, was made because the lake had been dappled with sun when the bride-to-be first cast her eyes on it and saw the waters like living yellow light, lambent, indescribable as light itself; and because of the view that would be had from the front bedrooms on the third story, of those faint blue distant hills beyond which Lisadill, her childhood home, stood amid its trees by a shallow sea.

The superstition about not observing a custom, as well as the fear about the evil effects of "night air"—worse if it comes in from the south after nightfall through an open window—were overridden at last. And now, the house looks over lake and island, coppice and upland, so far southwestwards that the mountains can hardly be distinguished from the low bright clouds that shine over Lisadill.

The great house would be ready for occupation by its proud owners when cleaned of the débris of the builders who had had to live in it as it arose (and who showed by their habits how little used they were to any decent house). A green bough waved from the tallest chimney stack. It could not be seen from the village, but the carters who brought stones from the quarries and lime from the kiln and the slates that came by sea from Wales, and the men who were building the demesne wall, could see the bough in the chimney and they knew it for a sign that the builders' work was done. All that remained to do was servants' work—to wash the floors, air the rooms, put fires in all the grates to dry the new-made chimneys and help them to draw and then to stretch and put down the carpets that were waiting rolled in canvas at the station in the village by the mail coach road.

The mile-long drive from the highway to the house was a sorry sight. Great ruts were grooved in the heavy soil. There would hardly be time to make a road and to cover it with gravel before "the family" moved in. At any rate, there was a double row of young lime trees already planted to border the avenue.

It did your heart good to look at the house now when ladders and scaffolding and hods and those four-handed barrows that meant hard work had been put out of sight and the house stood clear in its pride, the biggest house for twenty miles around, with the mortar new between its cut stones and the balustrade looking fine on each side as the steps swept up to the pillared hall door.

A flush of rain would do it no harm. It would wash the spilt mortar away and bring out the deep colour of the stone, blue-black that turned light grayish-blue when the sun came out again.

Here was a living symbol of the life of a family: a house built to last for hundreds of years, a house of pride, a decent house, a house that might outlast the family itself, though God forbid. A house that was built, with no thought of its falling, to last forever. A house that showed that its owners were lords of the manor, and was as substantial and immovable as the soil on which it stood. A house built by people who had no idea of leaving the place, a house, in fact an establishment, that was the outward sign for all to see of worthy ones within.

Now the workmen who built the house and the tenants who dwelt on the twenty thousand acres of its fields eagerly awaited the celebrations that would mark the completion of the house in which everyone had had a hand.

A labourer could live on the bowl of midday porridge and save the fourpence until at the end of the week he had two shillings, that is to say if he did not have his pay stopped for absence, or for turning up too late. And that was enough to entertain himself and a few of the boys. But now there was no question about that for there was not a man for miles around who wouldn't have as much as he could drink and lashings more, and the women too would be entertained. Every house was to have its keg of whiskey. There was to be bacon and cabbage for every man, woman and child. But they must supply their own crockery which, when you came to think of it, was reasonable enough.

There would not be room in the barn for the dancers, but even if there had been, the foreman said that he had orders to let no one near the new buildings for fear of fire. The village would be a better place to hold the celebration, after all, for the house was a long way off and it would be lying on your mind to think that if you are a bit of a distance out in the country, you would have to make your own way home after all the gaiety. The highway was firm enough for dancing if the weather gave the boys and girls a chance. The fiddlers and the fluters could sit where they always sat during a fair —in the barn that was used for a court-house during the assizes and so was hardly ever filled with hay. There was a fine floor on it— polished, you would think if you saw the shine on it—and benches could be brought in from the houses hard by.

As if the stuff from which it was made had become conscious, the great house was taking its first look now through shining eyes at the landscape. Aloft, over the lake, saffron now from the sunset, the evening star was shining as freshly as a daffodil in the June night's warm blue. Soft clouds in the west opened and revealed it growing bright in the deepening vault of heaven.

The wooded islands at the end of the lake had lost their translucence long ago, for the sun had set, but they floated still upon the yellow water. The woods darkened as the half-light came on over the gray fields by moat and rath and fairy ring. As if aware of what was mannerly and proper, light left the upper windows and the new house shut its eyes on a magic landscape older than that of any country in Western Europe that retains its heroes' names. Darkness fell on the land of Ossian, Finn, Oscar and the everliving, youthful Angus Oge. From cairn and cromlech and ruined castle, the light faded and gloaming soothed the sleep of unforgotten warriors beneath their gigantic stones.

But within the house neither darkness nor silence reigned. The new house, that had drawn into itself the peace of the evening fields, was alive with the ructions Biddy Early made in giving out her orders. As housekeeper, she had to prepare the linen against the coming of the bride. She had to warm the rooms and air the beds and have the basins filled with water, and how could she do that when nobody knew where Maura had put the brass cans for the hot water? They were unpacked in the coach-house last night. Coortin' she was with one of them Eyetalians that was ruining the place with their singing and smiling and their good teeth and not getting their work done.

Maura's arrival made these querulous questionings seem, by contrast with the outbreak of invective which it caused, gentle as the fancies of a girl. Maura was a little out of breath. She had rushed up three flights of stairs and with half a dozen two-gallon brass waterpots in her arms. She was about to announce her discovery when the words were taken out of her mouth, with the natural result that she became more breathless.

"You found them, you did? Leave them there and go back to hell out of this and wash the muck off your feet before daring to come into decent peoples' houses. Where the hell do you think you were raised?"

And so poor Maura, blushing as red as her ankles that looked like pink hosen under her white calves, took herself and her mud-splattered legs out of the room. Shouted instructions were launched at her as she ran down the stairs.

Meanwhile the work went on. Evidently the bedroom chimney was rightly dragged, for it drew well. Logs of an old crab-tree blazed finely in the brass-rimmed fireplace; and there were more logs in the copper bucket. When Maura came back she could be got to fix the curtains on the four-poster. Biddy was too stiff for playing with curtain rails.

She thought that she heard something moving overhead, but you could never tell with all the horse-hair packing between the floors. A new house like this could not be haunted, yet, for all that, she began to feel an eerieness which could not be explained. A groan? Was that a groan she heard? It sounded like some sort of suppressed cry. And what sort of drumming on the floor was that, like the heels of a hanged man? It might be that "they" were coming over. There were dark doings in the Lynch family that went far back. One of them, Lynch Fitzstephen, hanged his son with his own hands for killing his Spanish guest-friend, and went mad after it. The Martyns too had every reason to be haunted. Nobody knew where Nimble Dick Martyn was buried, who was stabbed to death by the O'Flaherty's men. Not alone that, but there was an old Lynch who compelled his wife to sit at table so placed that she could not take her eyes off the tomb he had built in the lawn over the stepdaughter he suspected her of poisoning. And Hyacinth Martyn had added his uncle's name to his own. There might be ghosts in most of the old families, but there was none that had earned them better than this connection of families.

What was keeping that girl? Maura could have washed a dozen pairs of feet in the time she had been gone. Impatient, Biddy went to the stairwell and called the girl's name again and again. When at last she appeared, it was, to Biddy's astonishment, from upstairs that she came. That explained the ghostlike noises, but it came far from explaining what the jade had been doing there.

"And what might you have been up to?" Biddy demanded angrily.

"To no good, it is sure. When I see your father, I'll tell on you and your pranks."

"We . . . there was torches. We went to look at them out of the window."

"It's easy knowing who 'we' is. I'll tell his Reverence about that good-for-nothing Eyetalian and have him sent away. Torches, indeed! When you can't see the house from the mail road, how could you see torches on the road? Gallivantin' with an Eyetalian in a decent married woman's house! But get on out of that and fix the curtains as you should have done long ago if you had not been gallivantin'."

VII. THE RISING OF THE MOON

IF MAURA THOUGHT to impress Biddy and divert her anger by news of the sight of torches, she was mistaken. The old woman knew well that if she saw torches it was not on the mail road they were. And yet she thought it better not to pursue her tale too closely. The girl had probably seen torches, but they were not those of a procession to welcome the Martyn-Lynches to their new mansion.

Biddy knew that there might well be torches in lane and short-cut, bringing the boys to the field by the river. Biddy knew that if your sight was good (and thank God hers was and she was able to see farther the older she grew) you might catch here and there a glint of torchlight on the dull steel of a pike or spear. On nights such as these, there were as likely as not men going by the lanes and the short-cuts to the fields; the less said about them the better. It would never do for a talkative girl like Maura to have her story questioned or to have the lie given to her direct. Information could be squeezed out of a girl like Maura if she fell into the hands of the militia. Torches there were, no doubt, and there would be movement in military formation to be observed if a spy followed the boys to the low field by the river at the rising of the moon.

The times were disturbed enough in all conscience. The boys had lost much of their gaiety. There were secrets about, and the worse for anybody who stumbled into them. Unfamiliar faces were to be seen here and there. The country was restless, and the blacksmith was busy day and night even when there was not a horse to be seen near the forge. And he wasn't making gates for Martyn Hall. It would never do to doubt the slut and so fix her in her conviction. It would be best to pretend to believe her so that she would forget the sight quickly, thinking the torches were there to light the Master's coach down the side road.

The Master should indeed be here by this, even though, when the coach got to the driveway, the horses would be taken out of the carriage and the tenants would haul home the bride. And it would be just as well that they arrived once and for all before the fire fell low in the grate and the half-furnished house lost its air of welcome. There was no sound of cheering, however, and no one on the front lawn.

Though, if you looked at it another way, it was just as well perhaps that the party did not come at a time when half the boys would be missed, away as they were at the drilling. Not that the Master objected to it altogether, for he was one of the few of the gentry who sympathized with the national movement for freedom. If he didn't object in some ways to the English, he would be fighting for them in their foreign wars. The boys were aware of how his sympathies lay; not that it increased his popularity and got him any more respect, but they knew that he wouldn't report them to the militia if he actually discovered them drilling or found them creeping back from it before dawn. What he did object to was that they were bringing boys in from other districts, not to mention other counties, some of whom had Frenchified notions that purported little good; upsetting a place that was peaceful and law-abiding, if let alone.

But what was worst of all, there were French agents going here and there and getting shelter, who were preaching a new and disruptive doctrine which said that there were no "superiors," and that servant owed no allegiance to master, that to talk of "those in high stations," as the priest did at the end of mass, was slavish nonsense. It was the people's own fault if there were men in high stations. They should be pulled down and levelled and then everyone would be equal, and there would be land and food and work for all. Once they got rid of landlords there would be no rent to pay. The People would own the land and divide it fairly and equally, and everyone would have his or her share once you got rid of the Quality, beginning at the King. The Quality called the People louts. But now the lout was as good as if not better than his lord, by virtue of the generosity and nobility so long suppressed in him. So ran the reasoning of the rebels.

Hyacinth, between the razing of his old house and the building of the new Martyn Hall, had been an absentee landlord over the vast acreage. He had to put up with the rebel sentiment because, if he caught and expelled a French agent from his part of Mayo, the tenant who sheltered him would, likely as not, be hanged; and he did not want to be instrumental in having one of his own people—so far as they could be called his own people, for their loyalty of late was precarious—handed over to the Government and executed. Thus he turned a blind eye to the unrest and forbore to root out the causes. Things had gone too far for that. Even if a man knew the cause of the distemper which had spread like a plague from Paris, he could do nothing to cure it. To attempt to stem the flood and dam its stream was the best that he could do.

Unfortunately his forbearance, as signs of clemency often are, was taken by the country people to be a symptom of fear. So, instead of making them grateful, it made them arrogant. This was always the reaction of those subjected. He felt sullenness in the air. He felt that the gap between master and man was widening and that the more he did to close it, the more suspicious the people became.

One instance had brought this out clearly. He had dismissed his former agent Aiken, a man of Scots descent, who, though righteous and strictly honest, was too rigid to get along with easy-going, well-meaning, backsliding people like the tenants of Martyn Hall.

When Aiken was in office, all sorts of tales were circulated about him. It was said that he condemned several acres of potatoes as being "scrub" and sold them for his own profit. This story was without foundation, but there was a half-truth in it, or a side to it that could be distorted to look like truth. What Aiken did was to order that no potatoes were to be sown in any of the unmanured fields. One particular field of three acres was "in potatoes," and Aiken knew that if it was to be put under potatoes the following year the soil would be exhausted. Therefore on finding the field sown against his orders, he had the whole field dug up and the crop sold before it was fully ripe. This was intended as a lesson to the disobedient cottagers who were wont to take the easiest way the moment supervision was relaxed. Aiken had seen famine ensue among the crofters in Scotland by the very same practice of exhausting the lighter land, and he took farseeing precautions against any such occurrence in Martyn Hall, knowing that it would cost more to feed the people if they left themselves without resources. He cursed the potato mentally because he knew that cheap food meant a low standard of living and overpopulation of the land.

Yet in spite of, or rather because of, his wisdom and honesty, he was dismissed, in that country of contradictions and paradoxes which is Ireland, where honesty and foresight can lead to a man's undoing. And his master suffered from a decline in his revenue after the departure of his just steward.

Months afterwards, when Martyn realized this, he sent for the man who gave the false information. Martyn upbraided him for his calumny. After the usual preamble of denial, the fellow exclaimed, as if in justification of the tale which led to Aiken's dismissal, "Well, he had a long jowl on him, and, anyway, he looked like the nailer on Calvary."

Thus was revealed an ineradicable prejudice of the Gael: a worship of physical beauty with a dislike for its opposite, the ugly or the uncomely. So honest, ugly Aiken went and pleasant, untrustworthy Crosbie took his place. Martyn's rental fell. And that was the total effect of his commiseration with the poor.

Crosbie stopped the mail coach at the hundredth milestone out of Dublin in the morning. He knew the coachmen well, as everyone did for the whole length of the run which started at Athlone. The driver knew what the question was before it was asked.

"He'll be here before meself," he shouted. "They left before I left Athlone. They can't have broken down or I would have passed them."

"How were they going?"

"Smooth and purty, like the ribbons on Feeney's whip."

Crosbie meant by his question to ascertain in what direction they were going. He overlooked the professional interest in appearances of one coachman for another's coach. The driver of the mail coach whipped off before Crosbie could find out the probable cause of the delay.

At all events, he thought, they were within a radius of at most thirty miles and they could not be long in arriving. Of course, they might have turned aside to stay with some of the gentry whose seats were between this point and Athlone. He should have thought of that before.

Wherever Martyn-Lynch was, he would be here in a day or two at the outside. Crosbie had better give orders to have tents erected that evening on the lawn, limy and bald as it was with all the traffic of the builders. The harpers would smell a wedding feast from afar. They had their own means of communication, even without the tinkers, who were the chief distributors of news. Already half a dozen of them were in the village, together with story-tellers whose invention never failed them even when their memory gave way, tinkers, jugglers, and card-tricksters as well as a balladist or two who could improvise a ballad upon a wedding better than a wake dirge if he got enough drink in him to float his intellect.

It was unfair of Martyn-Lynch to be so unpunctual, Crosbie thought. If the celebrations were premature or the rehearsals too thoroughgoing and enthusiastic and fighting ensued, it might lead to a garrisoning of the place by the militia; and if that wouldn't kill joy as well as, likely enough, some of the wedding guests, what would? Here was Crosbie with a wedding feast on his hands with no help for organization and neither groom nor bride. All he could do was to get everything ready. The more extravagant the better. The Master should be made to pay for his unpunctuality. There would be three fiddlers and three harpers, half a dozen flautists and a piper or two, as well as representatives of the Tenants' Committee to present an address of welcome to the bride.

Strictly opposed as Crosbie was to the giving of money as largesse in cash, he could not refuse a little charity here and there over and above the charity he practised in delaying the notices to quit served under Aiken's stewardship, and in remitting the rents of the very poor; and it was hard enough where nearly all were on subsistence diet to tell who was poorer than his neighbour. He had to enable some of these whose families increased annually to clothe their children so that they could all appear in the open air at the same time. If he did not do this he knew well that many a mother would leave her offspring's faces filthy and appear holding them naked above the half-door as the bride and groom drove past. They were quite capable of doing this to spite him and shame the estate. There was enough opposition to landlords without exhibiting the reasons for it. It would never do to let his master down before the old Galway family of Lynch, into whose tribe Martyn had married after he had assumed the name when he fell in for his uncle's estate. Crosbie must give money here and there. He could not give it out, however, until the whiskey had been issued free. It might be diverted into a *pourboire*.

He took a bag full of groats and shillings, mounted his horse and prepared to ride round the estate. He would not be back until nightfall. If the newly-wedded couple came in his absence they had only themselves to blame.

VIII. HERE COMES THE BRIDE

FEENEY REINED THEM in before the two-storied house of Mrs. Ellice St. George. Its sunken basement was bridged by a gracious flight of steps ascending to the pilastered hall door. The walls of Attymon House were dashed with a mixture of gravel and lime that had once been coloured like the yellow sunlight. Its chimneys and roof were high and, set back from the ornate parapet, five gables could be seen if you stood on a knoll and surveyed the house from a distance. The high, graceful roof gave the pile a somewhat French appearance, recalling the Mansard roofs of the chateaux.

It was a lovely and ornate house, as ornate as the times of the second Charles. It had a not ungraceful line. Obviously it did not date back to the devastating days of Red Elizabeth, in whose reign there were but three houses built in all Ireland; and it was not built when the cowardice of James razed the houses of the gentlemen of Ireland, whose loyalty to his throne was their undoing. It had been built by and occupied by the same family since the days of the Merrie Monarch, a dark fellow in spite of his pleasant sobriquet.

Feeney reined in the four lathered horses and was about to put his whip in the socket at his side when his eyes caught something that brought them staring from his head. His son Timsey, the postillion, was asleep. He could hardly believe his eyes. Feeney solemnly took the whip in a deliberate grasp and with a long lash welted the damp pipeclay from the exposed seat of the postillion, whose breeches were put to the stretch as he lay along his horse's neck.

The boy woke with a start and instinctively urged on his mount, only to be corrected and cursed by Feeney, who had difficulty in managing the startled horses.

Feeney shouted in Irish to the postillion to leap down to hell out of that and let the lady out by opening and putting down the folded carriage steps. As the boy was running to obey, the hall door opened and a servant came out in such haste that he was still shouldering himself into his livery. When his coat was buttoned, he plunged down the steps and assisted the bride.

Out she came, dressed in a dark costume of olive green of a simpler mode than fashion dictated. She had a little cap of the same colour with a jaunty feather on her head. She stretched a dainty limb in search of the step and exposed a high boot, a white stocking and a tapering leg on which a faint encircling weal could be seen on the smooth skin above the knee. With a little cry she turned and ascended the steps and entered the coach, the door of which she shut with a bang. Extraordinary as it appeared, this action had a very simple explanation. The bride had taken off her garters, which pressed too tightly for comfort, as she sat in the coach on her long journey. She had forgotten them in the ease their doffing gave her and she now had to put them on before making a friendly call. Hastily she gartered herself. She would not accept her husband's help again with the golden buckles: what went on in the coach was plainly visible from the steps and windows of the house.

She had not to try the steps once more. The coach door was no sooner opened than she was seized bodily by a tall youth and swung merrily to the ground.

"Welcome to the bride!" Denis St. George exclaimed. And then, seeing her husband, "Come on, Hyacinth. *Caed mille failthe!* Come in, come in!"

When Hyacinth Martyn-Lynch reached the ground, he turned and carefully removed a parcel, covered with a dark cloth, that had the shape of a wicker cage. He held it half behind him as he gave his friend his outstretched hand.

"I have something here for you, Denis, that will help you to maintain your position in the county. We brought it all the way from Longford in Mullingar."

"Come on in! Come on in! It will keep. What about a drink and a bath? The journey must have been dusty." And he looked at the windows and panels of the coach. "My mother is all in a fever to see the bride."

"Just a minute. Tell your man to take this to the stables and not let an eye behold him on the peril of his life. Isn't he a beauty?" he asked as he drew back a part of the cover. "Look at the way he is eyeing us. I believe that he would go for us if he had his spurs. Feeney will tell your man how to treat him. Feeney knows as much about a game-cock as he does about a horse. And that means there is no more to be known."

"Give me your coat," Denis said.

The black oak panels and the dark, close banisters of the ample staircase made a fine setting for the young couple. A full-length portrait of some gallant in plush coat of blue, waistcoat of yellow-flowered poplin (made by some of the Dublin Huguenots) and blue knee breeches, could just be seen at this moment, while the hall door was open. Except for the full arrogant eyes and the periwig, the subject of the portrait might have been either of the youths who talked so cheerfully in the hall.

Martyn's coat was deposited beside the bird cage on a black table with great thick legs, which took up the middle of the hall. The bride was taken by the arm and led into a large bright room with Chinese wallpaper that contrasted pleasantly with the gloom of the entrance.

"There's claret, sherry, whiskey and tea. And a seat for herself."

"Did the pigeons bring you the result?" Denis asked.

"I forgot about the battle. Thanks to—" Hyacinth nodded towards his wife.

"What!" Denis exclaimed in surprise. Turning to the bride he said: "Don't reform him, Ninon, whatever else you do to him. He has only one personality and we must leave him that. What would he be without it?"

"Oh, do tell me all about the fight," Ninon requested.

"Deaf Burke, your uncle's fancy, won, but not until he had given us all a fright. He fell and lay on his back for nearly half a minute.

His head hit the post in his falling. That is what probably saved him, for Wallins was afraid to fall on him because of the nearness of the post. Had he lost, I might as well have resigned from the club."

"Why? What club?" Ninon inquired.

"Oh, a little refuge in the hills. No upstarts are admitted and no stewards or land agents, money lenders, bankers or lawyers of any kind. A truly pleasant place if you want a respite from carking cares and so on."

Ninon, puzzled, looked anxiously at her husband. "Where is this club?" she asked, puzzled.

He was spared, for at this moment the cock began to crow loudly from his seat in the hall.

"The poor warrior's crop is empty," Hyacinth said. "He must be watered and fed with the horses wherever he goes."

St. George pulled a long, red-tasselled bell rope. He told the servant that Feeney would instruct the next keeper of the cock.

"I am afraid that if you do not go upstairs and allay my mother's concern for you, she will endeavour to come down from her bed."

"Run along, Ninon, my dear," said Martyn. "Mrs. St. George must not be kept any longer in suspense."

IX. TUNING UP

Biddy Early had been foster nurse to the Master. She was assured of her holding of three acres; no steward could put her out. While she lived, it was as good as freehold. On the strength of this she had a "shop" in the town. The "town" was a miserable village that stretched intermittently along one side of the mail-coach road from Athlone to Westport. The other side was open for the most part of its length, though every fifty yards or so some indiscriminate building could be seen. These few buildings were slated, which meant that they were store-houses. One of them was the station at which the mail coach stopped. Another was the largest shop in the village, the ground floor of which carried everything, as it proudly boasted, "from a needle to an anchor." Here could be bought butter, eggs, flour (that is, India meal), bacon, spades and forks, hay forks and dung forks, from England or Henshaw's in Dublin, oil, hardware, and a collection of hats, cloaks, rolls of frieze and the scant miscellany of goods that a poor community could afford. Above, there were bedrooms from which the owners could be removed to make room for any benighted traveller. It was "Mulcahy's," the principal and only hotel.

Some of the "houses" on the opposite side of the street could hardly be distinguished from a decayed one with mould-covered, cracked walls, which had been long abandoned.

These cabins were built of mud save for a few foundation stones, and roofed with sods or "scrawl," that is oaten straw. They were built, not as the mud houses in England were, with good oaken frames showing their dark patterns through the mud. In the miserable Irish cabins the floor of mud was often at a lower level than the ground without. Some of them had a hole in the roof which reversed the function of a chimney and drove the turf-smoke out through the half door, which was left open night and day to admit light. Air was not considered indispensable, for it brought in the winter cold. There was no furniture, unless that name were given to an inverted bucket or milk pail, or a three-legged stool and a wisp of straw wrapped in canvas. The hearth was a flat continuation of the floor, baked into a rough brick from the perpetual turf fire, which, though allowed to fall down nightly in ash, never lost its "seed of fire." The indispensable kettle hung from its hook.

Inside the huts would be a large family of pallid-eyed children—often with fever-flushed cheeks—and a friendly sow which had to be sheltered, for on her and her progeny the subsistence of the family depended. The pig paid the rent.

By contrast, Biddy Early's house was thirty-three feet long. It had a partition at either end, which did not reach up to the ceiling. Protruding like enormous hat-racks from the wall on each side of the entrance were three or four beams of wood. These were racks on which visitors might hang their saddles.

In the wall at one end near the hearth was a recess boarded up so as to form a kind of bunk, or bed. A few boards in another recess made shelves for a dresser over a two-doored cupboard, or sideboard, which was gay with a show of dishes and blue teacups and plates. Around the dark walls were three benches separated by two chairs. The floor, though made of earth, was dry and smooth. A few planks laid on the rafters made a shelf for anything that was not required for daily use. A large carved oaken chest that at one time might have been a chest for silver stood out some distance from the wall opposite to the hearth and supported a bowl of flowers. This chest was an article unequalled in all the village. Many a bit of female apparel given to Biddy in expansive moments, or left to her in her late mistress's will, lay within. Chief among these was a Paisley shawl fine enough "to pass through a wedding ring."

Three men sat on a bench. Two were of the far western type, with eagle faces and dark eyes, whose foreheads were not as ample as the promise of their brows. Between them sat a thinly haired, red-headed fellow in his early forties. His head was intellectual and egg-shaped. His forehead rose high and when seen sideways his countenance was endowed with a fine nobility that was not borne out by his manners or address. But for his thin sandy hair he might have been the descendant of some stately survivor of the Spanish Armada, the wreckage of which strewed the coast for many a mile nearly two hundred years ago. Had his education kept pace with his appearance he would have been superior to many a rich shoneen or many a member of the Galway Blazers' Hunt.

"But, Biddy," he argued, "tell us what rules you will be breaking if you broach a keg now? The whiskey is free to all and there is no stipulation as to when it may be drunk."

"That will do you now, Roddy. The whiskey was entrusted to me for the haulin' home and, until there's someone to haul home, a drop of it will not pass the lips of anyone in this house. Sorra one. And that's final, as the hangman said."

"There have been one or two hangmen who thought that in this country before this, and it was far from being final: either the rope broke and the boy escaped or the hangman had to keep on hanging the next generation. And to tell you the truth, it would be as well to be hanged in a country where you cannot get a drop of the drink that cost a woman nothing but was given out free. Isn't that right?" he asked, turning invitingly to the man at his left and giving him a friendly, rousing blow. "Isn't that right?" he repeated with a broad, disarming grin which showed the weakness of his face. The heavy-browed man broke into a laugh.

"It's free, right enough; but it's in Biddy's keeping." Biddy, as women do when they want to temporize or to refuse, pretended to see a slight where none was intended and to read an insult into the simple-minded fellow's speech.

"What do you mean by 'It's in Biddy's keepin'?' Do you mean to suggest that Biddy is going to keep for herself what was intended for the people?" she asked. "If you don't, what the flames do you mean?"

"I meant nothing."

"No. Nor you couldn't mean anything. Well, yez'll get no free whiskey until I set eyes on the coach and four."

Roddy assumed an attitude of great concern. He patted his companion's thigh as if to soothe him and to prevent him from insulting Biddy.

"If we only had the brains to explain ourselves to Biddy, she would be up and busy handing out the glasses and not forgetting that she was always famous for her hospitality, especially on a day like this."

"What brains do ye want?" Biddy asked, caught by curiosity. Roddy whispered to the man on his left: "Back me up."

"It is we that lack the brains to put the case to you. The whiskey is free. We don't deny that you will ladle out every drop of it honestly and hospitably when the bride appears. But by the time she appears every house in the village will be doing the same; some are doing it already to welcome the pipers, for well they know that on the pipers and the fiddlers, our good name, not to mention the success of the entertainment, depends. I would never have it on me to be stingy with a fiddler."

"What about the fluters?" asked the man on his right.

"Whist," said Roddy, "I'm coming to you presently. Well they know in the other houses which are not as good nor half the size of this one, that on the fluters, the fiddlers and the pipers the whole thing depends. So, Biddy, if we bring you in later on, when it's flowing in the meadows, the few glasses of liquor that we take out of your barrel now, when the time comes you will have lost nothing and you'll have the same amount to give away."

Suppressing a smile, Roddy looked at his friends and then at Biddy who, confused, became elusive again.

"Wouldn't it be better for yez to betake yourselves to them hospitable houses and not come bothering me?"

"Ah, is it put us out ye would?" And a big fellow rose to go.

"Stay where ye are!" Biddy commanded, and shot an angry glance at Roddy for bringing all this trouble on her house.

Smoothly Roddy resumed.

"My good woman of the house, we all thought of that. Didn't we, Phil?"

The fluter nodded with great solemnity. Roddy continued:

"It was I who stopped the boys from preferring any other house to this house because, sez I, when the fiddler comes from Galway who never plays to anyone but to the Quality and he cannot get into the big house here yet, where in the name of God are we to put a man that is accustomed as he is to be treated decently by decent people? We cannot let him go to Mulcahy's, a gombeen man's hotel."

Biddy was divided between suspicion and concern.

"Where is this fiddler?"

"He is coming from Auchnanure," Roddy said, ground-baiting for the next bite.

"But where is he now?"

"Just down the road at the one-hundredth-fifth milestone. We thought it better to send out the boys for him to give him a welcome and a fresh horse. We asked them not to let him wet his lips until he could do it in a decent house." Turning to his friend, he said: "Cock your eye out for him, Shaun. He ought to be here now."

But before Shaun got to the door, a dark head was bent over the lower half of it.

"God bless all here," it said.

The head drew back immediately. There was a sound of excited voices.

"It's Festus Kyle, the blind fiddler from Auchnanure, and no mistake," said the fluter, rising.

"Sit down there, can't ye?" said Biddy as she advanced rapidly to the door for the honour of the house. It would never do to leave it to a visitor to ask a Galway man into her house when she was at home.

They pushed the blind man before them as if he were a ram at a fair.

"Here's himself from Auchnanure, Biddy Early, God bless you."

Once in the room the great, gaunt man straightened up to his full height.

"And welcome ye are, Festus Kyle," Biddy said. "Sit ye down over there in that seat." She led him to the oaken chest. "Get out of his way, boys, and sit by the wall. It's tired you must be after that long journey. Fifteen miles beyond Galway, isn't it? Where's yer manners, Roddy? Get the glasses. And you, Shaun, put the spigot in."

"He's the boy that has pleasantness on the top of his fingers. He's the man that can make the heart leap in the chest of those who are sitting down," Roddy commented, helping the blind fiddler to the seat of honour on the chest. While Roddy was looking for the glasses at the dresser, he kept up a commentary of remarks that might have been addressed to himself or to the room as a kind of chorus:

"If people won't come to their own wedding celebrations where decent and famous men are assembled to give them a welcome, we ought to give ourselves a treat and do the honours for them that are absentees."

So he spoke to keep himself before the audience, for instinctively he was jealous of anyone who was getting attention, guest or no guest. He could not keep in the background. There was too much attention lavished on the fiddler. As he went on with his search he continued:

"Let us all break out and start the party so that when the Master comes we won't have to warm up but he will find us all in full blast, the boys whooping and all the girls dancing and everything going grand in honour of the loving couple. If they don't arrive at all, nothing will have gone to waste, and all the honours on our part shall have been done!"

He opened a door in the lower part of the dresser. He looked in and shut it hurriedly. Biddy shouted:

"For God's sake, come out of that and leave her alone. She turned the eggs yesterday. You can't trust that old goose. If I let her out, she'll be off skedaddling down the town. The tumblers are forninst you on the top shelf if you can reach them. What's come over the men nowadays, Mr. Kyle? They're not breeding them as tall as they used. We don't see many of them now the full of a door."

Roddy was annoyed at this reference to his lack of inches. Somewhat chastened, he brought the glasses over to Shaun, who by this time had the barrel tapped and the spigot in.

The first gill he carried over to the distinguished visitor. The fiddler raised his glass to the level of his face and saluted his hostess, inclining his head and making a motion with his glass in her direction. Before drinking he said:

"Here's to you, Ma'am, and to this house and to all in it. May it be full of good fortune and roofed over forever with the Blessing of God." He swallowed the gill without moving a lid of his sightless eyes. Pausing to savour the drink he took a deep breath.

"It's John Locke himself from Kilbeggan, by all that's holy," he said. This made a deep impression, which was increased by the testimony of Shaun.

"Begob, he's right. Here is the name branded in on the barrel."

"It looks like it's going to be a great wedding by the same token," Festus remarked, basing his judgment on the quality of the drink.

Roddy said, jealous of the fiddler's knowledgeable palate:

"Before we went cubbing at Dunsandle last September, the lady of the house served brandy and claret to all the hunt at dawn with her own hands, and she dressed in her hunting dress. 'Try this brandy, Roddy,' she says, coming up to me on my hunter. 'You must be tired of whiskey,' she said! 'I want your opinion of this.' 'Thank you,' sez I. 'That never seen a gauger,' I remarked as I tossed it off."

"I hope you called her My Lady," Biddy said, for Biddy, who had served the Quality all her life, knew the proprieties. Roddy did not answer, but asked, "What about a glass of whiskey now that there is no hunting?"

As Shaun filled his glass again, he said:

"Them sort could not have been too pleased with its never seeing a gauger. That was as much as saying they were friendly with the

French smugglers and as bad as ourselves in the eyes of old Isaac Weld and the Parliament."

"Mr. Kyle will think this was smuggled if you make it so hard to get," she said to Roddy, directing his eyes to the fiddler's tumbler, which had been empty for several minutes. At this the fluter drained off his glass to have it ready for the second round.

"If I'd known you were coming I'd have had the salver out," said Biddy with a show of concern.

"Don't mind me, Ma'am. Good stuff like this is its own salver, butler and all," the blind fiddler replied.

At this moment an urchin put his face over the half door, and said in a mixture of Irish and English:

"Mr. Mulcahy's compliments and he would look after the fiddler's horse."

"Be off to hell out of this. We are well able to take care of all the horses in the country," said Roddy.

"Can you beat that?" exclaimed Biddy, resenting Mulcahy's invitation, well knowing that he only wanted the fiddler to draw a crowd to his hotel.

But no such subterfuges were required to draw a crowd. The wide street was filled with people, and the crowd had extended its depth beyond the hotel. From the barn at the back of it the skirl of the big Irish bagpipes could be heard. It was the piper from Ballintubber tuning up. The head appeared again above the half door. Excitedly it exclaimed, "Things is starting," and was gone.

Festus the Fiddler, accustomed to the excitement preceding routs, country wakes, and such festivities, ignored the remark.

"It's a fine party this Mr. Martyn is about to give from all accounts. I never heard of such lavishness—though I live in Galway—as a pig for every five families and a sack of flour and a pound of tea apiece."

This was another puzzle for Biddy. She had not been told anything about the details of the festival. It was just like Crosbie to leave her to a Galway man to find it out. But it would never do for the housekeeper of Martyn Hall to appear uninformed.

"There was never a mean Martyn," Biddy affirmed, taking the subject from the particular to the universal, where anything might be true.

Festus the Fiddler nodded his head.

"Well known is it to me, woman of the house," he said, "that what you say of the Martyns is true and proper. Even in the troubles after King Seumas Ochocagh let us all down at the Boyne, they never dared put a finger on a Martyn because in his humanity he sheltered many a Protestant swaddler who wasn't fit to live. And years before, in the times that old red-headed bitch Queen Bess was scheming with those behind her in London, the Martyns had a house in Galway with oblong windows. That's two hundred years ago and they're only catching up on them in England today."

Half a dozen Galway men were looking for their fiddler. Biddy could hear the urchin running ahead, shouting directions.

"Maybe, Ma'am, you'll come out and join us," Festus the Fiddler coaxed Biddy. Side-cars were rocking down the road, from Ballinarobe, Westport and from as far as Newport and Ballina, swaying with their loads. Jaunting cars that had not been painted or varnished for years rolled and pitched on the dusty uneven street. Fawny shawls and buttoned knee-breeches, black stocks and, here and there, a beaded bonnet with a patch of purple ribbon, proclaimed that this was a white holiday, that it was more than race-meeting or even the wake of a famous character. You would never see so many bonnets at a wake. The little children had ribbons in their hair and the little boys' faces still bore signs of the solemn ordeal of soap.

But on all the side-cars, and Biddy recognized many of them as they came one after another in a continuous procession, she saw no shawl that could be compared with the one in the box on which Festus the Fiddler sat.

"Thank you kindly for your hospitality, Mrs. Early," Festus said, and the boys rose too and shook her hand.

Roddy interposed with a shout, "What are ye doing? You are tempting Providence! You can't go till she takes a drop herself. She has been so busy entertaining the company that she forgot to respond to the healths."

Biddy shook her head.

"And particularly she never drank to the blessing the Fiddler of Galway called down on her own roof-tree. It's enough to bring bad luck to the place to pass a blessing by." None could gainsay that.

Shaun was quick enough when it came to handling drink. He had a glass in Biddy's hand before she knew it. Glasses were filled all around, and Roddy took the floor as if he owned the place.

"It's not every day such distinguished company comes to this part of the country. Distinguished as we all are, we can get on better with added distinction, so here's to the greatest musician in the land and his hospitable hostess, Biddy Early."

Outside, the men from Galway were growing restless. It was unusual for Festus to separate himself from his friends, so Roddy, as Master of Ceremonies, went to the door:

"We'll all be out in a minute, boys. Biddy Early is drinking his health."

As such a ceremony could not be interrupted, the boys outside possessed themselves in patience.

Shaun insinuated another gill into Biddy's hand. Biddy looked at it askance. Suddenly recollecting herself, she raised the glass as any decent woman should do, whose health and that of her house had been drunk, and said fervently:

"Here's to you, Festus Kyle. May there be as much joy in your fingers as in Carolan the Bard's. More power to your elbow. I'll be seeing you all, please God, later on."

Solemnly the gaunt men from Galway bowed, and taking their dark hats, went out through the door. As one of them turned round before closing it, Biddy called aloud to Roddy:

"Here, you red-headed huntsman. Give the Fiddler his fiddle. And"—pointing to the cupboard—"you may go over there now and let out the goose."

X. MR. WELD

MR. WELD REINED in his mount. He had caught sight of the yellow coach nearly half a mile away, the splashing horses, the postillion lying to it, and even Feeney's *coatie mor* with its double cape. He turned into the fields and cantered behind the hedge-rows seeking concealment. From behind the beeches which made a screen to his estate he could watch unseen the distant cross-roads. He could hear the galloping four-in-hand. What were they doing on this road? And what was the meaning of their desperate pace? It was faster than the mail coach with a new span of horses. They were on the Dunsandle road when they should be making for Balla and Westport. There was something strange in this avoidance, particularly at such a time. Why did the coach turn off the mail road? Why did the bride and bridegroom delay their homecoming? Were they headed for Attymon House, the residence of Martyn-Lynch's friend St. George?

This should be investigated. Mr. Weld was not without means of getting information, however ambiguously and inaccurately it was given. Meanwhile it would be better to return by the back drive to his own house. He must avoid if possible the invisible rows of resentful eyes that gazed from every hovel on his wide estate. He must amble back leisurely. He skirted the two-mile estate wall which had been built by starving hands.

But the well-bred hunter felt the elastic sod springing under his hooves. He knew that he had been turned before he had had the exercise that was always his at this time of day. He put down his head and began to gallop. Weld held him in, but something unusual must have been noticeable to the invisible, watchful eyes. They could read much in the condition of a man's horse, and would wonder at the reasons for the horse's turn for home an hour before the accustomed time. Weld could feel the smouldering eyes upon him. These people were so primitive that they could almost with truth be said to be in collusion with the animal kingdom. He would have a stiff back in the morning. He had never felt his hunter to have such a hard mouth. Perhaps Shauneen was feeling him with oats when he ought to be fed on second-crop hay. He would look into the matter.

Now that he came to think of it, he was on the Martyn-Lynch property. As if twenty thousand acres within a ring fence had not been enough, the Lynch property, far more extensive, had recently passed into Martyn's hands. And it marched alongside Weld's estate, making an entering angle that interrupted the continuity of his demesne. It would not be hard to acquire it when the easy-going Martyn felt the pinch which his extravagance and ambitious building were sure to bring in their train. Weld could afford to wait. By waiting he had acquired the present estate from one of his own countrymen who, demoralized by living among a servile population, had gone to ruin through arrogance and improvidence. Ireland undid many a gentleman, as it put many a beggar on horseback. Though his English ancestors had not fought at the Boyne with William of Orange, Weld could hold his head as high as any of those of such descent: his estate was unencumbered. It was being slowly rid of the incubus that brought all landlords' property to ruin: the peasant squatter on the land. These slaves would not demoralize him. Though he was in a land of serfs, he had none of the vices of their masters. He neither drank nor gambled. And above all, he rarely visited Dublin. He sought no favours, for he wanted none.

He called to the keeper of one of the gates of the three avenues that led to Castle Weld. No dirty children played or sprawled here. The keeper was a Protestant, and did his work well. He kept his place and the drive clean. He was a trustworthy fellow. Weld raised his riding crop to his hat as the man saluted. He rode in silently, revolving in his mind the extraordinary occurrence he had witnessed. Why had Martyn-Lynch turned aside on the road home, where all the countryside awaited him?

You could never trust one of those whom the country people called "the old stock." For all their friendliness and devil-may-caredom they were of a different kidney from himself and from the other landlords whose in-coming like his own could be remembered. The Martyns, the Dalys, the Lynches and Burkes could not be got to keep the peasant at a distance. It was a classless community as bad as the outrageous commonalty of France. Worse, even, for the custom of fosterage made it impossible for you to know whom you could trust. The commonest woman may have suckled one of the native landlords who asked you to his house. This familiarity probably accounted for the absence of any expressions of disgust among the older families for the doctrines of the Revolution. That Revolution could add nothing to the equality and fraternity which was rampant here. They were hand-in-glove with the natives. You could not trust them. At a pinch they would side with their tenants against the law of the land.

And yet this fraternizing with their tenants did the tenants little good. Out of compassion, they subdivided the lands and gave every tenant a small holding. They ruled by favouritism, not by justice. The results were increased population and abject poverty. They never evicted tenants or took advantage of the facilities for transporting them. They could have cleared them out and sent them in shoals to Virginia or Van Diemen's land, where they would have a chance and where the climate was dry and suited to rheumatic peasants. But you could never get one of the Martyns, the Dalys or the Lynches to look at the problem sensibly. They said that there was room for everybody, or that there should be, in his own country. He had heard that kind of talk even before the new, pernicious doctrine came over from the French Revolution. There had been revolutionaries in this country from time immemorial, and he could not satisfactorily exempt even his own acquaintances, gentry though they were. The Irish always strained themselves to give their sons the best education they could afford. What did it avail if they came back from Oxford and Cambridge with the same notions with which they went over, and relapsed into the same way of life and cherished the same old reprehensible customs? It was money spent in vain. Actually most of their money went in ostentation, gambling and drinking.

Their sympathy with drink, which apparently excused every form of backsliding, gave you an indication of the way the country as a whole was going the road to ruin and decay. Yes, the way things were going was ominous, to say the least of it. What were the cardinal causes of Revolution? Lucan, the Roman poet, a poet of the Decadence (he lived in Nero's reign), Lucan could tell you that the two things that led to Revolution were famine and discontent. Discontent was here already. Famine would ensue unless the country was thinned by transportation to the bountiful colonies.

But Weld could not evict people merely because their hovels were unsightly excrescences on a gentleman's park. He could transport only the guilty ones, those who were proved guilty by incontrovertible evidence in a court of law. As he was the magistrate, he would have to see that the evidence was incontrovertible before he imposed sentence. He had as yet no evidence about Martyn-Lynch's loyalty or lack of it. But his suspicious instinct made him very much concerned by the strange happening which he had accidentally witnessed in the afternoon.

Could it be that Martyn-Lynch had been summoned by one of his cousins to a consultation, or, to be more precise, a conspiracy, in connection with enemy agents from France? That would account for the sudden turning aside. Some messenger might have just landed from the Continent, and those at the head of the conspiracy been called to assemble immediately. What else could divert a man from his own house, and take him to Dunsandle on his honeymoon? Mrs. St. George had been on the Continent as a girl. Her house might be the seat of Treason.

XI. MRS. ST. GEORGE RECEIVES

Ellice St. George sat up in bed examining the panels of her fine Condor fan, awaiting the arrival of the bride. If that tall son of hers was twenty-three and if she had been married at seventeen as many young ladies were in France, Mrs. St. George could not have been more than forty-one. And she had the appearance, on this evening at all events, of a woman of thirty. Her remarkable air of youthfulness was abetted by the pleasantly shaded candles and the soft glow of the wall lamps that lit the long mirror. Her youthfulness was heightened by interest in the arrival of the bride, and equally by her desire to meet again the courtly Chevalier who had helped her out of France to safety. Indeed, the latter consideration had more influence than the former on Ellice's decision to descend for dinner. She could let Ninon visit her in her bedroom; but to see Constant d'Estournelles she must go downstairs.

Ellice seemed to have suffered no harm from being confined a great deal of the time to bed. Health bloomed on her forehead. It caused her eyes to shoot deep hidden glints and her auburn hair to curl gently with a soft brilliance around her coral ears.

Steps sounded in the lobby, and presently the door opened.

"Oh, Ninon, Ninon! How well you look in spite of your long journey. How fast you must have driven! How lucky not to break a spring! But come here at once and let me look at you closely, you lovely thing. Sit there on the bed. Give me your hand. Now tell me everything."

Ninon bent to kiss her and then she seated herself as she was ordered on the rich coverlet of the bed.

"Oh, dear. We did come fast!" she said. Then she blurted out,

"We were held up and rudely searched by soldiers at Athlone."

The news had a startling effect on the older woman. She was about to ask an anxious question about the Chevalier's safety, but restrained herself and maintained an air of indifference.

"Tell me about it," she said quietly. Ninon proceeded to describe the disturbing incident.

"You got away in the end without any loss?" Ellice asked when Ninon had finished her account.

"Oh, we got away, but we had to drive far too fast to make up for lost time, for Martyn said he could not pass your house without showing me off to you."

"It was very sweet of him. Are you very tired, dear? Did they give you any refreshment?"

Ninon said that she was too tired to think of refreshment. She had sipped a little negus. But now that she had arrived at last in this house, everything was restful.

"You do look pretty in that little coat. Now tell me where you stayed in Dublin before your wedding, and whom did you see?"

"Aunt and I stayed in Drogheda Street near the bridge. We could see as far as the columns at the entry to the House of Lords. Then we went to Lord Charlemount's place at Marino. Then we went to Blessington and we stayed at Russborough House. Oh, it is so lovely, all with wings and urns and pillars and such wonderful views of the Wicklow hills which turn quite pink in the evening. Then we came to Dublin for the wedding and we were no sooner married than Martyn got word that Constant and Clemente were about to land at Wicklow."

Ellice shook her head, lifted it and smiled happily.

"It must be all but impossible to reach here from France just now," she said. "You know with what difficulty and danger I got out of it. It took Constant nearly a week to get into touch with his friends in Brittany and then we were handed on by night from house to house by the queerest peasants you ever saw, like satyrs in their hairy goatskins. . . . But you— A glass of negus is little good. What you will have, if you will do me the kindness to join me, is a refreshing dish of tea. . . . Where is that bell-rope? Oh, here it is. . . . And after tea Lucille will be your maid and you will lie down and close your eyes for some hours. I am going to surprise the household by going down to dinner tonight. Be sweet and stay for it."

"Oh, I am so glad you are coming down. You will be quite well again very soon."

"I know you must be burning to see your new home. You only saw it half built."

"I would love to stay. We can go before it gets too dark."

When Lucille returned from attending to the bride, Mrs. St. George was already out of bed and sitting in front of her great mirror, combing out the lovely hair which was soon to be oiled and hidden by powder.

"Get the men to help you with the water," said Ellice.

Bath water had to be carried in large cans up the stairs of the tall country houses, a great hardship for the servants, particularly the serving maids. Lucille softened the turkey sponge in tepid water as she filled the bath.

Sitting once again before her mirror after bathing, Ellice drew towards her the lotions and washes which Lucille had laid out. She applied a light wash first (for she was not pitted with the smallpox and never used the heavy French washes). Cochineal, which the *vendeuse* in Paris had told her came from the Americas, made the paste-rouge and served to redden her lips as well. And a small pellet of kohl darkened the line of her brow.

While Lucille shook the dried verbena from the folds of her dress (and tried to shake out the creases), Mrs. St. George gathered her powder sheet, her jar of powder and her brush and went into the powder room. Lucille attended carefully to the process of powdering. Fastening the sheet around her mistress's shoulders, she made free with the powder over the oiled hair till not a hint of the auburn showed through. Putting her lady back in the bedroom, she fastened her into the great hoop, pressing in her waist till she flushed red, so that the waist-band might be hooked. Over that went the skirt of yellow moiré (watered tabby, they called it in London), caught up to show off the fine underskirt of Brussels lace. With a last look at her hair (for once in the basque she could raise her arms no higher than her shoulders), she hooked on her earrings, and dotted her lobes and palms with cochineal.

The yellow basque costume required more deep-drawn breaths before it could meet. The square neck was cut, after the French fashion, wider than the English decolletage, but not so deep, and edged with an embroidered braid from Italy.

She took a last look in the pier glass at the brilliant, white, high-piled heap of hair and the porcelain-white skin, the delicate veins showing through the light pearl wash. Eyes and lips were a bit too brilliant, perhaps, but safe enough to pass discreetly under the high candelabra of the downstairs rooms. Ellice blessed the current fashion that showed to advantage a neat waist and a full throat and bust, and the brilliant silks from France that had saved fashion from the puces and drabs of home-dyed stuffs. She approved the fabulous width of her hoop, which meant that the slightest movement tilted the hem to show her golden-clocked stockings, and the neat line of her ankle and instep's arch. She approved of herself for twisting the obvious complement of auburn hair—yellow cloth—and making it twice as brilliant with a well-powdered head.

At the top of the stairs she paused for a moment and drew a deep breath against the prisoning stays—the last deep breath she would have for some hours—and held her hands as nearly shoulder-high as she could to let the blood run out, and leave them white for a salutation.

A footman had just lit the last wax candle in the white China brackets that illuminated panels of tapestry set in an overmantel of pear-wood carved by Grindley Gibbon, and was withdrawing the long red wax lighter into its thin metal case as Mrs. St. George entered the drawing-room. As yet none of the gentlemen had appeared. She sat on a small gilt couch at right angles to the hearth in which a log fire was blazing in spite of the season. It was customary to light a fire every evening in the great mansions of the land, more for ornament and homeliness than for the need of warmth.

A dark-featured man with a military bearing entered. The Chevalier Constant d'Estournelles came forward eagerly to where Ellice was seated, and bowed over her hand. Ellice arose.

"Oh, Constant!" she exclaimed. As he was about to enfold her in his arms, she pointed to the door which he had left open on entering. He closed it and came forward again to press her against his bosom. Then gently, reluctantly, she stepped back.

"Ellice!" was all he said.

"So you are safely arrived?" she asked casually in French, seeking to control her voice. "You came direct from Paris?"

"Yes; through La Vendée to Brest. Last week I slept at Les Fougères and here I am on the edge of Europe tonight."

"It must have been a beautiful journey at this time of year. I am not well acquainted with Brittany."

She smiled at him as one who shared a secret. For it was through Brittany he had helped her to escape from the Terror some years before.

"The country is all flat from Rouen. The beauty of the scene was marred for me by the shut and deserted chateaux, not one of which, I could see, had been opened since the owners were guillotined or driven into exile."

"You were not united. You might have defended yourselves."

"Are you united here?" he asked.

She sighed.

"We, who represent what is left of the few native landlords, are divided between our allegiance to a government that once confiscated our estates and the aspirations of a people who are ignorant and oppressed," Ellice said.

"I see it. You must support the government against your inclination, if you wish to continue to exist, or else throw in your lot with your own tenants at the risk of being reduced to their condition."

"There should be a middle course," she sighed.

"Dearest, it is all too sad and too old a story to be experienced once again. The middle course, if such it can be called, is to hold what you have and incline neither to one side or the other. If you identify yourself too closely with the government you will be exposed to the vengeance of the insurgent tenant. If you go out of your way to take his part you will be guilty of high treason to the government you dislike. All the signs that preceded the revolution in my country are here today in yours. I have come to stand by you while there still is time."

Ellice listened as though reluctantly. She knew that what Constant said was right, but the position of the country at the moment was so full of confusion and cross purposes, that she felt a repugnance to any deep consideration of it at all. Like that monarch whose court still influenced the fashions and outlook of the Irish gentry, she contented herself to accept things as they were. "After us, the deluge. Only do not let us do anything that will bring it nearer."

"The powers that be, shouldn't be," was all she said, and she laughed and shrugged the subject away.

"If we could see any evidence that if the powers that be were overthrown, the native chieftains would be restored, even then the prospect would not be more hopeful, for, as you know, the native chieftains were even worse landlords than the present Cromwellian fry."

"Oh, do explain it all to Martyn and Denis. Save Denis, who is only interested in politics because he admires Martyn. I wish that Martyn had been able to get to France . . ."

"Why?" he asked, surprised.

"Because it would have taught him a lesson. Surely it would have shown him how hollow and selfish and bloodthirsty a revolution for Liberty, Equality and Fraternity can be."

"Had he gone there he could only have returned as a fugitive and a suspect, as I am. Youth never learns any lesson which the emotions do not teach. His enthusiasm for the doctrines of the Revolution reinforced by instances of oppression all around him in his native country would blind him to the self-interest of agitators who have grasped the fruits of revolution in ours. He would never be content to accept an object lesson from one country until he had experience in his own."

"Hush," she said. "I will leave you early at dinner so that you may give the young men your advice."

There was no opportunity for the conversation to grow more intimate, for Hyacinth and Denis entered. It was noticeable that they had brushed the powder out of their hair to be in keeping with the condition of their guest. Denis advanced and bowed to kiss his mother's hand.

"Has he been cooking up any plots?" he asked lightly, punning on the disguise of Italian chef under which Constant had been brought to Attymon House.

His mother smiled, charmed by the gentle carriage of her son.

"Ninon, my dear!" Mrs. St. George exclaimed as the radiant bride entered the room. "You have had a beauty sleep, I see."

Denis essayed a gallantry inspired by the presence of d'Estournelles.

"Can we not testify to the beauty without giving credit to the sleep?" he asked.

Ninon made a little playful gesture with her hand as if to encourage him and to acknowledge the compliment.

"Sit beside me, Ninon, dear," said St. George's mother as she made room on the settee.

Ninon had no sooner complied than the butler appeared to announce, "Dinner is served."

The mistress gave her arm to d'Estournelles. Ninon followed on the arm of Denis, who released her with a bow to enable her to precede him through the door. Hyacinth was the last to leave.

They crossed the great hall, dimly lit by two lamps, into the reception room off which the dining room was situated. Panels of Venetian glass in a door caught the reflection of the table's candles before they entered the dining room.

A long shining table of Domingo mahogany glowed, its dark grain flowing through a mellow ground. Tall, unshaded candles in silver branching candelabra lit the table center. Crystal glass and shining silver made sumptuous the gleaming board. An Adams sideboard, dark and austere against a wall, glistened with silver. An urn in dark wood stood on a plinth at either side. On each wall a single picture hung, collected during a last visit to Italy by some member of the family. One picture frame of dark blue and gilt wood looked the worse for its journey from Leghorn. Mementoes from Italy decorated the room. Not the least of these were two magnificent fire dogs which stood in the hearth, masterpieces of Cellini. The ceiling was slightly arched, coloured with panels of stucco work which revealed the fact that the dining room was an addition to the older part of the house.

"Take my place at the head of the table," Ellice St. George bade Denis. "If you sit at the other end, you will be too far away."

"No, mother. On an occasion like this, your first dinner downstairs for nearly a year, the place of honour belongs to you."

"Well then, the next place belongs to our visitor."

And she motioned to Constant to sit at her right hand.

"I am putting Ninon next to you," she said, addressing him. "Hyacinth sits here and Denis opposite Ninon. And now," she said, as a signal to the servants.

Following d'Estournelles' gaze, she exclaimed, "Don't look at that frame. It was broken before it reached Dublin. But luckily the picture is undamaged. It is said to be a Leonardo da Vinci. It is certainly not a copy, as you would realize if you saw it in good light."

"Even in this light one can appraise the composition."

Constant looked at Ninon.

"But you can see that the wall was never made for pictures which hide the design of white festoons. I have nowhere else to put them. So there they are. Don't you like the simplicity of that girl's head?"

"Yes. My father had several like it," Ninon said. "They are in the gallery at Lisadill."

It was true. Into the seventh city of Christendom, which was Dublin, the masterpieces of the continent were continually being gathered. The taste of the Irish landlords who had town houses in that city, and of the officials who resided there, was in advance of any city save Paris, and Paris rarely went to Italy for its treasures. Hence it came about that Dublin, with an aristocracy of Anglo-Irish blood, had houses furnished with the finest examples of art, which extravagance enhanced rather than vulgarized. This elegance, while owing nothing to the colony of Italian artists in marble and stucco work that had taken up its residence in the city, may have been contributed to by some knowledgeable member of the colony who was able to put the leaders of the social life of the city into touch with the needy Italian owners of masterpieces of painting, statuary or Capo del Monte ware. Be that as it may, the great houses of Ireland were treasuries of antique and contemporary art. The great self-contained country house of Ninon's family was no exception: quattrocento paintings could be found on the extreme western shelf of Europe, on an isthmus where the oak boughs touched the tide twice daily at Lisadill.

While the ladies and d'Estournelles were discussing art, a subject more engrossing if less aesthetic engaged the minds of the young men. They discussed the prospects of the coming race at the Curragh, and of Denis' newly acquired fighting cock.

D'Estournelles held his glass against the light and smiled. Mrs. St. George nodded to a servant and smiled too. "Do not drink for a moment," she requested.

On the table a stand of gold was placed. The butler went to a long box which lay at the back of the sideboard and opened it with a silver key. From within he took a long object that seemed to be composed of twisted ivory, lifting it out by means of the faded purple velvet cloth in which it rested. Followed by the two footmen, he carried it round the table counter-clockwise, for that was the way in which its spiral went, and when his stately walk was ended placed it with great ceremony in the golden socket in the middle of the board.

"Ah, my dear lady, you have not forgotten, *'Le lichorne, garnie d'or, pour faire essay,'* "—the Chevalier quoted. "It brings to mind the stateliness with which it was surrounded when His poor Majesty had it borne and placed about his table (quite unnecessarily) to test the wine. It is a test I hold superfluous here." He raised his glass and drank to his hostess, gratified by the thoughtfulness which made her remember to bring out the royal alicorn in his honour.

"When mother brought that horn back from France we could

not make out what it was," Denis volunteered. "'The horn of the Unicorn, a fabulous beast, seld' seen, solitary and untakeable!' she would say. 'This is the very place for it.'"

The Chevalier looked at it and again at Ellice.

"You see, it does not perspire." He laughed. Legend had it that the horn of the Unicorn perspired in the presence of poisoned wine.

"Egad," said Martyn, "I know a drop or two at Weld's that would make an anvil sweat. There's nothing fabulous in that."

"Constant obtained it from a dealer in Paris when all that was graceful and customary went down in ruin after the murder of the King," Mrs. St. George explained.

The Chevalier continued, "I love to think of that beast, fabulous or not. The more fabulous the more true; for it proceeds from the creative instinct of man. Wild, but no beast of prey, a beneficent beast, for it sweetens streams with its horn so that the waiting animals may drink. And, as the old verse in Mediaeval Latin has it:

"Capitur rhinoceros
Virginis amplexu—

It can be led into captivity only by a woman whose heart is pure. I believe in it, for I believe that the mind of man cannot imagine any distinct thing which cannot exist."

If he addressed himself to Hyacinth, he spoke in vain. Hyacinth was heeding the play of light that brought out the copper glints in Ninon's hair, and the way her long lashes almost touched the line of her eyebrows as she met his gaze.

As though catching Hyacinth's mood, the Chevalier turned to regard Ellice with the same look of warm absorption. For a moment she seemed not to notice his attention. Then she turned to look at him with glowing eyes, her frail beauty heightened by a sudden flush of colour. At that moment something passed between them that said more than all the words they had exchanged since their meeting. Gone now was the reserve that had made Ellice mask her true sentiments with a ladylike show of casualness, that had led her to direct the conversation to impersonal topics.

Once before, after Constant had helped her to safety through Brittany, he had seen this same depth of feeling shining in Ellice's delicate features. He had never forgotten that look, and now that he saw it again, it seemed as though the intervening time had passed in a twinkling. This moment of pure contentment, with its promise of deeper happiness to come, made up for all the loss Constant had suffered in attaining it.

The spell was interrupted by Denis' ridiculous, embarrassed cough. Made uncomfortable by the brief silence, the youth again engaged Martyn in a conversation about the chances of the various entries at the Curragh.

The coffee was served and the "dumb waiters" placed in position. These were circular shelves of mahogany supported by a central pillar of the same wood. They rose in three decreasing tiers and they were employed so that the guests might help themselves in the absence of the servants, who could not always be trusted not to carry to dangerous ears any unguarded conversation.

Denis opened the door for his mother and Ninon to leave the room. Returning to the table he took from a dumb waiter a large cut-glass decanter of port and placed it on the table in front of the seat lately occupied by Ninon. Into this chair d'Estournelles moved, and having filled his glass, passed the decanter around the head of the table, according to usage, from right to left.

"Are you quite sure that I will not embarrass you if I visit Martyn Hall?" Constant asked.

"By no means," Hyacinth replied. "But you will very greatly embarrass our neighbour Mr. Weld, who will be woundily puzzled about you when he sends the Government his secret report. If he be an émigré aristocrat why is he not in England? What is he doing here among scoundrelly emissaries of the Republic? All that he will want to know."

"If I were to visit England at this time," said d'Estournelles, "with that country at war, it would destroy whatever chances I may have of recovering my French estates. In fact, were it to become known that I, who was attached to the Embassy during the reign of our lamented King, was again in that country, the Directory would see to it that I never returned to my native land; whereas, in the eyes of that egregious body, it is quite a patriotic act for a Frenchman to be in Ireland now."

The two young men exchanged glances. At length Hyacinth spoke. "As you know, there are some half-dozen agents of the Directory in Ireland just at present. The English government is well aware of their presence but not of their whereabouts. Men like Weld, who have cause to fear an uprising, are busy hunting them out and have means for discovering where they are. And they do not lack information, which in some cases is supplied by the people themselves."

"Irishmen?"

"Yes. You cannot know the condition of these people and how divided and half-hearted their loyalty is. The ideals of the Revolution make little appeal to them. They are too abstract. But misery and starvation are not abstract."

"Starvation in this most fertile land and amongst a population—what is the number—?"

"About four million and a tenth."

"How then is it that they come to starve?"

"The exactions of rent. Some of the poor devils here have three landlords. First, long-lease holders, as they are called; then middlemen, and then the immediate owner of the estate, who collects through an agent whatever remains from the hard industry of their undernourished bodies."

"Though as a Protestant I should not remind you," Denis interjected, "you have forgotten a fourth landlord, the collector or farmer of the tithes." Turning to d'Estournelles, he continued: "You see, Sir, Ireland might be called the Island of Landlords—though most of them do not reside in it; they are absentee landlords. Thus the long-lease holder is rarely seen except in cases like Martyn's: Martyn holds his land hereditarily and lives on it without a middleman. He deals directly, or almost directly, through a residential agent, with his tenants."

"What are tithes?" Constant asked.

"Tithe," Martyn volunteered, "means one-tenth. A mulct on the peasant of the tenth bag of potatoes, the tenth sheep and the tenth of the pig's litter, of one-tenth of the value of the crops."

"Ah, I remember. The great 'tithe barns,' as they are called in England."

"It is different here, very different. The Englishman pays tithes to support his own church. Here the poor peasant has to pay for the support of a church in the religion of which he does not believe, for a rector whom he has never seen, and for a university which he and his sons are not permitted to enter. So you have two absentee rent collectors but no remission of the rent. I might add a third rent collector, who is usually a solicitor or an attorney, as you would call him. He is another of the ravens who sit pecking at the peasant and is the most voracious of them all. It is he who arranges loans or mortgages on the estates of the long-lease holder and increases the interest than has to be paid every time the mortgages are renewed. They are always renewable at compound interest and short-term as well. All this presses down on, and has to be paid for by, the unfortunate peasant in the end."

D'Estournelles meditated upon this situation, which, so far as exactions went, might be likened to that which preceded the Revolution in France. Having suffered from the uprisen "People" (to him a few conspirators), and having seen the sufferings they in turn inflicted upon themselves—wholesale atrocities far more excessive than anything the Monarchy had ever known—he had lost all belief in plausible aspirations and, though he did not fully realize it, had become contemptuous of liberal sentiments, even when not in the mouths of those to whom a liberal life was unknown.

Though his work had kept him absent, he went among his tenants on every occasion of his return to his estate in France, and had a first-hand knowledge of their conditions and their requirements. There were neither murmurs nor complaints. On the contrary, there was the loyalty of many generations to his family. He could not but consider that an uprising on his estate was an act of the sheerest treachery. Little did he know, nor had he the patience to listen to it, that the explanation of such acts lay in the very formula of such upheavals. It lay in the way revolutions are organized. Sore-heads, rascals, patriots and mean men who exploit the "plain man" might be few in numbers, but their organization had to be wide to succeed. Given an organization among peasants, all must obey the Central Council without question, in spite of old ties and even the association of centuries. This was the method in all cases of revolt, whether it were nation-wide or only local.

Thus, under the threat of death and the destruction of their own property, tenants were forced by orders from the distant Commune to rise against the families with whom they had dwelt peacefully for many generations. If they did not rise in murderous revolt, peasants who owed no local loyalties would be turned against them.

D'Estournelles did not consider that. Had it been explained to anyone who had not suffered and might be considered impersonal, it would not excuse the neglect of the retainers to whisper a warning. To d'Estournelles, the fact that not even a hint of the upheaval was heard in his château was unforgivable. It cost the lives of his mother and his sister, and left him a lonely and embittered man, loyal to what was now become nothing more than a memory and an ideal. He was still too young and too hurt to win through cynicism to detachment.

"The reasonable remedy would seem to lie with the Government. A fair rent should be fixed and the long-leases and the rest of them who are absentees or land-exploiters should be compounded with and bought out. That is the reasonable way. But when did Reason take the place of Revolution in the world's history?" he added disdainfully.

St. George asked:

"But what are you to do when it is the lessees and middlemen who constitute the Government? Is the peasant to starve while he waits for them to vote themselves out of power? Is a Government that made the iniquitous land laws to renounce them? Since 1641, four-fifths of the native landlords of this country have been dispossessed and their estates planted by Cromwellians and Dissenters—'Swaddlers,' as they are called—and Scots Presbyterians. No upholder of the unreformed ritual—that is, a Catholic—was permitted to own land or to have his children educated, except by the ministers of the church of those who dispossessed him. Martyn there can only hold his land on a thirty-years' lease, although his ancestors were treated with special consideration on account of their humanity to the Protestants during some of Queen Elizabeth's devastations and the ensuing bloody revolts. It is only by the connivance of the Irish Government (though it is a puppet of England) at the abeyance of the laws, that there has not been a bloodier revolution long ago. There is one brewing now."

D'Estournelles sat silent and helped himself to brandy from the dumb waiter.

"The worst scoundrel of them all," Hyacinth said, "is the attorney who tangles even the most straightforward and simple lease and makes himself indispensable in straightening it out again. It is he who arranges mortgages and arranges that the borrower shall never be out of debt. His compound interest sees to that. I have not passed my debts on to my tenants, neither has St. George. We have to pay by what my agent calls the fortuitous hazard of the race course and the dice."

"That will not save you," said d'Estournelles.

"From what?" they said at once.

"From the vengeance of your tenants when they catch the contagion of vengeance from those who have worse landlords. As one who has some experience of the *canaille* in revolt, I know that it is not so much their wrongs that makes them destructive as the very sight of culture and refinement. Perhaps these are associated in their minds with superiority and aristocracy, and I suppose to some extent they always will be," he said with some slight sarcasm; adding, "It is advisable to put one's pictures and silver out of the way when one goes to the aid of the People."

An unfamiliar object had been attracting his attention as he was listening to the younger men. It was a circular ring of concave open-worked silver, about four inches high and ten in circumference. The design was one of birds in flight through flowers.

"They should hardly fall out with that," Denis said, "for it is only a potato ring. It has been introduced quite lately by two silversmiths in Dublin. You cannot get them anywhere else—we use them to keep the rough surface of the wooden potato dishes off the mahogany."

As he spoke he went to the sideboard and brought the latest example of the Dublin silversmiths' art to d'Estournelles. The Chevalier took it and examined it closely.

"A new object of art? How lovely and unique," he said. "And rather symbolic, I am afraid."

"Symbolic?" asked St. George.

"Yes; it is a symbol of life in this country: riches and high refinement on the one hand and poverty and the potato on the other. I know no country where the disparity is greater between elegance and misery." And he laid down the crown-shaped silver ring.

"As for riches, they are absent," Denis said. "The refinement comes perhaps from a realization that with insecurity all about us we must live for the day. The English government has destroyed the shipping and wool trade of this country, part of the revenue of which goes to Dublin Castle to corrupt the politicians of the Irish Parliament. As far as I can see it will end with the suppression of the Irish Parliament and the rigging up of a union with the English constitution. To Irish nationality then, goodbye. It is against this system that I would willingly take up arms and welcome any assistance from your countrymen."

D'Estournelles sighed.

"My countrymen! And what price do you think you would have to pay for that assistance? Do you think you can pay an avaricious gang of guillotineers merely with your hatred of England? They have already got that commodity in full measure and flowing over. Think of whom you are inviting, a rabble of red-handed Revolutionaries mouthing sophistries, absurdities, impieties and blasphemies. A mob whose 'social progress' consists in uprooting the only foundations on which society can exist. An outrageous gang constituting itself the nation and usurping the powers and rights of all the rest!

At this very moment, the *Directoire Executif* is being petitioned ceaselessly by one of your own countrymen. His wounded pride has turned into patriotism and he is endeavouring to avenge himself on all England with the help of France. He may obtain a force of fifteen ships of the line, ten frigates and at least ten thousand of the best troops in France."

"I hope he does!" said Martyn-Lynch.

The Chevalier seemed not only astonished but affronted, so sudden was the apparent transition. He had taken Martyn's attention to his views for acquiescence in them. He was as yet far from realizing that in the Irish character the charms of politeness and refinement could go with an utter extravagance and abandoned recklessness. Only his solicitude for Mrs. St. George's son made him continue.

"If your wish be granted, you will see all symbols, honours and privileges swept away, all that is poetic, romantic, venerable and noble. This is an immemorial land in whose chapels a whore set up as the Goddess of Reason will, to say the least, be unbecoming. It is significant that no man of your station is conspiring to sell his country to the *Directoire Executif*. And your priests, who are the guardians of tradition, prefer the present state of things, bad as they are, to a regime of the Committee of Five Hundred. Out of commoners cometh nothing glorious."

Hyacinth was silenced.

"Pray forgive me," said St. George, "just a moment. I must ring for a man to snuff these candles."

After a while Hyacinth spoke, a little chastened:

"There are those, in a far higher station than I, a mere country landlord, who are sympathetic to our cause, which is the cause of our country. One is a nobleman of exalted station. If I do not name him it is not from any distrust of you, needless to say, but from an observance of one of the conditions on which his security depends."

The entry of the servant broke the tenor of the conversation.

"Before we begin drinking I must go to say goodnight to my mother," Denis said.

"May we not follow you?" his guests asked with one accord.

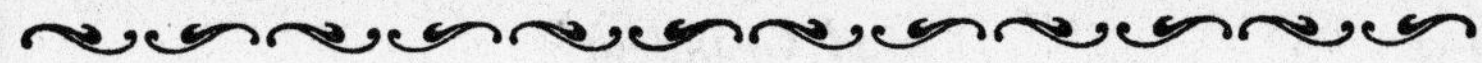

XII. ANTICIPATION OUTDOES REALITY

RODDY WAS ADDRESSING what he called the "meeting" from the roof of an old and sorry coach. His red hair, thin against the sunset, blew up in one long wisp from his balding scalp.

"Men of Mayo!" he shouted. "Many a time and oft you have heard speeches from all kinds of people on all kinds of troubles and oppressions, but now ye are going to hear a short discourse on the course of true love. And while I am warming up to my subject, don't you think we might have a little music? That's right, make a ring there for the fiddlers in the middle of the road! And it would do no harm if to the music we were to add a few cruiskeens of usquebaugh. Drink is free tonight and there's an ox to be roasted in Cudahy's at twelve o'clock."

The unsmiling faces turned. Two fiddlers were hustled in from the rear.

"Stray the stick over the strings, boys! That's right, tune up! The bride and bridegroom are delayed, but that we should delay the rejoicings is the last thing that they would wish, and I will bear witness to it. It would look bad if the celebrations hung fire. Let us see, Phil," he shouted to a piper, "how much you can bring out of an empty bag. Play up, boys, and give us 'The Hare is in the Corn.' . . . We were not at the wedding but here we are. Aren't we, O'Hara?" O'Hara, one of the pipers, in reply blew a series of suggestive jig-notes from his "empty bag."

"Where the hell are the colleens?" Roddy continued "They should be jigging it now. Put that tinker out and let the girls in!"

There was no tinker as yet. But the orator was bent on popularizing himself by turning his invective against that elusive, slippery and uneducable tribe that correspond to the gypsies in other lands.

"Ah, I see a long-snouted lean fellow over there," Roddy continued.

Darkly the gaunt faces turned to look behind them. They could distinguish no tinker. But a grim figure on a dappled gray reined up on the outskirts of the crowd. Silence fell like a cold sweat on the assembly. The figure wheeled his horse. Mr. Weld rode silently away.

Father Colyer sat in the parochial house, a thatched cabin distinguished by one window of glass which went from the roof to the ground, a distance of about six feet. Father Colyer sat in an armchair of tattered horsehair, reading a pamphlet by the light of a tallow "dip." He heard the knocking of a horsewhip on the door. A red-legged servant opened it.

Mr. Weld bent down and said:

"I would like a word with His Reverence."

The frightened girl shut the door in the horseman's face.

"Let him in," said Father Colyer from his room beside the door, for the house had no hall.

The red-legged maid returned and opened the door. The rider dismounted and fastened his horse to the ash-tree which grew beside the house—for it is unlucky to have a detached house without an ash-tree hard by. He stooped and entered. The priest received him seated. Weld carried his hat and riding crop in his hand. Father Colyer motioned him to the only other "chair" in the room, a three-legged stool beside the fire.

The man Mr. Weld took it upon himself to interview was one of the most highly educated men left in the country. He had been for more than ten years on the continent, at Paris and Louvain. Offered a chair at each of these universities, he had elected rather to cast his lot with the most oppressed and degraded race in Europe, his own people, a race deprived of all the opportunities of civilization and held by England, as its Prime Minister, Mr. Pitt, admitted, in a "cruel and abominable restraint."

"I have come, Sir," said Mr. Weld, "to inform you that if you do not use whatever influence you possess to disband this disorderly meeting of the Martyn tenants before it becomes a disgusting orgy, I shall have to put in motion the powers which reside in me and proclaim it an illegal assembly. Three suspects meeting together, as you are well aware, constitute an illegal assembly in the eyes of the law. If this drunken meeting is permitted by you, who are their accredited spiritual director, you will be held as an accessory to it and will have to answer to the military powers that rule this country."

The priest sighed but did not answer.

"You are responsible for the behaviour of your flock and I for one shall hold you so. You will have to answer to Dublin Castle for the conduct of this crowd who are riotously drunk at the present moment, disaffected, and in process of being roused by an agitator."

The effect of Mr. Weld's harangue was apparently lost on Fr. Colyer.

"You do not answer, Sir?"

Fr. Colyer took a pinch of snuff. He smiled, and said, leaning forward:

"Since when have you concerned yourself with the spiritual welfare of a race that your country can hardly tolerate and from whom it has until quite lately withheld instruction in its own religion? Since when have you been flooded by Christian and commendable sentiments of solicitude for the serfs you hold in subjection? Why should you choose this fleeting hour, which holds out food and merriment to them, for the exercise of your solicitude? Can it be that you have been moved by the words of that youthful genius, the Prime Minister of England, who says—"

He picked up the pamphlet he had been reading:

" 'I denounce in the strongest terms the past treatment of Ireland by England. Until these last very few years the system has been that of debarring Ireland from the use and enjoyment of her own resources; of making that kingdom completely subservient to the interests and opulence of this country; without suffering her to share in the bounties of nature, in the industry of her citizens, or to contribute to the general interests and strength of the Empire. This system has counteracted the kindness of Providence and suspended the enterprise of man. It has been a policy of keeping the smaller country completely subservient and subordinate to the greater; to make the one as it were an instrument of advantage; and to force all her efforts to operate in favour, and conduce merely to the interests of the other. This system of cruel and abominable restraint—' "

"Sir, you have not answered me," interrupted Mr. Weld.

"I am afraid that I am entertaining one who not only seeks to be more authoritative than the Holy Father, but who is also in disagreement with the head of the English Government. You are free as far as I am concerned to indulge your spleen. Justify it to your authorities as you may. You will not find me putting out one finger to interfere on the too rare occasions when my flock is able to forget for a moment the subhuman conditions to which your England has reduced them. Do not seek to provoke by your interference passions of which you may be made the victim. And prithee terminate this intrusion on my privacy."

Weld grew pale with fury.

"I take it that you are instigating rebellion. You shall hear more of this!"

"If you go up the road—it will be against my advice—you yourself will hear more than is good for any man who is separated from humanity by sanctimoniousness and conceit. Mary Ellen! Open the door for Mr. Weld."

Mr. Weld was no coward. His avoidance of the crowd was due more to a disinclination to see hundreds of faces gloomed with dislike for him, than to any fear of physical danger.

Never had it been known that a country wedding was the occasion for bodily violence. Even men who were wicked in their liquor became mellow for the joyous festival. Weld felt that his passing would act as a killjoy and, to preserve his self-respect, he took a lane that led round the crowd encamped upon the highway. Across the dim fields he could hear the merry squeals of the fiddles as they struck up a jig.

Roddy was having a difficult task. It was hard to prevail, even on friends, to coöperate and take hands in dancing or singing with strangers come from as far as Kiltullagh or Clontuskert or Kilmeen.

The Irish peasant girl is shy to a fault. It was this as well as the awkwardness of her possible dance-partner that prevented Roddy from infecting the crowd with his own enthusiasm. In every cabin that was roomy enough to house ten or twelve, there were five or six of both sexes sitting separately on benches against the wall, the girls whispering in monosyllables to one another to prove to the mute young men opposite that they were not ill at ease. Nobody had the courage to begin dancing.

Roddy knew that if he were to inaugurate a premature celebration —and he was bent on doing it if only to annoy the land agent, Crosbie —it would be necessary to devise some means of getting the girls and boys out of the cottages and away from the constraint which the presence of their elders imposed.

"There's room enough up here for a colleen to come and dance a jig," he said, and at once, independent, as it seemed, of his body, his legs began to move like lightning and his heels to tap out the lively opening measures of the Irish jig.

Before he could whoop out "Whurroo!" at the first turn, the fiddlers caught the fever and the irresistible strings awoke others in every cottage that housed a waiting fiddler. Roddy tapped out the rhythm on the top of the ancient coach, turning on one leg and emphasizing with raised elbow and hand the intricacies of the ritual of sound and movement. As Roddy whirled, cheers were heard from the opposite side of the road and a very reluctant partner was being pushed forward to the challenge by her admiring and mischievous friends.

"Go on, Molly, acushla, and dance the red head from off av him!"

"Do, be Jayshus," a tall fellow, with a face already inflamed, called out. "A little spalpeen the likes of him has no right to challenge the whole of Mayo and the half of Hy-many."

Blushing, with her hood of dark blue cloth fallen back off her head, a country maid was pushed forward and lifted to the top of the coach where Roddy pranced and cavorted. For a while she gazed at the twinkling feet, then, forgetting the prominence of her position, her eyes still fixed on the floor, she slowly and mechanically undid the strings beneath her chin and let her cloak fall. Roddy, it seemed, was caught up by the ancient magic. Out of a trance of speed all he could do was to cry in a hoarse whisper, "Come on!"

Demurely at first, with hands modestly holding skirts and petticoats, Molly advanced tentative feet to catch the time of Roddy's, then her face became transfigured while her erect body was moved up and down by the invisible feet below. Wheeling hand in air, she felt for Roddy to turn and touch her fingers momentarily with his fingers. Roddy was jigging it with one hand on his hip. The old coach echoed like a drum and the drum taps re-inspired the dancer.

Molly retreats, Roddy advances. Failing, he turns, she turns. His overtures begin again. Now the partners are in unison. And the double vortex continues. As she retreats he comes on. Neither apparently is any longer conscious of his or her own identity. They are part and parcel of the cosmic swirl.

And now here and there, from a low door with its yellow light behind him, a fiddler or piper came to investigate the sudden clearness of the uninterrupted music outside.

Silently, slowly, with a few whispers between them, fiddlers and pipers joined the ring in which their colleagues sat. They had to play as the others went. There was no time for tuning up. Who dared break the harmony or disturb the dream of the trees of Tir nan Og whose apples fall as swiftly and as invisibly on earth as the heel and toe of the dancers on the stationary coach?

The fiddlers bent their backs to it. The pipers forced it out with elbows almost touching ribs. In the long summer light the two figures dancing aloft seemed to be denizens of no common land. Even the calls of encouragement were no longer heard. The individuality of each dancer was merged in the cosmic chorus.

At last the music began to ebb, the lightning died out of their tread, the action of the dancers' feet became visible as with slow grace they returned hand-in-hand to earth, as it were. To a gentler movement they bowed to one another, each regaining his personality. Roddy's paleness left him. As he looked at and recognized his partner, he blushed.

A pair of great square wrists were upraised with palms stretched backwards. Molly trusted her bird-like feet to the great hands. She stepped upon the palms and was lowered without effort.

Roddy was too exhausted to lead the revels for a while.

"Give us a jorum," he commanded, acknowledging fatigue. Ready hands held the whiskey to his lips. He retained the glass and entered into a conversation with the musicians, but there was never a word about the recent performance among them all.

"It's about time that we had the ox that Cudahy is roasting."

"It's not roasted yet," said a fiddler. "He is waiting for Mr. Crosbie's commands."

Roddy, with another swig, rose and went to remonstrate with Cudahy, who was at times a butcher but more usually the cobbler or shoemaker of the village. When Roddy met Cudahy, he found him in those realms where arguments no longer hold and conclusions are not necessarily logical.

All that Roddy had to say was, "And who the hell is Crosbie, anyway? There were Cudahys here before that twister was ever heard of."

That settled it.

"Come here, boys, and give me a hand with it," said Cudahy.

The whole ox was already in position below iron stanchions which the blacksmith had placed behind Cudahy's house. The turf and wood were already collected. Long boards were placed to serve as tables in a tent or booth with one side open that fronted the street.

"We'll send a leg to His Reverence anyway," Roddy remarked airily as he set the heap alight. He said this to assuage any misgivings the more sober of the tenants might have for this open defiance of the steward Crosbie.

Bad as it was to proffer drink to boys, Roddy thought it was called for by the exceptional occasion. The girls he left alone, well knowing that they could dispense with any stimulant once they got excited. All he had to do was to dispel the lethargic shyness of the boys.

Soon there were yells and screams as night descended. Grave men who had taken advantage of their long drives to the meeting to transact business, as they would at a fair, were exhorted by Roddy to drink the bride's health—which was tantamount to a challenge to drink yourself drunk and no heel-taps, "in honour of the bride." It was a spell laid upon you by a custom ages old, and everyone knows what happens to a man who defies an old custom. Reluctantly enough at first, for they did not want it, some of them having taken the pledge, they began to drink the bride's health, and that reminded them of many a bride and many a wedding and many an unaccountable occurrence or mishap.

"And now what about a bonfire?" said Roddy. "Be heavens, I never thought of that!"

It is never too late to start mischief in Ireland. The gossoons were not lending a hand in the rejoicings, and little boys, as Roddy knew, loved nothing better than setting things ablaze. And he did not mind where they got the timber or the turf.

"Set it where we all can sit around it," Roddy directed them.

The village was ablaze. The main street was like a bivouac. Half a dozen bonfires lit the dry road and shone on the patient horses tethered to wall, post or cart. A dark body could be seen intermittently, pushing its way through the masses of the tenants and their friends. At the ring in the center of the road it rested. The flame revealed Father Colyer.

"Now, boys, don't waste the whole night in aimless drink. Get yourselves together into a pipers' and fiddlers' band and play some of our own old airs—who knows them better than you whose ancestors composed them? When the bride and bridegroom drive up in the early hours, as I hope they will, they should hear something that is incomparable when it comes to drinking songs or songs of joyful praise. I'll leave you as soon as I have blessed the meat."

"What will we give them, Father?" the blind fiddler of Galway called out.

"You're the authority yourself on that. And a better one than myself."

Festus screwed the turns tighter on his fiddle and raised his dark eyes to the gray light before the dawn. Gently he laid his bow across the strings and nestled the fiddle under his chin. His foot began to beat softly.

"What will I give them?" he asked, as if the bride and bridegroom were already within earshot of his strings.

"Fair Mabel ni Kelly" stole into sound.

It was a song written by the famous harper, O'Carolan the Bard: a man with a remarkable genius for improvisation. He was the inventor of many movements and rhythms and innovations in verse, fine tests of a poet. Planxty after planxty he wrote, and the "planxty," or Anacreontic, is associated with his name in Ireland forever. In no poetry is there such praise of drink. Well could he make returns and pay for hospitality by conferring immortality on his hosts with the tribute of his song. A true bard was he. And this was his praise of the chieftain's daughter, the lovely child of The O'Kelly who entertained him at Gallagh half a hundred years ago.

Whomever Fate may favour
To have his right arm 'neath thy head,
Through all his life he never
May sickness fear or danger dread.

Oh, head of the beauteous curling hair,
Oh, breast like the swimming swan so fair:
Love and hope of lover
All the island over,
Fairest maid is Mabel, here or anywhere.

The sudden change of tempo at the end of the stanza suited the fiddle as well as it had suited the harp on which it was composed. The last lines rushed together in an ecstasy, as if the stream of song burst its banks spontaneously from the spate of beauty and the implied challenge brought to being by the bard.

The blue night glowed with the memory of fair Mabel and built again in dreams the beauty of that swan-white breast which the earth covered long ago.

XIII. HAULIN' HOME THE BRIDE

CROSBIE'S MOUNT HAD cast a shoe. From a swelling over the hoof, the blacksmith whom he consulted concluded that the horse would be unfit to be shod for some time. Could he tell Mr. Crosbie where he could get a mount and a boy to lead his own horse home? Well, he could, but he would have to consult some of his friends who would be sure to be coming over the fields on their way to the village.

Thus it came about that Mr. Crosbie was late, very late indeed, by the time he had ridden behind a tenant on a hollow-backed steed, bowed down further still by the double load. If the steed was heavy, the tenant behind whom Crosbie rode was light-hearted. A favour such as this to the agent of the Martyn estate could not be without its fruits.

By the time the agent reached Martyn Hall it was after two in the morning. His errand had been ill-timed. He should have realized that the tenantry to whose homes he was bringing relief would be on their way to the festive meeting in the village. He should also have realized the proportions such a festival would take. The countryside was assembled with all the tenants from the estates of the neighbouring gentry, from Lenasilla, the Meadow of the Willows, from Lisheen-anoran, the little Fort of the Cold Spring, from Moyoon and Drimcong, the Ridge of the Narrow Straight. How the secret was kept from the couple in whose honour it was held was a mystery, but to some extent it accounted for the continued absence of the principals. Had the bride been aware of what was awaiting her and her husband she would never have delayed and brought about what might be taken as an act of discourtesy.

Crosbie decided he must hurry to the village and give orders that no one was to touch the food or drink provided until such time as he gave the word. After all, he was the immediate host and it was just as well that the fact should be impressed on the tenants.

He had to find a saddle in the dark and go into the house for a lamp because the bit he found, though it was hanging up beside a hunting saddle, belonged to one of the cart-horses. Which of the stable boys was responsible for this gross carelessness and untidiness? A cart-horse's bit and blinkers in on the hunters' side of the harness room! Now where were the proper reins and bit? Up for the summer of course; and the hunters in the fields. What chance had he to catch a horse at this time of night? If he were to ride at all he would have to take a cart-horse and lose face thereby if seen mounted on such a charger. He could stop at Mrs. Early's house and fasten the horse to her palings and approach the street on foot. The damned reins would not fit without the blinkers, and these in turn required the horse collar, to which they were carried back by a chain. He would look like a farm-hand lolling on horseback coming in from the fields. The night was dark. In such a crowd no one would be likely to know or care how he looked. Damn it again! If troubles never come singly, absurdities have an even greater ratio of multiplication: Biddy Early's house was at the end of the street farthest away from the direction of Martyn Hall. He would have to ride through the multitude on a horse heavier than the chargers that bore the Crusaders to the Holy Land.

Contemptuously he selected a large roan with feathered feet, only to find trouble with the saddle girths. They could be lengthened, but how was he to stretch under the beast to gather the buckles on the opposite side? It was enough to ruffle anyone's temper, and it getting on to three in the morning.

Mounted at last, he took the heavy mare up the lane and steered her as best he could with reins of rope. The boreen, or little road, that led from the gates of Martyn Hall to the mail coach road, was a mile and a half long. Beech and ash trees met or almost met overhead, making a narrow gray lane against the dim sky. By watching this Crosbie could steer, but, filled as he was with exasperation, he left the finding of the way to the mare. She could be trusted to avoid the ditch on either side. The ground was deep with dust, kept from rising only by the dampness of the dew which was heavy under leaves, or from the dewfall from the leaves themselves. The mare went on in absolute silence broken only by the jingle of metal in the harness and the large horse collar she wore. This jingling irritated Crosbie and added to his ill temper. It prevented him hearing clearly sounds which came from beyond. This accounted for the fact that he was unaware of something walking in the dark until he was right upon it. The mare slowed a little. He could hear heavy breathing and was aware, now that the harness no longer rattled, of something breathing and advancing with strange thuds.

Suddenly the night was startled by a shout.

"Dismiss!"

On both sides in front of him he could hear the crash of men making quickly for shelter through the hedges in which they floundered in the dark. What their numbers were he could not make out. That they were considerable was evident from the crashing of the undergrowth through a wide area for a minute. Then all was still again. He peered into the darkness, trying to catch sight of the man who had given what was undoubtedly a military command. There was no one to be seen. After a while he urged on the mare.

His mood had changed from one of exasperation to one of grave apprehension. He had surprised a secret company marching in military formation through an unfrequented lane at night. This was revolution under his very nose. Evidently tenants on the Martyn estate composed the company, or whatever it was, that was marching; for none but those who had an intimate knowledge of the terrain could have disappeared so suddenly and so completely through the black woods without betraying their presence. After the first rush, there was no sound of anyone splashing through any of the numerous brooks that went through these woods, as strangers to the territory would certainly have done.

Crosbie reasoned that the sound of metal jingling on the mare had made the men mistake him and his mount for an ambush of dragoons into which they imagined that they were walking. In the darkness they could not possibly tell who was on horseback, least of all suspect that the estate agent would be patrolling on a cart-horse at three o'clock in the morning.

As he rode on he meditated more. What discipline must there be which drilled men at night into the small hours, men who had to be up early to resume the arduous labours of the day? It revealed the existence of strong discipline not only to do this, but do it at a time of feasting and rejoicing when the whole countryside was on holiday. If he could only make out whose was the voice that gave the command "Dismiss!" It came so suddenly he had no time to note it, but it was significant that the word of command was given not in Gaelic but in English. The officer may have been one of the English renegades lately come who were getting recruits and drilling them to help the enemies of their own country. Ireland was not the only country to suffer from English traitors. Perhaps, though, they were *agents provocateurs*. One way to end rebellion was to cause an abortive rising. This the Government had done successfully in Wexford.

Crosbie would be one of the first to suffer from a rising, successful or not, for it was he who was in immediate contact with the tenants and it was he who collected the rents. The tithes' proctor would be the first to be assassinated, then himself. Goodbye to his plans to rise by diligence and industry to the ownership of one of the estates which were falling into ruin through the recklessness and extravagance of their masters. An estate such as Weld had now was owned a generation ago by Matthias Burke. Horses and dice and the Hellfire Club were Burke's undoing and the making of his land agent, Weld.

There would be no need to undermine Martyn. He was undermining himself. But even though Crosbie could not purchase the mortgages and take over the estate, there were six hundred acres of marshy woodland which he could acquire and there was enough duty labour due to him by the tenants to divert the little brook which kept the wood marshy, and clear the six hundred acres of scrub and rotting timber. That could be done for nothing. Then give it a year or two to form a sod and it would be the best grazing land in Mayo. He would leave trees enough to provide a shelter and, once sheltered, there would be winter grass for the cattle, and sheltered cattle would give that commodity rare in winter, milk.

Mrs. St. George would be grateful to him if he could pull her son's estate together. It was in as bad a way as his friend Martyn's and St. George was making it worse. And a grateful woman is easily won.

It was rumoured that she had had a love affair in France with a nobleman who had barely time to get her out of the country after the Revolution broke out. Some said her lover had perished on the scaffold. At any rate that was what her French maid had told someone in French who told Mrs. Brophy in confidence—which went further than French.

One thing was certain: dead or alive, her lover could not be connected with the agents of the Directoire, who were over from France endeavouring to get an army of peasants sufficiently drilled to be a support to any French forces which could effect a landing.

If an insurrection were successful, the Irish character could be as cruel and revengeful and bloodthirsty as that of the "citizens" of Paris. They would permit no one but the commonest to own land. They would be "the People" to the exclusion of every other part of the state, to the exclusion of nobleman, aristocrat, inferior gentry and the middle classes who composed the rest of the community. They would imitate if they did not exceed the bloody frenzy of the French Commune. They would turn on their masters, interpreting the help that any one of them lent during the revolution as an effort to curry favour with the People and save themselves from the righteous wrath of the oppressed. If it did not succeed—and how could it?—the suppression would decimate the tenants, crimp those under suspicion, send them to serve in the Fleet, and leave the estate with nothing but the labour of boys and old men. Who would drain the Killyloughavoy wood, the Wood of the Lake of the Drowning, then?

The sooner he reached the village the better. He could note those who were present and note those who were absent. This would give him some idea of the numerical strength of the revolutionary movement of the district. The men he had encountered drilling in the dark must have been missed from the celebrations; perhaps he could learn the names of the men whose absence had been noted. He was soon to learn the utter unpracticability of such plans. Discrimination between those present and absent was impossible. He had not counted on the size of the assembly which attracted balladists, tricksters, vagabonds and musicians from all the neighbourhood within a circle of fifty miles and more.

Once on the broad highway he cantered to the village. What a sight met his eyes! The broad mail coach road was completely blocked by a vast assembly, huddled silent, sleeping in their coats of gray frieze. High on tables stretched across the street were half a dozen dark forms fastened to their chairs by suggauns or ropes made of twisted hay passed round their chests. They looked like the wounded felons who have to be shot in chairs. These were the musicians. The ropes were fastened by friendly hands to prevent their falling from the seats. Only the middle one was awake.

Crosbie rode, as it were, through a sleeping auditorium. The wakeful musicians' eyes rolled in the intermittent light of the dying bonfires. Let them sleep, thought Crosbie; but who the hell broached all the casks and who was responsible for the smell of roasted beef?

A keg under his horse's hoof nearly threw him on the road. As she plunged to recover, the mare awakened a score of sleepers. Dimly they saw him and slowly it dawned upon them who he was. But what a mount! What could Crosbie mean coming mounted to meet his master like this? Drink does be quare in some people.

"Av course it's a joke to amuse the Master," one grim fellow assured the rest.

The idea was greeted well: Crosbie's contribution to the general "divarshun."

"Cheers for Crosbie!"

Cheers which may well have been derisive greeted his ear. But to call him "Crosbie." Such insolence could only come from the spirit of insubordination which was being spread through the land by the agents of France. Soon there would be no respect even for the priest. The fellows looked like Westport men, and the revolutionary ideas came in at the ports. Lately suspicious-looking vessels had been cruising off the coast. That cheer was certainly derisive, coming as it did from the men who were not under his jurisdiction. What the real feeling among his tenants was it would be impossible to gauge. The fact that the celebrations began and were over without his express permission was something that could not be overlooked.

There was a light in Biddy's house. He dismounted and led his cart-horse to the back of the place. Returning, he knocked at the half door, the upper part of which was open. Through the window he could see two lamps burning brightly. He knocked again, but there was no sign of Biddy. He drew the bolt and went in.

Propped on a chair with her back to the fire lay Biddy, dressed in the most ostentatious finery he had ever beheld. Her bonnet rose like an enormous shovel rising from the back of her head. She wore a gaudy Paisley shawl. He tapped his boot against a chest. Biddy stirred in her sleep.

"Through a wedding ring," she murmured, and slept again.

Chagrined, he left the house. He would find Cudahy if he could make his way through the masses of gray coats who were bivouacking sound asleep. As he passed the roadside booth he looked in. Behind a long table a red-haired fellow was busily engaged in filling a row of glasses, assisted by a pair of grinning small boys.

"What the devil are you doing, Roddy?" Crosbie asked.

"Have a drop for the dawn," Roddy replied without looking up.

"What is all this about?" Crosbie demanded.

As he entered, a piper who was lying on the floor rolled over on the bag of his pipe and a wailing sound came forth in sinking semitones.

Suddenly his ear caught the sound of galloping horses and faint cheering from the far end of the village. In the gray light there was no mistaking the yellow coach. Feeney was laying about him with his whip. As those on the road got up to make way, the village arose as one man.

"Turn me round, boys," Festus the fiddler prayed. Willing hands turned the fiddler round on his table to face the oncoming coach.

"Ask them to whist a bit."

In a silence broken by women straining over the doors of the cottages and shouts from within, Festus Kyle played. The thin delight arose above all the noises of the wakening sleepers.

"Whist, can't ye, for the fiddler from Auchnanure!"

> Whomever Fate may favour
> To have his right arm 'neath thy head
> Through all his life he never
> May sickness fear or danger dread.
>
> Oh, head of the beauteous. . . .

But they were unspanning the horses to the tune of Feeney's curses. Gossoons were rushing from yards and houses with coils of rope. Crosbie's reins were gone. With surprising speed, speed undiminished by the night's festival, ropes were hitched where the traces went and paid out to willing hands at either side. The coach began to move. In vain Feeney strove to dismount and put an end to the absurd position in which he found himself.

The coach was gathering weigh.

"Mind yerself, Mr. Crosbie, or come on and give us a hand," a tenant shouted.

A red-headed figure stood up in the guard's place behind the coach. He acknowledged the cheers and wild huzzahs which were meant for those within. An old boot struck him on the back as showers of that lucky talisman fell on the coach.

"Can't yez go aisy, there? Ye'll break the windows."

But the windows were well open. From one side the bride bowed, from the other the bridegroom. Showers of golden guineas reduced the pressure on the coach as the besieging brats and gossoons fought for them amid the rolling kegs.

Fresh as the morning itself, the crowd ran beside the horseless carriage. Old women waddled in the direction of the Hall. Barefooted gossoons leaped and danced. Turning the corner to the left at the end of the village, the lines of haulers collided. Roddy jumped down and re-formed them at once. A rope was attached to the rear to act as a brake as the coach entered the down grade of the lane. From the top of the coach Roddy beat time as tension on the rope was required. Now and then he called for relays.

The first beams of the sun caught the yellow panels at the turn. Under a mist of greenery the coach disappeared from view as the haulin' home proceeded uproariously to Martyn Hall.

As Crosbie was following on foot at the head of the minstrels (through no fault of his own), a little boy rushed up to him holding a golden coin on high.

"Will you change this for me your Honour, Mr. Crosbie, please?"

Crosbie's pleasure at the child's good manners gave way to consternation as he recognized in the grubby hand a *louis d'or*. If proof had been needed of the presence of French agents in the vicinity, here it was.

A piper played, by the way of no harm:

The French are on the sea
  Says the Shan van Vocht,
The French are on the sea
  Says the Shan van Vocht.
The French are on the sea
  To set ould Ireland free,
And fight for Liberty,
  Says the Shan van Vocht.

"The Shan van Vocht," or "Poor Old Woman," was one of the many poetical synonyms for Ireland.

It would have seemed to a stranger that Mr. Crosbie was leading the martial band that played the rousing tune behind him. Actually, knowing Mr. Crosbie's sentiments full well, the pipers had chosen the tune as a musical taunt to him.

BOOK III

XIV. AN OWNER AT THE CURRAGH

Sir Richard de Vesey sat in his gazebo at Lucan House and looked along the river. The summer house was built of stone in an octagonal shape. This was apparent from the outside, but within its contour was circular. The design of the architect had been to give the building the rectilinear appearance of a house from without and the circular shape of a planetarium within. The window door, which was made of plate glass, was curved and the inside panel or door which could close over the glass was fashioned so that it might slide in a curved groove hidden in the floor. Once the inner door was closed the place was sealed and all signs of an exit hidden. Light was admitted from windows concealed under the dome. The walls were panelled in cedar wood of which the door was a part. The roof, painted blue as a July night, was raised in a cupola set with golden stars. The signs of the zodiac in heavy golden relief were depicted in a dado, or circular band, from which the domed roof sprang. In the centre of the room was a card table, also circular, while hidden behind sliding panels were books and decanters of cut glass. It was a pleasant place for a lady to pass the sultry hours, or for the men to gamble through a summer's night.

Sir Richard sat gazing along a reach of the river which was as tranquil as a mill pond, thanks to the work of Grattan's Parliament, which had lately "weired" and otherwise treated many of the rivers of Ireland, beginning with the river on which the capital stood. This river had a great interest for Sir Richard de Vesey. Not only had he chosen to build a stately mansion within fifty yards of its banks, but to its water-meadows and rich limestone soil was entrusted the raising of his horses, the rearing of his foals and the maintenance of his stud. Had he been asked to name from memory one of the golden zodiacal signs that circled over his head, in all probability all that he would have remembered would have been "Sagittarius, the fellow with the bow and arrow," and this only because Sagittarius was depicted as a centaur, like that wise man-horse who taught archery to the stripling son of Peleus. Horses were in the mind of Sir Richard de Vesey, and the river occupied his thoughts only because, not far away along its banks, his stallions roamed and his brood mares bent their necks to drink of the bright, black water. Not the beauty, then, but the utility of the river filled Sir Richard's mind.

Poetry was known to Sir Richard only through Virgil and Alexander Pope, and this not so much from natural inclination, but because it was the accomplishment of the time and the fashion in politics to drive home an argument by an apposite quotation from the classics. Suffice it to say, the only thing that could be counted poetical in the person of Sir Richard at the present time was his costume.

He wore a gray cloth spencer over his coat, which was collared and cuffed with fur. His riding boots of black polished leather reached high above the knee—boots such as the prints represent King William to have worn at the Boyne. Large gauntlets of yellow doeskin reaching to his elbows resembled the armour of a knight, and a three-cornered hat completed the costume, in which he had intended to ride on a visit to Simmondstown, where his horses were kept on both banks of the Liffey's stream. A twitching in the great toe of his right foot had made him change his plan for riding this morning, yet if he could not ride out for the fear of being unable to ride back, there was nothing to prevent him from driving. He ordered the tandem and went to the "River House" to wait for his man, not bothering to change his clothes. There would be a greatcoat in the gig against the evening cold.

Sir Richard had property in England and Ireland. The English property, which was rapidly being covered with labourers' cottages and improving in value, brought in a yearly sum sufficient to compensate for any year's deficit in the rentals of his West of Ireland property near Lisadill. The rents of that he could enjoy in diminishing proportion until his niece Mabs' coming-of-age, which, by the terms of his late brother's will, was not to be until that young lady was twenty-three. By then she would have had time to make up her mind about the young gallants who were sure, in an impoverished country, to buzz about her like bees about a linden. At seventeen, she was wild as an unbroken filly. The deeper in the country and the farther from the city she was, the safer she would be. And Lisadill was on the western shore of the island, a place singularly blessed for climate and good weather, situated as it was on a shelf of land but ten miles wide between the mountains and the ocean. Here Mabs stayed with Aunt Penelope and Madame de Ronquerolles, when she was not visiting her sister at Martyn Hall.

If Lisadill was too far for the training of race horses, there was blood enough in the stables to supply a mount whenever his niece wished to go on horseback, which was every day in the week. There was enough to keep her quiet there, since she was forbidden to ride any of the saddle horses to Dublin following her last escapade.

The tandem was heard on the gravel. If, when he stood up, the blood went into his toe without hurting him, he might outdistance the gout yet; but he had not had gout for a year and the damned thing was overdue. It had not begun to attack him until he turned fifty, and that was more than the less active members of his acquaintance could say. Why, there was a young fellow, a newly elected member of the Club, who had an attack of it in the eyes, and he could not yet be in his thirties. (Some said it was gunpowder got by fighting a duel across a handkerchief, a method which was outside the rules and to be deprecated, anyway, for its tendency to reduce the number of sportsmen and thus spoil sport.) No, on the whole, if the gout got Sir Richard without preventing him from visiting his manager, it might take him in charge for a week or two. He had earned it.

But it was all-important that he should see Perkins without delay. He pulled open a panel at hand. Yes: The Racing Calendar gave room for no ambiguity about dates. The second day at the Curragh was the day of the big race, which was already as good as won by Sir

Richard's horse Agincourt in spite of rumours from the Curraghstown stable about some entry by St. George.

Uneasy and anxious about rumours as to form at the Curragh, Sir Richard got up to climb into his gig at the entrance to the rose lawn where the tandem waited. Grooms held wheeler as well as leader by the head. The tandem drove off, and, when the sounds of the smartly trotting horses had died away, the river resumed its song.

As he drove along, Sir Richard speculated on the proverbial dishonesty of horse dealers, horse copers and horse trainers. He had come to suspect the sincerest assurances of any trainer. He knew that they could not go straight, that their code of honour was to outwit their supporters.

Perkins was no exception. Ignorant but full of mother wit, he knew on the instant he saw him the character of the "owner" with whom he had to deal, and decided on his course of action—whether it should be cajolery or flattery and adulation (a good way with a *nouveau riche*) or, as a last reluctant resort, deceptive honesty. In this last recourse he always felt diffident, being unfamiliar with its usage and distrusting that which limited his imagination and restricted his activities. Knowing this, the wise owner did not push him too far or question him too searchingly. He left him to the devious ways he took to achieve victory, with a tacit proviso that a certain proportion of success was to be expected if the horses were to remain in his charge.

The difficulty was that the successes, though they aggregated a certain proportion during the year, were anything but predictable. No owner could tell when his horse would win (though he knew when it should). If he had ten triumphs for ten horses in the year, the trainer could point to a victory each for his ten horses in training. But one certainly would be better than an average of chance wins, especially as some of the victories seemed to come as a surprise to the trainer himself.

Knowing these things, Sir Richard did not attempt to get a straight answer from Perkins, and yet Perkins, because of his English blood, perhaps, was at a disadvantage when it came to winning the confidence of an owner. Sir Richard had to be content to let Perkins spin his yarns and try to extract any hint of information that they might conceal. This mannerism of Perkins' might have been attributable to long residence at the Curragh, had Perkins not graduated at Newmarket before he came to Ireland. Probably any little diffidence in Perkins' traffic with the truth had been acquired from the disdainful manners and customs of that English University of the Stables.

There were those who thought that Perkins' straight-forwardness, when it appeared, was due less to his sincerity than to his shortcomings as a linguist. These were rivals.

The tandem was hardly in the yard when obliging stable hands ran to hold the horses. Tulip, the coachman, jumped down from behind the gig and said, "Whoa there," to steady the leader. "Hould him like that, now!" he directed, as he assisted Sir Richard to the ground.

Perkins appeared from nowhere. He was a middle-sized man kept from corpulence by his trade rather than by his habit of life. He had a large head with small blue eyes set wide apart over high cheek bones, which, being rounded and broad, gave his red face the abundant look of a pumpkin. The lids under his eyes were full like those above.

With steady deference and a certain mystery in his bearing, he waited for Sir Richard to reach the ground. He made as if to give a hand but thought better of it. He did not want to make it appear that he thought Sir Richard lacked anything in activity and youthfulness.

"Now, Perkins," said Sir Richard, grunting from his exertion, "I want a word with you."

"The office is open, Sir Richard, if you care to come in."

The "office" was part of a long building of loose boxes which was boarded off from the rest. It contained a safe, a high desk such as those hideously plain ones seen in the scriveners' room of an attorney's office; three or four chairs and an armchair with the horsehair stuffing showing at the edges. Dusting the armchair deferentially, Perkins motioned Sir Richard to it.

"No, no, man. I want a higher chair than that." Seated to his satisfaction, he regarded Perkins steadily. Perkins, to avoid the stare, with a "By your Honour's leave," opened a cupboard which exposed many glasses and different kinds of wine and spirits.

"No, no!" Sir Richard said impatiently, then added, as Perkins closed the cupboard, "Now what is all this I hear about young St. George's horse?"

Perkins' broad face could not betray all the astonishment which he billeted in it. Blankness took the aspect of surprise. With a note of innocence he returned the question:

"St. George's horse?"

"What the devil you think you will gain by looking like a mentally defective child when I ask you a question that has an immediate bearing on this stable, I cannot imagine. This is no time to play the fool, with the race not a week off."

The left side of Perkins' leg apparently began to itch. He put his fingers between the buttons of his leggings and scratched it. When he raised himself up he shook his head solemnly.

Sir Richard exclaimed, "Do you mean that you never heard of the horse?"

Keeping the tempo of the interview well in the slow movement, Perkins said, as if filled with solicitude for Sir Richard's interests, "Did I hear of the horse? I heard too much about it for all that I heard to be true." Again he scratched his leg.

"Then why the devil didn't you inform me before I laid ten thousand pounds on Agincourt?"

"On Agincourt. I never pays no heed to stable rumours," Perkins said. He rose and went to a drawer in his desk and took out a stubby little black notebook.

"There's twenty thousand on Green Glint."

"How comes that entry in your books?"

"There ain't no entry in my books, leastways no bettin' entries. This is a stable memo, and I sees that on the twenty-fifth of May last they sent over from Medlicott Anderson's to borrow weights."

"From St. George's trainer?"

"Exactly, Sir Richard."

"I have no intention to spy on another man's horse's form. You doubtless have lots of the lads doing that dawn and evening; but what I fail to see is what this rigmarole about borrowing weights has to do with the form of St. George's horse, which must be in pretty good fettle to have twenty thousand on his back and to be sure of beating anything this stable has."

"This stable has . . ." echoed Perkins, a trick very annoying to an impatient listener. "This stable has sense enough not to be taken in like that," he finished.

"Where is the dodge?" Sir Richard asked.

"Where is the dodge? When I rode for Lord Londsdale, the Stanley stable sent over to borrow weights."

"Borrow weights? To what are you leading?"

"To what am I leading? To this. A stable borrows weights to make the opposition think that they have to weight their choice above ten stone when running against the clock. They are making you think that they have to do this to deceive the spotters hidden all around the Heath. Then you are supposed to think that his form is so hot that his saddle has to be weighted for the trials of their horse while all the time they are counting on you seeing through the trick and discounting the chances of their animal. This keeps the prices long."

Sir Richard, who had little knowledge of the inner workings of training stables, failed to see how a trivial trick like that just described by Perkins could have such a vast effect. He did not realize that trivial minds were influenced by such slight and obvious subterfuges when overt acts of greater significance might fail to set them to work. A rumour had more influence with these suspicious racetrack people than circumstantial evidence of fitness and form.

"But surely, Perkins," Sir Richard said after a long pause, "you cannot attribute the shortenings of the odds—some of the bets have been laid off on London bookies—to a silly gesture such as you describe, which did not succeed in discrediting their horse's capabilities. The horse has form, and well you know it. All I ask is this —if you are not sure that Agincourt can beat Green Glint, give me time, I ask you, to lay off some of the money you encouraged me to put on. . . . Here, damn it, man, have you got the itch? Answer me straight—if you were I, would you keep ten thousand on Agincourt?"

"If you were I" was an unfortunate phrase. It was unthinkable, too, that by any possibility Sir Richard could be Perkins and receive a straight answer in spite of the change of character.

"There's a lot in the jockey," said Perkins at length.

Sir Richard tried to rise, so indignant had he become. Instead of getting up from his chair—for to do that would require assistance for which he was disinclined to ask—he merely glared at Perkins and said solemnly:

"So it comes to this, then, that it is on a jockey and not my horse that my victory depends?"

"Victory depends on a jockey in every case," Perkins replied soothingly. "One that knows his hoss can make him talk."

"Who have they got for Green Glint?"

"Green Glint? Ah, that's just where what I said about jockeys comes in. They have not got nobody up to date to ride Green Glint. There's talk of putting Feeney up what broke him in down in Mayo."

"Feeney that won at the Curragh twelve years ago for Matthias Burke on Burke Aboo?"

"Burke Aboo. That's him."

Sir Richard had food for thought. What was the significance of the fact that up to this it was not known who would ride Green Glint? Did it mean that the horse had tricks which no jockey brought over from England could be expected to master, or did it mean that only Feeney knew of what the horse was capable; and out of training and perhaps overweight as Feeney was, they were risking their fortune on his skill?

"Feeney must be fifty now," Sir Richard guessed.

"Fifty now. He doesn't look it. But Mr. St. George said that you should never count on age to handicap anyone in the West who wanted to do what he had set his heart to do."

Sir Richard started. Indeed he was learning slowly how much information the beginning of the interview promised to withhold. Perkins, who had begun by knowing nothing, was revealing much.

"When was Mr. St. George at the Curragh?"

"At the Curragh? It was about a week ago. It was either himself or another young friend of his, about the exact spit of him, a plenipotentiary if you like, for Anderson put him up for a gallop over the level mile at the back of the hollow. Don't think I couldn't see what was going on from where I hid."

This evidence of Perkins's zeal was somewhat reassuring.

"And your impression?"

"My impression was that he can carry eleven stone."

"Eleven stone! So there may have been some reason why they wanted the weights after all?"

"After all, if they had not got none. But they has. All stables has."

"If I cannot lay off now," Sir Richard said, "I am sure that there will be no difficulty in getting Barlow to divide my money and put five thousand on Green Glint."

"Green Glint. What about the whole packet each way?"

Sir Richard made no reply. He struggled to rise. He held out his hand for assistance. He had learned all that he had come to know. He was satisfied that he knew as much as Perkins, and all was shaded by uncertainty. What else can the gambler expect but uncertainty? Where would there be room for Fortune's favours if all were as certain as a pensioner's pay?

From the glib way in which Perkins made his suggestion about placing the bet he suspected that that was precisely what Perkins had already done for himself: backed the opponent. It would account for the sudden shortening of the odds if a bookie knew that the trainer of the favourite had backed a horse from a rival stable.

"How did Green Glint go?" Sir Richard asked.

"When they brought him out he was restive. There was no weights in the saddle as far as I could judge from the way the little slip of a lad wielded it. I had a spy glass and could see quite clear. They held him for the tall young gentleman what was to ride him. Once he was up they led him from the yard and let him loose. He turned right round at the start."

"I hope he keeps up that trick," said Sir Richard fervently.

"Then off he goes as if he was bolting. That he wasn't bolting could be seen from the way the young gentleman steered him past where I was laying. I thought he'd have seen me lying in the furze. He's a wicked one to go: long in the legs and full of fire."

"To which are you all alluding, horse or rider?"

"The hoss, Sir Richard. He is long in the forelegs and he has a long level gait."

"There is no advantage that I can see in too long a foreleg."

"No, Sir Richard, but remember the finish will be downhill and I counts a long foreleg downhill somewhat like a long hind leg, as hares has, for running uphill."

"Did he try him over the full journey?"

"No fear of it, Sir Richard. About a mile."

Sir Richard made to go. Ostlers came to the help of Tulip to hold the horses until Sir Richard reached his seat.

As he took ribbons and whip in hand, Sir Richard said, to terminate the interview:

"Very well Perkins, I'll be over in the morning to see Agincourt tried out."

Perkins screwed his puffy under-lids up so that they almost met his upper eyelids and left but a slit of an eye. With a look of momentous confidence he said:

"You'll see summat, Sir Richard."

XV. THE MISSING GUN

DURING THE FIRST few months of the Martyn-Lynches' occupancy of Martyn Hall, Ninon rose rapidly to a sense of the dignity that her marriage with Hyacinth Martyn-Lynch conferred. There were servants to answer directly to her bidding. Her authority was no longer divided with members of her family as it had been at Lisadill. All at Martyn Hall were ready to obey her will with joyous alacrity. Perhaps a partial exception was her housekeeper, Biddy Early, who showed some signs of resistance. But it would be out of the question for Ninon to resent one so long entrenched in her husband's family.

Biddy's conduct exasperated by being the opposite of anything that could be called a shortcoming. Her faults, if faults they could be called, were overzeal and an endless amount of ostentatious fuss when any trivial duty was to be done. For instance, she would evince far too much solicitude about the temperature of her mistress's sheets and, when her mistress was about to retire for the night, linger far too long on the lobbies and floor of the bedrooms after her mistress had retired, "to be there in case My Lady wanted anything." And Ninon could not very well thrust her head out from the nuptial chamber and order her downstairs or tell her to stop making a noise, when she was not making any noise. It was hard to rebuke a well-intentioned servant no matter how superfluous her self-appointed task. Nor was this conduct a subject that could be referred to the steward Mr. Crosbie.

If Ninon lay late of a morning, Biddy would be sure to avail herself of a servant's privilege of entering without knocking. She would be armed with a tray on which "morning tea" and thin wafers of bread and butter, after a fashion coming into vogue, would be displayed. While placing the tray at her mistress's bedside she would chatter familiarly of her own introduction to marriage. That would remind her of how she went to hear a monk preach on matrimony during a mission without coming away any the wiser, and that in turn would remind her of the mother of a dozen children who exclaimed after hearing him "I wish to God I knew as little about it as he does!" It would be more suitable if the Church were to employ married women to give instructions on the non-ecclesiastical aspect of Holy Matrimony. From such solicitude and reminiscences Ninon at last guarded herself by the employment of a French maid and by strictly confining the housekeeper's duties to the care of the house rather than of its mistress (things hard indeed to distinguish, she found). She would be left in a position of insecure peace while her maid would find the ways of the house increasingly more difficult to comprehend.

Ninon spent much of her time familiarizing herself with her domain—walking about its vast grounds, planning improvements in the new house and its landscaping, and learning to assume the position of gracious mistress to the tenant population of the estate.

Never were the pride and privilege of married life borne in on Ninon more than when her sister Mabs and Aunt Penelope came from Lisadill to visit her in her new home. Clemente, pleading fatigue, stayed behind to enjoy the peace of Lisadill, now that Mabs was away. Though she did not for a moment regret that she had volunteered to act as Mabs' preceptress, a short vacation from her sometimes trying charge was very welcome.

Mabs' and Penelope's delight in the beauty of the site and the spaciousness of the establishment of Martyn Hall was a pure joy to Ninon. Her new home compared favourably with her old, Lisadill, one of the loveliest houses in Ireland, and she had her aunt's testimony to that. The effect of its novelty and freshness on her relatives and their pride in her she did not discount. Her only concern was what the effect on her sister of the display of such independence would be.

Hidden away in Lisadill with foals and saddle horses, dogs and guns, as she was much of the time, Mabs could be as much of a tomboy as her heart desired. There was no envious old gossip to report any unladylike behaviour, any undue familiarity with the stable boys or the underlings. "Underlings" did not exist at Lisadill. It was only when the grooms came up to the Curragh that the chasm separating mistress from servant was noticeable. This was a lesson learnt when she "ran away" to follow her colt Green Glint, when he was being taken from the loose fields of Lisadill to the strict training ground of the Curragh of Kildare.

Green Glint was the first and only get of Burke Aboo, whom Feeney had steered to a resounding victory twelve years ago in that place famous for training stables and horse races. Feeney had smashed his knee against the paling as he came along to win on the inside, a feat of horsemanship which gave him the lead when he appeared to be shut in by the rivals, who, knowing that they had no chance by fair play, had agreed to spread out and leave him to go round outside them so that any horse at long odds might take the race. Burke Aboo was at long odds on that day, for he had strange faults. For one thing he was a one-man horse; for another, he went mad at the whip and was likely to swerve off at a tangent if so much as touched with it; and lastly, he often turned right round at the start of a race. Trial after trial with stable boys had proved this. In fine, no one but Feeney knew how to control him. And at the last moment, when Feeney took his seat, his master was able to take advantage of such rumours as these which leaked from the stables, and to get fourteen-to-one against his unbeatable stallion. Seven thousand pounds Feeney had won for Matthias Burke on that afternoon. Was it any wonder that Feeney could do as he liked in the county which was all sib to the ould families?

"Talking of wonders," as Biddy Early used to say, was it any wonder that when Miss Mabel's pet Green Glint was transported to the same hard school, the only person he would suffer on his back save Feeney and his son Timsey should wish to follow him? It was not Mabs' motive but her method in following him that brought on her the disapproval of her aunt and of Sir Richard de Vesey, her uncle, who was thus forced to take serious notice of her escapade. The golden-haired girl had taken the risk of county inns and county roads, crossed Ireland in three days and put up at a training camp without attendant of any kind. That escapade was, in spite of the tradition of Irish chivalry, dangerous and unladylike. From that day she was more or less a prisoner at Lisadill. That was why the sight of the freedom and independence which marriage brought, and the effect this knowledge might have on Mabs, was a cause of anxiety for the elder sister.

"Ninon, dear," said her Aunt Penelope, "what day have you decided on for the party? Of course you know you must devote a day to the celebration of your occupancy of Martyn Hall."

"Dear Aunt, all the county has hardly had time to call upon me yet. And even if everyone did, I would hate to have them assemble formally at Martyn Hall until the trees are more grown and the place losses the signs of its newness."

"It is all cleaned up and all it wants is a little grass and time for the mortar to be washed from the limestone. But what does it matter how new the house looks? It will appear all the more desirable to those who have not built large houses for themselves and are unacquainted with modern furniture. Your Adams tables and Heppelwhite chairs and your lovely French escritoires will be such a delight to the Hemphills, who are hesitating to build because of the uncertainty of the times, and as for the Dalys, the times can hardly be called a consideration to James Daly. He would build, if the fancy struck him, in the middle of a revolution. The D'Arcy's and the Burkes will be full of curiosity. You simply must hold a salon before the winter makes it impossible to drive abroad."

"Dear Aunt, you cannot know how uncertain and anxious everything is until we get the results from the Curragh."

"Green Glint? St. George's horse?"

Ninon smiled. Between them it was well known that, though entered in his friend Denis' name for a variety of reasons and precautions (chiefly not to arouse the envy of jealous landlords), Green Glint was Hyacinth's horse and Mabel's too.

"It must be an anxious time. But please God, Green Glint will rehabilitate you all."

Ninon said nothing. Her aunt, noticing this—for she had not been brought up among horses without gleaning some knowledge of the effect of a great house's stables upon a great house—asked:

"Oh, Ninon dear, don't say that anything has happened to Green Glint. Did not Hyacinth take him for a mile gallop on his way down here?"

"It is not the horse but the jockey that gives us cause for anxiety and even for alarm. You know Green Glint only behaves quietly for three riders—Feeney, Timsey and—" she stopped.

Her aunt swung round on Mabel. Mabel smiled, flattered at her sister's silent tribute to her horsemanship.

"Oh, Feeney, I mean only Feeney knows his racing secret, and even Timsey does not know it, though Green Glint loves Timsey to ride him."

"Why on earth cannot Feeney impart the mystery, if there be a mystery, to his own son?"

Ninon shook her head and looked at Mabel.

"There is no use asking me," her sister said. "The only secret I know is that he likes to be talked to; and he loves to hear me sing. . . ."

Her aunt laughed. "So that is what you have been doing with your voice, you naughty girl, singing to horses when you should be taking lessons with Madame de Ronquerolles."

Suddenly she asked:

"Is Hyacinth thinking of putting Feeney up?"

"All I can tell you is that Feeney volunteered. He told Hyacinth that it would be too great a risk to try his county horse, as he calls Green Glint, with any of the English jockeys—apart from the fact that fee and present may cost us one thousand guineas."

"Poor Feeney. What hope has he? Is he not over fifty years of age and overweight? How ever does he expect at his time of life to make ten stone again? He has been sitting on the box seat too long."

But Ninon did not know. She only knew that Feeney was starving to reduce weight for the Master's sake and that Hyacinth was more than anxious lest he should lose what strength he had. Feeney should concentrate on fighting cocks at his age, as Hyacinth said.

"There must be some mystery after all," Aunt Penelope said, half aloud. "I do detest those jockeys they bring over from Newmarket. Our subservience has given them a prestige that makes a horse seem second-rate if he is not ridden by an English jockey. Your uncle, as you know, Mabel, is bringing one over to ride Agincourt. He says that the horse deserves it."

"Damn deserving it!" Mabel exclaimed before she could check herself. "His English trainer Perkins insists on it. Probably he has a relative among the stable boys in Newmarket and he wants to give him a chance to rank as a first-class jock by riding in Ireland at our expense. I heard it all when I was at—" She checked herself. A reference to what her interest in sport had brought about would have been most unfortunate at this moment. It would in all likelihood have reminded her aunt to make her promise that she would make no attempt ever again to visit the Curragh unaccompanied.

The light was dancing on the yellow lake. Lost in white light, the low hills far down to the southwest would be invisible until the upshot beams of the setting sun would raise them into sight. On the long slope that fell to the water side from the centre of the crescent which the woodland formed, the summer grass was springing green and lush, shadowed here and there by purple clouds of tufted clover flowers, as becoming to the new meadows as the bride was to her spacious house.

"How well you chose the site of this house. I never could believe the view could be so lovely. How could you tell what it would be like from the level of the drawing-room floor when there was as yet no house?"

"She climbed a tree," Mabel announced irrepressibly, to Ninon's confusion.

"Climbed a tree?" Aunt Penelope repeated thoughtfully. For Aunt Penelope knew what times Ninon had visited the old, squat, two-storied house that had stood near the site of the Hall, and a knowledge of the scenery as seen from the height they commanded now implied either that Ninon had gone up to one of the bedrooms in a bachelor's establishment, an act of impropriety, or that she had climbed one of the trees on her second visit, when her aunt's attention was distracted, at a picnic held by the lake two years ago. This would imply that Ninon was choosing a site for her house long before Hyacinth had even proposed. No wonder Ninon's face became suffused. She was so embarrassed that she did not even glare at her sister.

"Now if it had been Mabel who had climbed a tree on another person's property it would have been not altogether so surprising. But . . ." Aunt Penelope caught sight of Ninon's face and finished, "Hyacinth should be here now unless he has adopted unpunctuality as a habit."

As so often happens, he who was spoken of appeared as soon as his name was pronounced.

"I heard you, aunt," he said. "I hope you did not think it another instance of 'talk of the Devil?' "

"No; but of the adage 'better late than never.' "

Hyacinth had been in the gun-room, fitting new flints on some fowling pieces—for soon the season would open—and had been delayed by the discovery that one of his guns was missing. There was one flint more in the flint box than there were guns. He distinctly remembered placing in the box one spare flint for each lock. Now which of the guns was gone?

It could mean only one thing, and that was more or less excusable. What was not excusable was that the gun should have been stolen from a sympathizer, such as Martyn considered himself to be, of the struggle to emerge from starvation, pestilence and ignorance, the struggle to win as free and prosperous a life as even the lowest menial enjoyed in England. The theft of his gun brought in an overwhelming sense of ingratitude and potential treachery to himself. It suggested that there were cynical influences at work which would come to rate even him as an enemy of the revolution. It was not from Mr. Weld that these conspirators stole a gun, but from their own fellow-countryman. What trust or confidence could there be between him and such people? Likely as not, it was one of his own people who took the gun at the order of an "organizer" from Dublin. Had they come boldly forward and asked him for a gun or for half a dozen guns. . . .

No, no. He forgot. Openly he could never have allowed himself to be a sympathizer with, much less an abettor of, a repetition of the French Revolution in Ireland. If they wanted the gun they must take it in the only way that would leave its owner beyond the suspicion of being a supporter of the revolution. But there again he came to a crossing of the ways in his mind, because if he wanted to put himself above the suspicion of comforting insurgents he should report the theft to the Captain of Militia stationed at Castlebar. This he was loath to do. So all the greater was his exasperation.

Hyacinth refrained from mentioning the discovery to Ninon, Mabs and Aunt Penelope, lest they be disturbed by the thought that the peasants were arming themselves.

"I saw Father Colyer coming out of Myles's forge and stopped to have a word with him. What an excellent fellow he is."

"Hyacinth, you should not call a priest a 'fellow,'" his aunt rebuked him. "It sounds disrespectful."

"I meant it in all good nature. I will ask him to dinner if you wish.

"Ah," he said later, seeing no invitation in his aunt's face.

"Mabs," said Ninon in a whisper to her sister, whom she had cornered near a window, "why will you always be blurting out stories about me?" There was a slightly vindictive note in her voice. "You knew quite well that Auntie knows that the only time I had a chance of surveying Martyn Hall unescorted was long before our engagement. Now she thinks me a calculating hussy."

"I only said you went up a tree. I have often climbed a tree but nobody wanted to marry me when I came down."

"Oh, silly," Ninon said.

"I have a present for you, aunt," said Martyn, as he led Penelope to a buhl china cabinet which fitted into a corner of the room. The cabinet was crowded to confusion with Dresden and French porcelain. But standing out from the exquisite medley were two marvellous magpies with tails erect, a perfectly matched pair.

"Oh, Hyacinth, look at that blue at the root of the wings. I never knew there was such a rich colour, nor that dull green, in a magpie. What a pair they are! Can they be Dresden?"

Martyn opened the cabinet with a key.

"I fear that they may be a little dusty. But I prefer dusty to broken porcelain. And these are 'rare birds.' They would be much rarer if one of the heavy-handed country girls whom Biddy Early recruits could get her duster on my precious pair. Yes; you were right the first time, aunt. They are Dresden. Seek the mark: the crossed swords. There is an earlier way of marking which I think is in white, not blue. They will look cheerful on a mantel-piece in your boudoir."

"How can you think of everyone?" Aunt Penelope asked in thanking him. "But you know the old saw about magpies? 'One for sorrow, two for joy.' How can you expect me to carry off symbols of what I hope will ever be the state of your married life."

Martyn looked disappointed.

"When I got them," he said, "I had your mantel-piece in the black-and-white lacquer room in my mind's eye, and I thought—"

"Martyn, dear, was it of me and my room you were thinking? They would look lovely and surprising I admit; but you know how superstitious I can be, and in the face of the strange notion about two magpies bringing joy, I could not think of taking them away from your home. But give me something else. This cabinet is so crowded with treasures that I can hardly see how precious they are. There! Is there a match for that shepherd lad in his blue coat and golden gartered breeches, ogling some simpering shepherdess?"

"How often have I vowed that I would thin out these figures and set them about the room; but between fear of housemaids' dusters and the work to be done outside, I have not so far succeeded. Here, I think, is the wench who puts that simpering smile upon her shepherd boy."

He drew out from the back of the cabinet a little figure of a shepherdess, full of the charm which comes from the highly artificial simplicity of the Dresden designs. "The original of this may have been some lady at the court of Le Roi Soleil, when they loved to dress up as rustics, with a refined simplicity which no rustics could ever know. I imagine that it was the *fêtes champêtres* of Versailles which gave rise to the Dresden series of shepherds and shepherdesses."

"Ah, the gay elegance we find in Fragonard!" Penelope said enthusiastically.

"Here, now, you have your pair of courtly lovers dressed up as those whose care was flocks. If sheep had depended on such frivolous creatures there would have been little mutton or wool."

"The hungry sheep looked up to Le Grand Monarch and were not fed," Aunt Penelope suggested.

Mabs made an inaudible remark. She seemed to be listening to some sound outside.

"What do you say, Mabs?" Hyacinth asked.

"I thought I heard a saddle horse, but maybe it's only the phaeton."

A few moments later, Constant d'Estournelles appeared at the door. Surprised cries of welcome greeted the unexpected visitor. It was apparent at once that Constant was in a serious mood and wished to talk to Martyn alone. Therefore, the ladies soon withdrew.

As soon as they were alone, Constant said to Hyacinth, "Little did I think, when I asked you if my visit would be an embarrassment, that I should have cause to visit you so soon. I would not have done so were I alone involved. My case is a very simple one; but you may not know what is in store for you."

"Out with it," Hyacinth said.

"In spite of the way the revolution in the counties of Wexford, Wicklow, parts of Dublin and Meath was crushed last May, the Shannon is said to be guarded again, and neither man nor news is permitted to pass it. There's a new revolt in the air."

"Revolt has been in the air for some time," Martyn said.

Dropping his voice, Constant asked, "But did you know that the French are expected to land on the coast here within a week or two and that you are to lead them?"

The blank surprise on his face would have reassured d'Estournelles, had he had reason to doubt that Hyacinth was unaware of what was expected of him.

"Who told you this?"

"A stranger in the night. I was on my way to inquire the direction from the nearest forge when I was accosted by a tall figure on horseback who spoke to me in French, not native French, but quite understandable."

"A stranger in the night?"

"I might have thought that he mistook me for someone else—one of the French agents, no doubt—had he not addressed me as 'Chevalier,' and that for the moment threw me off my guard. I answered cautiously, but I acknowledged that I was an officer. My very caution seemed to give him confidence. He assured me that the rebellion, though crushed with brutal severity in the East, only wanted an armed ally and a leader for the West to rise again to a man, and that you were ready to lead the men of Mayo to rally to whatever port of disembarkation the French forces would choose."

" 'Tis news to me," said Martyn-Lynch.

"I am sure it is. But is it not an extraordinary thing that all this has been going on in secret and that you are chosen to lead the local contingent, without being consulted or informed?"

"I can't see how anyone could have taken it on himself to appoint me as a leader of a revolt without taking the trouble to inform me."

"Excuse me, I can," Constant said.

"Who, then?"

"Some subtle mind who knew that, once chosen and acclaimed, you might just as well go forward as not make any move to go at all. In either case you would be arraigned in the event of the failure of the expedition."

"An enemy has done this," said Hyacinth. "I'll lay fifty-to-one the man you met was Weld."

"Oh, Weld has been pointed out to me. I have been keeping out of his way for some time. It was not Weld, who, by all accounts, is ignorant of French, but someone who is very fully acquainted with the conditions in the district."

"Father Colyer speaks French, but he could hardly have the temerity to appoint me captain of a venture of which I am not sure that I approve at all."

"True," Constant answered, "but you would be placed in a very difficult position if you found that not only your approval, but your actual participation in the movement was taken for granted, on account of your old affiliations with the country's religion and the country's cause. In which case your inclusion in the rising might be interpreted as an honour which you could not refuse."

"When all necks risked a halter, it would not befit me to shun that risk? That is their idea?" Martyn asked.

"Exactly. Let us examine the point of view which would include you in the movement. It would be of interest to know who are the hidden leaders who can put such as you and St. George, too, in this invidious position, which can be stated thus: 'Either join the country's cause, or declare yourself its enemy and the ally of its oppressors; and lose your house and land.' This was not done by any friend of yours. Had he been a friend he would have consulted you first in private."

"They may think that the only way to maintain secrecy and to enlist the help of the 'Quality,' as they call us, is to stampede us into the rebellion at the last moment."

"True," d'Estournelles agreed, "but don't you see the corollary to that?"

"Not at the moment," said Martyn-Lynch.

"If, as I think, their intention is to stampede the gentry into rising with them willy nilly, they must expect powerful assistance from overseas. Otherwise no one could be prevailed upon to join them."

"Of course they expect great help from the French and a successful landing of troops and cannon this time," Martyn said. "The failures of Hoche's expedition to land in Bantry Bay the Christmas before last, and the loss of the French fleet at Camperdown last year, have only encouraged them to expect that the third attempt will be more fortunate. They look upon the defeat at Vinegar Hill in Wexford last

May as the defeat only of a sporadic outbreak which had neither arms nor support."

Constant thought for a moment. "From what I have just heard, it would appear that they expect a landing somewhere on this coast and they are determined that this time the country will rise in support of its allies and that the gentry will fight for their country just as Lord Edward Fitzgerald did. This time, the stranger in the dark assured me, victory is certain."

"A pretty hope, when the country supplies its own McNallys and other traitors and spies to frustrate the efforts of their dupes," Hyacinth said sourly.

"One thing is certain," d'Estournelles continued. "Some adventure is at hand. The Shannon has fenced off East from West. Both Parliaments, the Irish and English, have determined to locate and to isolate any invasion of the country and to crush rebellion with all the ferocity of which England is capable."

"Damn their risings!" Hyacinth said. "With the Shannon closed, Feeney and I may not be able to get to the Curragh to race Green Glint."

They drew up before the fire and prepared to sit late into the night speculating as to what the future might hold for the West of the country.

XVI. LISADILL

IRREGULAR LITTLE PROMONTORIES, covered with low woods, entered a landlocked bay of tawny sands. The setting of Lisadill was not large enough to overwhelm one with a feeling of loneliness, but it was spacious enough to afford seclusion. It was remote from the world, and unknown. This was just as well, for had the beauty of the spot been revealed to visitors at large, it would have become a national haunt of landscape lovers and have been as public as its counterpart in beauty, Killarney.

Here Colonel Lynch had reigned alone until his recent death. The demesne was not open even to the few travellers who penetrated to what was Europe's extreme western edge.

Lisadill had charms of a different nature from the hill-hemmed lakes and broad-leaved hanging woods of Killarney. It was on the sea, but when you viewed the tawny sands, over which shallow waves rippled and delighted the eye with myriads of little rainbows, it was hard to believe that the water was salt unless you took it in your hand and tasted it. The beach might be a lake's shore: there was little sign of waves upon it; no sea wrack or jetsam flung up by any storm. And how could there be when the bay was so land-locked that, as the gardener put it, "there was hardly time for the tide to go out till it was time for it to come in again"?

Thus it was that the trees dipped their leaves twice daily uninjured by the quiet tide. The trees or, rather, the woods, seemed peculiar to the place. These were so low that they might have been chosen of a size that would not dominate the promontories but would remain in due proportion to the little kingdom.

The woods were paved with the yellow flowers of some sort of small sessile rose. They were lightsome, happy and unhaunted woods: joyful and free from gloom. One might wander there all the morning, treading on this deep soft carpet and seeing lovely pictures of warm sands and blue waters framed by boughs, or lie down in the shade by the quivering water, that in the sunlight trembled with colour as iridescent as the sides of the fleeting mackerel shoals that sometimes dusked along the surface as they sought the refuge of the bay.

Aloof, in an opening giving on the water, the House stood square, gray and two-storied: a large, unromantic house, it seemed, ornamented with pilasters in the perpendicular style. A square gray pile, enclosing a courtyard on three sides, its aspect was somewhat uninviting. From the size of its windows, which were as large as those of the library in Trinity College, the beholder could guess the spaciousness and grand proportion of the rooms within. Four of its tall windows lit a fine library in the east wing. Here it was that Mabel spent whatever part of her day was left after riding through the woods and copses or rowing on the water in quest of fish, or going through her rather cursory lessons in "singing, dancing and deportment," gratuitously given by Madame de Ronquerolles. Though the task of turning the headstrong girl into a lady often seemed to Clemente a thankless one, she felt that in undertaking it she was repaying to some extent the hospitality extended to her.

The library at Lisadill was as fine as could be found in any of the great self-contained mansions of the land. Here for years before his death, the old Colonel had delighted to read to his little daughter (his excuse for orating them aloud) extracts from the more sonorous of the poets of Elizabeth's boisterous time, or, lost behind the ages, stories of the heroes of the land whose battle shouts echoed amid the hills a thousand years before the first syllable of the English language was uttered.

At first the little girl listened without understanding, but, as she grew, the thunder of the lines caught her and caused her to shudder deliciously. From this to an inquisitiveness concerning the subjects of Song was not a wide way; nor was it long before she rode in triumph with Tamberlaine through Persepolis or recoiled at damnation with Dr. Faustus. Thus she learned history from inaccurate and desultory study; but most of all, deeds of arms delighted her, deeds of arms with or without the chivalry of Lancelot to ameliorate them for the girl, until 'twould

> . . . waken Caesar from his Roman grave
> To hear war beautified by her discourse.

The great library became associated with romance and battles and with her father, until in the back of her mind the great room was a kingdom which her father governed, and which rang with hero lays and war unlimited by time.

For a year after her father's death Mabs was forbidden to enter the room, for Aunt Penelope realized, and with correct judgment, that so long as she was allowed access to the great library her grief for her father would not be assuaged.

But now that her father held his victorious place with the men who ranged the hills, or swung the battle axe with Ralph the Wode, or rode through Arthurian and Elizabethan literature, and jousted at Aspermont, the library became once more a battle-field and no longer a scene of grief and brooding. Mabs was re-admitted to the library, which in fact proved to be a sedative to that wild creature's nature and a welcome alternative to her exploits by land and sea. And yet, as Madame de Ronquerolles knew, in spite of the way that her pupil could submit to routine, there was a wild heart untamed in that gentle breast. Clemente, after she had learned of the girl's early years, explained to Aunt Penelope in her lucid and logical French way:

"It was not fair to the child to have been an only daughter, as she was while her elder sister was in the city, away on the Continent or in Town. Her father's desire for a son had to be endured by his younger child and, *voila!*"

There was Mabs, at any rate, with a studious mind and a wild heart, shut away in a fairyland undiscovered by any of those who were in a position to impose on the public their opinions about landscape, and so sheltered from the common eye.

Madame de Ronquerolles was walking on the strand by the shallow waters. She had the forefinger of her left hand in the pages of a book, "Candide," by the notorious cynic Voltaire. The French was after her heart but with the sentiment of the writer she felt that, in spite of his unanswerable persuasiveness, she could not agree. Why, she did not know: and the less she could explain her dislike, the more it grew. Why she disliked the book her instinct could not inform her in words which she might repeat to Mabs. She hoped that that young lady's unconducted excursions through her father's large library had not brought her into contact with such an author. She felt that she would need clear and succinct reasons for repudiating a writer accepted and acclaimed by all the intellectuals who had a hearing on the Continent. She trusted that Mabs had not read Voltaire. She felt that her charge, fresh as a wild rose sprung from a rock, would be taught before her time and therefore aged before her time by a perusal of that sour and cynical man of the world.

By what arguments could she confute his obvious logic? By none. But there was one statement by which she could throw him out of Mabs' interest. It was far from being an argument (the farther the better) but it would prove effective. How she thought of it she could not tell. The answer came as she was turning to retrace her steps along the sand. Suddenly she thought of an argument which to an Irishwoman would prove unanswerable. Should the question come from Mabs as come she felt assured it would, "Isn't Voltaire marvellous? Who can answer his philosophy? Even Frederick the Great—"

"Yes, my dear," Clemente decided that she would say, "but look what it has done to his face."

No woman could answer that. And why should she, or a man either? If your way of thinking turns your countenance into obtruding eyes and a maze of crafty wrinkles, there must be something radically wrong. If Voltaire's casuistry and cynicism came from those who gave him his early education, it behooved her to exercise the greatest care in the upbringing of her sprightly pupil. Few responsibilities are greater than the training of the young—to keep youth sweet!

This task would have been less difficult had it not been for the illimitable library. To allow a young girl to wander there was as bad as allowing her to enter an unknown wilderness without a guide or guard. In fact, it was much worse. For a wilderness could but endanger you in the present, but a library could bring back all the ages and rank them against you and leave you at the mercy of unrefuted errors and old-world allures.

Clemente had hidden the translations of Apuleius and Lucian behind the large albums of woodcuts of the Ruins of Ancient Rome. Rabelais she left where it was, among the sixteenth-century folios, for she was sure that for Mabs there would be little attraction in the over-robust and unromantic code under which the monk concealed his mockeries.

With the Tales of the Fianna, the ancient Irish heroes, and the Exploits of Finn she could do nothing, for Mabs knew where they were and her marker marked many a page in the old sagas. Would the attractive way in which ancient paganism was presented, in contrast to the Christianity of St. Patrick, upset the growing mind? The only symptom so far was that Mabs had obtained a young wolfhound through the good offices of her cousin's coachman; and she called the rough, gray-haired puppy "Bran."

Yes, in a library all the ages are ranked ready—ready to edify, ready to seduce, or ready to inspire. So far, Mabs seemed to have derived nothing wilder out of it than Bran the hound of Finn.

Milton was a sound and edifying poet to study, and should provide enough of that urgency and incitement to action which Mabs loved. She could charge harmlessly to her heart's content with Charlemagne, and go down with him and all his knights in the sand:

> When Charlemagne and all his peerage fell
> By Fontarabia.

After such excitement she could lull her spirit by the sight of:

> Where the great vision of the guarded mount
> Looks towards Namancos and Bayona's hold.

What ominous necromancy is in that vision, that *guarded* mount! Milton, the greatest wielder of proper names in the English language!

Clemente heard something behind her. It sounded like the galloping of a horse. How could it be? Not in the woods, surely? It died away. She looked back. Good gracious! Clemente blushed. Look at the track of her own footsteps on the sand! There she had charged with Charlemagne, here she had walked with her feet out of line, one foot was not exactly in front of the other. She feared that she was as bad as Mabs, whom she suspected of riding astride when there was no one to see her.

There it was again, that sound! The hooves had left the silent sands; on the harder knoll they rang out. Silhouetted against the level light went Mabs with her hair flying out straight behind her, borne by the wind of her own speed. She was riding astride and barebacked.

Mabs at that moment, if Clemente only knew it, was Niav, Queen of Fairyland, and she was leading from Knocknaree the Hosting of the Fairies or, as they are called in their own country, "The Shee."

XVII. A DOMICILIARY VISIT

D'Estournelles and Martyn-Lynch had no sooner pulled their chairs together before the fire than the door opened and two servants entered in a state of agitation.

"Anything amiss?" Hyacinth inquired.

"The house is surrounded by troops, Sir," one of them answered.

Martyn broke out laughing as he turned to d'Estournelles.

"With Mr. Weld's respects to you," he said.

Thunderous noises rang from the echoing hall door as it was pounded by rifle butts.

"Let them in at once," Hyacinth said to the frightened servant. "And tell the officer in charge that I would like to see him." And Martyn sipped his wine.

As a young ensign in a foppish periwig and smart uniform led his men up the stairs, Martyn went to the lobby and called out:

"Hey there, officer. Is there any need to bring those dirty-booted Hessians into my dining room? What is it that you want? And who the hell sent you here?"

For a moment it appeared as if the officer would halt. He was only a youth, and quite confused. Never in all his experience of raids on Irish houses—and they were many—had he raided such a house as this and been so scornfully and fearlessly received.

"The house is surrounded, Sir," he ventured.

"Well, send those Hessians out to surround it more. I don't want them in my house. I want you, though; and I want to know by whose authority this outrage is being perpetrated."

"I am under orders to search the house," the officer answered.

"Whose orders?"

The officer was silent; and, as is the way with many incompetent people in authority, when he found himself outfaced to confusion, he adopted a bullying role.

"Stand where you are, men!" he said. He began to ascend the stairs.

Fury made serpentine veins stand out on Martyn's brow. He moved to the top of the grand staircase and folded his arms.

"If you advance one step farther without producing your warrant, I will fling you down among your men."

The young ensign halted.

"I will see your warrant, Sir," Martyn repeated.

Again the youth was confused. At last he muttered:

"I have no warrant."

"So no business here. I demand that you get out at once."

"Mr. Weld—" the youth began.

A sneer from d'Estournelles, who had come to stand by Martyn, distracted him.

"So it's Weld after all. And I bet a guinea that he wants me. I am a Frenchman. Is that of interest to you?" he asked, addressing the ensign. "Perhaps the magistrate does not even know my name. I am sure that he doesn't know whom he is ordering into custody."

The officer recovered his poise.

"In this case no warrant is necessary. We are within our rights when we raid a house for one of the King's enemies, or shoot him and those who shelter him if he resists arrest."

"I have no intention of resisting arrest, but I have every intention of calling Weld out and shooting him the very moment my position is made clear to Lord Cornwallis." He turned to ascend the stairs.

"I must request you to remain where you are. You can send a servant for your travelling cloak. You will spend the night in Castlebar, where I must await further orders."

Martyn looked scornfully at the German troops employed by the British Government to protect Ireland from the majority of its inhabitants.

Turning to the ensign, "'Within your rights!'" he repeated, releasing some of the rage with which he struggled. "'Within your rights,' to come armed into a gentleman's house without warning, having smashed at his door with unnecessary violence and ruffianism? It is well for me that I am not some poor famished peasant with little children and a shivering woman in his hovel, and hard on you that you are not now in such a place, with your bullying 'soldiers,' your mercenaries, blackguards who sell their bodies for pay. Whores are more honourable. Bah!"

A servant came with d'Estournelles's coat. As d'Estournelles was being helped into it, Martyn snapped his fingers in the ensign's face and pointed to a soldier who was indulging in horseplay with a maidservant at the head of the servants' stairs.

"I pray you to tell that fellow, if you have any authority, to let my housemaid alone," he said.

Hearing her master's speech, Maura broke loose from the soldier who was holding her. D'Estournelles advanced.

"Wait for me," said Martyn. "I am going with you, friend. Weld will not get off so lightly with this adventure. You will oblige me, Sir, by ordering those men to wait until I order my carriage. Neither I nor my friends will submit to be marched on foot through the night under arrest."

The officer hesitated. "I would be exceeding my duty to permit a prisoner to be driven in a private coach."

"Damn your duty, exceed it then!" Martyn exclaimed. "You cannot expect a French Chevalier to walk through the night to some damned barrack-room for no reason on earth but the cowardly envy, spite and hatred of Mr. Weld? Put as many Hessians on it as the coach will carry, and Castlebar will see a mixture in the morning such as it has never seen in its life. Hessians standing where my servants stand behind my coach!"

That apparently decided the young officer.

"Your friend must accompany me. If he does not wish to walk, he can be driven in the military wagon. It is a matter of a court-martial for me if in any way I contribute to his escape."

"I give you my word," d'Estournelles interjected. The young officer shook his head. A deep flush overspread d'Estournelles features as he looked, humiliated, at Martyn-Lynch.

"Bear up for the present," Hyacinth counselled. "I shall see it through with Weld for this outrage, which is staged as much for my humiliation as for yours." Turning to the ensign, he said, "If you are afraid to trust yourself alone in a gentleman's house, at least order those louts of yours to behave themselves. Tell that fellow to take his hands off that clock." It was a valuable piece by Thompion.

"Form up, men!" the officer commanded. "Surround prisoner! Forward!"

Martyn was paralyzed for a moment between impotent rage and a desire for action. He remembered the ladies in the drawing room, and locked the door.

"I will gallop after you presently," he said loudly, without mentioning d'Estournelles' name.

As the troops turned to move out with d'Estournelles in their midst, the hall door refused to open. A tall Hessian strove to turn the key in the great brass-bound mahogany lock. The key could not be turned, possibly because it had already been turned to its fullest extent. Swearing at his clumsiness, the ensign looked around for the butler, but no servant could be seen.

"If this door is not opened in one minute I will blow out the lock."

Martyn descended the stairs.

"My house is in an unusually hospitable mood tonight," he sneered. "It is loath to release my uninvited guests."

"Open the door, Sir. You heard what I said."

"I am not in the habit of attending in the hall. Your men were not slow in battering the door and straining the lock before you gave my butler time to open it."

This was not an accurate accusation. The fact was that everyone in the house but the family and d'Estournelles knew that the house was surrounded and no one wished to let the soldiers in.

After an angry delay it dawned on the clumsy Hessian to turn the key in the opposite direction. The door opened and the party filled out into the night.

At a signal from the officer, men who were posted in the grounds and stables fell into rank and followed the company with its prisoner. Torches were lit, although the moon was full. With all the elegance of an officer of the guard, d'Estournelles marched, conspicuous among his captors. He was led to a lane where a large military wagon covered with canvas stood waiting. To its floor was attached a chain. Some instinct forbade the young officer to subject the Chevalier to the indignity of being fettered. The cart rumbled away amid the trees.

When Martyn went to the stables to find a groom he heard a faint call from the room above him. Thinking that some maid servant had been maltreated by the troops while they were besieging the house, he listened.

"Mr. Hyacinth, Sir, is that you?"

It was Feeney's voice coming faintly from his room.

With the lamp he carried, Martyn lit his way up the stairs and opened the door of Feeney's bedroom. On his bed lay Feeney, fully dressed save where his clothes were torn from his back. He was bleeding and half-conscious. Evidently he had been badly mauled and battered by some of the soldiers who filled the stables before the house was attacked.

"Feeney, my poor fellow, what has happened to you?"

"They was asking me questions, Mr. Hyacinth," the faithful fellow replied.

Hot rage swept Martyn's being.

"Where are the boys?" he asked.

"They all run to spread the word when they seen the sojers."

Dazed with anger, Martyn stared round Feeney's modest room. He hardly saw the few coloured prints with which it was decorated: a series of horses and game-cocks.

"I cannot leave you out here all night, my man. You must come into the house. Is there a bone broken?"

"It's me poor knee," Feeney groaned, overcome by pain and the sympathy of his master.

"Let me put the lamp at the head of the stairs and I will carry you down." Lifting the now ominously silent man, Martyn bore his emaciated body down the stairs and through the back entrance into the house. He was met by the butler.

"Here," he said, letting Feeney down on a bench. "Let you and Mrs. Early make Feeney comfortable. I will fetch Dr. MacDermot myself." Turning, he asked:

"Are there any troopers in the house?"

"Not as far as I know, Sir."

"Not so far as you know!" the exasperated master repeated. "Have it searched from attic to cellars before I leave; and bring me my pistols and my riding boots. I will put them on here when you come back. Haste!"

On the man's return with the assurance that no soldiers were hiding in the house, Martyn ordered that as soon as a boy could be found he was to go at once for Mr. Crosbie, for whose absence nobody could account.

As Martyn rode out in pursuit of the cart which bore his friend, a glare behind him to the left caught his eye and made him turn back. A haystack in one of the haggards was in flames. Not a stable boy was to be seen. If the fire spread—his new home, his horses! The first thing to do was to let out the horses and to turn them loose, but before this could be done he would have to open the yard gate: horses could not pass through the wicket.

Voices sounded in the night from beyond the blaze. There were Mabel with three servants and a maid, already carrying buckets. Ninon joined them.

"Quick!" Martyn shouted. "Use the trough and some of you take turns at the pump. Get a ladder at once," he said to the floundering men who came from the house, "and pay the buckets up to me."

When the ladder was brought, he mounted and from his perilous place poured the water into the blazing hay. Someone cried out. One of the maids, Maura, was working the pump when her place was taken by a drunken soldier, belated, or on purpose left behind.

Martyn was in no mood to speak.

From one of the outhouses another soldier appeared, leading a horse mad with fright. When he had turned it loose to follow the others into the grounds, he relieved his companion at the pump. After an hour the fire was extinguished, with the help of those who had caused it to be lit.

It was, Martyn reflected, a pretty symbol of the state of affairs in the land at large.

Dr. MacDermot was sitting up late, if one were to judge by the light in the two windows of his one-storied, well-thatched house. He was in his cozy but ill-kept "study"—his sitting room, dining room and consulting room combined. He was engrossed in his studies; that is, he was collating figures which looked as if they were statistics, and were in fact, but they had no reference to disease or death. They dealt with the performance of certain horses and they gave certain measurements for which the doctor had written to a secret "friend" at the Curragh, Toucher Plant. At a cost of one guinea for each sheet of "information," these papers gave a horse's "form" as well as his chances of winning.

He was reading that Green Glint measured eighty inches round the chest. "And you, doctor, know what that means," wrote his friend.

Therefore when he discovered that the loud rapping on his door was made by one who knew as much about Green Glint as its owner, St. George, annoyance fell from him.

"You are just in time for a glass of punch and a warm welcome, Mr. Martyn."

Martyn explained the reason for his call and for his inability to delay and partake of the kind sportsman's hospitality. That sportsman was only too ready to go to the Hall when he was told under a vow of secrecy that the man whom the Hessians had so maltreated because he refused to give them any information about his master or his master's visitor, was none other than the jockey who was chosen to ride Green Glint.

As Hyacinth went away into the night, the doctor lit a lantern, and went to the yard to saddle for himself, for he was loath to waken his man. He rode to Martyn Hall with what medical equipment he could gather—laudanum to ease pain, belladonna to soothe a bruise (providing that the skin was unabrased), splints for a broken limb, and many a boxwood-covered phial. "Eighty round the chest," he repeated to himself as he rode, and though the measurement could hardly have referred to any human being, his attention was not far dissociated from Feeney.

Hyacinth galloped on by the light of the moon. As he passed places where the hedges were sparse, he thought that now and again he could catch glimpses of a deep glow in the distance.

"More burnings by the Yeomen or Hessians. Whose place can that be?" he asked himself. He knew that there was no considerable house for many miles around Martyn Hall, and yet—the fire was framed as by a great door.

The hedges ended where the road was fenced. He saw a deep glow, as if there were a fire in a cavern. It was hard to judge either distance or locations at nighttime when the landmarks were gone. But he had often been across country and had seen the forge of Myles the Blacksmith at the corner where the boreen, or little lane, left the mail coach road. The flames rose and fell, as is the way with the intermittent glow in a forge. Working late, Martyn thought. Now, as he approached, he could see figures of men dark against the light.

Either it is surrounded and they have taken away Myles, he thought; or this activity is due to the fact that the soldiers long ago have passed by.

He urged his horse forward.

He did not hear the rustle that a hare made as it left its lair aroused from sleep, or the noise of a corn-crake scuttling like a little ostrich through the grass. He had no thought for the whispers and voices of a night made magical by the moon. He could not have heard them if he would, because of the sounds made by his going. He was thinking of the cursed state of things in a country rich in natural resources but blighted by its overlapping Governments, a country where a generation back no Catholic was permitted to continue in the condition of a gentleman—even to possess property exceeding the value of five pounds—though his ancestors were affluent in the land for hundreds of years. He thought of the "bossthoons" who had usurped their place, and he thought all the more angrily of his own position—

a Martyn on sufferance in his own country, permitted to own the very horse under him only by the apathy of a Government that preferred to wink at the breaking of an inhuman law than overtly to abolish it; a Government suppressing a rebellion that its creatures instigated, by "means that they dare not avow." But what was the use of going over it all again?

Apparently the militia were not roasting a poor peasant caught with a scythe-blade fastened to a pole, or another whom they might have suspected of sheltering a man "out on his keeping." It was only the fire in the forge.

He had not passed the forge by a mile when he overtook a dark, silent figure seated on a horse and ambling slowly in the same direction as he himself was going. Martyn pulled a pistol beyond its hammer out of his pocket, so that there would be less risk of its getting caught in the lining in case of emergency. He came up with the horseman, and was about to pass him.

"It's a fine night to be out, Mr. Martyn-Lynch." Father Colyer said.

"If you want to talk to me, kindly put spurs to your horse, Father. I am in a desperate hurry. My house has been surrounded and raided and a guest friend of mine carried off to Castlebar by a troop of Hessians or Yeomen or some sort of ill-disciplined scoundrels in uniform. I am pressing on to have him released."

"To Castlebar?" repeated Father Colyer.

Martyn assented.

"He may not be detained very long in Castlebar," the priest said equivocally, with a little mocking laugh. The remark was, however, lost on Martyn. He was more in a hurry than ever, now that he was prevented by courtesy from breaking away from the priest, who made no attempt to accommodate himself to the pace of Martyn's horse. Finally Martyn could tolerate the delay no longer.

"Father, you must hold me excused if I bid you good night," he said, and rode away.

Castlebar, like any other town in Connaught not situated on the coast, was a picture of misery in gray. It was even grayer than most of the hamlets, called towns, in the West of Ireland, because of the recently-built, hideous limestone barracks, which looked like a malt house or an old mill.

With the absence of every grace and without even the little contribution that austerity of line and mass can make to the aesthetic sense, the plainness of the barracks was beyond description. It seemed as if the whole horrid structure were designed by an automaton devoid of heart and soul.

As the horseman approached, a sentry challenged, in the old formula that years of occupation of other people's lands had prescribed:

"Halt! Who goes there?"

"A friend." The title sounded ironical to Martyn-Lynch as he gave it.

"Approach, friend, and be recognized."

Martyn dismounted and passed his arm through the bridle of his horse.

"I have come to see the Commander of the barracks," he said. Through a peep-hole barred with iron a soldier peered. Presently he and two troopers came out through a wicket. They had been listening to the challenge. One of them seemed to be a sergeant. He spoke with an English accent and seemed intelligent. He recognized Martyn's station at once.

"Have you a letter to him, Sir?" he asked.

"I have not but I wish to see him personally on a matter of importance which will not brook delay. Will you present my compliments to the Commander and say that Mr. Martyn-Lynch wishes to see him at his earliest convenience."

The sergeant seemed at a loss to know what to do. He looked at the gray light in the east. "It's very early," he said; then, "Just a moment, Sir." He disappeared through the wicket in the great door that looked, in its coat of dull gray paint, like a prison door.

After a quarter of an hour—it seemed longer to Martyn—the guard was changed. It was six o'clock. The sergeant who changed the guard was the same man who had interviewed him. Martyn wondered what would become of his message now that other and more immediate duties confronted the sergeant. After another quarter of an hour, an orderly appeared.

"Come this way, Sir," he said.

Martyn secured his horse to a chain which joined other chains in festoons, supported by stone posts. He stooped through the wicket and found himself in a stone-flagged hall. It was cold and badly lit, for there were no fan-lights in the barracks. The wicket door was secured behind him. The orderly opened another door which gave on a room as bare as the hall, and disappeared. His tread rang on the bare boards as he traversed the room and apparently entered another off it. Again Martyn had to wait.

Presently a young soldier, evidently British from his complexion and build, came out with a strip of paper. He stopped before Hyacinth and asked, accenting the names foreignly:

"Are you Mr. Martyn-Lynch of Martyn Hall?"

On Martyn's declaring that he was, the young soldier withdrew. Up and down the dark forbidding hall Martyn paced, waiting for the exasperating formalities to end.

Twice he had given his name. It had been taken by two persons, and he was no nearer to obtaining an interview with anyone in authority. What was all the delay about? True, he had come early, but it was now six o'clock and someone must be taking duty for the first part of the day. Why this endless—?

Ah! A thought struck him—a very serious thought indeed. How had he named himself to the sergeant? Had he said anything about Martyn Hall? He did not think so. But there was no mistake that the young soldier had asked him if he was Martyn-Lynch of Martyn Hall. Who had added the Martyn Hall? Why the address, if he had not proffered it himself? The thing came clear as day. He had been identified as the host of the captured Frenchman by some unseen official somewhere in the barracks, who probably had to write a report about the raid overnight.

"Sheltering and comforting the King's enemies." He could see the charge and he could see the impossibility of clearing himself until d'Estournelles had been cleared of all complicity in fomenting rebellion. A pardon or a letter of rehabilitation would have to come through Dublin Castle from London and from London through Dublin Castle. It would take months. Meanwhile they were making up their minds to detain him in the barracks, waiting only until the Commander woke from sleep. He could be of little help to d'Estournelles and, once arrested, he could be of no help at all to himself.

A Roman Catholic was the next thing to an outlaw—outlawed from half the laws—in his own land. Martyn-Lynch stood now a full outlaw. Had he not sheltered a Frenchman? What was to be done? They had kept him waiting three-quarters of an hour. Let their delay be their undoing! He would let them all go to hell. He would preserve his freedom, at least until he had seen his fortune put to the test on the Curragh turf. What would Ninon do if all she could ascertain of him was that he had gone to the help of d'Estournelles and had never come back? His pistols? Yes. He was armed; and that was enough to have him hanged for illegal possession of arms: a gentleman could not keep a brace of pistols to defend his honour in the land!

He had walked into the enemy's clutches like a fool, but it was not too late to walk out. He would retire like a wise man. A cunning man, for once in a while. For the benefit of the sentry, he played a little pantomime. As he departed, Martyn turned to bid a friendly goodbye to someone within the wicket who was not there.

Dublin Castle would be the most direct channel through which to go to the rescue of his friend. Things there might not be as subject to officialdom as in a disaffected area. He must go to Lucan House at once and get Sir Richard's help in freeing Constant, but on his way he would stop briefly at Martyn Hall. He lost no time in mounting his horse. It was the fleetest in the country.

With sun-cast tree shadows barring the road, he cantered down from the barracks and went at a walk through Castlebar. At the end of the straggling town, screened by its morning smoke, which was coming sideways from the half-doors, he turned and skirted a long wall. On the Dublin road, once well out of sight of soldier and peasant (if anyone was ever out of sight of the latter), he turned into a field and made across country for Martyn Hall. It was the last place on earth that the military would go to look for him. Far inside, in the fields, he could not be seen from any of the highways. Here he would be safe from anyone who, in his innocence, might acknowledge that he had seen Mr. Martyn-Lynch riding through the morning towards Martyn Hall. One would have to be a civilian to get an answer from anyone from the Shannon to the sea, and even a civilian would have to be well known or the question a very general one, for neither soldier, yeoman nor stranger could obtain any information from man, woman or child in the West of Ireland at a time like this.

He was cold, hungry and uneasy as he rode. The case of d'Estournelles would not prove so simple after all. Months might elapse before the English families, some of whose members Constant had rescued from the Terror in France, could be found, to give testimony to his loyalty. And it would be necessary to bring forward some influential witnesses to his integrity in England in order to convince the Justiciary in Ireland. Both Governments were in a state of hysterical fear lest the French Revolution be repeated in their countries. They crushed rebellion with "means that they dare not avow."

The May outbreak in Wexford had been crushed and burnt out with ruthless ferocity. Those who lived in the districts where it took place were, if they were young men, crimped for the British Navy or transported to Australia in coffin ships. In such an atmosphere of martial law it would not be at all a simple matter to clear the name of d'Estournelles. He would have to explain why he had chosen to come to Ireland clandestinely instead of approaching it through England. He would have to explain his disguise and why he did not discard it when he was with friends in the country. He would have little difficulty in obtaining Mrs. St. George's testimony as to how he had rescued her, from a little convent, from the fury of the ruffians of Paris. Madame de Ronquerolles, who had escaped by his aid from the south, would be only too willing to tell what she owed to the

Chevalier d'Estournelles. But these would not be enough, Hyacinth thought.

The first thing Hyacinth had to do was to inform his wife of his plans, and arrange for her to come up to the races later in the coach, bringing Feeney and the Lisadill cousins with her. Once he had seen to that, he must lose no time in getting Sir Richard to use his influence to have Constant freed.

XVIII. DR. MACDERMOT

THOUGH FOR THE time being all thoughts of the Curragh were put out of Hyacinth's mind by the Chevalier's emergency, there were those to whom the coming race remained the most important object of speculation.

Dr. MacDermot, for instance, was concerned about more than public health. He was concerned about "form," that mysterious thing which may be said to be the result of perfect health and to bear the same relation to health as style does to writing. Dr. MacDermot, when in the full professional garb he wore at the numerous sporting events in the country, looked like a sporting parson. His subfusc clothes were ultra-fashionable. His large head and square, red face surmounted broad, straight shoulders and a flat chest. He was a spare man of about middle height. Nobody throughout the length and breadth of the land could have said that he ever let brandy get between him and his work. This was due in part to the nature of his work, and in part to his own nature, which was extraordinarily tolerant and which could extend an enthusiastic and untiring welcome to brandy with unflagging hospitality.

His work? What was his work and when had he time for it? These were questions that had long since been set to rest in the minds of the sporting cônfraternity. There was not a horse race, cock-fight or encounter of pugilists in the country which he neglected to attend. He may have lost a patient or two—and sometimes their death was due to the will of God—but he never lost a race-meeting. Nobody could complain, for the continuous health of his district testified to the success of this practice of his, if not to his skill.

In a country where a doctor's skill is estimated by his stature, Dr.

MacDermot had a great reputation, even though he fell short of being "the full of a door." He had endeared himself to the people by his good nature and his sporting propensities, if not by any mental quality he possessed. Nevertheless, had his mind been made manifest to the nation at large, it would not have lessened by one jot the esteem in which he was held. In fact, if the truth were known, it would have endeared him further to his people. For that mind of his went to extremes; it wavered forever between heroes and "villains of the world." If there was no middle way in it, neither was there mediocrity. Only those who sought to balance themselves between good and evil or to be reserved in their judgment, might abandon hope: for them there was no entrance to the mind of the sporting chirurgeon.

What made him choose to live in a little Western village near Martyn Hall, when he was called so far abroad by frequent events around the capital of Dublin, would be hard to explain to folk less sapient than his countrymen. "His people came from there." That was enough.

That was one thing; but there were those who were shrewder, and would not have been at all surprised if it wasn't the limestone in the grass that kept the doctor in self-imposed obscurity. That is to say, supposing you had wanted to raise a foal on the quiet to beat the blazes out of those raised in Meath—where the limestone was so strong that the kettles grew solid—where could you have raised it—and no one any the wiser—but in the County Mayo? Where else?

His rustication was no source of loneliness. He was well liked and known among his own people. For society he had the local tavern, Mulcahy's, where you could always rely on finding him (racing events barred). As the local jokers used to say, "Try the tavern; and if he is not at home try his house."

But on this occasion he was going to attend a patient.

"Eighty round the chest," he repeated as he rode along; aye, but it was the postscript, in different handwriting in the illiterate communication he had received that caused him to entertain grave misgivings: "He spins round at the post." A horse that turned round at the starting-post obviously could have no chance of winning. True, that vice might be due to some stable hand who could not manage Green Glint in his morning gallops; and it may only have been a result of fitness or form that made the horse caper and cavort in his own length as he was being put to the measured mile. It was some such performance as this, undoubtedly, that his informant had witnessed as he lay, "gathering information," among the gorse bushes that stud the boundaries of that long plain which is the Curragh of Kildare. Feeney's riding would put an end to Green Glint's "bad habits."

Thus weighed down by considerations of human health and equine form, Dr. MacDermot drew nigh to Martyn Hall. Another consideration, this time for the ladies, made him, in order to avoid wakening them at so early an hour, approach the house by the back drive and enter it by the back door.

The back door was ajar and lights were already alight as he walked to the house after turning his mount into one of the loose boxes. The stables were empty! This was, to say the least of it, astonishing. But the house was up. The sooner he ascertained Feeney's condition, the better; one weight would be off his mind.

Mrs. Early met him at the door.

"Ah, and Doctor, is it yourself? Come in, agrah, and don't look at what's in the kitchen. Prussians or Russians—have it your own way—but a finer pair of blackguards you never met. Anyway, we couldn't leave them without their breakfast, and they after putting out the rick. It's up all night we were and likely to be, for the Master found Feeney near murdered and I had to help him to bed in spite of himself. He says he never felt better in his life, and his face cut and his eye closed."

Biddy Early took a lamp, and led Dr. MacDermot up a dark stair with but one small, square window to light it, till they reached a windowless closet. It did not occur to the doctor that better provision might have been made for the servants, any more than it had to the architect who designed the house.

The bed on which Feeney lay was clean and comfortable. The lamp beside his bed was turned down; but Feeney sat upright smoking a short pipe. His face was only half visible under a mask of white cloth, covering a raw beefsteak which was applied to his swollen and blackened eye.

"How am I looking?" he asked automatically, even before greeting the doctor. Then he bethought himself.

"Well, God bless you, Doctor, and may He forgive the likes of me for bringing you out at this time of night."

The doctor turned to dismiss Biddy, but modesty had already overcome her curiosity, and she had withdrawn.

"What have the villains of the world done to you?" the doctor asked.

"Three or maybe four of them came up the stairs with a dark lantern. When I heard them I called out, 'Timsey, what do you want?' Thinking it was my son. 'Silence,' they says, and come into the room, all in uniform.

"'You are the coachman?' one of them asked.

"'And what harm if I am?' says I.

"'You will tell us who it was you drove from Dublin to Attymon House on the fifth of May.'

"'Red Dander,' I answered back. They looked at one another after that.

"'Where is he now?' At last the leading fellow said.

"'As far as I know he's at the back of Attymon House at the present moment.'

"'You lie!' the big fellow whispered through his teeth, and made as if he was going to shoot me with the pistol in his hand. He put it into my chest.

"'It might go off,' sez I.

"'It can be loaded again,' sez he.

"'But I can't,' sez I.

"Then he hit me on the eye with the handle of it.

"'Liar,' sez he again. 'At the present moment he is dining in the house!'

"'May it do him good,' sez I. 'If they don't give him potatoes, he won't get too soft!'

"'How many of the stable boys are drilling at night?'

"'How would I know?' sez I. 'I never drilled in me life, save a hole in a barrel. It's a game leg I have, bad cess to it.'

"With that they dragged me out of bed and jumped on me. One of them gave me a kick on the other leg, and it's now like the bad one was when it first got hurt."

"You have no pain in your back?"

"Not now. It's easy I am."

"Then why are you sitting up like that?"

"Oh, that's a tip I heard from Deaf Burke. 'When you get a welt in the eye,' sez he, 'plaster it with a raw steak and keep upright to let it go down.' I'll be all right in the morning. Thank you and the Master, all the same, for sending for you."

"Let me see your leg."

Feeney threw down the clothes and exposed the thin legs of a jockey, small, steely, with bony tendons on the inside of the thighs.

"Can't you straighten it out?"

"Sure I can, Doctor, I was keeping it like that so that it might match the other when it set."

"Match the other? Don't be foolish, man. You don't want to have two bent legs."

"I'd be better balanced with two bent legs than with one straight, when it came to riding a horse."

Dr. MacDermot paused for a moment, debating whether he could with propriety reveal to Feeney what his master had confided to him. As soon as he realized that with Feeney it would hardly be considered a breach of confidence, for the secret was unlikely to go farther, he said:

"If you want to be fit to ride Green Glint, you must bandage that knee."

The effect on Feeney was unexpected. Feeney was no fool. At once he dropped his affectation of being slow-witted. He jumped to a conclusion immediately.

"The Master told you that?" he asked.

The doctor nodded.

"In the name of God, Doctor, get me up out of this in time. Can't you let the water off the knee? Pain matters nothing to me."

"Get this into your head, Feeney, and you will go half the way towards curing yourself. Drawing the water off a knee never does any good. It sometimes kills the man. All I can do—and it's the best I can do—is to strap it and raise it up and leave it on pillows for a week. If you cut down the amount of fluids you take, it will help to dry it up."

"And the race is coming near," Feeney groaned.

"I'll tell you what I will do," said Dr. MacDermot. "I will come over here myself every day for a week or more, I will give you a bottle and make Biddy give you raw beef chopped up, and beef tea, and you'll be dancing at the end of it."

The doctor was silent for a moment, then continued:

"When the news of my daily visits gets up to the Curragh, the odds will lengthen on Green Glint. And that won't do any of us any harm."

Feeney cogitated for fully a minute. Even though the doctor was a confidant of the Master, it was none of his business to imitate his master by continuing the confidences. So he kept the talk where it was without introducing another theme.

"There's no news that can leak over the Shannon."

"Ah, Feeney, I thought better of you. Leave that to the boys. All the troops in England and Prussia can't stop the spread of a tip on a horse."

XIX. MAJOR CRABBE

"WHAT'S THIS YOU say, Cole?" asked Major Crabbe.

"I say, Sir, that this Martyn-Lynch is probably the owner of Martyn Hall, the house that was raided for the French agent last night."

"Well, let him go to the devil. We have his guest."

The young ensign hesitated. The Major was not open to suggestion from a subaltern "in the field," and he considered that he was on the field of battle even when in barracks, in a country so disturbed and dangerous as Ireland. Additional decorations, he hoped, would record his garrisoning as a campaign. Medals were given for every campaign regardless of success and this was a campaign that well might be considered more strenuous than the usual campaign in the open field. It had the characteristics of a siege, a beleaguerment of a fortress in which he was shut up. Punitive and other expeditions were like so many sorties.

Therefore Ensign Cole refrained from suggesting that Martyn-Lynch should be taken to the cells for the insolence of his manner, which was tantamount to "resisting arrest." At the same time, he thought that Martyn-Lynch must be pretty sure of his innocence or his influence with the Government authorities (which were more or less the same thing), or else he would never have put himself into the lion's jaws by a visit to the barracks at Castlebar. As for himself, he had done his duty. He had captured his man. He had sent in his report. He had been up all night. It was time to lie down and to sleep. Martyn-Lynch and the Major might go to the devil for all he cared. Thus it came about that no answer was given to the orderly who had taken the message to the orderly on duty before the office of Major Crabbe. The first orderly returned to the orderly room off the hall. Nothing suggested that he should explain the cause of the delay to the visiting horseman in the hall. He would be off duty at 6:30 A.M. If there were any answer to the message it must come in a few minutes or else come to the man who would take his post.

In the same way, such was the discipline of the British army, the sentry on sentry-go at the gates of the barracks saw Martyn re-mount without giving it a thought. If he noticed the matter at all, he looked upon Martyn as one of the many gentlemen who had come to pester the Major for armed protection in their isolated and lonely steads.

But Martyn rode away obsessed by the conviction that a hue and cry would be raised after his departure was discovered. He never dreamt that his absence was not even noticed by any of those concerned. All his misgivings and precautions might have been forgotten. He might even have entertained Major Crabbe, secure in the knowledge that if the dinner were up to that gentleman's standards of what was to be expected in one of these rich, mad Irishmen's houses, he would go unmolested as far as the Major was concerned—for no decent Englishman ever avails himself of any knowledge or information that comes to him through nonofficial channels, nor permits it to influence his private behaviour. Had he to take official notice of a report, when "on duty," that would have been a different thing.

So Hyacinth unwittingly rode on with a sounder reputation for loyalty since his visit to the barracks than he could have hoped to obtain by inactivity.

At Martyn Hall, Feeney was his first care after Ninon, Mabel and his aunt-in-law. It would be easy for them, now that they were all at the Hall, to send the coach to Lisadill for Clemente and to proceed straight to Kildare and the races.

Leaving the members of his family to arrange the details of their journey at their own convenience, he set out to cross the River Shannon at a spot where it was deep and slow running, a spot that was unlikely to be guarded since it was not considered fordable. Though for the Quality military passes were not needed to cross the Shannon, Hyacinth was afraid to cross the bridge because of the hue and cry he supposed had gone out from Castlebar over his "escape." The river was all the more a barrier between the disaffected East and the rapidly rebelling West since the officer commanding the Castle of Athlone had burnt all the river boats.

With the idea that he was being pursued and watched for by sentries the question uppermost in his mind was, "Would it be safe to ride through Ballinasloe?" He was well known there, but it was not known that he had escaped from the barracks at Castlebar. One friendly hail or greeting and his identity would be divulged and he would never reach Sir Richard to enlist his influence in favour of d'Estournelles. In spite of the swampy ground, he would have to go south of Ballinasloe and cross the Shannon at Clonmacnoise, where the famous old cemetery was situated, the final hosting place of the kings of the Gael. If the moon held, he would swim his horse and tow his clothes across the Shannon that very night. There was not a native in Ireland that would not help him once he heard that the soldiers were after him.

His first place of call must be Attymon House. St. George must be informed of his own plight and that of the Chevalier.

For a long time he deliberated as to the advisability of keeping his arms. To be taken with fire-arms meant death on the spot, if taken by armed forces, and by the hangman's rope, if captured as the result of "information"—that is, by the treachery of an informer. The death of Lord Edward Fitzgerald last May was an example of the latter method.

And yet, suppose that he was stopped by a picket of only two or three, what chance would he have without his pistols? Whereas armed, he could shoot his way to freedom for the time being, if not to safety. If he were about to be overtaken by a troop of dragoons, he would have time to dispose of his pistols.

This latter consideration decided him. He kept his pistols, and rode away.

Through many gaps in the road-side hedges, Martyn, a fugitive in his own country and on his ancestral land—for he had not as yet passed the boundaries of his property—could see over a wide champaign. Not a red-coat was in sight and, what was more assuring, he received more friendly salutations from the peasantry than he had for the last three months. No surly face greeted him with a mere "Good day." Now it was a smiling, "God be with you, Sir;" and "God speed you safe." So they had evidently heard that he was "on his keeping" now, he thought, when in reality all they were aware of was that his house had been surrounded, a French officer taken prisoner in it and his hayrick set on fire secretly by the military. He had suffered with the humblest. They were united by persecution. He was one of themselves.

In order not to embarrass St. George by being seen visiting his house and possibly rendering it subject to a raid such as he had experienced, he entered by the long lane that led from the stream to the yard. A boy took his horse and was undoing the girths when Martyn forbade him.

"Give him an armful of hay and no water," he said.

He went through the back door into where Mrs. Brophy was cooking for the men. Thinking that it was one of them who sought his dinner prematurely, she remarked without taking her eyes off her work, "I'll fill yer guts in a minute, but you'd be better out of this till the bell rings."

"I am afraid," said Martyn smiling, "that I cannot wait for the bell."

Hearing his accents, Mrs. Brophy turned.

"May the Saints guard us! God forgive me! But you put the heart across in me, Sir," she said. "Were you looking for himself? He's gone to Dublin, Sir. He left Tuesday morning; but the lady's in the house. And all about it she is and fully recovered, it's like a hare she is, she's that light on her feet. I'll send word to her if you come into the house."

"I'm in my boots and not very presentable in this garb. Pray ask her to excuse me if I wait in the hall. I have ridden hard since the middle of the night."

Mrs. Brophy's face beamed with admiration for the horseman.

"Have they landed?" she asked eagerly.

Martyn shook his head. Everyone, he thought, thinks I am in the "movement"—to solicit help from the French. But why, he thought, should it be taken for granted? All along his path as he rode from his home, he was hailed by friendly greetings, friendlier than he had ever experienced before, not even excepting at the revels, which were in the nature of a benefit to his tenants. He had now a place in the heart of the people who had always nursed a longing for freedom and a slow unremitting hatred of the oppressor. Of the oppressor he had had recent experience, enough to make him wonder if his attitude of aloofness from his own people was right.

Mrs. St. George came down the stairs.

"My dear Hyacinth, why all this mystery? Has anything happened? Do not keep me in suspense."

"Forgive me for coming to visit you like this. The reason was a compelling one. I had to come here to tell you that my house was surrounded by the military last night."

"Oh!—and Constant? Tell me, what of Constant?" Ellice asked anxiously.

"He was taken and is now in the barracks in Castlebar."

"Is he alive and safe?"

"Yes, yes," he answered, but his answer was not heard. Ellice fell fainting into his arms.

Hyacinth did not know what to do. To ring for her maid was the first thought he had, but he was checked by the consideration that to do so would leave the maid a witness to her mistress's perturbation. And his tale was but half told.

He bore the fainting woman into the nearest room, the door of which was open. He laid her gently on a couch. Unsummoned, a manservant appeared.

"Bring water and brandy here at once."

"Mrs. Brophy has the keys and I—"

"Damn you, bring me water."

But Mrs. St. George was sitting up on his return.

"Forgive me," she said. "I will be myself in a moment."

A discussion in the kitchen had delayed the bringing of the water so long that Martyn could with propriety curtly dismiss the man when he came. This disappointed the menial greatly, for it reduced the drama of the situation and detracted from the interest his narrative would have in the servants' quarters.

"I am on my way to see Richard," Martyn resumed. "He will have him released."

"Cannot he be released at once? He is a Royalist and as such a friend of England. Why can he not be released at once?"

Martyn was at a loss what to say. He was responsible to some extent, if not for d'Estournelles arrest, at least for the delay that must occur before he was liberated. By driving him down from Dublin in his coach he had directed to d'Estournelles some of the dislike and distrust that Weld felt for Martyn himself.

"He is under suspicion because of his irregular mode of entry into Ireland," Hyacinth said at length.

"Can you not go to Castlebar before going to Dublin?"

"I have been to the barracks—"

"Oh, Hyacinth, you are so good and kind. And what did they say?"

Here was another dilemma for Martyn-Lynch. He could not tell her his own difficulties without making her feel that he had embarrassed her friend's claim to freedom.

"I found that I must visit Dublin with all dispatch. At Castlebar nothing can be done. A caller at the barracks is liable to be detained there. The garrison is in a rather panicky state and ignorant of the country. The Staff considers everyone an enemy who resides here. I must go to Headquarters, or enlist someone whose influence is greater than mine," he ended with a wry smile.

"Cannot I go to Castlebar and tell the officials how Constant saved me from the Terror in France?" Ellice asked anxiously. "Would that not be proof enough of where his sympathies lie?"

"Do not think of it!" said Martyn in alarm. "Your health would not permit it, and furthermore, you might meet with the same reception as I was given."

"My health has greatly improved," said Ellice. "In truth, I no longer consider myself an invalid," she paused. "But tell me—why had you to come in by the back of the house?"

"So as not to risk being delayed. It is quite possible that, with the Shannon guarded and all the East shut off, no one will be permitted to leave this part of the country without a special permit, which would probably have to be obtained from Dublin after many recognizances, and that would take time, weeks maybe. I intend to cross the Shannon at some lonely and unguarded spot. There is no possibility of reaching Dublin otherwise." Then he added, "For me or anyone else."

Ellice St. George sighed.

"I could go to Dublin myself. I could go and get Grattan to interfere in this high-handed outrage. I will go myself!" she exclaimed; then, seeing for the first time Martyn's gaunt expression, "You are famished!" she cried.

"Mrs. Brophy has already offered me food, but—" he laughed.

She rang the bell. When the servant left with the order she turned to Martyn. "Do you think it practical? I mean my going to Dublin at once? You could come with me. If the Commander at Castlebar is panicky he may execute Constant summarily to prevent any attempts at rescue."

Martyn waited. Evidently she had not grasped the situation at all. At length he said.

"I told you that the two Governments are highly frightened. The English Government has had to deal with a mutiny in the Fleet for which it blames, and perhaps rightly, the thousands of Irishmen whom it has seized and carried off to serve at sea. The Irish Government has just escaped from what might have been a nation-wide conflagration. Both governments are in a panic. They know that the French intended to land troops and endeavour to rouse the West. I have been told that they have taken steps to shut the West off at the Shannon. They want no communication whatsoever between West and East. No one is permitted to pass. Even the troops are not moved back. They continue to pour in but they do not go East again for fear that if a landing does take place the news of it would spread and the country would be up in arms as Wexford was. No, I intend to adopt the only means to reach the capital. Even if I do reach it, my petition may be invalidated if the way I came were known. I must not be seen here. I must leave you. I can get refreshment in some cottage."

"Food in a cottage! You would starve. You cannot swim the Shannon on potatoes and buttermilk. Hyacinth, do wait until you have had a meal and a bottle of wine and a hamper packed for your secret journey."

Martyn hesitated. "May I speak to the men in the yard? I want to give directions about my horse and send a few of the stable lads on an errand."

In the yard he saw Kelly, the coachman, who thought he had come to inspect Red Dander, the fighting cock.

"He can give a crow out of him like the blast of a horn," Kelly assured Martyn.

"I want you to send some of the boys to keep an eye on the road and give them mounts so that they may gallop back here if they catch sight of any of the red-coats."

"God bless the day," said the coachman fervently, "and me that I lived to see it! Sure, Mr. Martyn, I'll go meself. 'Tis I can see them a league off and smell them ten miles away. I wouldn't trust a gossoon, not with Weld's men out on all our tracks."

Hyacinth thanked the man heartily, gave him a guinea, and said before returning to the house, "If you see any cause for alarm send in word that you are back. I will know what that means, and it will not alarm the household."

During the meal he repeated his assurances to Ellice that Constant would not be shot out of hand. He had to put aside many suggestions from the anxious lady. One was that he should try at Athlone to get a permit to pass, before putting his more daring plan to the proof. He could not reveal, without giving cause for increased concern, his belief that the military were after him and that at the moment there was probably a price upon his head as on those of a dozen men in the district.

Before he left, he hinted that Attymon House might be searched, and tried to make Mrs. St. George believe that, if it happened, it would be but part of the new precautionary routine.

"They may be seeking d'Estournelles' papers. You should tell your men to give them what little information they possess. After all, what can they say but that Constant was your guest, and that when your son went to town he came over to stay with me?"

This was far from reassuring to her. She paled and Martyn feared that she would faint again.

"I am glad you told me," she said.

Kissing her hand, he took his leave.

In her boudoir, Ellice opened a secret drawer in a bureau, took out two letters tied with blue ribband, placed one in the fireplace, lit it and waited until it was consumed.

Rivers, when seen on the map, look as if they had definite margins. No allowance is made for the rushy banks or the swampy sides of many a stream. It has been said of the river Shannon, that chain of lakes and marshes which represents the extreme western margin of the central sea which filled Ireland in an earlier geological era, that it possesses hardly enough energy to take itself out of the country. In this it resembles many of the inhabitants. The river Suck is an even more softly-sliding stream. At Ballinasloe, the Suck divides and ripples widely, but south of the town, before it turns to enter the larger river, it resumes its fuller and easier way, seeping into the rich land for a space as wide again as its stream is wide, sheltering snipe in the winter, and providing in the summer a cool pasturage for cattle, udder deep in its lush and grassy edge.

Martyn knew of this marshland, but he thought that a place as old and as famous as ruined Clonmacnoise would be approachable from both sides of "the quiet watered land," and that the river would be deep and more firmly banked.

Still under the impression that he was being pursued, and comforting himself with the thought that, once across the river, the obstacles that he had surmounted would act as temporary safeguards, he took a line across country which he calculated would bring him to the river about thirteen miles south of Athlone. He must make it

during daylight and trust to night to conceal him and his swimming horse. Some farmer's hovel would shelter him until darkness fell.

Meanwhile, in Castlebar, things were going well for d'Estournelles. The bearing of the Chevalier, and fear of an adverse account of the conduct of his arrest and the burning of the hayrick, moved Ensign Cole to placate him as far as consideration for his comfort in prison could be counted on to placate him. Therefore, before going off duty, Cole gave the order that the Chevalier should be removed from the stone cell into his own room, in which he directed that a fire should be lit. Satisfied that this afterthought of his was sound, Cole threw himself down on a brother officer's bed and fell asleep.

The Major would interview the prisoner at nine o'clock. The explanation of this delay lay in the character of Major Crabbe. "Early" (in the early hours of the morning) "to bed, and early to rise" was the Major's guiding slogan. Breakfast never agreed with him. It took two bottles of claret to efface the memory of the meal.

This morning's meal being by this time completely forgotten, he sent for the prisoner who had been taken, an avowed Frenchman, at Martyn Hall.

The Chevalier appeared between two guards.

"Has the prisoner been disarmed?"

"Yes, Sir."

"On duty at the door. Leave him to me." The guard withdrew.

The Chevalier bowed.

This action, without a word from him, as well as that indefinable "influence," which the stars and some human beings are supposed to shed, had a strange effect on Major Crabbe. Afterwards he explained his feelings in terms of prescience saying that he knew a gentleman when he saw one.

"Be seated, Sir," said Major Crabbe.

The Chevalier remained standing.

"The report here reads that you entered this country in disguise, that you travelled from Dublin or its environs, still in disguise, as the servant of Mr. St. George of Attymon House, that for weeks you lodged with Mr. St. George, from whose house you went about the country on horseback on errands unknown, and that last night, after Mr. St. George had left his house, ostensibly for Dublin, you transferred your quarters to Martyn Hall, where you were apprehended by Ensign Cole. Is that correct?"

"In substance, yes; in statement, no."

The Major overcame his astonishment at his prisoner's polish and perfect English.

"May I trouble you to explain?"

"I entered this country in preference to England, where I have many relatives, refugees from the Revolution, because whatever small chance I have of regaining part of my estates would be prejudiced if it were known to the Directory that I was in England. Here I have friends and kindred, and here, were it not for the Government's obsession that every Frenchman is an agent, I could visit my friends until the danger subsides in France. Instead, I find that the fact of being French fills the minds of the gentry with suspicion, and in one case, that of Mr. Weld, with prejudice against me on account of my friends, to whom he is no welcome neighbour.

"Yesterday, when my host found it necessary to leave for the Curragh where he has a horse in training, I took my leave of him and of Mrs. St. George and repaired on an invitation of long standing to Martyn Hall. There I was followed by the unofficial spies of Mr. Weld, by whom this absurd report was prepared, and as a result of it the house was forced with undue violence while I myself was subjected to unnecessary insults, the grossest of these being a refusal to accept my parole."

"I wish you would sit down, Sir," Major Crabbe said not unkindly. "In a country such as this, which may be made the landing ground of the enemy at any minute, it is impossible to discriminate between friend and foe and quite impossible all of a sudden to make oneself conversant with the petty politics of the place, even if it were the business of a soldier to do so. I will have you released at once as soon as the formality of having you identified is concluded."

Crabbe rang a bell. To the orderly who answered it he said, "Ask Mr. Martyn-Lynch to step this way."

The man withdrew.

"And now, Sir," said the Major genially, "might I offer you a little claret? This is one thing I can forgive the scoundrels round about here for: their connection with France. They smuggle in good wine. I wish it was their only traffic with that country.

"They tell me that French troops, given their proper ration of wine, will go anywhere, storm any redoubt; but once try to curtail their red wine— Ah!" He gestured at d'Estournelles as if he were a general vainly trying to rally an immense army.

"Is that your experience, Sir?" asked Major Crabbe.

"I have not seen service since my King was murdered five years ago." He paused. "If I might be permitted to shave and to make my toilet? I came away somewhat unprepared for the amenities of social intercourse," d'Estournelles said to the Major in a tone that was disturbingly equivocal.

"But of course, of course," Crabbe exclaimed. He rose and opened a door. "My room, such as it is, in this awful place, is at your disposal."

He returned to his desk and rang a bell. A man appeared. "Attend to this gentleman and bring up some hot water."

D'Estournelles bowed and, thanking the Major, withdrew.

Again the Major rang his bell. To the soldier who appeared he said, "I asked you to fetch Mr. Martyn-Lynch."

"He can't be found nowhere, Sir. He went riding away."

Damned uncivil, thought Major Crabbe, forgetting, as he had forgotten his disturbing breakfast, the length of time that Martyn had been expected to wait while the cure of the meal lasted. But, since he had chosen not to remain to testify regarding his French friend, it would be necessary to detain d'Estournelles until satisfactory identification could be made and his bona fides established.

XX. A JOURNEY BY NIGHT

HYACINTH LOOKED IN over the half door of a house on the barely raised knoll opposite to Clonmacnoise. His long tabinet waistcoat and his rich clothes were objects of suspicion to the farmer who confronted him. Martyn-Lynch knew his countrymen too well to offer a bribe, at least as an introduction.

"May I come in and talk to you for a minute?" he asked.

The farmer opened the half door. "The childer's in the way but I'll put them out. Herself is gone back to a neighbour's." Like the University of Oxford, the house of an Irishman is the capital from which one goes back and forward as Oxfordmen go up and down.

Hyacinth dismounted.

"Hould on, your Honour, till I take your horse. It's yourself is well mounted entirely."

When the farmer returned from the stable he dismissed the staring children. Martyn stooped into the house.

The farmer produced a three-legged stool.

"Aye, indeed, but she is the fine beast."

"I hope that she'll remain in good condition, as you may too when I tell you what I have to do with her this very night."

The farmer shrewdly watched Martyn's face, trying hard to place him in any one of the particular classes with which he was acquainted. To elicit information of the other he proffered his own name first.

"Me name is Martin Coyle, Sir. And I'm sure you're welcome." He said this although he had just made up his mind that Martyn was a highwayman, a gentleman of the road with pistols in pocket, a skirted waistcoat and braided hat. Who else could possess such a fine horse and talk so darkly about what he had to do with her "this very night"? It was better to take him aisy, though, and no harm would be done. Maybe he was being hard-pressed and wanted to hide his horse and change it for another. What would he himself be doing if the horse were to be found in his stable by the militia after his guest had gone? He remembered that this morning he had put his stocking on inside-out and his right boot on first. See what luck it had brought him!

"My name is somewhat similar to your own. I don't want to tell you what it is, in case you might be questioned about me. If I don't tell you, you can safely say that you don't know it. I came here because I want to cross the river when night falls. I will put my clothes in a barrel and swim over beside my horse. I chose this place because at one time there must have been a ferry, and that means firm landing ground."

"Faith, then, there was a ferry, and many's the honest penny I used to get bringing pilgrims to the graveyard, until the sojers came here and burned me boat because I wanted to paint me name on it to get it back when the troubles would be over. And I have a patch of land and a few sheep on the other side."

"So they took your boat?"

"Aye, burnt it, Sir, as I was saying. 'Troubles, indeed,' said a whippersnapper of a young officer, 'is that what you call rank rebellion? Here,' sez he, 'burn that boat.' "

"I had no expectation of finding a boat here," said Hyacinth. "I thrust myself upon you in order that I might not be seen on horseback at this unfrequented place. The soldiers are after me for entertaining a French friend."

The farmer's face showed relief crossed with some disappointment.

"And I thought—"

"You were wrong to think it. I am neither Collier, the highwayman, nor Tiger Roche lying low from the result of some encounter."

"May I shake yer hand, yer Honour? I'll hide ye safe. There's no sentry for miles back, but there passes by a lot of troopers one after the other about once a day. They went by a long time ago just as herself was leaving the house."

"I must make Dublin if I can before the morning. It's eighty miles from here, and I cannot take the highroad until I get beyond Moate. I can get a fresh horse at a house I know. I must reach the city in order to have my friend released before it becomes known that I broke what was about to be my own arrest."

"And did ye escape from the Yeos?" the old man asked, youth welling in his eyes.

"Not exactly, but I called into the barracks of Castlebar, having these pistols with me, to demand an interview with the officer commanding. It was early in the morning. I was kept waiting. It suddenly dawned on me that I would be held for entertaining the Frenchman. I was armed and that alone is now punishable with death. It might take weeks to clear myself and it might happen that I could never wholly extricate myself from the toils of a Swaddler magistrate even if I was sent to the civil court. So I took to my heels. I have an interest in a horse that bids well to win at the Curragh."

Complete confidence now reigned in the mind of Martin Coyle.

"You don't tell me?" he asked, inviting details about the race horse. "There's great horses back at Ballinasloe." And with the thought of horses in his mind, his voice unconsciously dropped into a whisper of secrecy such as seems to be universal in the ritual of the horse.

"Would it be any harm to ask the name of yer Honour's beast?"

"Not at all: Green Glint."

The old farmer muttered, fondling the names:

"Green Glint out of Madora by Burke Aboo. Glory be to God, isn't the world very small? I knew his sire and his dam; and I seen Burke Aboo come through at the Curragh from last place to first, and Feeney rubbing him against the rails, it was so close. He balked at the start. But he sent the country home talking to itself. Am I right?"

Hyacinth assured the old man of his accuracy.

Herself came in and Martyn's position was explained to her.

"There's a barrel in the dairy," she began.

"Ah, what ails you? Is it that little barrel for the gentleman's fine clothes? How could we get the grease out of it?"

"Well, as for that, it's scalded and dry and fit to hold a bishop's mitre."

"It's about boots we ought to be thinking and not a hat. The butt at the corner of the house, though heavy, will float and bear up the gentleman if it's a cramp he gets in the could water."

"Have no fear on my account. The distance is short and there is no current."

"Sorra a current; even in a flood you could hardly tell which way she was flowing," he said.

It was the good wife who thought of putting a sheet in the barrel to protect the gentleman's clothes from the damp sides and to dry the creature when he came out. Saddle and holsters went into it with Martyn's pistols and his bottle of wine, a roast grouse and half a loaf.

"She's forgotten the butter and the salt," Mrs. Coyle exclaimed, reflecting on an absent servant. She added those commodities as a gift from the house.

"We'll shorten the reins to keep them off her feet," Martyn advised Coyle, who was preparing the mare for the water.

"Whoa there! And not a sound out of ye," Coyle said to the mare. "Aren't ye lucky to be going to the sea-side?"

"It's hardly dark enough yet?" Hyacinth asked.

"It's often more deceptive before the moon comes up than when it's in the sky." And Coyle turned a wise eye along the river.

"Down there under the bushes there'll be no seeing you. All I'm afeard of is the sound of the barrel when I'm fitting on the lid."

"We can hammer it through a damp cloth."

"We may have to bury it a bit or it will sound like a drum."

"That sound would be unwelcome," said Martyn-Lynch.

"There's few around to hear it and them that does will take no notice. There's quare things does be going on and they all can't be put down to the fairies," said Coyle, excitement moving his fancy.

"I cannot deprive you of your barrel and your wife of her fine sheet.

I will put it in the barrel and leave it in a corner of the churchyard."

"Any corner will do. There's a neighbour has a duck boat on the Suck; maybe I could borrow it to go for the barrel."

By night a river rejoins the primordial things, the winds and the darkness. Its substance feels stranger, wilder and more magical than by day. Even the light of the moon cannot gladden it into any friendly affinity with humanity. It remains elemental and like palpable night. In its depths dwell the nameless things, things that are seldom seen but whose centuried existence is known and handed down by word of mouth from those who have seen either the Phouca, that white horse of the river, or the great water snake that survived in spite of all St. Patrick had to say.

River banks look unfriendly to a man swimming in the black water. They seem to rise suddenly like walls and not to slope helpfully to the reach of an exhausted swimmer. As the naked man swam through the black water, he anticipated with horror the fleshy touch of the cold obscene things that rise from the slime at night.

Yet Hyacinth had no choice. He could not care. He was too occupied with his mount to let his mind be caught by such fears. He held his horse in front of the withers by the crest, where a hammer and chisel were fastened. The left-hand rein he held in his left hand, and his body floated horizontally as he encouraged his horse in the journey across. Far behind them the barrel floated, towed by a rope. Hyacinth had instructed Coyle to pay the rope out gradually before launching the barrel, lest it foul the mare's hind legs.

Through the cold blackness they journeyed slowly, lost in the middle of the stream; but Hyacinth had taken precautions against the loss of bearings with which the night swimmer has to contend. A candle-light in the cottage window gave him his distance and a lantern hidden under the bushes where he had stripped gave him a bearing for the length of drift. The little round tower by the church would be a guide while it could be seen: when no longer visible he would know that he was nearing the bank beneath it.

All was going smoothly. Now for the landing and the outward plunge of the restive horse. It would never do to have his foot trodden on by the submerged hooves.

Out! He held her with one arm through the shortened leathers. There was some difficulty in salvaging the barrel. He feared to take it out by pulling. It would be necessary to lift it for fear of breaking the rope. If it went adrift, he would be left naked on the bank to fall a victim to the morning patrol or to haunt the churchyard in the vain hope that he might find some unterrified pilgrim who would wait to listen to his story and bring him help. Getting the barrel ashore was by far the most difficult part of his feat. He dared not let go the frightened horse and, with his reach shortened by the closely-looped reins, he could not touch the barrel without bringing the mare back again to the river's brink, to which she refused to go. He solved his problem simply enough by tying some of the slack of the rope to the reins and so getting sufficient freedom to rescue the barrel. Once he had that out of the river it was a simple matter to roll it to one of the white thorn-bushes, tether his horse and proceed to pry the barrel open.

He blessed "herself" for thinking of the sheet for drying him, for the night was bleak and cold. He took the bottle of claret out of his boot and revived himself with the wine. Nothing remained to be done now but to bestow the barrel, dry his horse, saddle her and find the boreen that led from the graveyard to a point on the Coach Road five miles east of Athlone. He calculated that once on the high-road, even at that distance from town, it would not be necessary to skirt the Mail Road as far as Moate, a thing which was almost impossible at night, for the fields, where they were not knolly, and covered here and there with scrub, were marshy bogland, outlying pools of the great central bog of Allen in which it would be impossible not to lose one's way.

Suddenly the sound of a chain startled him. A trooper's bridle? But it seemed to come from where no horse could approach—the middle of the churchyard.

There it was again! The mare trembled. What the devil could it be? Some of the United Irishmen at a secret meeting? Most unlikely. They would have provided themselves with a boat so as to slip across the river. They were the boys that were hard to surprise. Whatever the noise, Hyacinth was glad that the barrel had kept his powder dry.

Like his learned ancestor, Alexander Lynch, Hyacinth was a Roman Catholic. Though he practised his faith infrequently, he believed in it and had never thought of changing it for another.

Absurd as the idea was that an apparition from Hell or Purgatory could revisit the earth and rattle a chain, Hyacinth nevertheless found himself thinking of ghosts. The churchyard of Clonmacnoise had been a great centre of learning. To this, the "Secluded Recess of the Sons of Nobles," the chieftains of Connaught had sent their sons. Here lay, as in Westminster Abbey, the sagest and the bravest of the land. It had been a scene of more sorrow and regret, heartfelt or formal, than any one spot of the immemorial Isle of Destiny. If yearning for life was ever strong enough to break the bonds of death, if ever a graveyard gave up a ghost, surely this was the place for it to happen.

Again the chain shook; this time nearer to Hyacinth. It was no bridle spliced with chain such as the troopers use to prevent the pikes of rebels from cutting through the leather. The chain seemed to be loose and running by itself. Now a crash accompanied it and it jingled loudly over the ancient tombs. Against a faint patch of lighted sky he saw it. A white phantom with horns! It stood erect for a moment, turned and plunged and disappeared.

It was a goat! Some goat, tethered so as not to eat dead man's grass, had got free and entered the ancient graveyard.

"I can stand almost anything but the loss of sleep," Hyacinth explained to himself, and so restored his self-respect.

There are worse experiences than riding through Ireland on a summer night, that is if you are warm and comfortable and do not suffer from loss of sleep. Martyn was neither warm nor comfortable. He was cold and anxious, his mind crowded by a dozen disturbing thoughts.

Would he be overtaken before he got Sir Richard to release his friend? Would he be disgraced before the stewards and forbidden entrance to the enclosure at the Curragh? Would they accept an entry of a horse whose jockey could not be named? How could he account for his unshaven appearance and travel-stained clothes and boots, if interrogated by a military patrol? From what house this side of the Shannon could he say that he was coming and to what house going, without embarrassing their owners unfairly and dragging them into a plight like his own? Might he not be mistaken in the dark for one of the soldiers or for one who belonged to the governing class, and be ambushed by United Irishmen before he had gone another ten miles?

The hills to the left between Horseleap and the road to Mullingar were said to be infested with stragglers from the defeated and disbanded armed gangs of Wexford and other parts of Leinster. Already he had been taken for a highwayman, even in a good light. Might he not be taken for one again in the dark? Mail coaches were being held up almost every night now, and after the occupants had been robbed in the name of a non-existent Republic, letters were carried off in the hope of finding military dispatches addressed to Dublin Castle. Troopers escorted the mail coach from Athlone, through which town all communications from the Connaught Command passed. Even they were ambushed and overpowered.

His only comfort at the moment resided in his brace of pistols. It would be a wise precaution now that he was past Moate, with its broad village street, the broadest of any village he knew, to loosen his pistols before entering the dark and narrow road that led to Kilbeggan. This he did.

With every village he passed, he left behind him roads other than those that led directly from Athlone. He could be regarded as having come from any of these. At every village the risk of his being apprehended grew less.

There were no lights. The "strong farmers" and shopkeepers lay sound asleep behind barred windows and doors. He envied them their warm beds. They had not sixty-five miles to ride alone in the night, forty-four hours without sleep and still six hours to go.

His mare whinnied and threw up her head. She stopped still

and brought her head down to her knee, pulling the reins nearly out of Martyn's hands. While gathering them, he felt a pistol slipping. He caught it in his right hand, felt the flint, and was about to replace the weapon in his pocket when a command rang out.

"Stand!"

Walking his horse slowly from a recess in the dark, high hedge, a dimly-seen horseman approached. Martyn saw with relief that he was not accompanied. "He is only a highwayman," flashed through his brain. "Only"—he had not time to realize the irony of the thought.

The fellow had a pistol in each hand.

"I don't want to kill you needlessly but I must have the contents of your pockets. I don't want your watch. I want what you are carrying in the breast of your coat or waistcoat."

"I am armed," said Hyacinth, "and if you don't stop your horse, I will shoot you dead, whoever you are."

Hyacinth's mare threw up her head. At that moment a shot rang out and a bullet entered her brain. As she sank Martyn fired, aiming between two shining objects he glimpsed in the dark. He barely saved his thigh from fracture as the mare rolled over. Expecting a shot to be returned instantly, he took cover behind his dead mount and held his second pistol ready. With every nerve tense, Hyacinth listened for any movement. He heard a horse's breathing in the dark. He heard close by the dragged breathing of a man.

Caution! His enemy might only be knocked off his horse and have enough life left in him to shoot if Hyacinth approached.

"Don't fire again!" the man gasped. "I'm done for."

The breathing of the man on the road began to bubble. There was no mistaking that. Hyacinth advanced towards him, feeling the way with his feet. His foot touched the head of the dying man, hatless now. Martyn stooped and felt his forehead. There was no need to feel along his arms to see if he had dropped his pistols. The man had heard the last pistol shot he was ever to hear.

"Have you more orders to hang them?" the dying man asked feebly.

"Hang who?" Hyacinth asked. "So you are not Collier the highwayman?"

"I am; but I was doing a service for the boys that done many a good turn for me. I wanted to intercept the orders to execute, that they send by secret messenger from Athlone. They are sometimes carried by the local Quality. I got one of them hereabouts tonight."

"Strange as it may seem," Hyacinth answered in a way the man would understand, "I am on my keeping from the militia at Castlebar; and you have shot the horse from under me that was bringing me to safety in Dublin."

"Take mine; but no, no. Not Dublin! Not there!" the dying man adjured. "Strike a light. The tinder's in my waistcoat. I hate the dark. God, is all this my blood? Empty my pockets before I faint. Don't leave my money to the sojers. Is there water anywhere? Water—air—water! Why didn't you tell me who you were?" The man babbled incoherently, and then he was still.

Hyacinth struck the tinder. As he lit the match he caught a glimpse of the long, furrowed, equine face of the highwayman. It had that high degree of distinction which is found in many uneducated but mentally endowed Irishmen.

A warm breath over Hyacinth's shoulder almost blew out the light. The highwayman's horse was looking at his master.

Hyacinth looped his arm in the reins. He stooped again and, as the man had requested with his dying breath, removed a packet from his coat which he placed in his own breast pocket.

If he could get his own saddle off the mare! But it is a difficult feat to unsaddle a dead horse that lies on its side or back. He must make haste, lest someone from the military camp at Athlone should surprise him.

Now his only mount was the horse of a notorious highwayman probably well known in a dozen counties. He had been mistaken for a secret messenger with dispatches from Athlone. It was unlikely that such a one would take the great risk that Martyn had just taken, of travelling alone so as to appear dissociated from the military.

He pulled the dead body of the highwayman by the arm-pits to the grassy side of the highway, propped up his head on a tussock, folded the arms across his breast, and left him lying by the side of his precarious kingdom.

The highwayman's horse was tall and moved at an awkward hand gallop. The owner must have been as tall as Hyacinth, who found it unnecessary to lengthen the stirrup leathers. When Martyn found how fresh the horse was, he let him out, and found to his surprise that at a full gallop he was easy and restful to ride. Without effort he could do twelve to fourteen miles to the hour in the glimmering dark through which he seemed to know his way.

They had travelled hardly ten miles when the horse stopped of its own accord beside a shieling hidden in the bank of the roadside. A light appeared. Thinking quickly, Hyacinth called out, "Wait a while, can't you?" and urged on his reluctant mount.

What will they think in that den of thieves at such a strange command, Hyacinth wondered, grimly amused, as he galloped past.

He would have to pass through Kilbeggan on the highwayman's horse. It was an important town, full of rich merchants, and the home of the famous distillery of John Locke. It was sure to be well guarded in times like these. Would he take it at full gallop in the dark or amble through as many an honest benighted traveller must have done before him? No. The fields were sound above and below the town. There would be few obstacles in his way if he skirted it. All the rolling, gentle hills were not as great a barrier as one turnpike would be. At Kinnegad he would take the risk of putting up and of getting some refreshment for man and horse. Possibly no one would know the horse there, or take Martyn for Collier the highwayman. But it meant putting all his fortune on one throw. If he sent his horse to the stables, he might be refused possession of it after his meal. Ostlers are a society all to themselves. They know every horse on the road; aye, and the history of many a one whose career on the turf had ended long ago.

To the right there still lay low and boggy land, outlying parts of the great midland bog. The road from Athlone lay on the summit of the esker, the great ridge of gravel dividing the island of Ireland into two almost equal portions north and south. It ran from east to west above the great central plain from near Dublin Bay to Galway Bay, where it ended one hundred and thirty-three miles west of Dublin.

The coach road was not hard to follow, undulating from Horseleap to Kilbeggan, where it turned north for Tyrrell's Pass.

At Kinnegad Hyacinth saw a light in the little inn near the church on the Kilbeggan side of the pass. As his horse's hooves became audible the light disappeared. There was no doubt of it, this was the place. The owner must have been afraid of some mounted night wanderer. No. There was the light again.

Gently he tapped on the shuttered door. To his surprise it was opened at once. A man wearing a night-cap held a lamp high and so prevented himself from seeing the horseman clearly, though he had a good view of the horse. "Come in," he whispered.

Hyacinth dismounted and put the reins on a hook. He entered a small hall made like a sentry box. Passing through a door at the side of this he entered a room which apparently ran the full length of the house. A long bar went the whole length of it, leaving a space for the bar-keeper to walk up and down as he served customers. A flap in the middle gave access to the space behind the bar and immediately in front of it was a fireplace. In this a bright fire was burning. A small recess for a window went into the wall on either side.

Passing through the counter, the landlord pulled back a little curtain that concealed one of the windows, and waved his lamp two or three times. Soon a dishevelled ostler appeared through a door at the end.

"He's at the door," said the landlord sharply, referring to the horse. Then he turned to Martyn.

"Holy Christ! But you're covered with blood," he exclaimed, and lowered the lamp.

"But it's not Larry Collier at all!" the ostler cried out. Then, recollecting himself, he ceased, suddenly terrified lest he had given offence.

"I am not Collier," Hyacinth said, "but I have messages from him. As you can see, it is his horse. Leave him where he is and give him a bucket of oats. And get me a basin of water at once to clean myself, and a razor, as quickly as you can."

The landlord turned to the ostler. "Get them at once," he repeated the order. He placed his lamp beside those on the wide mantel-shelf, and turned to Martyn-Lynch.

"Is he caught?"

"No," said Hyacinth.

"Sure he must be hurt?"

"He was. And there is no time to lose. Is there anything in the larder that a man could eat?"

While the landlord was out of the room, Martyn re-loaded his pistol.

Partly to give an impression of nonchalance, and partly because he was tired, Hyacinth passed through the counter, and stood with his back to the fire. He noticed that his hands were covered with blood. There was blood on his waistcoat, on his breeches and on one sleeve, the lace of which was a brown mass. Was it any wonder that the landlord got a fright? But what would they do with his horse? He could hear him occasionally as he moved his feet. He would hear him if they attempted to lead him off, but at the moment there was no fear of that. Neither master nor man knew who Hyacinth was, and his declaration that he had messages from the highwayman would secure him good treatment whether the landlord was a friend of Collier or afraid of his associates.

In came the landlord with a steaming bowl, a towel, a razor and some yellowish soap which was melting in the middle of the basin.

"If you have a little looking-glass, I'll shave where I am," Hyacinth declared. This statement seemed to reassure the landlord in some strange way, perhaps because it was in keeping with the picture he had in his mind of the men who have to be ever on the alert. The thought that Hyacinth was afraid of being deprived of his horse, and that all these precautions were taken to prevent his being spirited away into the dark by suspicious people, never entered the landlord's mind.

The act of shaving was a good excuse for not being able to reply, even if he were asked a direct question, and if direct questions had been the landlord's way of obtaining information.

As a matter of fact that simple man was so greatly impressed by the quality of the aid he imagined that Collier had enlisted, that suspicion was far from his mind. All his efforts were directed towards speeding the mysterious stranger with Collier's horse on his mysterious way.

"And you forgot the pig's cheek?" a woman's voice called from beyond the doorway. "It's cold, but would the gentleman have time to stay for a few duck eggs fried with a bit of bacon?"

Martyn-Lynch nodded assent. The very thought of food cheered him.

"Of course he will, if you hurry up," the landlord answered for his guest. Then, dropping his voice, he asked Hyacinth:

"Would you like Cherry to give him a rub-down? It's far and hard he must have gone by the looks of him."

"Let him do it where he stands. I may have to mount at any moment. Has he got the bucket of oats?"

With his face scratched and somewhat blotched from the uncouth shaving, Hyacinth sat down to one of the most enjoyable meals he had ever had. Behind him the landlord busied himself with some of those thousand and one irritating little tasks which such people invent when they wish to put their victims through a seemingly harmless questionnaire. Examined singly, not one of the little tasks could be pronounced utterly unnecessary. The fault was in the timing of them and their extension beyond the endurance of a restless guest.

"He looks as if he came from Kilbeggan within the hour," said the landlord. "Twelve Irish miles it is. And in the pitch dark is there a beast in all the land that would as much as look at it, let alone come on here, mebbe, in twice the time?"

By ignoring him, Hyacinth raised himself in the landlord's estimation. "Leave them alone," the landlord thought, referring to the outlaws, "and they'll not be long in learning what a good turn I did for this one, whoever he is. He must be as grand a man as Lord Edward."

Those who would "not be long in learning" about the landlord's kind offices were, to him, almost imaginary beings who inhabited the land darkly. In his mind they required somewhat the same kind of treatment as the "Good People." While it was hard to win their good graces, it would be madness to thwart their plans.

Greatly refreshed by his meal, Hyacinth rose abruptly.

"Good night!" he said, and examined his pistols as he went to the door to mount.

The landlord came as far as the hall-shelter with a lamp. When, on his return, he found five gold guinea pieces beside the bit of a looking-glass on the mantel-shelf, he decided that the unknown stranger was the hero of some enterprise far too desperate to be revealed to his wife.

XXI. AIDING ORDER

It was nearly noon when Hyacinth completed the last lap of his long and adventurous journey from Castlebar to Sir Richard de Vesey's country house, at Lucan.

"But how the devil did you get here and what have you been doing to your face?" was Sir Richard's greeting. When he heard the narrative told to him briefly, but without reservation, he said:

"This means that you cannot turn up at the races."

"As you know, Green Glint is in St. George's name."

"Oh, the horse can run, damn him," Sir Richard said, "but you will be harassed unless I can get them to understand at the Castle how the land lies. I suppose this French fellow is in love with Ellice?"

Martyn thought long. At last he said:

"I don't think that that has anything to do with the state of affairs at present."

"If he were in love with Ellice it would give him some excuse for being in this country, just at the moment when the Government imagines that all the land is stuffed full of French recruiting agents and instigators of rebellion."

"As for that," said Hyacinth, "there may be one or two in the Castle who are related to people d'Estournelles helped to get out of France four or five years ago. We cannot very well bring in the name of Madame de Ronquerolles, for her presence in Ireland is as much in need of explanation as the Chevalier's."

At mention of Clemente, Sir Richard's eyes lit up.

"We must not embarrass Madame la Baronne if we can avoid it," he said. He coughed and continued in a somewhat admonitory tone. "Then there is all this nonsense of Constant's disguise. Now why the devil did he wear that and sit with your fellow out on the box seat?"

Hyacinth was momentarily embarrassed. At length he said with a shy laugh: "I suppose out of consideration for the honeymooners who occupied the inside of the coach."

"Meaning the pair of you? Yes, yes. A Frenchman would think of things like that."

Relieved, Hyacinth went on:

"He could not wear his uniform, and the clothes he had when he landed were little better than my servant's box coat, which he said was at any rate a cover for his shabbiness."

After a pause, Uncle Dick asked: "Where did you say he is being held?"

"Castlebar. I did not wait—"

"You certainly did not. No need to report your Shannon swim. Makes you condemn yourself. You could easily have got a pass. Get your boots off and go and have a bath and a rest if you are not too tired to sleep. I know that I should be after such a journey. We can go to town later, after you have rested and eaten. No harm or danger in being seen with me. No one would connect you with a fellow who broke gaol yesterday in Castlebar. Andy will do something for your face."

The road from Lucan extended to the traveller one of the most beautiful drives by any river in the country. Its beauty was not ended when it ran by the Phoenix Park, so called by a mistake of one of the Stanhopes. He erected a graceful monument to the fabulous Phoenix, under the impression that the traditional name of the park was derived from that bird. Actually it was named for the well of *foinn uisge* (at its western end near Knockmaroon Hill) meaning "clear water" and pronounced *finnisk*. However, the monument was unique not alone for its unostentatious grace, but because it was the only instance where English ignorance benefited Ireland, as some of the Dublin wits declared.

Sir Richard drove from Lucan to his town house, which looked down Great George's Street over the river and the riverside roofs to the long line of the Dublin mountains and to those heights of Killiney and Wicklow which resemble waves of amethyst.

"Tell you what," he said to his nephew. "You remain here while I do a little reconnoitring work to see if there is a hue and cry out. I'll send back for you if the way is clear. You will find me at Daly's. Dashwood and his lady are staying at Morrison's. He may be able to do more with the Viceroy than I can. I will look in at Morrison's first. There may be a half a dozen friends of mine there. Stretch yourself for two hours. I will not keep you more than that. But I know very well that you have come so far ahead of the news that you might as well possess your soul in patience for a day."

Hyacinth lay on a short, uncomfortable ottoman and stared at the ceiling, which was covered with pictured amorini attending a recumbent Venus. They could never get away from Rubens' wife, he thought; and fell fast asleep.

Sir Richard called first at Morrison's. He knew that a house which received all comers and was a station for every incoming stagecoach would be the most likely place to find news.

He caught sight of d'Aubrey lolling in an armchair and sipping a glass of wine. D'Aubrey was a young Englishman attached to the Castle staff, a position he owed more to the influence of his family than to talent. Though young, he had one of those strange and harmless delusions which are found more frequently in the aged. He was under the impression that he had business to attend to which kept him always in a state of hurry. He could spend all day in a coffee house and all night at a gambling table, but no sooner would an acquaintance accept his invitation to drink or invite him, than he "must be getting on." It was said of him that he kept a watch to mark the hours on which he prayed to be excused.

"Hello, d'Aubrey," Sir Richard greeted him. "Surprised to see you here. No, no. Do not rise. I will take a seat. What is that you are drinking? Port? No, no. I will take some sherry. Do not let me drive you away."

D'Aubrey resumed his seat and said in a drawling tone:

"In the future there will be less risk of your being waylaid when you visit your place in Galway, by all accounts, Sir Richard."

"And just what are those accounts?" Sir Richard inquired.

D'Aubrey, delighted at the attention he aroused, drew out the travellers' tale as long as he could.

"The stage came across the dead body of a highwayman presumed to be the notorious Collier, but of course it did not suit either the driver or the guard to identify it beyond doubt."

"No, the rascals!" Sir Richard exclaimed, irritated by the sympathy of the lower classes for every kind of breach of law.

"There was also the body of a strange horse. It was not the horse the highwayman was in the habit of riding. Of that the coach guard was sure."

"Of course. The rascal would swear to the horse when he would never pretend that he knew its owner."

"From which it would appear," d'Aubrey went on, "that whoever killed Collier took his horse. That will go far towards leading to his identification."

"But who the devil wants to identify him? You don't mean that the Government would prosecute a man who rids the roads of a highwayman—a thing that, let me remind you, they found more than they could do themselves. Identify be damned!"

D'Aubrey rose with, "Sir Richard, I must crave your indulgence and beg to be held excused. My time is pressing—"

"Oh, I know all that!" Sir Richard said testily. "But you have not told me why the Government wishes to identify the man who slew Collier. Do they mean to reward him? There was a reward on Collier's head at one time."

"They are making inquiries concerning the ownership of a bay mare and a pig-skin saddle with a horse pistol in one of the holsters, in the other a half-finished bottle of claret."

"Damn it," Sir Richard exclaimed, "where can that waiter be?"

D'Aubrey, who was infecting his companion with his restlessness, ceased brushing imaginary specks of dust from the heavy cuffs of his tunic. He joined his fingers together, pursed his lips and appeared as if he had much information and many reserved opinions.

The waiter came with Sir Richard's bottle.

"Will you change to this?" Sir Richard asked. "Or would you prefer to continue drinking port?"

"I will join you, Sir Richard."

When the glasses were provided, Sir Richard tasted his wine, made no audible comment, then suddenly asked:

"To whom are you attached now, d'Aubrey?"

For a moment d'Aubrey did not know whether the question conveyed a slight rebuke from Sir Richard; but he concluded that there was change enough at the Castle to warrant that the question was asked in all good faith, without reference to his obvious idleness.

"To General Lake," he drawled, as if already overpowered by the responsibility.

"To that fellow? He is in charge of all the dragooning operations. Let me see, now. Succeeded Ambercrombie, didn't he? I know that he is causing no end of trouble by not looking after the discipline of his troops. Plunder and outrage and so forth. Never heard of such things in any regular army."

D'Aubrey sipped the sherry and said with a drawl that would have been insolent had it not become second nature to him, so often had he employed it to give his frivolous and shallow spirit some appearance of weight:

"Have you no idea of the state in which he found the country? I am only on his staff two days, and already every dispatch we open tells of more and more lawlessness and rebellion. Last night a land agent from somewhere round your western estates was held up and robbed outside Moate. He was bearing a report to Headquarters. His horse was probably shot or stolen to prevent him giving the alarm. Fellow called Crosbie. The highwayman Collier may have done the robbery before he was shot, and Collier's assailant may have taken the papers stolen from Crosbie, who, fortunately, escaped with his life."

Sir Richard, who was anything but a good dissembler, said nothing. He was trying to remember if Crosbie was his nephew's steward. He did remember that Martyn had dismissed someone or other.

The fact that he found himself in a position in which he could not speak his mind to a brat of a boy made him restless. Not to be able to say whatever he had to say was a position in which he had rarely found himself.

"And is Lake responsible for law and order west of the Shannon too?" he asked as he rose.

"We are General Headquarters," d'Aubrey drawled, piqued that he had not made as if to go before Sir Richard rose.

"One thing, young Sir, would greatly oblige me—if you would use your kind offices with your General to grant me an interview tomorrow." Sir Richard departed without waiting for a reply.

As the chaise drove back, he wondered what was the best course to pursue. "As I told Martyn," he assured himself, "he will have to wait. He has arrived before the news. No use looking in at Daly's."

It was late afternoon when Hyacinth woke on his uncomfortable ottoman. He found that a lumpy object pressing against his side was the cause for some of his discomfort. He reached into the pocket at his breast and drew out the heavily sealed packet he had taken from Collier. It was addressed:

General Lake
General Headquarters
Dublin.

There was no further address. Evidently the original bearer had known where to find the General, and would have found him and delivered his communication had he not been intercepted by Collier.

"Orders to hang them." The words came back again to his mind from the lips of the dying highwayman.

Martyn was in a predicament. If he opened this package addressed to another person he would be but little better than a highwayman who intercepted His Majesty's mail. It was highway robbery, not to mention the breach of honour which would be incurred by opening and reading another's letters. And yet the highwayman had risked his life to get this package, to which, evidently, great importance was attached by the disaffected. It contained orders or evidence on which the lives of unknown persons depended.

He turned the packet. On the back of it were the marks of four bloody fingers. Hyacinth had been too tired to attempt to clean his blood-covered hands when he arrived at Lucan House.

The sound of Sir Richard's carriage was audible above the street noises, the splashing of a drove of swine and the curses of the swineherd, mixed with the whoops of helping street urchins.

"Rested, Hyacinth?" inquired Sir Richard as he entered. "Lake is the fellow to go to. He has command of the whole business from Dublin to the Atlantic seaboard. Never had heard of any General Lake—did you? By the way, they found your saddle horse and your highwayman. We must see Lake tomorrow."

Hyacinth, who was rising, said, "General Lake? This is a strange coincidence. Here is the packet. I should have told you that Collier asked me to take it when he heard that the troopers were after me. It is addressed to General Lake."

Hyacinth handed the packet to Sir Richard.

"Still in a bit of a mess. If we are going to deliver this in person we had better have the thing cleaned. Looks as if it had been in the wars, eh? All the same, delivering this to General Lake should provide the strongest possible evidence of your good faith, if any is needed. Meanwhile a little food would not be unwelcome, eh?" Hyacinth assented readily.

Hyacinth was not destined to see General Lake.

Sir Richard went to bed early, leaving his nephew-in-law sitting up. Hyacinth read until, by the silence which descended on the city, he judged that it was late. Twice he had tended the candles and turned up the lamp. As he was about to take a sconce and go to his rooms, he heard a scuffle and voices in the street. The rioters, whoever they were, must have come suddenly into the highway. They seemed to be fighting beneath the very windows of the room. He drew back the heavy red rep curtains, raised the window and gazed out. As he peered into the street he could see a dark mass of men surrounding a tall figure who fought with a bright blade, backed against one of the torch posts of the hall-door. There was a cry from the street.

"Lend your sword arm, Martyn-Lynch!"

Hyacinth, looking from the lighted room into the dark street, could not see who had recognized and called him. All he could see in the dimness was a swordsman surrounded and hard pressed. That the others were roughs was apparent; that the swordsman was a gentleman went without saying. There was but one thing to do.

Hyacinth rushed down to the hall and took his sword from the settee as he went. He also took the whistle that was kept hung on a nail in the hall, to summon the Watch on occasions of emergency. As he opened the door he blew loudly and then took his stand by the side of the tall, broad-shouldered swordsman. He recognized Tiger Roche, and knew that the Society for Aiding Order was in action.

There was something laughable in the fact that law and order depended on such a character as Tiger Roche. But the country was disturbed, and as a result, law was lax—except military law, and that did not deal with foot-pads or highwaymen. These were left to the force of utterly inadequate watchmen who were nightly falling victims to rogues, outcasts and deserters, concealed in the dense lanes of the Liberties. To help the guardians of the law, Tiger Roche had set up his Society.

A staff, thrown from the back of the crowd, came hurtling through the night. The torch flickered and gave light. Tiger Roche lunged. A burly ruffian fell back. Hyacinth's sword was almost broken by the blow of a stout stick. He pricked the striker on the shoulder. With his foot, Roche threw off a drunken rogue who tried to grasp him by the legs. He made as if to run him through, but instead caught his companion unexpectedly in the breast. The crowd drew off, but only to rally and to gather cobblestones. One of these broke a window beside the hall door. One struck Hyacinth in the waist. He heard Tiger Roche say in a voice that was calm but sinister:

"Don't hesitate to run them through. But don't let them come to grips." And again the Tiger smashed with his sword-hilt a face that had been pressed too close by those who shoved from the rear.

A backhand slit another face as the fine point grazed across it. A whistle blew. Several of the ruffians slid off down the lane on the east side of Rutland Square, which would give on Cavendish Row and provide a way of escape. Further off the whistle could be heard frantically blowing its shrill double note.

"The Toucher's in the offing," cried Tiger Roche.

A scurrying was heard at the top of Great George's Street. The cause of this was not long obscure: cavalry were coming to the rescue. From three sides they came, guided by the few night-watchmen who had run for assistance as soon as they heard Hyacinth's whistle and saw that Tiger Roche was beset.

With the flat of their swords they laid about them. An officer drew up.

"Just in time, gentlemen. Whom do I address?"

"My name is Roche."

"And mine Martyn-Lynch."

"Some pretty sword-play, I perceive," the officer remarked as he pointed to two wounded and dying men lying in the street.

Protest as he might, Martyn-Lynch had to accompany the officer. As he was about to be taken into custody a carriage appeared. It was Roche's chaise. On the box sat Toucher Plant.

"I couldn't find your coachman, Sir," he said to Roche. "But I found the cavalry and your coach."

So with a cavalry escort Tiger Roche and Martyn-Lynch were led away to spend the night in gaol and explain before the magistrates in the morning how and why they had been attacked by a crowd of ruffians at night, and what had led to the slaughter of two and the wounding of many men.

As Hyacinth lay in the guard-house he asked that the Captain of the Guard be brought. This was out of the question. There would be a new guard mounted at six in the morning. There was nothing untoward about which to waken the Captain. Hyacinth explained to Roche the absolute urgency of his interview with General Lake.

"Sir Richard will see to it. Leave it to Sir Richard," the Tiger assured him. "And let this comfort you: If you had not to explain the émeute of last night you would have to explain how you came to have a highwayman's horse without reporting the fact to the Military."

"How long will they detain us?"

"Until they find the body of the murdered watchman whom I was too late to save at the corner of Hill Street. I think that the body has been concealed. I have never been interfered with for so long." Then he asked nonchalantly, "Do you play écarté or bezique?"

Hyacinth played both, and in the next two days had ample opportunity to demonstrate his skill. For two days the evidence was taken. First the Tiger was exonerated. Then the magistrates exonerated and commended Martyn-Lynch.

But two days were lost—two days during which Hyacinth was made miserable by the imagined sufferings of his guest, the Chevalier, who had been so rudely taken from under his roof; two days in which he kept wondering if Sir Richard had gone to see Lake alone. His guest Constant, a French émigré, to be left where he must think himself deserted, in a country barracks in a warring land! It was an unbearable reflection. And for the two days neither he nor Tiger Roche was permitted to communicate with the outer world, until all the evidence had been amassed.

The incident of the horse was child's play compared with the Coroner's jury he and the Tiger were to attend. That might last another two or even three days. And he had protested such friendship to Colonel le Chevalier d'Estournelles, only to leave him forgotten in Castlebar barracks! Held as he was, he could do nothing, and the thought of his impotence galled and maddened him. The aplomb of the Tiger made it worse.

Roche's suggestion, "You must permit me to enroll you in our Society for Aiding Order," did nothing to assuage Hyacinth's exasperation. Who would make it clear to the Chevalier that he had not been betrayed?

XXII. IDENTIFICATION

To conform to official requirements, it was necessary that d'Estournelles be identified. Identifications by the residents of Martyn Hall could not be accepted, for it was there that d'Estournelles was arrested; and evidence from such a source would be considered unsatisfactory. Nor, apparently, could evidence be obtained from Attymon House, for Denis St. George was in Dublin and it was reported that his mother was a semi-invalid.

Still, perhaps her indisposition was not so serious that it would prevent her from making the journey by chaise. Major Crabbe, without informing the Chevalier of his move, dispatched an ensign to Attymon House to make inquiries and, if feasible, to bring Mrs. St. George to Castlebar.

"If I am to be of service to you, I must proceed so that you will not be troubled again." Thus the Major explained to d'Estournelles his need of a reliable witness. When Crabbe named the person he sought to bring to Castlebar to fill this rôle, the Chevalier showed extreme agitation.

"But Mrs. St. George has not been well!" he protested. "I will not have her incommoded for my sake. I should sooner stay in your gaol as long as you see fit to hold me."

"I instructed my ensign," said the Major soothingly, "that if Mrs. St. George feels the trip will incommode her in the slightest, she is not to make it. I also instructed him to make it clear to her that it is I, and not you, who make the request, and that it is entirely subject to her convenience whether she comes or not. You may prefer to stay in gaol rather than disturb Mrs. St. George, but it is my duty to make your status clear, and she is the only available person who can satisfactorily identify you."

Ellice St. George looked anything but an invalid when she arrived at the barracks. Her desire to help Constant out of his predicament had overridden all considerations of inconvenience to herself. Indeed, the opportunity to come to his aid seemed to have acted as a tonic on her. Ellice's previous indisposition might have been largely of the spirit, since no doctor had been able to find an organic cause for it. If this were the case, it appeared that her rapid recovery had also come about through some medium other than the purely physical. At any rate, there was nothing the least bit sickly in the indignation she lavished on Major Crabbe over Constant's arrest, once the Major had explained his position in the matter.

"The fact is, Mrs. St. George," he said, "that I am the very unwilling victim of circumstances and officialdom. The circumstances are that I am placed here to prevent a repetition of such disgraceful occurrences as were witnessed in Wexford last May, instigated by the example of the French Revolution; and officialdom makes it incumbent on me to clear your friend of any complicity in disloyal activities directed against his Majesty's Government and the peace of the Realm. My information is that there are French agents abroad in this neighbourhood instigating the peasants to revolution. Acting on the information of a magistrate, I sent a party of men—I had no other course—to apprehend a French agent who was reported to me as having entered this country in disguise. We thought that we had the fellow. Now it turns out that I have arrested—"

Ellice broke in with an asperity unbelievable to anyone who had judged her character by the frail gentleness of her voice, as it had sounded in her first words with the Major.

"It turns out that you have arrested the Chevalier d'Estournelles, Colonel in His Majesty's Household Cavalry and saviour not only of myself—he devoted a week to smuggling me out of France—but of at least a score of English gentlemen and gentlewomen who, but for his help, would have fallen into the hands of the sans-culottes. Some of these aristocrats he was able to transfer from France to England, others he succeeded in getting into Brunswick, where he himself served under the Duke in the army intended to restore legitimacy to the throne of France and to avenge the death of His Majesty King Louis. Why an English Major should confuse a French Royalist with a Revolutionary, you yourself can perhaps best explain. The least exercise of intelligence would have been enough—"

"But Mrs. St. George, you misunderstand me." The Major rose from his seat. "Pray give me a chance—"

"I pray you to remain seated." Ellice said. "You must hear me out. Misunderstanding? Any misunderstanding was on your part, not on the part of anyone else. You are a soldier, are you not?"

The Major was about to speak when he realized that the question was but a rhetorical one, or that it had to be taken as such for the moment.

"The merest ensign would have recognized the character and bearing of a soldier, not to speak of a gentleman and an officer, commanding, until the murder of his King, the Household Cavalry—"

"Damn it, I can tell a gentleman—" the Major interjected.

"Then it is all the less excusable for you to offer as gross an insult as could be offered to a soldier: confusing him with a sans-culotte!"

"This is unfair!" exclaimed the Major, attempting to rise.

"Sit down, Sir, and if it is unfair, take it as part punishment for the greater injustice you have done to the Chevalier d'Estournelles."

"Ellice—" d'Estournelles began.

Turning to him, she proceeded, "And it was just as much your fault! Had you no record of your services, no medal, no experience which you could have related so that this man would have been satisfied that you were a soldier and not an *agent provocateur* for the Directoire? It is your own fault and you deserve to find yourself in a predicament like this, in this dungeon."

"France, just at present, is not a country through which to carry Royalist decorations nor, for that matter, is this," said Constant, amazed at the heat Ellice was showing. He sensed that her manner might be due to a desire to hide her genuine concern for him.

"I am sure that it is not!" the Major echoed, heartily glad of his French ally.

"No, I suppose not. Everyone has to masquerade here as someone else. Everyone is afraid of his own identity."

"Really, Mrs. St. George," the Major exclaimed.

"Yes, you! You are afraid to show your nose out of this fortress. What is the use in pretending to protect a country in which you are a prisoner? If you were not afraid to leave your barracks, why did you not come over to visit me, instead of requesting me to come here? Oh, I know, your ensign couched the request in gracious phrases, but nevertheless you would have shown far more gallantry by coming to me with the Chevalier, who should never have been arrested in the first place."

At last tears relieved Ellice's overwrought emotions. She shook with sobs. Both men were afraid to make the least remark, fearing to provoke a storm of even greater invective.

"I have not a damn woman in the place to take her in hand," the Major whispered. Ellice may have heard the whisper. She rose suddenly, with her face composed.

"I presume I am at liberty to leave?"

The Major bowed. He considered silence the wisest course.

When Mrs. St. George was ready to leave, Crabbe rose and opened the door for her, hiding his face by the depth of his bow. With his disengaged hand he took d'Estournelles gently by the elbow and guided him to accompany the lady. Hardly had they both left the room he rang a bell.

"See that the lady and gentleman have every facility to leave these premises."

Seeing the inane look on the orderly's face, he shouted, "Tell Ensign Cole to get up and see his protégés, the prisoner and his lady companion, safely out of the barracks. Immediately and without delay. At once!"

"You will come back to Attymon House, of course," Ellice said to Constant as they entered the chaise in which she had travelled to Castlebar. "I have sent to Lisadill for Clemente, and you two will join Mabs, Penelope and Ninon in their journey to the races."

"Thank you," said Constant, "and once again I must accept your hospitality. It would not do for me to return to Martyn Hall after the trouble I have already brought on that house and its master."

"Poor dear Hyacinth!" Ellice sighed, with as much tolerant humour as concern in her voice. "He has gone to Dublin to seek your release. We must let him know as soon as possible that it has been accomplished."

Ellice laughed, and allowed a slim hand to fall against Constant's on the chaise cushions. The tenseness she had showed in Crabbe's office had given over to relief and a happy fatigue. She rested her head back against the seat and closed her eyes, while a gentle smile played over her lips. Constant clasped her hand in his.

"I would have done anything to spare you this journey," Constant finally said.

"Then you do not like to see me happy?" Ellice asked cryptically, without opening her eyes.

"How is that?" The Chevalier was honestly puzzled.

"Because it has made me very happy to come to your aid, as you came to mine in a far graver situation in France, and with far greater risk to yourself."

When Constant raised her hand to his lips, she made no effort to draw it away.

As soon as the trying journey to Attymon House had been made and the travellers had taken refreshment, Ellice St. George gave in to fatigue and retired at once, begging her guests' pardon if she should keep to her bed for a good part of the following day.

Constant found Clemente in a mood of gentle melancholy.

"I wonder if the Château du Moulin is still standing?" she asked after they had finished discussing Constant's arrest and ultimate release. "And who occupies it now?"

"Some real miller, I suppose, who will by this time have undone the restorations you made, and restored the mill to its original condition of darkness and disrepair."

"He would have some work to do and I do not grudge him that.

To clear the mill-pond of lilies would be a task in itself. And to take the floors out which I put in, build up the windows and doors and darken the place would be as costly as to buy another mill. There must be others on the brook lower down the hill."

She began to show signs of agitation, so Constant changed the subject as soon as he could.

"How wise you were to take my advice and come with me. Had you stayed on you would have joined *Les Noyades* in the Loire or your own pond. Here our only problem is what clothes we shall wear to the Curragh."

"Clothes?" she said, and laughed.

Constant, never impatient when the subject had to do with feminine adornment, which he considered one of the most important aspects of civilization, said:

"I hope that I am not going to invite your disapproval, but, knowing that it would not be the first time that you and I have worn clothes that we borrowed, I suggest that you might wear a costume of Mrs. St. George's or any of the ladies', if your own wardrobe contains nothing suitable to wear to the races. Am I making an outrageous suggestion? I feel that anything would be better than to be deprived of your company at the gay race-party."

Clemente smiled at the thought of the clothes she had worn and those she might have to wear.

"Mabel is taking only two frocks, and even if she had one for every day we shall be in Dublin, I would look too young and too much like a school miss if I wore hers."

Knowing that Clemente was too sophisticated to be rallied on the subject of her youth, and that for the moment she was intent on the very practical side of the problem as it presented itself to her, he forbore to say that she was not too old. It was obvious that any woman over eighteen would be too old for Mabel's girlish costumes.

"The best clothes I have were given to me by Ninon. I suppose that she has something she can spare, but any ambitions I have had to be fashionable are gone."

"Ah, my dear Clemente, we must not lose heart. In fact, now more than ever it behooves us to be 'fashionable,' to be different from the canaille. We have suffered the loss of all we ever had and the greatest loss is the loss of rank and all that made for it. We are here in a strange, kind country where no one knows or cares who we are. But it is a land whose aristocracy lacks both dignity and distance, a land where the gulf between rich and poor is as great if not greater than in our country, a land where even the Throne is a make-believe. Penniless and dependent as we are, and perhaps must ever be, we must not yield for a moment that which it is in our power to sustain."

"And what is that?" Clemente asked almost inaudibly.

"Our pride," he said.

XXIII. DUBLIN CASTLE

DUBLIN CASTLE OWED its origin to the "Danes," those Scandinavian pirates, for the most part Norse and Danes, who set up their Steyne, or standing stone, to commemorate their landing on the firm southern bank of the Liffey between the site of the Castle and the mouth of the river Dodder. On the eastern end of the highest ground—the long ridge running from Kilmainham eastwards to the side of the river Poddle—they built their strong stockade, which became Dublin Castle. Since the year 832 it has been the site and the symbol of the natives' subjection to better organization and arms.

This was true up to the moment when Sir Richard arrived there, save that the organization now was better only because the opposition could not have been worse. The arms were still superior to the pikes and pitchforks that in May had sent the disorganized English and Hessian troopers running 12,000 "strong," with their cannon, from the fortified town of Wexford, before a few thousand farmers and a priest.

Organization in the Castle consisted largely of cross purposes and officialdom. No one knew where any department but his own was, and nobody knew the name of any official save the one with whom he was either in immediate contact or the one to whom he was assigned, usually two different officers.

This morning something must have been overlooked in the routine, or perhaps Sir Richard had come so punctually as to surprise the Castle out of any possible excuse for delay. He was ushered at once into the ante-room of General Lake's private sanctum. The room was distinguished by the absence of all ornament with the exception of a broad arrow on the door, and the presence of all ugliness, which in military circles was considered to be a sign of efficiency.

"Never heard of such promptness in my life. Why, when Cornwallis was here you had to wait a week. Of course we have not got into the 'presence' yet," and Sir Richard laughed at his own satire as he spoke to the officer on duty.

But he was at once admitted. D'Aubrey came for him and ushered him in. This was a good mark for d'Aubrey, in the opinion of Sir Richard. "You did not forget, I see," he said to that youth, who was now so overcome by his own importance that he waved all acknowledgment of unofficial acquaintanceship aside.

General Lake was a pleasant person. He was even of a kindly disposition, in marked contrast to the conduct of those under his control. Many Irishmen have been amazed at what appears to them a paradox and an insoluble problem—the difference between the private personality and the official performance of one and the same Englishman.

"Ah, Sir Richard, I have been talking to my aide about you. He says that your horse is the favourite for the Curragh next week. I hope to see him win. See you there, at any rate, if I can get a little respite from all this." He pointed to a heap of memoranda on his desk.

Sir Richard laughed.

"Glad to hear he's a favourite. It puts a bit of responsibility on an owner though, with all the poor fellows following my horse in the betting."

"And now," said the General, "will you kindly tell me the object of your visit?"

Though it was hardly the time to spend precious moments of conversation on the packet, Sir Richard said, "First let me hand you this. My nephew took it from a highwayman the other night. It is addressed to you, and its safe delivery should have a favourable bearing on the case which I have come to discuss."

While the General was slowly examining the packet Sir Richard said, "You were good enough to grant me this interview so that I might have an injustice, arising from a mistake, no doubt, immediately undone. On Monday night the house of my nephew, Martyn-Lynch, was raided by troopers."

"Where was this?" the General inquired.

"In Mayo."

The General looked at his aide, who thereupon disappeared, to return almost immediately with a map, which he placed in front of the General. The two bent over it while they went campaigning in whispers on its irregular surface.

"Ah, here it is! Castlebar Command. You may proceed."

"Chevalier the Colonel d'Estournelles, who was staying at a friend's house some twenty miles or so away, came over to visit my nephew by marriage, Martyn-Lynch, while his friend St. George preceded him to Dublin for the Curragh races. D'Estournelles arrived just after dinner, and as they were awaiting some refreshment for him, the house was surrounded and the Chevalier was carried off with unnecessary roughness. The house was subjected to bad usage, but a complaint about that is not the immediate cause of my visit."

"Which is?"

"To have my friend immediately released. He was Colonel in the Household Cavalry under King Louis of France until the king was assassinated. Then he joined the army of the Duke of Brunswick and—"

"What did you say his name was?"

"Le Chevalier d'Estournelles."

The General looked at d'Aubrey, rolled up the map and, presenting it like a field marshal's baton, repeated, "D'Estournelles."

While the aide searched for the dossier that doubtless existed, and the daily report that should have arrived with the morning mail from Castlebar, the General undid the secure wrapping of the packet. Before he could examine the contents, d'Aubrey returned with two sheets. The General perused them, laying aside the packet Sir Richard had brought. "These are dated Tuesday and the raid took place on Monday. There is no account of such an important personage being concerned. The only report is about the malicious burning of a rick on the estate of Martyn Hall. This is what we are here to prevent, malicious attacks on and the destruction of the property of landlords. We have had a pretty bad example of the insecurity of Irish gentlemen and of their property in the last few months.

"Crabbe says that it was very quickly and efficiently extinguished by a picket of his troops. Good for Crabbe. Must have gone about things very expeditiously. It doesn't take very long for a rick to burn out. Is that all?"

That was all from Castlebar for Monday and up till noon on Tuesday. The burning of the hay-rick was reported as the work of local mischief-makers, but there was not a word about the raid, the arrest of the Chevalier or Martyn's visit to and departure from the barracks. Officially they did not exist, nor had their adventures taken place.

"Now this is the kind of thing we like to get," Lake said as he read the papers he had taken out of the packet delivered to him by Sir Richard. "If every landlord had as loyal and as staunch stewards as the owner of Martyn Hall possesses, instead of Masters Facing-Both-Ways, there would be more security for their physical existence in the country. Here we have a list of the disaffected in the Castlebar Command area." Lake passed the papers to Sir Richard, who read:

Myles, a blacksmith.

Father Colyer, a Romish priest.

Roddy, an agitator, said to have served in the English Army.

Feeney, a coachman, and his son Timsey of little consequence, being a half-wit.

Cudahy, a butcher.

Mulcahy, an inn-keeper; his brother; Dr. MacDermot who communicates almost daily with an address near the Curragh. All of these on the property of Martyn Hall. Drillings take place almost every night on this property.

On the estate of Mr. St. George, the next property of note:

Kelly, a coachman.

Mrs. Brophy, a cook (comforting and entertaining the King's enemies).

All the male indoor servants from butler to pantry boy.

All the men connected with the stables or the farm. This house, Attymon House, is a hotbed of treason. It is at Attymon House that a mysterious Frenchman is staying.

Meanwhile every blind fiddler or piper in the country is a go-between. Some of these fiddlers cannot be as blind as they pretend to be. They go about freely. On account of their infirmity their subversive activities are not suspected. They are the principal agents of information and they travel from the sea-ports to the inland villages and hamlets.

All these named should be immediately apprehended in the interests of public security.

"This is from a man named Crosbie," Lake continued, "who has been recommended by the local Magistrate, one Weld, as a loyal, honest and trustworthy person. You see by what we are confronted. Real treason. Compared with this the alleged arrest of your friend is only a trivial matter. I cannot act on it until I have notice brought to me officially. Up to this there has been no report." He indicated the papers which his aide had placed before him.

D'Aubrey assumed a languid air which had an immediate and unpleasant effect on Sir Richard's temper.

"But damn it, General, is my nephew's word not good enough? His house was raided; his and my friend abducted. That 'mysterious Frenchman' in your list is the very one who has been arrested; the only mystery about him is how such a staunch foe of rebellion could be mistaken for an agent of treason. He risked his life to rescue a noble Irish lady, Mrs. Ellice St. George, from the Terror in France. Why, man, the Chevalier d'Estournelles is a cousin of mine, and I would vouch for his honour as I would for my own. Is not my word as good as the gratuitous report of a denunciator?"

The General smiled at the generous precipitancy of Sir Richard. "That is not the point," he said. "When Crabbe, who is in command, does not mention any such prisoner or any such event, how am I to become aware of it officially without going over the heads of all my departments and causing dissatisfaction, not to say resentment? If you tell me how it is to be done I will gladly do it."

"Tell him if he is in, to let him out."

"That would be simple, did it not constitute a dangerous precedent."

"May I ask what precedent?"

"The precedent of proceeding on private and unofficial information over the heads of my officers. It's hard enough, as it is, to hold things together."

While Sir Richard argued and attempted to circumvent officialdom, he was inwardly cogitating on the news that had just been revealed by the opening of the packet—Crosbie's treachery. He was again placed in a false position. How could he accuse Crosbie openly, without possibly implicating his own nephew? Martyn-Lynch was to all appearances a loyal subject, without sympathy for the forces of insurrection. And yet Crosbie had sought to involve both him and Denis St. George in the net of suspicion at a time when the slightset hint was enough to have its victim cast into prison or shot without trial and their lands estreated. And what right had Crosbie to desert his post and try to reach Headquarters with this informer's letter? What was the reason for this course of action? Evidently Crosbie had some information which had led him to believe that trouble was imminent in the neighbourhood and he wished to remove himself to safety. But, and this spelt black treachery, how many instances in the recent past had there not been of agents' informing on their Catholic masters and as a result inheriting property which, on the letter of the unrepealed Penal laws, it was illegal for any Catholic to hold? Did Crosbie think that, by informing on Martyn-Lynch and impugning St. George, he would have both landlords and their estates estreated for high treason and obtain them as a reward for his loyalty and solicitude? That, not to go very far away for an example, was how Weld's father had got the Burke property on which the present magistrate resided. Another insurrection and another reshuffle of the old for the new would have Martyn's estates confiscated and "planted" with new landlords.

It would be best, Sir Richard realized, to give General Lake no intimation of these disturbing thoughts. Hyacinth had rescued the packet from the highwayman who had taken it from Crosbie, and, by delivering it intact, had demonstrated his good faith to General Lake's satisfaction. To discuss Crosbie's real motives would only confuse the issue.

"There may have been a report on d'Estournelles' arrest which was intercepted," said Sir Richard at length. "Could you not act on that supposition without unduly offending your subordinate in Castlebar?" This mildness was a great mental effort for the old soldier, who had never been a diplomat.

Wearily General Lake replied:

"How do you account for the report I have received about the attack on the property at Martyn Hall?"

"It seems rather inconsistent," said Sir Richard.

"In what way, may I ask?"

"If Martyn Hall is such a seat of disaffection, it is incredible that the men who are reported to be drilling there should be guilty of malicious injury to that property," Sir Richard answered with a sneer. He felt his blood rising, and would have openly denounced the Castlebar Command, under the "protection" of which Martyn had lost his rick—but would the General believe that the men who had reported the attempt to save the hay had themselves set it on fire?

"The tenantry of every property in this country secretly hate their landlords," said General Lake. "That fact would account for many an apparent inconsistency in their conduct. They hate the well-to-do. This has been the case from time immemorial, I am told. But Irish history from time immemorial does not interest me. What does concern me is the maintenance of the status quo. And I intend, to the best of my ability, to protect property owners, even those who endanger the whole body politic by not protecting themselves."

It would have been easy to ask, "Who can guard the guardians; save Martyn's household from the military?" Though the question was on his lips, Sir Richard restrained himself. He began to fear that he might be compromised by further questions.

He asked at last, "May I take it, General, that if and when you have an official report of the arrest of the Chevalier Colonel d'Estournelles, you will take my testimony as to his status in France into consideration?"

"I'll send for you the very moment I can proceed," said General Lake, smiling and rising from his chair. Then, with an unexpected change in tone, "Good luck at the Curragh!" he shouted cheerily as Sir Richard left the room.

Sir Richard consoled himself as he left the Castle with the reflection that perhaps it was the same excess of officialdom which had prevented General Lake from taking cognizance of the Chevalier's arrest that also prevented him from re-opening the question of how the Chevalier came to be in the country at all.

It was not until the coach from Martyn Hall arrived in Dublin, the day before the races, that Hyacinth and Sir Richard were able to piece together the whole story of misunderstanding surrounding the Chevalier's arrest and release. The coach bearing Ninon, Mabs and Penelope had stopped off at Attymon House to pick up Ellice, Constant and Clemente. Although Ellice had suffered no ill effects from her journey to Castlebar, she decided not to expose herself to the excitement of the Curragh races. She would rest at Sir Richard's town house while the others went to the Curragh, so as to feel fresh enough to join them at the Race Ball afterwards.

Immediately upon Hyacinth's release from the guard-house, Sir Richard had given him the details of his interview with General Lake, and now the two renewed their discussion of the whole incident. By this time Hyacinth had somewhat recovered from the humiliation he had felt on first learning that his impetuous actions had been largely to no purpose, and that by remaining at Castlebar he might have saved himself and the others concerned a great deal of trouble. Indeed, it seemed likely that the Chevalier would not have been detained at all but for Martyn's abrupt and unexplained departure. Now, as the party discussed the affair in the drawing room of Sir Richard's town house, Hyacinth was able to take their affectionate chaffing with good will.

"And so the poor boy swam the Shannon in the middle of the

night," Sir Richard was saying, "thinking it was barred by the military and that he was being pursued by Crabbe's men, when in truth the only barrier existed in his imagination, and his pursuers were figments of that imagination."

"With the country in the state it is in," said Ninon defensively, "one never knows when reality will exceed one's wildest imaginings."

"That is quite true," agreed Sir Richard, "and there is so little correspondence between our officials that it was only by happy chance that Hyacinth's fears were not fully justified. Quite possibly if he had waited, it would have suited the whim of the commanding officer to detain him until his own bona fides could be established by some roundabout means. Why, there was actually no report made from Castlebar to General Headquarters of Constant's arrest, although Lake was in possession of detailed lists of the supposedly disaffected in the Castlebar area."

By now, all the facts were known concerning the packet Hyacinth had taken from Collier at the cost of the highwayman's life. Shortly before Martyn's encounter with him, Collier had held up Crosbie at pistol's point, robbed him of the secret papers, and forced him to walk all the way back to Athlone, after taking his horse. When the military had found Martyn's slain mare beside the body of the highwayman, Crosbie, by identifying the horse, also identified the probable killer of the highwayman. The officer commanding the forces in the Castle of Athlone, whither Crosbie had gone for protection, had sent Martyn his personal congratulations for services which he did not hesitate to describe as of national importance, for the King's mails were not secure while such men as Larry Collier were at large. Unfortunately, these congratulations and the story attending them had not reached Dublin in time to spare Hyacinth his two nights in gaol with Tiger Roche.

Once again, now that the whole party was assembled, Sir Richard and Hyacinth discussed the problems that had been raised by the discovery that Martyn's agent, Crosbie, was acting as informer. Hyacinth, characteristically, was so anxious to see both sides of the question that he ended by taking no positive stand on it, and would not act on Sir Richard's advice that he discharge Crosbie.

"We should, of course," he said, "do our best to clear the names of Father Colyer, Feeney and Dr. MacDermot, against whom accusations of disloyalty are plainly ridiculous. I fancy that no action would be taken on such a report without rigorous investigation. As for the others named, I should not be surprised if the charges were justified."

"But, Martyn," Penelope put in, "have I not heard you defend the rebels for their desire to improve their lot?"

"Can I not defend their principles while deploring their practice?" Hyacinth asked. "As an Irishman, I sympathize with their hatred of foreign tyranny. As a landlord, I cannot encourage the insurrection of my tenants, when it threatens my very property." If there was inconsistency in his attitude, it was certain from Martyn's earnest tones that he did not suspect it. The others, accustomed to his vacillation, refrained with tolerance or resignation from arguing that he could not be on both sides at once without danger of being caught in the middle.

If Ellice took little part in the conversation, it may have been because she was afraid her thoughts, if spoken, would seem indecorous —even unkindly. Although there seemed to be no way of expressing it without danger of being misunderstood, Ellice was actually glad that Hyacinth had dashed off so impetuously from Castlebar, leaving Constant for her to rescue.

BOOK IV

XXIV. THE CURRAGH RACES

SIX THOUSAND ACRES of it, Sir, and it never felt a plow. That's, mebbe, what has it so cocked up. The sod's that springy that it sends the horses leppin' off it. It's hard set they do be to keep on the ground at all. It's going like flames they do be from start to finish. What chancet has a horse at all that wasn't born and bred to stay on the surface? 'Is it a steeplechase I'm in at this time o' year?' he'd be asking himself. There's six miles by two of it. They say it's hollow the Curragh is, and sodding the roof of a palace of one of them old fairy kings.

"For the love of God don't let them see me talking to you, Sir. Don't let them catch sight of me. It would be all up with me."

"What do you mean? Let go my arm, you rascal," Dashwood said to the famous tout, who was known as the Toucher on every race course in Ireland, as Plant seemed to be trying to hide behind him.

Totally illiterate but full of mother wit, the Toucher would single out a stranger at a race course and ingratiate himself. He could change as the circumstances required, from whining servility to an affectation of disdainful aloofness.

"What do I mean?" Plant repeated. "What I mean, Sir, is this." And he spoke in his broadest brogue to cajole the Englishman. "I mean that if the bookies were to catch a glimpse of me talking to the likes of you, 'It's a tip he's giving him,' they'd say. 'And if Gayoffo wins we'll skin Plant alive,' meaning me. The odds is five to one now but the price is fallin' fast; with the luck of God I might be able to put five on for you if you give me the money quick. There's no time to be lost. Don't let me out of your sight and meet me here after the race at the corner of the Stand."

If the trick succeeded (and the Toucher's first tip seldom lost), he would return with the winnings only one point less than the betting quoted, for which he would account by saying that, owing to a regrettable delay, the price had fallen a point, before he could get the money on. Thus, as he always bet on a horse the price of which was falling, there was no way of ascertaining what price the Toucher actually had received.

But to Plant's consternation Dashwood said, "Now, Toucher, look out for a stranger and leave me alone."

The Curragh was a grassy plain six miles long by two miles wide running north and south and inclining gently to the east. This inclination assured good drainage and kept the sod in the elastic condition described with Gaelic hyperbole by Plant. It also provided a natural amphitheatre with a stage set at its eastern extremity. This was the race course. Immediately around this oval enclosure were set the coaches, tents and private marquees of "owners" and wealthy sportsmen, who entertained half a countryside on the occasion of the races.

The multitude were roped off beyond the precinct of the privileged. "Jayshus, did you ever see such a day? Be Christ, if the best beast doesn't win on a day like this he'll never turn up at all!" Such exclamations, heard from the roped-off acres, expressed the contagious exaltation of the crowds.

Dublin, from its exclusive squares to its all-embracing Liberties, had poured out its thousands. Those who had no means of riding the thirty miles which lay between the city and the plain had started out two days previously.

Throughout the night before the race, "shawls"—young women whose chief and almost only garment was a shawl—lay out on the warm, firm sod unchilled by the first coldness of the moon, so closely were they packed. The Jackeens of Dublin, corner-boys, beggars, ballad-singers and vagabonds (for the word jackeen had lost its original meaning of a landless member of the class of little squires or squireens), sat up playing cards or telling stories against each other, and drinking themselves as thoroughly drunk as the members of the Hellfire Club were doing at the moment elsewhere. The lower classes were waiting for day to break, when they would stake out their claims for stands, for betting, card-playing or thimble-rigging.

In the city, the gentlemen did not think it worth while to sleep, with an early morning start before them. If a good four-in-hand could get to the Curragh of Kildare in three hours with the roads uncrowded, six hours were more likely to be spent, owing to the confusion on the roads, on this day. So they would have to start at five to be sure that they would arrive in time to greet their friends.

It was stranger than the vision of Piers Plowman to see this great plain full of folk lying like troops bivouacked before a battle, or like bodies prone after the passage of some battle-breaking lord. Here on the Curragh of Kildare lay thousands of men and women sunk in sleep. The ribaldry of the few who were "sitting out the night" and the drunken laughter or curses of the grosser sort were resented by those who, unaccustomed to the open air, were trying to snatch a night's rest.

At the edge of the massed sleepers a tinker was addressing his doxy, pleading for love which he, lacking poetry, did not name but called simply "it."

"Take yer hand out of that and go to sleep!"

"Mary, Mary!"

"Go to sleep."

"Mary, Mary! If you give it to me, I'll go to sleep. Mary, if you—"

Suddenly an impatient voice called out, "For God's sake, give it to him, Mary, and we'll *all* go to sleep."

Raucous laughter approved the sally. Then, save for the coughing of the old and ragged beggars, uneasy silence briefly settled on the plain.

Suddenly the ambrosial night was torn by perhaps the most hideous of all animal sounds, the braying of an ass, the broken silence of its endless servitude. It was answered from somewhere amongst the crazy carts that hemmed the fields on the city side. Ineffectual attempts could be heard to beat the beast into silence. A bottle crashed among the carts. Down by the course mallets thudded dully, driving in pegs for tents and booths. A night watchman was heard, driving away some pilferer. New arrivals who had started from the distant villages rattled off the road to the silence of the grass, refusing with curses importunate offers of help, and cracking whips at the vagabonds who raced along with a hand on the bridle.

Dawn touched the Hill of Allen, and soon the cheerful yellow coaches began to roll merrily into sight from the mansions around, from Castletown, Cloncurry and Clondalkin and from the city itself. They contained the house-parties held for the Races and were bright within and without with signs of good cheer. In place of luggage the coach-tops were piled high with hampers, the scraps from which would later on provide food for the famished vagabonds who hailed them with delight:

"Long life to you, Mr. Connolly!"

"And to the Missus that's to be!" an old crone added.

"Good luck to you, Mr. Lawless!"

"God blast you, Black Fitzgerald." This to the Lord Chancellor.

"Lave him alone. Isn't he coming to hang us for an illegal assembly?" Someone within the Lord Chancellor's coach raised a window, and the root of a furze bush was flung in amongst the occupants. This feat raised derisive cries and elicited mocking protests which brought to mind the ancient rules for such assemblies: that they be held "without deceit; without wounding a man."

The beggars pretended to take sides in praise and contumely; but in vain the brawling of the boors went on. Not a coin was flung amongst them from the coach.

In the tent for members, Constant stood by a long table waiting for a dish of plovers' eggs for Clemente's lunch. He was the first friend Martyn ran into when he entered the tent. Looking about, Hyacinth saw Clemente near by. He greeted her warmly as he and Constant joined her. They had come up from Dublin in separate coaches.

Hyacinth, in a preoccupied mood, took his leave of the two in a few moments.

"I will try to return to lunch when I find my own party," he told them.

But no sooner had he left the tent than he realized that Ninon, Mabs and Aunt Penelope would lunch on the roof of Sir Richard's coach. He went back and asked Constant and Clemente to join his party after lunch, seeing how uncertain it would be to find them again in such a crowd. It was evident that Hyacinth's mind was still confused over the happenings of the past week.

Now his chief concern was to find Feeney, and he set off in search of him. His box was beside the paddock. He would, most probably, be found beside his mount. It was necessary to keep guard unremittingly on the favourites.

He entered the paddock.

Denis St. George, who was with Medlicott Anderson, the trainer of Green Glint, could be seen at a bare space of the railing surrounding the paddock. A few horses were being led round. It was an hour before the first race.

Denis hailed him casually. His absence of surprise at their meeting brought home all the more to Hyacinth the realization of what a fool he had been.

Turning to Medlicott, he asked, "How is he?" There was no need to say that he was inquiring about Green Glint.

Medlicott was a tall man, straight and sallow, his head at a perpetual angle, as if the necessity of bending down to converse with the majority of mankind had fixed it there. His eyes shifted ceaselessly in a short horizontal movement as if he were examining each of his companion's eyes alternately in a single scrutiny.

His head was held over Martyn's and he answered with the solemnity of one who has weighed his judgment, in a voice as cavernous as an echo from the Sibyl's cave, "He could not be better."

The sound of the trainer's voice was so authoritative that Hyacinth hesitated to inquire again. However, he had to satisfy himself on a point of the utmost importance.

"How does he start?" he inquired.

The tall man looked down and examined Martyn's face while his own moved sideways once or twice as he shifted his balance. The effect of this was to waft away as if by a hand any cloudy doubts in Hyacinth's mind.

"He can start backwards and beat the field."

Martyn-Lynch had not the repose of St. George, who was one of those men who could companion difficult people like Anderson and yet indulge in no exchange of words at all. Anderson had the simplicity and repose of a ruminating animal. He was difficult only to highly strung men who took life in mouthfuls and could brook no delay in anything.

Denis looked carefully about him. He was about to emulate Anderson as far as he could, and give to the information he was about to impart an oracular ring, when he chanced to look behind him. There the Toucher stood examining a card which he could not read.

As Denis drew in his breath, Dr. MacDermot appeared. He nodded to the group of three, and going on without altering his pace, as if he intended to pass them with a cursory recognition quite out of character, he stopped, and drove his stick into the Toucher's ribs.

"Plant," he said firmly, "I find that the tips I paid for are common property all over the Curragh. What is the meaning of that?"

"Oh, begob, and is it yer Honour Dr. MacDermot I have the privilege to address?" the Toucher asked, and then exclaimed, "I wish to God I had that ballad-singer here who betrayed the pair of us."

"No nonsense. What has a ballad-singer to do with the leakage of information about form?"

The Toucher assumed a victimized air. "And you paying me for exclusive information," he said, as if the calamity to his integrity had come from circumstances over which he had no control. He hung his head. "The blackguard," he muttered. Then suddenly he raised his eyes and searched the crowd eagerly. "If I catch that ballad-singer, I won't leave a bone in his body sound."

The doctor was puzzled. Evidently someone had imposed on the

Toucher. "What has a ballad-singer got to do with it?" he asked, unconscious of the skill with which his wrath had been diverted.

For a second or two before answering, the Toucher searched the passing faces. Resigning himself at last to his inability to discover the ballad-singer, "Wasn't he me clerk?" he asked. "Wasn't it him that wrote me letters for me and stole the information for himself? But," he said, brightening, "he didn't steal no information on form a month ago when I sent you the early report, for I got a gossoon who is a bit of scholar to fill in the blanks for the name. Hadn't yer Honour plenty of time and to spare to get yer money on? And isn't it only this minute that the news leaked out? And much good it will do ye if ye just think. Be shortening the odds it will leave the bookmakers more money to pay ye yer ten to one."

He assumed an air of injured innocence. Suddenly collecting himself, "I think I see him!" he said, and went hurriedly away.

Owner and trainer were surrounded now and any conversation would be highly indiscreet. Eager eyes searched their faces for a hint of either confidence or concern. The inscrutable countenance of the trainer was proof against any such betrayal, and St. George's efforts to assume this protective impassiveness made his mood serious. Those who thought they could read coming events from a man's expression found their hopes drooping.

Mounted men with whips like huntsmen's kept the ragamuffins at a distance from the long line of coaches, but they could not keep the beggars' brats and the tinkers' children from crawling in underneath the coaches and uttering their piteous, whispering prayers for alms.

On an exclusive part of the great plain stood coaches filled with what wealth and fashion the land possessed. As far as the eye could see the rest of the plain was filled in a half-circle with dun figures representing a poverty and a squalor unmatched by any city in Europe. Bravely and gaily they rose against their misery, scoffing at themselves with mother wit. The deeper they were sunk in destitution, the merrier and more mocking rose their jibes.

"Brian O'Lynn," a ballad-singer began.

A whip cracked near him. He changed his tune as he fled and probably altered radically the words he intended to sing, as he shouted over his shoulder:

> "Brian O'Lynn had the pox and the gleet
> And he stank like a privy in Mecklenburg Street. . . ."

The horse guard rode down on him before he could finish his ribald song.

XXV. GLINTS

FEENEY SAT IN the dressing tent, clad in the St. George colours of gold and brown. From a peg behind him hung his golden cap. His saddle was supported on a portable saddle rest.

The tent was hot and oppressive with the odour of humanity. Its flaps were tightly laced to shut out curious eyes; its bulging walls revealed the pressure of the crowds without.

Feeney was pulling on his boots just as St. George, with Ninon, Martyn and Mabel, pulled the tent's flaps aside, entered, and tied them firmly again. The crowds were dense without and within. No one thought of airing the place, filled as it was with jockeys, owners and attendants.

At first it was difficult to see through the steaming air. Denis at last caught sight of his cap on a post. He knew that his jockey would be under it. He wanted a last word with Feeney before the race.

Feeney was pulling on his boots. He had a borrowed pair. His own hurt him when he was walking Green Glint round the paddock. He should have got them loosened over the calf of his left leg. It was too late now.

St. George said, "Good luck to you, Feeney. I have brought you a little brandy. Take a sip of it, man."

Feeney looked up. The doubt in his face was apparent.

"Doctor MacDermot's orders, you know," St. George said reassuringly. "You are probably fasting since yesterday."

Ninon patted the old jockey on the shoulder.

"Take it, it will give you strength," she said.

Mabel asked, "Have you had any food at all?"

He had tried to satisfy hunger with a few grapes, he told them, and added, "I'll be right enough, Miss, when I get out in the air."

"Damn the place, it's broiling," Denis exclaimed, realizing the effect it must be having on his man.

He held out his flask. Feeney stood up as straight as he could and, putting on his cap, extended his hand for the flask St. George offered.

Suddenly Feeney swayed and fell to his knees. The gold cap sank to the trampled, grassy floor. Feeney placed his elbow on the chair on which he had been sitting and supported himself as best he could.

Consternation seized Denis. He pushed back the would-be helpers roughly. Mabel took the brandy flask and knelt beside the jockey.

"Run to Timsey, in God's name, Miss," Feeney gasped, "and tell him not to lay a whip on him—for God's sake don't insult him with the whip. He's to keep muttering quiet-like, 'Aboo! Aboo!' in pace with his gallop. Just like that, 'Aboo!' But when he's in the straight let him lean far out on his neck and roar 'Burke Aboo!' That's better nor a whip, and God, won't he gallop! Tell him to ride high and hold hard when he bolts home down the straight. It's Burke Aboo!"

Mabel rose, her face pale.

"What's he been saying, dear?" Ninon asked.

But she did not answer. She held Feeney's cap in her hand.

"Get me out of this at once." Mabs said. "Give me his shirt. I have an important message for Timsey."

Fenney had struggled half out of the colors when he fell back again. Denis grasped the silk and cleared a passage to the door.

Mabel stooped before the canvas was fully opened and sped away on her last-minute errand to the stables.

"We cannot leave Feeney in this awful air," Ninon said.

"No, you're right, Missy. I'll get him out of it," the ubiquitous Toucher Plant volunteered.

"Hold that flap back, will you?" St. George said testily to the interloper, as he lifted the fainting Feeney into the open air.

"How am I looking?" the jockey asked at last.

The Toucher did as he was ordered but sped through the opening first, so that he might take advantage of the increase in odds that the news of a last-moment change of the favourite's jockey was sure to cause.

"Let us get him over to the coach," Ninon suggested, but her husband was so abstracted that he did not hear. "We cannot leave him lying by the tent," she insisted.

St. George was looking ruin in the eye. What if Green Glint failed to win?

"Stand back there, will you!" he shouted in exasperation, as too many would-be helpers crowded around the jockey.

The crowd repeated the order, each as if the rebuke were intended for his neighbour, not himself.

"Stand back there!"

Willing arms carried Feeney to the coach.

"Won't ye tell me, me Lady, how the race goes on?" he asked.

Ninon promised to keep him informed from her stand on the roof.

"Who is to ride Green Glint if Feeney can't?" Aunt Penelope inquired.

"His son," said Ninon.

"MacDermot, you devil, where the hell have you been?" Denis exclaimed, sighting the doctor.

"I got your message from Plant," the doctor said.

"From Plant? That fellow's everywhere! Throw your eye over Feeney. He is lying inside."

The doctor entered the coach, while the crowd milled around it.

Dainty ankles in white silk stockings could be seen as many a damsel climbed the stepladders to coach tops.

The Toucher approached Medlicott Anderson, to whom it was advisable, in the forwarding of his "business," to be seen talking.

"There's a tapering piece of stuff with a leg straight as a wand on the inside," Plant said, endeavouring to attract the attention of the trainer. "You would not think she had a knee."

Medlicott ignored Plant, who shook his head sadly as he walked away.

The Toucher had been entrusted with five guineas to "invest" as best he could while the odds on Green Glint were even. Now that his jockey was changed, he expected that the price would rise to three to one. Then he would invest. And by advancing the time of his investment when reporting to his client, he could make a little commission of ten guineas for himself—

In the coach, Dr. MacDermot had finished his examination.

"How is he?" Ninon asked from her seat on the coach top.

Dr. MacDermot said, "Can you open a hamper and give him a glass of milk and something to eat? It is starvation is the matter with him, and nothing else. Who asked him to reduce to ten stone? Green Glint could carry thirteen."

"Nothing could dissuade him. He had his heart set on giving Green Glint all the advantage in his power."

"And he left himself without power to ride."

"Ah, for God's sake, Sir!" Feeney moaned in gentle protest.

Sir Richard, who was fumbling in one of the hampers on the coach top, called down, "Can't you order him something else? Milk is about the last thing they would think of packing in a hamper."

"I would prefer to begin with milk. When he drinks that he can go on to something solid," the doctor answered.

"But where can we get milk? The race will start at any moment." Sir Richard's query was taken up by the crowd around the coach.

"Milk, is it?" a grimy tinker inquired. "Hould on there and I'll be back while you wink."

"Indeed I will hold on, placed precariously as I am," Sir Richard commented, smiling at the tinker's advice.

He threw the fellow a guinea when he reappeared with the milk.

"And now run off," he said. "A little brandy will counteract the dirt in this bottle."

When Feeney swallowed it he winced. "Ass's milk!" he exclaimed with a wry smile.

"Damme, I wish I had brought my spy glass," Sir Richard remarked. "The start is so far away, I find it hard to pick them out."

"If yer Honour would not object to me sitting on the box, I'll name them for yer Honour," Feeney volunteered.

"What about it, Doctor?"

With the leg of a chicken to give him nourishment, Feeney was helped on to the box seat.

"Where's the Master?" was his first inquiry.

"Beside us on Mr. St. George's coach," Ninon assured him.

By his tall figure Constant, standing up from the guard's seat at the back, could be recognized, though his face was averted. Hyacinth was with Denis St. George; owner and nominal owner could not bear to be separated. It had not occurred to either of them how awkward it would be for Feeney in the rival coach if his enthusiasm for Green Glint was accompanied by the defeat of Sir Richard's horse.

Half a mile away a strange medley of moving colour could be seen on the plain. It was the parade to the starting post. It was necessary, in order to get the distance, to set the start about five furlongs from the post. Under the bright silks the glossy hides shone as the handsome products of breeding moved on their slender limbs.

"Well, Feeney, what do you see?" Sir Richard asked.

"He's on the outside."

"Who is on the outside?"

Feeney, remembering that Sir Richard "had an interest," as the Toucher would say, and a very large one at that, corrected himself in time, and said:

"He's starting near the railings now. I can see your Honour's purple cap and stripe. It looks black from here."

"What the devil looks black? What do you mean?"

"The purple cap," Feeney replied. "It's hard to see."

"There's a gold cap on the outside. I can see that for myself," Sir Richard said.

"That's Green Glint, yer Honour. They're starting him farthest from the rails." And Feeney remembered how he had steered Green Glint's sire by risking his own limbs "on the rails."

"They're off!"

The best eyes in the country, younger eyes than Feeney's, caught that, and the cry was taken up by the vast assembly.

Feeney's eyes were straining now. He couldn't make out what had happened. One moment he thought that he saw Green Glint prancing sideways to the start. Then the bunch started when the starter had all but him in line. And now he was leading, if that were he, on the outside, forty yards from the railings, and with far more distance to go than a horse on the inside. He didn't undulate at all, whereas the other horses, seen afar, seemed to roll or rock like toy horses. He was chest-high as if reined in; but reined in as he was, he was still gathering speed.

"Timsey's gripping him hard," Feeney whispered. "But he cannot hold him."

"And why should he?" asked the doctor. "Isn't he eighty round the chest?"

"Where the devil is he now?" Sir Richard roared.

Quickly Feeney adjusted. "On the rails, yer Honour, on the rails."

"How can he be on the rails?" the doctor asked.

"Arrah, whist, Doctor, it's Sir Richard's horse. I'm watching it for him."

Silence hung on the assembly as the horses came into view round the first bend. Seen head on, the distances by which one led another could not be estimated. Sir Richard's horse was glued to the rails and appeared to be leading the field, as indeed he must do if his position was not to imperil his chances.

On they came, stretched out in their speed. The jockeys' intent, deathly faces, set like masks, were plainly visible to those on the coaches placed beside the finishing straight. The few sods thrown up by glancing hoofs had hardly fallen when they were gone for another circuit.

Now they were rounding the bend and would soon be far away.

"How is he going?" Sir Richard asked.

But Feeney's face was set.

"I asked you how is he going, over there. Are you deaf?"

"Flames!" was all Feeney could say.

His trance passed. "Yes, yer Honour. Going fine."

Sir Richard shook with impatience. "What is his position at the moment?"

"On the rails."

"But is he shut in? Is he leading?"

"There's nothing fast enough to shut him in."

"Hah! I can see the field now myself. They have still a mile to go. My colours do look dark in the distance. By Gad! There's a horse bolting off the track. Fellow lying on his neck. A bolter!"

"No, yer Honour, that's Timsey letting him out."

"Letting what out?"

"Flames, come on!"

Feeney stood up on the roof, forgetting himself. Again he shouted, "Flames, come on!"

It was Green Glint he adjured, Green Glint who had seemed to bolt when his jockey lay on his neck. Green Glint was now in the middle of the track, leading the field and gaining still.

The doctor squeezed Feeney's arm and whispered, "Christ!"

"Hold on, Doctor, wait till ye see him gallop. He's only beginning to stir."

"Will you ask that man to put down that chicken-bone? He is making a show of the coach," Aunt Penelope said, severely referring to the ecstatic Feeney. But there was no one to heed.

Into the straight now, leaving the field still behind the bend, came Green Glint—alone. And still he seemed to gather speed.

Out on his neck his jockey lay, head lower than the horse's ears, whip held in hand with the level reins. Green Glint flashed past, and past the winning post, and was lost in the far field.

"He's torn his cap," someone said. From the cap of Green Glint's jockey there shone a glint of yellow hair.

This was noted and forgotten. In their excitement about the next horse, the crowd raised another cheer. The horses came on now with a noise like thunder, from out of which the snarling cries of the jockeys could be heard.

Their thin rods flailed the air.

"Come on, Agincourt!" the crowd roared. "Come on, Agincourt."

"As if the race wasn't over," the doctor remarked. "Let us get down out of this," he added, unwilling to be a party to Sir Richard's disappointment. He climbed down and helped Feeney to the ground.

"God blast them sojers for bruising me knee," Feeney said, thinking of the glory of which he was deprived. Then with a change of thought, "Be Cripes, he had him leathered!" he remarked, referring to the way Agincourt's jockey rode.

"And what did I say?" the Toucher asked, appearing as though by magic beside the doctor.

"You said a damned lot of things, and the sooner you say nothing, the better," Dr. MacDermot answered, not at all pleased with what he recognized as an attempt to exact tribute for Plant's "information," now that Green Glint had won.

"Eighty round the chest, eh, Doctor?" the Toucher leered. "And the first horse to win by half a lap."

"So it was you was spying on Green Glint?" Feeney asked angrily.

The Toucher continued unperturbed: "To win by half a lap even without Feeney up—"

"Me son was up," interjected Feeney.

"There was no mother's son up. That shows what you know."

"What do you mean, Plant?" asked Dr. MacDermot.

"There was no mother's son up. Let him riddle that for himself."

"And who rode it if it wasn't Timsey?" Feeney asked, beginning to take the fellow seriously, seeing him so assured.

"Ye can ask your master that. He ought to know."

The doctor had no patience with conundrums. He said to Plant: "Come out with it, Toucher. I'm a customer of yours."

"It was Feeney's master's sister-in-law brought him home. And that makes Green Glint the first horse in Ireland to be ridden by a woman at the Curragh—and on top of that, to win."

"Holy smoke!" said Feeney. "Doctor, can you beat that?"

Ninon gasped, and left the coach, followed by her aunt and La Baronne. They hastened over to St. George's coach, but Denis and Hyacinth had already gone upon the field. The three ladies could only return and wait, in consternation and restlessness.

"It comes from the Dalys," the doctor was saying thoughtfully, taking account, as a scientific mind should, of cause and effect. Mabs was one of the Dalys on her mother's side. "It comes from the Dalys; and all the Dalys were daft."

In the press, where it was not noticeable, one horse ran riderless. Now that the jockeys were reining in past the post, empty stirrups could be seen flailing the lone horse's sides as it galloped, swerving and throwing up its head. Its rider had fallen in mid-career where there was neither help nor care for such a catastrophe.

But from the stand which the carriages formed, immediately opposite where he had fallen, he could be seen lying prone. He lay with his head slumped sideways. His face was in his cap. The arm that still retained the lash looped to his wrist was bent back over his body. He lay still.

One or two flying figures ran to his assistance, but the course-guards rode up and threw them back.

"Where is Doctor MacDermot?" voices began within the crowd. "Where is Doctor Mac?" Possibly the crowd held doctors, but they were not the doctor it wanted. The crowd wanted a man who had spent his life at race meetings and could best deal with what happened at them.

He was sighted near Sir Richard's coach. The crowd roared again. Youths ran on either side of him like acolytes, cutting a lane for his approach.

"Stand back there! Can't ye stand back and give him air till the doctor sees him?" those about the fallen rider were asking each other angrily.

The doctor arrived and knelt down. He lifted the head with its livid face. He rolled it on its neck. Fast silence awaited the verdict.

"He's dead," said Mac. "But I'll do all I can!"

Out on the field, Denis came up to Green Glint and grasped his bridle.

"Mabs, Mabbie dear!" he cried. "Are you all right?"

"Yes, of course," she said breathlessly, with a show of assurance which her trembling lips belied.

When Hyacinth caught up with them, he showed even greater perturbation than Denis, and something like anger.

"Mabel," he said in amazement, "what ever have you done?"

"I've ridden Green Glint to victory!" she exclaimed. "That's what I've done. I've saved the fortunes of both of you. Isn't anyone going even to congratulate me?"

"I do," said Denis fervently, "from the bottom of my heart. Oh, Mabs, you are the most wonderful girl who ever lived!" Catching a spark of Denis's enthusiasm, Hyacinth quickly echoed his sentiments.

As he led Green Glint in past the wildly cheering crowds, Denis turned his head so frequently to look up at Mabs that Hyacinth took the reins from him. Now Denis fairly danced along the sod. For perhaps the first time in his life, he knew the joy of being filled with pure admiration for another.

XXVI. TRIUMPHAL PROGRESS

RACING WAS GOVERNED by a committee of gentlemen and owners, not trainers or jockeys, and there was not a word about the jockey's sex in all the rules. They took it for granted, perhaps. No committee could bind you to race your horse with any particular jockey, and if that was the case, Green Glint's victory would have to be accepted.

"If I were you I'd collect on him now, before the bookies goes away back to England," the Toucher remarked to Dr. MacDermot. "If it wasn't against me principles I'd have had a bit on him myself. Thank you, Doctor," Plant ended, as MacDermot paid him off with a guinea.

"St. George is leading him in." Renewed cheers greeted the victor as he was led in, with his slender rider answering the crowd with upraised whip.

"What did I tell you?" the Toucher said, fondling the thought of his perspicacity regarding Green Glint's rider.

"That's a roan one for you, wid a heart as big as a beehive! O, bring me home!" The Gael's enthusiasm for a great horse broke out in Plant as he witnessed the stately stride of the triumphant animal. "Did yez ever hear such cheering? The change of jockeys has broke the bookmakers. We're game-ball now if Fosdyke doesn't appeal."

"And why the hell! What has he got to appeal about anyway?" Feeney asked. "Wasn't he only fourth?"

"Aye; but if the first is disqualified, the fourth will be third and his horse will fetch more when he becomes a selling-plater, don't ye see? Fosdyke is all but down and out." He tried to hurry off.

Dr. MacDermot said: "Hold a minute, will you?"

"I'd like to collect before the bookies get wind of any protest."

"Fair enough," agreed the doctor. "We'll all collect."

Against the partition that railed off the grandstand, which consisted mainly of the coaches, the bookies were lined up. They stood on boxes which gave them a preëminence above the crowds. These were the well known "Sons of Chance," who could not afford to "welsh," or run away from their responsibilities to the public, even in the disastrous event of an outsider winning at long odds.

They wore gaudy clothes: enormous overcoats or high hats in which favours were stuck or their names written on a circular band. Raucous men of open manners and liberal speech, whom no one could accuse of sanctimony. Honest they must be, and they accepted this solitary virtue with resignation because it was part of their stock in trade. Their business depended on it. Without it they would be cast out from the exclusive precincts of the grandstand. Some of them even boasted of the virtue of honesty to encourage investors. One bookmaker, for example, took bets under a pennon on which in brave letters was inscribed the legend:

"Bumbeigh never owes."

And the legend recorded a truth, because that bookmaker took the precaution to prevent any of his "clients" from winning considerable sums from him twice. If any client were lucky enough to win once he was rigidly excluded from his book forever—a method of bookkeeping which impinged on the Toucher's business considerably. You could win only once from Bumbeigh. You could lose as often as you pleased. His honour was intact.

Now the Toucher approached Bumbeigh, and produced a card. It was unnecessary. The Toucher was only too well known to Bumbeigh, but he could not be utterly ignored, for he brought so many pitchers to his well—on their last journey. Besides, Bumbeigh came to Ireland only once a year, and his losses on any one race-course could not greatly affect his year's profits.

"Yes," Bumbeigh shouted, "Yes! And the price was even until the last minute, and of course you waited until we heard that Feeney could not ride. Give him his packet." His clerk complied. "And to Hell with him!"

"Feeney or no Feeney, he'd have won even with yerself up—if ye was strapped on," said the Toucher, smiling and withdrawing.

"And now, Doctor, what can I do for you?" asked Bumbeigh. "Are you another three-to-one?"

"I am, and so is Feeney here; but I am a little more than that. I am ten to one. I dealt with you in London." And the doctor produced two tickets, Feeney's and his own.

"English correspondence will have to wait. We deal with that as we get it—that is, by mail. But Bumbeigh never owes. Give them their money, boy."

The great man got the amount of the debt inscribed on a scrap of paper, fumbled in a satchel which was in front of his belly, and produced a handful of golden guineas. Swiftly he counted them. "Count them yourself," said he, as he handed them to the doctor; and with a sing-song repetition to himself of, "A good loser, a good loser, a good loser is the best sportsman," he snapped shut his bag.

"Now, Feeney," said Dr. MacDermot, as he gave the amazed man a handful of gold, "I sent to put the money on for you when you were in the coach, and the Toucher brought me the tickets. There's enough there to keep you in your old age; but stop your thanks and give me a promise instead. Promise me that you won't get drunk until a month after you go home."

"I promise," Feeney said, after a long pause. "And in that case, Doctor, you had better keep the money for me."

It may have been his popularity, or it may have been that he was the owner of the runner-up, or both facts together, that made it impossible for Sir Richard to hide himself within his coach without giving offense to the cheering mob. He did not wish to delay unduly and to find the road barred to all but the slowest progress. He solved the problem of getting away quickly without giving offense by taking the coachman's seat and holding the reins himself. He saluted so often, with his whip held obliquely across his face, that it was useless either as a guide or goad to the horses. Returning the salvos of shouts and cheers gravely, he sat on the box-seat and directed the four-in-hand across the rolling acres of the Curragh. Sometimes the four stretched out in a trot as the way opened, and a gallus sight they looked, the four dappled grays. Then Sir Richard would stroke them gently with the whip while they maintained their even paces. Again he would lean back and straighten his shoulders as he reined them in from some sudden obstruction. Then with reins tight and tightening he would crack his whip till it sounded like a pistol-shot heard at a distance. He looked as likely a man as Nestor driving from the field.

"Eleven rounds
And nine knock-downs
And breaking his jaw bone,"

a ballad singer drawled slyly. The doggerel won him a shilling from Sir Richard. The lines referred to the victory of his protégé, Deaf Burke.

Tinkers jumped from their carts, and swerved their donkeys sideways out of the way. Strong farmers drew their cobs aside to permit the passage of the magnificent four-in-hand.

Curtly Sir Richard acknowledged their courtesy with lifted whip. And some as he passed said quietly, "A great race, your Honour!" This, coming as it did from solemn judges of horse flesh, pleased Sir Richard more than the uproarious approval of the crowd.

Within the coach the scene lacked gaiety. There sat Mabel. And Mabel was one reason for her Uncle's desire to leave the race-course as early as possible. There was a serious risk of the crowd's taking Mabel out and carrying her shoulder-high on the scene of her victory. Luckily, whenever she was recognized, it was from a carriage or high chaise in the open, when the grays were going apace.

Mabel sat with her back to the horses opposite Aunt Penelope and Madame de Ronquerolles.

"Now, do not try to run away. You cannot get out of the coach so you had better remain where you are and listen to me," Madame de Ronquerolles began.

"Listen to all those rowdies calling you by name. You might better be a play-actress than make such a public spectacle of yourself," Aunt

Penelope said, mortified by the acclaim, which even included herself, as the heroine's relative.

But Clemente felt she had to render, as it were, an account of her stewardship. She resumed:

"How often have I told you that to ride astride, even in the private grounds of Lisadill, is immodest and unbecoming to a lady, or, for that matter, any woman? And what did I see today? I saw you in the most public place in all the island, and before the greatest number of people it is possible to gather in one place, galloping—and not only galloping, but bending over in a most unseemly posture!"

"Nobody would have known me if my hair had not escaped from my cap."

"That is beside the point," Aunt Penelope said. "If you were not riding it could not have escaped."

"But what was I to do?"

Madame de Ronquerolles took turn.

"You must have known, if you had paid the least attention to me during these past months, not what you were to do but what you were not to do. Well, you should have known it. On one occasion you ran away unattended to Dublin. Had you been punished for that conduct, we would not be in the position we are today. We would be—"

"We would be in the Court of Bankruptcy," Mabs said sulkily.

Aunt Penelope knew how Martyn was situated. She had feared that his estates were encumbered beyond hope of redemption. What gentleman's property in Ireland was not held by attorneys, banks or other money-lenders? Pride forbade her to discuss it before La Baronne, her guest. Therefore she sought at once to put the conversation into another channel.

"Where was Timsey?" she asked.

"That half-wit was in the box guarding Green Glint when I came with Feeney's message. I knew that he would never understand, much less remember, what to say to the horse, in his excitement at having to ride him. I tried to tell him. He kept on chewing straw and when I asked him to repeat his father's message he looked as if he never had heard me. So I took his breeches."

Madame La Baronne screamed and clasped her arms. She bent her head down until nothing of it appeared but a range of little curls on her neck and behind her ears. Her shoulders heaved.

Aunt Penelope tried to speak. At that moment the coach was making its way through a thickly crowded part of the road. A tall man sighted Mabel. He seemed to jump straight up in the air.

"By Cripes, it's Goldie herself!" he yelled. At this exclamation the crowd almost stopped the coach. Sounds like pistol shots cleared the passage, as Sir Richard plied the whip left and right.

"A penny a peep. Tuppence a show!" shrilled a little girl, beginning an indecent catch, an echo of some old Charivari of the Dublin Liberties.

"Make way, men. Out of the way of the horses!" They made way for the horses. It is always Horses' Day in Ireland.

Mabel blushed and choked back a sob. She seemed on the verge of tears.

"What, what was I to do?" she asked her aunt. "Oh, if they only would go away and stop their shouting."

"How can they stop their shouting?" Clemente asked, her face still bent into her lap. Her shoulders moved gently.

"Some of it may be for Uncle Richard, dear," Aunt Penelope suggested comfortingly. "He is so popular."

Clemente's shoulders moved more gracefully. Had she been in evening dress they would have been a sight for the Lord Lieutenant.

Aunt Penelope asked: "What was it you said about talking to the horse?"

But Mabel shook her head. She could be obstinate. She was worn out with her day's work and with its aftermath. She thought of its implications—of all it meant for Hyacinth and her sister. She had saved Martyn Hall. She had managed Green Glint and had come to the scales without losing anything. She had hidden in a loose box that the Toucher guarded while she dressed and she had escaped as well as she could. She had had to leave her button boots, for she could not be seen carrying them, and had hidden them in the hay. She had had nothing to eat all day. She was dying for a cup of tea. And here she was, after all her efforts, being taken from the field of glory like a malefactor. Her tears dried. She was too angry and proud to weep.

"Where are we going?" she inquired at last.

"To Lucan for the Race Ball," Madame raised her head and said through a mist of tears, "at which I hope we shall all be ladies."

"I won't go," said Mabel and almost wept again, realizing the embarrassment of fame.

"And indeed it would hardly be fitting after your outrageous behaviour," replied la Baronne.

Gravel sounded beneath the wheels. The coach rolled on smoothly with a gentle whisper. Lucan House appeared with the Liffey behind it, and the coach pulled up before it. Tulip took the reins. Sir Richard slowly descended. Grooms ran up. A flunkey put down the ladder. Sir Richard let the ladies pass in silence. But when his niece appeared he took her in his arms and carried her into the house, his back braced proudly—regardless alike of his losses and his gout.

XXVII. VOICES IN THE NIGHT

CLOSE TO THE ground Roddy was tying a string. He had only one more gate to "fix" and all would be as secure as his ingenuity could make it. No one could enter the field after dark, or pass down any of the roads that led to the forge, or advance stealthily up a boreen, without fouling the string and thus giving the alarm to the boys who, under the cover of darkness, guarded the approach to the forge.

The thirty representatives appointed by the United Irishmen for the thirty districts of the county were expected to meet at the forge of Myles the Slasher this night. If, by the conditions laid down in Major Crabbe's "Proclamation," a meeting of three men constituted "an illegal assembly," what would thirty men constitute?

When Roddy had finished, he tested his handiwork. He opened a gate very cautiously. A bucket fell off a wall ten yards away with a resounding crash. If someone on his way to spy upon the forge were to find such a trap set, it would prove the guilt of all concerned. But it was no worse to be found guilty than to be found at all; for, in any case, when all assemblies were forbidden, all would be guilty of assembling illegally tonight.

Tonight was to be the last council of war.

A fiddler had ridden in with the news that a fleet had been seen off Slyne Head. It would be, with the Sou'wester gently blowing, off the Mullet and Erris Head in the morning. That did not mean that a landing would be attempted in Westport, for ships of the line could not possibly navigate shallow Clew Bay with all its islands—an island for every day in the year. If it should be sighted off Achill, it might send the troops ashore at Blacksod Bay or Broad Haven. There was, as the fiddler said, no knowing; but that was all the more reason to be prepared. The French had delayed long enough, God knew, and lost at least two golden opportunities. They were coming now. At last.

Roddy had stationed a gossoon in the centre of each of the five fields that surrounded the forge. The main road could take care of itself. Anyone coming by that would be reported at once, and the meeting would have ample time to disperse. It was in the fields that the danger lay. Any company of troops, given a guide—and a guide could be forced at musket's point to lead them—could steal up under darkness of night and surround the forge or any suspected meeting place. Against this Roddy had provided.

He whistled low. He was answered by a similar whistle. That was from the boy lying somewhere in the middle of the field. He repeated this signal in each field. From each he was answered. The boys were on the alert. If one of them failed, God help him! He would die a traitor's death. But there would be no surprise and no failure. It was a night without a moon. Roddy had to be on his way to guide the boys from the places where they were waiting. He cast a look at the forge. The door was open. Intermittently the fire flared up and sent its usual blaze into the night. That should disarm suspicion, for the first thing an illegal assembly would be presumed to do was to meet in darkness. Instead, the forge fire leaped and shone merrily.

The organization was arranged so that few of the leaders were known to one another. This was a precaution necessary to prevent unwitting or deliberate treachery. Three men were known to Roddy and each of them would have to recognize and vouch for nine men under him before they could be admitted within a mile of the appointed place.

"Is that you, Phelim?"

"It's me, Mr. Roddy, all right."

"Are the boys with you?"

"Every one of the nine of them."

"Follow me."

In this way, through the night, the leaders of the districts were gathered. They were guided by hedge and lane to the back door of the forge. Many of them had ridden thirty or forty miles. They would have to make the greater part of their way home before dawn, for their horses were borrowed and it was dangerous to travel ten miles from home without a special "permit" except on market days or on the day of a funeral. Even attendance at a funeral was discouraged by the Government. It revealed the manpower of the county to the French agents.

As Roddy led his men past each hidden sentry he would step back and whisper to him:

"Good! Now no one passes."

At last they were all assembled. But the assembly was not within the walls of the forge. The forge was but the rallying centre. The men met under a rick in the yard with the open fields all round them except for the wall of hay that hid them from the high road.

"Number!"

Myles the blacksmith, who was called "the Slasher," from his prowess with a bill hook in the fight around New Ross, and also to conceal his identity, whispered: "One, two, three!" Whispering voices answered him in Irish.

At the count of nine, a man stepped forward. He was the group captain. He had already been identified and vouched for by Roddy. The Slasher opened the meeting.

"Men of Ireland," he said, "the French are here to help us. There will be no sheering off this time. They will land tomorrow morning or the morning after. A letter came in from Clare Island this morning which was taken off the fleet by a crew of men in a curragh. The French will be on the old sod within twenty-four hours. Here is the message. It is in the French language but a good Irishman on board added his translation. It has been verified again by a friend not far from here. The two versions tally; there can be no mistake.

"The Admiral promises to put a thousand men ashore before morning. Let me explain: that means before the morning after tomorrow at latest; for the Admiral counted on the message taking two days to reach us. Little did he guess how the Mayo men can row. He expects that an adequate effort will be made by the people of this country to coöperate with those who have sailed so far to liberate them. He expects that Mayo alone will furnish three thousand men. The Executive of the French Republic will provide arms and clothing."

Silent as the company was, a sense of depression seemed to make it more silent. It was as if the sinking of its spirit brought with it something of the silence of death.

Myles the Slasher sensed it. At last he said:

"I know that this is impossible. We all know that we cannot find three thousand men. But for all that, it is better not to disappoint the French, for this is our last and only chance. If they turn back as they did from Bantry Bay, never will they come again. It is a wonder they have come this time. Now that they are here, they should be encouraged to land, and we will see when they are landed if we can raise the country to help them. I have brought you all together so that I might give you the message and take council with you. Will Number Ten speak?"

From the darkness at the corner of the rick a husky voice could be heard. Its intensity made the others fear that it might carry too far, though it was only a whisper.

"There's ninety men behind me, ninety men. In God's name let the French land. With their muskets and bayonets we'll be as good as a thousand of the English trash that's going to be put against us. What did we do at Wexford?"

Myles the Slasher said:

"We don't want history. We want to make it. You are for a fight?"

"And with ninety men, who wouldn't? All we want is the guns and we'll see to the fighting." He sat down at the end of the haystack. His dim form subsided from the dome of stars against which it had been painted cloudily like the figure of some gaunt Apocalypst.

"Ten's for fighting. Will Twenty speak?"

"Fight!" said Twenty above a whisper. "Fight!" he hissed again through his teeth.

"With how many?"

"Ninety men." Whether he sat or stood it was not possible to say. His voice came from the centre, quite close to the Slasher. To him he must have been almost visible, wearing a starry halo as he stood against the sky.

"Will Thirty speak?"

"Fight!" said Thirty.

"With how many?"

"Two hundred; and two landlords who will see us through and lead us."

"On what are ye sitting?" This was a code to ascertain where the men might be counted upon to muster, the moment the landing was accomplished. Anything over two hundred equalled in code a three-legged stool, each leg or support meant one hundred men. Thus the question, "On what are you sitting?" To those who could not bring up a hundred men and who had no "legs" the question was couched otherwise:

"Will Ten and Twenty tell me where are their buckets?"

"At Balla."

"At Killala."

"Balla, Killala and Castlebar, stand ready. Ye have spoken like Irishmen. The day for words is past long ago. The minute the French land, out in the open with ye! You won't require instructions and there will be an end to this secrecy. Only one day more, boys, and we'll see the light dawning. Till then the less said the better. Dismiss."

"Do not go," a strange voice called out of the night. Consternation seized the gathering. Some stampeded in the darkness.

Roddy's voice said hurriedly, "It's all right. It's all right. It's Father Colyer."

"On whose permit, Roddy?" Myles asked menacingly.

"Not on mine," Roddy answered in confusion.

"How did he come here?"

But before the embarrassed and suspected Roddy could reply, Father Colyer said:

"Never mind, boys, how I got here. That I got here in time to save you all is enough."

The invisible group stirred. He sensed that there would be a movement to disperse, for he quickly said:

"Stand for a moment, men, and listen to me. I ask you to think again before joining this adventure, before welcoming into your country men whom you will not have the power to put out of it if once they get a foothold. They will slaughter every strong farmer and burn every house in the country as they did in France. They will outrage your wives and sisters, for they believe in nothing. And you will not be any nearer to owning the land than you are at present. And if you fail, the English will seize the opportunity of emptying the country of all the men they do not hang, and sending them into the Fleet. You are bound to fail as you failed at New Ross."

Had Father Colyer left New Ross out of his appeal, it would have had a better chance of success. But Myles' fame was won at New Ross and to put him among the failures was more than he could bear, keyed up as he was for the coming fray. He was about to speak when the voice of Number Twenty said:

"We had no help at New Ross. We had to seize arms with our naked hands. And who wants to put the French out before they put out the English?"

"There are worse things than even the English," Father Colyer said.

"If there are that's news to me," Myles answered. "Could you tell us who they are?"

"They are ideas," Father Colyer answered quietly. "Ideas which destroy more than ever the English could or can—our Faith and our souls. Through centuries of oppression, in spite of the rack and pitch-cap, it was our proud and justifiable boast that Ireland never lost the Faith.

"I have here in my pocket an 'Address to the People of Ireland' on the present important crisis. It is written by one Theobald Wolfe Tone, no Irish name but fit for a Protestant who sought and failed to get a commission in the ranks of the English Army and went over to the French out of pique. I cannot read it in the dark, but I can assure you that this is what he says. He says that he looks upon the French Revolution as a thing which has to be; and, as all human experience has verified that the new doctrine ever finally subverts the old: as the Mosaic law subverted Idolatry; as Christianity subverted the Jewish dispensation; as the Reformation subverted Popery; so he is fully convinced the doctrine of Republicanism will finally subvert that of Monarchy and establish a system of just and rational liberty.

"Now this man, who seeks to proselytize you, and to take from you your hard-bought privilege and one which it took more courage to preserve than it takes to march behind the French, this man has compared our Holy Church, which like all Protestants, he calls in scorn Popery, with idolatry; and to promise you, if you imitate the French scoundrels who tore their own countrymen to pieces, a just and rational liberty. Do you know what 'rational' means? It means that those who were the loudest to cry it set up a common woman of the streets on the altar of the church and called her the Goddess of Reason. That is what 'just and rational liberty' will bring you to. Believe me, liberty is a mockery without God."

He paused. There was no sound from any of those on the alert. Myles the Slasher answered as well as his untutored mind could against established and ingrained ideas.

"You are wrong, Father. Wolfe Tone belonged not the English Army but to the Army of England—which is a very different thing. It is under an Irishman, General Kilmaine, and is called by the Republic 'the Army of England' because the French intend to invade England with it and has it stationed on the coast. There is another paper going the rounds that answers your objections."

"If there is that's news to me," Father Colyer said contemptuously, echoing Myles' earlier retort.

"Well, then, there is; but it means hanging, drawing and quartering to be took with it. I know where it is buried in a canister and it says this or something like it. That great pains have been taken to mislead and misinform us on the subject of the French Revolution by people who want to keep us in ignorance. These people make out that the people who killed their King and banished the landlords and plundered the clergy were a nation of furious, bloodthirsty cannibals without faith. That was only the French Government, and only for a time. They were not the French tillers of the soil, poor men like ourselves, who had to work on land, four-fifths of which was owned by the nobility and the clergy, and were loaded with rents, taxes and tithes just as we are. They now own their own farms, and can put the money to raising ten armies to beat off the kings from outside that is seeking to grind them back again. They at least own the land of their own country but we are not allowed to own the land of ours.

"No; all we can earn is sixpence a day barring Sundays and holidays and if it doesn't rain, and God knows it rains often enough; then we only get thruppence. At best we can only get six pounds a year and we has to pay two out of that for half an acre of bad land and we has to work for the owner and can't quit any more nor a galley slave chained to his oar. If we come by a cow it costs two pounds more to pay for her grazing at the edge of the big estate. Then sixteen shillings goes for a rood of potato ground, and where are we to get the manure? There's thirty shillings for an acre of worn-out land the landlord calls corn land. What with tithes and taxes at ten shillings, every man in Connaught is fifteen shillings out at the end of the year, with nothing left for clothing, firing and milk when the cow is raising her calf.

"That's what we will rise and put an end to, and not to the Faith. It did not damn the soul of America to throw England and her Hessians into the sea. Look to America and to the improvement in her condition since she asserted her independence—and on a provocation which, compared to our grievances, is not worthy to be named. She put all to the hazard, and despised every consideration of convenience when her liberty was at stake. The French helped her as they are ready to help us. They did not turn that great land into a land of atheists, nor did they seek to hold it once it was free."

"You appear to have learnt by heart another of those subversive pamphlets," Father Colyer interjected.

"See how America has been rewarded for her courage and endurance," the voice answered. "Compare her condition now with her condition before her independence, and see if every motive which actuated her in the contest does not apply to us with tenfold force.

Compare her laws, compare her Government with ours, if you can call that a Government which is the subversion of all just principle and a total destruction of the ends for which men submit to be controlled—"

"Are you the boy I christened and confirmed?" Father Colyer asked. "That will do, Heanue," he added reprovingly, using the blacksmith's given name. Again Father Colyer had make a mistake. It was a stern rule of the United Irishmen never to name a man. That was why the members of the organization protected themselves by numbers, with ten as a unit.

Myles said angrily: "We cannot have that, Father. We can have no man named."

"I do not mean to endanger you. If you cannot trust one another your efforts will not go very far. I ask you to think what disaster you are about to bring on your land by rising up to help atheists to take it. Is that what your fathers and mothers taught you? What did they pray for?"

"Revenge, be Jayshus!" hissed the voice in the dark. "My father was hanged publicly on the Bridge of New Ross. And my mother died from the sight of it. And if the French were a set of devils, which they are not, they are coming here to help us drive out a damneder set of devils which the English are. . . . And it's you that ought well to know it, that had to go to France for your learning when the English would have hanged you for saying Mass in your own country. Atheists, Moryah!"

"You could not speak to me like this in the light of day, Myles," Father Colyer said.

"I have told you before that we will have no names mentioned. Why are ye calling out our names? Why are ye here at all? And how did ye get in? Father Murphy rallied the men of Wexford and took the town last May. You come here to tell us to lie down in the dirt and let the English walk over us. Is the Church in Wexford different from the Church in Mayo?"

A musket shot startled the night.

"Steady, men. Dismiss quietly. No hurry. No panic. That was half a mile away. Follow the man who led you and disperse when he gives the word."

Many of the men had already gone when the first order to dismiss was given. There remained about half the number to be got away.

Roddy rose and said:

"Follow me, boys!"

As the boys were leaving in single file, a barefooted gossoon ran up and stood panting in front of Roddy. He was Paddy the Eye, who led the blind fiddler. His excitement at first prevented him from speaking. He pointed and caught Roddy by the arm. Myles came over and asked in a low voice:

"Who fired?"

"The sojers."

"Very well. Steady yourself. Where are they?"

"They were on the road to this house right enough until the captain met Festus the Fiddler. 'A blind man can see in the dark and he knows the roads,' the captain said. And he rode his horse over to Festus and ordered: 'Lead the way to Myles the Slasher's forge.'

" 'Is it that ye want?' said Festus. 'Is it yer horse ye want shod by the best blacksmith in the county?' he said, and he turned his horse and said, 'Follow me, gentlemen,' and led the sojers away. They were nearly here but for Festus. The officer said nothing for a while but he saw the fire. He looked around twice and without another word shot Festus through the head. He's down. He's dead. They'll be here in a minute by the road."

"Myles, we had better go into the forge which you left open and unguarded," Father Colyer whispered, "and if it will be any help to you I will stay with you and let them find us playing a game of cards. Slip away now, Paddy the Eye, and don't let them catch you."

As he spoke, from two directions the sound of falling buckets reached their ears.

"Those are my traps," Roddy said. "The troopers are trying to surround the place but they are making such a noise about it that I think these boys and myself should not be moidered by such clumsiness. We must be getting off."

Two gossoons ran up as he spoke. When Roddy learned from which fields they had come, he steered his men in the opposite direction and had them safely dispersed before daylight.

The priest and the blacksmith had half an hour to wait before the troopers appeared. Myles knew that the forge had been surrounded long ago, but evidently the captain thought it would be an excellent ruse to keep his men in position at a distance for some time, with a view to capturing late-coming conspirators before rushing the building.

"A little whiskey on the table between us will look natural," the blacksmith said as he led the priest, stooping very low, past the little window which, uncurtained, sent a beam of yellow light along the road. They took up their places on either side of Myles' table, and still there was no sound from without.

"It would look natural, too," said Father Colyer, "if there were to be a kettle simmering on the hob."

"A true word, Yer Reverence, and easily obeyed." He set the kettle on the fire and was returning to his seat when whistles shrilled in the night. Tall men—made taller by their shakos—rushed the house with drawn swords. Lieutenant Cole entered the little sitting room Ensign Cole had recently been promoted to lieutenant for distinguished service in capturing a French *agent-provocateur* (the service apparently no less distinguished for the quick release of the prisoner). Fear and the need of becoming self-reliant had promoted him far on the road of cruelty and terrorism.

"I want Myles the Slasher," he cried.

Myles said lazily, "I am Myles the blacksmith, at your service."

"Where is the meeting?"

"Here it is," said Myles. "This is Father Colyer."

"Now, I will tolerate no evasions. If you do not tell me where the secret meeting is being held, I will put a bullet through you."

"Fire away," said Myles the Slasher. "I cannot provide a meeting for you. But you are free to search the house, barn and stables and everything in the place."

He would not have spoken with such equanimity a week before, while the hay was full of pikes and nailed boards for stopping cavalry.

Lieutenant Cole hesitated. "That will be done in any case. Come out here!"

Myles, thinking he was going to his death, went out fearlessly. In the forge itself were half a dozen horses which the troopers had evidently seized or "collected" from various houses in the neighbourhood.

"I want you to recognize those horses and tell me who their owners are."

But Roddy had provided for what he had seen to be a too obvious way of betraying the whereabouts of the United Irishmen. He had forbidden them to come to the meeting on mounts from their own locality. Instead, local horses were sent to them which they could leave with their owners when they reached the appointed place. So it was quite admissible for Myles to name the owners. This he did with a readiness that quite disarmed the little lieutenant.

"There was a horse taken from Mr. Crosbie's stable this evening. Is it among those?"

"I don't see it," Myles said innocently. "I'd know it if I saw it. I shoed that one over there only the other day. The shoes are fresh, if you take a look at its hooves." It was the poor old horse of Festus Kyle.

Wavering, Lieutenant Cole said:

"Let the owners collect their beasts. There is not one of them that is not suspect and as disloyal as yourself. Even the information about a meeting of conspirators at this forge this very night was sent to us as a decoy. The meeting is somewhere miles away—that is, if there is any meeting. How do you account for these horses being tired?"

Myles examined them very carefully. He stood back and raised the wick in the lamp.

"There's many ways of tiring horses. The first way would be a long journey. The second way a short, but swift, race. The third way, a slow funeral. Do you know of anyone who died lately in these parts?"

The speech was bold in the extreme but so incapable was the

imagination of the conceited little lieutenant of grasping the enormity of such impertinence that he was taken in by the apparent innocence of Myles' remarks.

"Have you a horse for me, or must I walk?" asked Father Colyer, coming through the back door of the forge at the moment when the lieutenant was pondering whether to give up the quest or take Myles into custody. He decided that with the blacksmith left at large, his forge would yet prove to be a meeting place. The cool inquiry of Father Colyer gave the additional air of ordinary and accustomed business to the place and saved the blacksmith from further molestation.

As he went on his way in the growing light, Father Colyer came across the body of Festus Kyle, the Fiddler, who had led the troops away from the forge. His eyes were still fixed on the sky as they had been in his life, by Death made no darker now.

Kneeling beside the body, he realized that the fiddler's murder was due to the fact that when he led the soldiers away from the forge his imagination failed to picture—how could it?—that there might be a glow from the furnace through the open door which would mark the forge to anyone with the slightest acquaintance with the locality. Gently he closed the eyes of the blind man who had died the heroic death of a patriot.

It gave him some consolation to think that the first light on which those eyes would open would be the Light Supernal, unsullied by the memory of substantial things.

XXVIII. TIGER ROCHE UNCORKS THE WINE

"Damn it, man, not like that! That's no way to uncork a bottle of port. The cork of a bottle as old as that should be knocked off with three or four gentle taps with a knife without disturbing it. You have shaken the whole thing up with your awkward corkscrew. . . . No! No! Bring another bottle—and bring it gently in its basket."

The flunkey, a new servant of the Hellfire Club, left the room in some confusion. He was only beginning to learn how many mistakes there were left to be made in this deceptive world. Sir Richard looked up from his chair and saw Tottenham. In pursuance of his remarks he said:

"I've seen many a fellow shootin' the top off a bottle: as good a way as another if you don't shake the bottle when standing it up."

Tottenham drawled, "That would require good shootin.'"

"Tut," said Sir Richard. "All depends on the range and the amount of wine already in the marksman. There's hardly a man in the house who could miss the neck of a bottle at ten feet by good candle-light and a bright background."

"I will blow it off for you with the greatest pleasure," said a tall, broad-faced man with brown eyes as gentle as those of an Irish setter. He was dressed in a coat of brown velvet, a long flowered poplin waistcoat and brown velvet knee-breeches which displayed pillar-like legs. He did not bow as he addressed Sir Richard. His manners were somewhat casual.

"No, thank you, Roche. Later on in the evening, perhaps, when the whole place will probably be blowing itself up. You may have duty to do on an evening such as this, when every ruffian is at large. Save your powder."

"The smell of burnt powder goes badly with port," he said sadly. "As for duty, I have backed myself for ten thousand against twenty to bring Larry Dooley, the highwayman, into the room within one month." Then, lurching his body, the burly fellow turned away.

The hilt of his sword was peculiarly fashioned. It was more heavily made than the swords usually worn with dress. It was made to fit a broad hand, and was meant to be a serviceable weapon, not an ornament.

"Now give me that," Sir Richard called to the returning flunkey who was unfamiliar with the nice conduct of port.

Wrapping the neck in a napkin in case of accident, Sir Richard tapped the neck of the bottle with a table knife, turning it slowly, with the touch of an expert. The part of the neck that contained the cork came off at the ridge. Sir Richard examined it.

"Just as well I did it. Look at the cork. It was mouldering; and just think what harm a screw driven through that stuff would do." Tottenham appeared to be much impressed; so much impressed, indeed, that Sir Richard invited him to join him at table.

"Thanks," Tottenham said. And when his glass was filled, he added: "What a surprising race!"

The thousands of guineas which Sir Richard had lost through the amazing enterprise of his niece were now counter-balanced by the glasses of port which he had imbibed. He was in an expansive and forgiving mood. Any enmity he felt was for his trainer, who was said to have made a "packet" by backing the horse of the rival stable.

"Surprising is the word, sir," he replied. "The first time a lady jockey ever rode in such a classical event as the big race of the Curragh. Or rode anywhere," Sir Richard added complacently.

"That is what makes it so futile for Fosdyke to lodge his appeal," Tottenham said.

"Quite so, quite so. There is no rule to prevent that of which nobody ever dreamt," Sir Richard said. "If it comes to protests, I have the first right to lodge one and you have the second. Damned ungallant it would be. Wouldn't think of such a thing." Sir Richard did not like Fosdyke.

Fosdyke talked unpleasantly about women, and his exhibitions before the members of the Blazers with country girls after a hunt supper were not to be described. They were more than men of the old school could stomach. He was not much of a sportsman. At cards he won consistently, too consistently. He could not be a good loser. And even Bumbeigh could tell you that a good loser was the best of sportsmen.

"I don't see how the stewards can act," Sir Richard continued. "So much money has been paid out already and there is no way of recovering it. Bookies would avoid the Curragh if my horse were declared the winner and they had again to pay on it. And what would become of Irish racing if there were no betting?"

Tottenham looked down at his silver shoe buckles.

"I lost ten," he said. "I'm afraid I lost Hazelwood."

"Ten thousand?" Sir Richard said. "So did I. But whoever heard of a fellow being ruined by gambling?" he asked, laughing at his own preposterous conceit. "That fellow on the wall there ought to be an encouragement to us all."

"Buck Whaley?" Tottenham asked, looking at the portrait of the Prince of the Bucks.

"None of us has been imprisoned yet for debt. He was, and yet for all his extravagance, he is said to be worth a hundred thousand." Sir Richard laughed. His spirits were lightening at the thought of the greatest gambler the century had produced, and especially at the thought of an exception to all moral maxims. "'These are our failures,'" he quoted to himself, thinking of Whaley's valet's proud allusion to a trayful of cravats which had not folded satisfactorily and so were being discarded. Sir Richard applied it to his lost bets. "Where is Martyn?" he asked. "I must congratulate him on his winnings."

"Coming along after the ball," said Denis St. George, who had been sitting quietly at the table in a mood of pleasant abstraction. In his mind's eye was the image of Mabs as he had led her from the field on Green Glint. "He won't be here for hours."

"See him before morning," Sir Richard said. Then to a man who was snuffing candles: "Tell the butler I wish to speak to him." To St. George he said, smiling: "Have we time for another bottle of this excellent wine?"

The butler could be trusted to open a bottle that had a dosed cork. As they were enjoying the wine a tall, stooped man, richly but carelessly dressed, came walking through, rather than into the room. He wore his travelling clothes. He was sandy-haired and carried himself with a stoop, as if he were near-sighted. His calves were long and he set them wide apart as he walked. He scanned Sir Richard and, as he caught his eye, nodded to him. He nodded also to St. George and swinging on his heels went into one of the rooms. Presently he emerged and passed through another door. He emerged again.

"Ha, ha! My muddy vesture," he exclaimed by way of an excuse for his travel-stained costume.

"What the devil are you doing, Domville? Have you become a catchpole or a bumbailiff? Come and sit down and have some port."

The tall man turned and said excitedly:

"I am looking for Tiger Roche. Have you seen him anywhere? He was here a moment ago. I have been robbed and there may still be time to catch the thief. Where is Tiger Roche?"

"Oh, if you have been robbed, all the port in the world won't comfort you. You will insist on fussing. Cannot you sit down and compose yourself? You can send someone for the Tiger. Now tell us your tale."

But the tall man was in no mood for narrative. He walked over and kicked a log in the open grate. He opened a window, and seeing the effect it had on the candles, ordered a man to shut it again. Aimlessly he wandered about the room.

"My father lost a trunk full when the Buck returned from Jerusalem," Tottenham said.

"Who the Hell has returned from Jerusalem?" Denis St. George called across the table.

Fearing that Sir Richard might resent the interruption, Tottenham accepted it and answered:

"Buck Whaley. Not either of us."

"The fellow who played hand-ball against its walls and challenged the Grand Turk," Denis said, with admiration for the Buck shining in his face.

"Think of challenging the Grand Turk to a duel!" Tottenham raised his glass to the portrait of a full-eyed man with a lobed nose who stared dully at them from the wall. On the tablet beneath it was inscribed "Jerusalem Whaley."

"I am an older man than any of you," Sir Richard said, "and I lost a little on that bet eight years ago."

"What were its terms, Sir, do you remember?"

Flattered by the opportunity to show his powers of memory, Sir Richard said:

"Its terms were these. He was to walk to Jerusalem, play hand-ball against its walls, and return within the space of two years. Of course he was permitted to take ship where he could not walk."

"But the duel, Sir?"

"Seems that he omitted to get a permit or firman or whatever it is called, from the Sublime Porte, so the Sultan had him arrested. When asked for an explanation of his conduct, he offered to give the Turk satisfaction as any Irish gentleman would. He produced his brace of pistols and extended the case to the Grand Turk.

"At first the Turk thought they were a present and he began to admire the chasing on the locks. Then, when they explained the meaning of the gesture and interpreted the Code of Honour to him—broke the news as it were—he jumped up and exclaimed: 'What! Do you mean to say that in your country you give your enemy a gun to shoot you? You must all be mad!'

"The Grand Turk found it hard to understand this custom of Christian gentlemen. He knew that the Christians were peculiar people; but when he learned of the custom of duelling, he thought that not only was it dangerous, but self-effacing and more suicidal than chivalrous."

"They exchanged presents, I believe?" Tottenham asked.

"Oh, they got on very well together, by all accounts. Playing hand-ball against the walls of the Holy City may have raised the Buck in the opinion of the Sublime Porte and counteracted the effect produced by the account of his other Christian practice. Judging by the gems he gave him, the Grand Turk must have thought that the Buck was a good fellow. And Whaley admired the Turk and loved paynimry ever after."

"But he is a Christian?" Denis asked.

"Well, yes," Sir Richard assented. "But he never lets that affect him. Talk of the devil!" he exclaimed, as the subject of their discourse came out of one of the card-rooms. "Here, Whaley," Sir Richard called. "Come and join us—you know Tottenham and St. George? Of course you do. We were talking about your journey. What was it that struck you most when you were travelling through the Holy Land?"

The Buck glanced at the members of Sir Richard's party. His eyes smiled, though his face remained unmoved, almost sullen. It was an impertinent and haughty face.

"I think I was most amused by my man's disappointment. He used to stare at the landscape. After a day or two he asked:

" 'Sir, are there *no* gentlemen's houses?' "

When they ceased laughing, Sir Richard asked: "The same fellow, I presume, who was proud of your failures?"

"Must be. They don't leave me. I am resigned to them by this time." Catching an eye on his portrait, the Buck added:

"I am resigned to that, too. The honour you did me by having it painted compels me to bear up." He refused wine, explaining that he had to find a partner and then join his friends.

"I would give an arm to have been his second if he had succeeded in calling out the Grand Turk. By Gad!" Denis exclaimed. The incongruity of the situation was too much for him.

"And yet the Turks invented chivalry," said Tottenham, thinking of the Soldan. "But he couldn't get the idea of honour being satisfied."

"Then," Sir Richard resumed, "to show the Buck what he did with his enemies, he called for a criminal, sent for his silver hammer and, ordering the poor wretch to lie across his knee, he proceeded to break his spine. 'A much better way than giving your enemy a pistol with which to shoot you,' he remarked as he did so."

"Ugh," St. George exclaimed, "what a brute!"

"Nevertheless he let the Buck go. He is probably puzzling out to this day what the Buck meant."

The place was beginning to fill up with those who preferred drinking and dicing to the gentler excitement of the company of the fair sex. Silk stockings, plush coats and powdered wigs coloured the club-rooms like a miniature Versailles.

Sir Richard took a pinch of snuff from a capacious snuff-box composed of the hoof of Burke Aboo which stood on the centre of the table. He was struck with the idea. Turning to St. George he slid the snuff-box over the darkly grained mahogany.

"That is the hoof of a Curragh victor that was owned by an old friend of mine," he said. "You must get one of Green Glint's shoes mounted in gold and present it to the Club with the date and details of the race."

"I will have one cast solid," Denis said. "Thank you, Sir, for the idea."

On catching sight of the tall wandering man, Sir Richard exclaimed: "Dammit, Domville, sit with us. One would think that you were suffering from St. Vitus' Dance."

This drew no smile from Domville, so occupied was he with his own affairs.

"What the devil did you lose?" Tottenham drawled.

"He lost nothing on the races, I'll warrant," Sir Richard growled. The tall man stood behind Tottenham's chair and looked at Sir Richard. "Tell us now the how, what and where of the outrage," said Sir Richard, with a smile that deprived the adventure beforehand of any tragical or momentous significance. "What was it you lost?"

"A piece of paper. . . . Nothing that would mean anything to you." He moved his legs uneasily. "Where is Roche?" he asked again.

"How the devil do we know? He is not at this table. That you can see. Go out and take off your riding boots and then come and join us,

Domville. That is," Denis added, "if you are not exercising total abstinence or any new foible."

"Perhaps if you come along later we can make up a little card party," Sir Richard said, smiling.

The invitation had the effect of a dismissal. When the restless fellow had gone, Sir Richard asked:

"What do you think he meant with his 'something that would mean nothing' to me? A salesman's list of kitchen utensils?"

"He may have meant, Sir, that you cannot read or write."

"Oh, damme, hardly that!" Sir Richard said, then added: "Though I am not so sure. For all his foibles he is the greatest writer since Brinsley Sheridan."

"Well, here's to the contemplative life!" Tottenham said, laughing.

The moment was an unhappy one for his remark. Through the open door of a card-room, shouting voices could be heard distinctly.

"Damn your objection, Fosdyke. It was won by a furlong."

"It was won by a hoyden, Sir. And well you know it."

Sir Richard rose to his feet. He crossed the floor with surprising agility. He held the door of the card-room open.

"Was that your voice I heard, Sir?" he asked sternly.

"It was, and what the devil has it to do with you?" Fosdyke answered.

"Only this, Sir. You have called my niece a hoyden."

"Listeners never hear good of themselves," Fosdyke said with a sneer. Tottenham and St. George, who had followed Sir Richard, now stood beside him. To each he turned. In turn they nodded.

"My seconds will wait on you, Sir."

Sir Richard resumed his seat and ordered another bottle.

"And you damned well deserved it," the first voice said to Fosdyke. "She is a brave, sweet lady."

"She should remember that," was all Fosdyke said.

"You can get someone else to represent you. I will not." The voice spoke again.

When an unpopular man leaves a room, the company takes on new life. Thus it was that when Fosdyke called for his coat, gloom seemed to be lifted from the clubhouse.

"I'll tell you what we will do," Tottenham suggested.

"And what is that, Sir?"

"Just this, Sir Richard. It is simplicity itself, and calls for no skill, thought, calculation or any pestiferous thing of that kind. We will play as Buck Whaley used to play when he could no longer see the pips on his cards."

Sir Richard smiled.

"I have played with him," he said. "Let's get a dozen or so of the members to join us. A-hundred-guinea squares?" he asked. "I'm ready."

Servants cleared the furniture from one of the rooms. White chalk squares were drawn on the broad, waxed deal floor-boards, along the walls. A delicate table, a small card table made by Sheraton and worthy of a nobler end, was carried into the centre of the room. The twelve players who had agreed on effortless and honest play each placed a pile of coins—one hundred guineas in each pile—in the middle of the table. The piles were all of the same height: no need to count when gentlemen were playing. The odd man out was to be Master of Ceremonies, or, as Whaley called him, "The Keeper of the Mint."

"Leave me out; I can't kick for the gout," Sir Richard prayed. "Is that agreed? It cannot make a difference. Any Mint Master will do."

"Agreed," they echoed.

Tottenham was chosen.

"Now, gentlemen, to your posts," he ordered. Each player stood in a chalked-out square. "When I kick, I'll dive for my square before the shower descends. Are all you gentlemen ready? Stand as close to the wall and as steady as you can so as to let the coins fall off." With that, he took a flying kick at the table. One thousand two hundred guineas went flying up against the ceiling and spreading sideways against the walls. Tinkling against the crystal candelabra they fell, recoiling off the pictures, showering over the players in the extravagant game. One guinea sizzled in the waxen grease of a taper in a wall-sconce and stuck fast. One or two were held aloft behind picture frames or over the curtain valances. These would be shaken out later or left there for the servants.

At last the shower of gold subsided, leaving three pieces on the table from which they had flown.

When all had come to rest the member with the fewest coins in his square acted as teller. It was not Tottenham, for Tottenham had won.

"I've seen the Buck lose a hundred thousand when every guinea represented a hundred, and win it back again," Sir Richard said. "What about another round? We can use the coins again."

A commotion in the great dining room interrupted the game. The door opened. Tiger Roche, holding the Toucher by the back of the neck, inquired:

"Has anyone seen Domville?"

"He was with us but a moment ago," Sir Richard said.

"Save me, Sir Richard!" the Toucher whined.

"And from what, pray?" asked Sir Richard with a smile.

"That has not yet been determined," said the Tiger. "We will give him a fair trial in the guest-room. In the absence of the plaintiff, I think I will have a bottle of port," he declared languidly. "Who would like the honour?" he asked with a strange smile.

Many members ordered it together and the butler fetched it quickly.

"This Sensitive Plant," Roche said, indicating the Toucher, "will act as my cup-bearer. Over there with you, against the fireplace, and do not shake the bottle, or my hand may shake with the next shot. Just like this—" he said, as he held the bottle at a gentle angle. "And you will hold the glass there—just so— A little less trepidation, if you please. . . . Now, then!"

But the Toucher could not hold bottle and glass without trepidation. Seeing this, the Tiger turned to Dashwood and asked: "Might I have the honour of your confidence and invite you to hold the glass?"

"Vastly obleeged, I'm sure," Dashwood answered in his English drawl, and he took the glass from the trembling Toucher and held it where he expected the wine to flow.

The Tiger fired. The bottle was decapitated. The wine poured into the glass Dashwood held. "That will do. Don't spill it, man," he said to the Toucher, who forgot in his agitation to raise the broken bottle. "What ails you, fool?"

"I'm cut to the bone," the Toucher said as he began to suck a finger which a splinter of glass had scratched. If he sought sympathy, he found none.

" 'Cut is the Plant that might have grown so straight,' " said Domville, entering.

"What do you say?" Sir Richard asked. "Is he hurt?"

"No. It's only a quotation from an old play, with 'plant' for 'branch.' "

"That deserves a bottle of the best," Dashwood remarked as he carried the glass to the table.

"Thank you. I am being served," said Tiger Roche.

"Have you recovered my property?" Domville asked.

"What property? I have searched him. There is nothing in his possession but some faintly cancelled betting tickets."

"Oh, what has he done with my poem?" Domville inquired disconsolately.

"Produce the poem, please," Roche drawled to Plant.

"I haven't got it. You took it with my pistol."

"Now, now!" warned Tiger Roche.

"It's in the barrel of it, yer Honour. I was keeping it for my financée," the illiterate wretch confessed.

The effect of this was decisive. It completely mollified Domville. His anger turned into clemency for one who had such an appreciation of high poetry that he stole it first and then tried to smuggle it out of the stagecoach and use it to advance his suit. A servant brought the Toucher's pistol from the pocket of the Tiger's greatcoat. A piece of paper tightly rolled was extracted from it.

"Is this your property?" the Tiger asked.

Eagerly Domville grasped the paper and unrolled it.

"Egad, it is!" he exclaimed and smiled with satisfaction. Still smiling, he turned to the company and inquired eagerly with an inviting smile:

"Would you care to hear it? It is an address to a love-sick maiden who is supposed to be living in an inaccessible castle and pining for her swain. If I have your permission I will—"

"Oh, damme, Domville, is this the time for love poetry, with all its amorous blandishments?" asked Sir Richard testily.

"Begob! Sir Richard, you took the very words out of me mouth!" said Toucher Plant.

At that moment Hyacinth entered and said:

"Oh, yes it is! It is the time for amorous blandishments."

He came resplendent from the Race Ball. He pirouetted on his toe and said: "We cannot have too much love poetry on this occasion." He waved the port aside. "Brandy, please. This occasion demands brandy and a love poem."

"But not one of Domville's," Tottenham said.

"What the devil is wrong with you?" Sir Richard asked.

"St. George is about to have a step-father!"

"He seems to have all the luck," Sir Richard commented, turning to St. George.

"Do be serious, Hyacinth," Denis said.

"I wouldn't take it as if it were a calamity. I have the permission of the happy couple to announce their engagement. Here's to Colonel le Chevalier d'Estournelles and Madame Ellice St. George, the betrothed."

"He's a fine swordsman," said Tiger Roche.

"There was something symbolical in the shower of gold after all," commented Tottenham, pensively. "Think of a courtier of the descendant of Le Roi Soleil finding a lady in the remote fastnesses of the West."

"Oh, so damned remote they are—are they?" St. George said, smiling. "Wait until you visit us at Attymon House and you will see that it is the centre of the known world."

Member after member gathered in. Such a toast was a rare thing in the Club upon the Hill, as they euphemistically called their meeting-place in the Dublin mountains.

"A winner and a wedding!"

"Egad," Domville said, "I have another little poem here which would suit this occasion. If you stop that noise I will recite it."

Sir Richard winced. Seeing his grimace Tottenham asked:

"Is there anything amiss, Sir?"

"This damned gout is back again."

Concern overcame Tottenham's countenance. "But you will not be able to stand to Fosdyke in the morning."

"I will fight him from my chair. I've had to do it once before from this same pestilential thing. See that you provide for it. And find out if it suits Fosdyke's seconds to fix the time after the cocking main in the morning. The later in the morning, the higher is the sun and there need be no tossing for positions."

On hearing the instructions, a bland smile overspread the broad face of Tiger Roche. He bowed to Sir Richard:

"May I have the honour of offering my services, Sir?" he said.

"No, no. I have seconds; but I'll tell you what you might do, Roche. You might second Fosdyke. He will find it hard to get anyone to act for him. It would be a pity to let a fight fall through for the want of seconds."

"Delighted," the Tiger exclaimed. "Of course, you will bear me no ill will?"

"Nonsense, man. Of course not. I shall be vastly obliged."

XXIX. SIR RICHARD "BLAZES"

THERE IS A long island to the north of the Liffey's wide estuary, known as the North Bull. It corresponds to another similar bank of sand on the opposite side, off the Rocky Road to Dublin, which is called the South Bull. The northern of these sand banks was chosen for the meeting. Nearby, the coaches could be concealed under the leafy lanes of Clontarf, while the principals and their friends could pass over a rickety gangway at low tide to the long southern shore of the island, which concealed any occupants of its lonely beach from the highway by its dunes.

Secrecy was of the utmost importance. If a word were to leak out, and any but those concerned in the duel to assemble, it would bid fair to spoil the meeting. This was true of any meeting, and it was all the more necessary to exercise the greatest precautions in preventing any intrusion upon a duel between members of the Hellfire Club.

Therefore it was taken ill by Sir Richard's friends that Fosdyke should have invited the most fashionable surgeon in the city to attend on him while he fought. There were those who were of the opinion—and did not hesitate to express it—that by so doing Fosdyke hoped that the publicity which might be aroused by the fight would come to his aid and spoil the meeting. If that were his hope, there were two things he failed to realize: one, that Sir Dominick himself had "blazed" and was well aware of the importance of secrecy, and, two, that the etiquette of the Faculty was no higher anywhere than in Dublin and that gossip about those who consult a doctor is forbidden by medical etiquette.

Sir Richard had said, "MacDermot will do." And that doctor was unlikely to be unprofessional. The fact that he had attended more race meetings than patients made it unlikely that, even if he were seen in a coach at sunrise, anyone would conclude that he was bound to a duel. It was more likely that the observer would take it for granted that the doctor was returning from a race meeting rather than setting out to a meeting of another kind. It was said of him that although he may have lost members of the human race, he never missed a horse race. MacDermot's presence would cause no suspicion. It was a different thing with Sir Dominick. Were he to be seen in a coach with other occupants leaving town of a morning, the secret would be out. News would travel quicker than a horseman, and the ground would be filled beforehand by those undesirable spectators who are ubiquitous.

Sir Dominick drove to the rendezvous alone. MacDermot followed him in a borrowed chaise. The Tiger's coach was rarely followed. It was known that he would not brook inquisitiveness on the part of friend, foe or stranger. Fosdyke was as safe from prying eyes in the deep chariot of Mr. Roche as if he were already coffined in a hearse. To Fosdyke, the very depth of the coach was disquieting. It filled him with a sense of close obstruction. The feeling that there was no escape and no way out, save by the ordeal of putting his life in jeopardy, was increased. The best he could hope for would be a harmless wound. The human body, though large, was not large enough to afford much of its surface that was not dangerous to wound. A bullet in the region of your fob, for instance, was almost certain to prove fatal. It was better to be shot above the waistline than below it, even though this region included the heart and head. Below meant a wound in the abdomen and men died, lingeringly, from fever, after being wounded there. It was not that Fosdyke lacked courage, but it was impossible not to take things like this into consideration when you were taking an even chance on your doom.

He would be better when he reached the field. He always felt better in action. Here in this gloomy coach there was a funereal and oppressive atmosphere. It travelled so silently. The very blandness of his second began to get upon his nerves. And the things about which Roche spoke with such assured satisfaction were disconcerting in the extreme. For instance, there was nothing reassuring (except to his second) in the fact that Roche had set up half the night moulding bullets in the mould provided with each brace of pistols, and oiling the weapons fastidiously. "I greased the leathers myself," he said, as if that provision for making a bullet fit more tightly in the barrel was something from which Fosdyke could derive comfort, and for which he should be grateful to his solicitous second, who seemed to expect some acknowledgement.

Fosdyke felt that Roche resented the presence of Trulock, the gun-maker, who was sitting beside his coachman outside on the box seat. It was quite true. Roche resented it because he feared that it might draw attention to his carriage and give an indication to the inquisitive as to its mission; and also because he felt that Fosdyke's insistence on bringing an "armourer" was in some sort a reflection on the loving care with which he had treated the weapons overnight. But he suffered this undesirable addition to the field, for he realized that the armourer was introduced less as a reflection on his skill and solicitude than as an attempt on Fosdyke's part to show those at the meeting that he was not reduced to only one "friend," and that a person with whom he was known to be barely intimate.

That Roche was thinking about Trulock was made evident when he said, "If you prefer my pistol to Trulock's, it is my duty as your second to tell you that you must grasp it firmly, in spite of its hair trigger. When a man is shooting with a hair trigger he is apt to hold the stock of the weapon lightly. This is a fault. It should be grasped as firmly as a horse pistol, otherwise it may cast upwards a little and spoil your work and thus bring discredit and opprobrium on you. For instance, if you intend to shoot your man through the neck—where death is certain, instantaneous, bloodless and probably painless, for his spine is shot through—and you do not hold your weapon correctly, you are liable to shoot him through the mouth. This is disfiguring. Relatives find it hard to forgive a man for mutilating his adversary. This accident happened to me. It is a thing I do not wish to see repeated. Therefore, I say to you, a firm grasp and a light forefinger!"

The great coach bowled along.

They came from under cover of the trees. They reached a space from which the Bay was visible.

The coach came to a halt.

"It's a pleasant morning for a duello," said the Tiger, cheerily. "This is where I usually leave the carriage." He put a fine brass-bound mahogany box under his arm as he spoke.

"Trulock had better carry this," he said, and added in a loftier tone, "for the sake of appearances."

"Will you be pleased to hand me the mallet and the pegs?" He led the way down from the wood to where the seaweed met the short, coarse sea-grass among the small black flints of the beach.

They crossed over to the island by a gangway made of planks fixed on tarred piles.

Soon they came to the place from which it was possible to see the southern shore of the island. A long beach of powdered sea-shells and firm sand spread endlessly, as it seemed, to the east, and appeared to reach to the Hill of Howth, which was still shrouded with the unrisen mists of dawn. To their right, as they advanced. the leaden sea lipped the firm sands and ran far in over the level shore.

"They are here before us, I perceive," Roche remarked, as a little group came into view. "I have always found Sir Richard punctual. It must have caused him considerable pain this morning to put his foot to the ground."

"Good God!" thought Fosdyke. "What kind of second have I got, who is condoling with my opponent?" Yet the Tiger only gave credit where it was due.

One hour earlier, "Easy, easy, Tulip!" Sir Richard had groaned, as that careless fellow had squeezed Sir Richard's foot between the chair leg and the door of the carriage.

It was not Tulip's fault. He could not see from the back what the coachman was doing, as between them they lifted Sir Richard's seated form into St. George's coach, which had been selected for reasons of greater secrecy, in preference to Sir Richard's too well-known chariot.

"It's when I lower the foot that it pains like the very Devil," he explained to Tottenham. "No, no! Don't raise it. I shall have to keep it lowered if we are to get on with this business. This must be the second time I have had to fight from my chair. Let me see. . . . There was Jocelyn Lucas; and there was another fellow, a member of Madmenham, who suggested that I was trying to evade a meeting by pretending to have an attack of gout. I suppose that he thinks differently now." Then he added reminiscently: "He never heard of a fellow fighting from a chair. Tried to object. His seconds over-ruled in my favour, as became gentlemen. 'Just like an Irishman!' was all they said. That was in England. It is nothing to be astonished at over here, of course. That is why I asked Roche to second Fosdyke. No wriggling out of a fight when the Tiger is your second. He will not hear of exception being taken to my chair. Wonder is that Fosdyke did not insist on 'Advance and shoot at will!' " Sir Richard took a drop of physic which was prescribed for the purpose of baffling the gout. Then he continued:

"Talking of seconds, Roche is the most thorough second a fighting man could desire. Remember when old Matthias Burke had his shooting arm broken and had Roche hold it up for him to continue the fight, Roche took a damned serious chance of being wounded or killed himself, for Burke's opponent was shooting rather wildly, being also in great pain."

"Is it somewhat the same idea that makes you carry a second chair on the roof, Sir?" St. George asked. "Do you expect to have the first one blown away?"

"No. No. It is at Roche's suggestion that I bring a chair the fellow of this one, so that if Fosdyke objects to a man fighting without standing, he can have any advantage he thinks I have in being seated. I think that we have forestalled Fosdyke prettily." Sir Richard twisted his mustache and added, reflectively, "I think that we have thought of everything."

But Sir Richard and Roche between them had not thought of everything. They had not thought of the legitimacy of Fosdyke's possible objection to the presence of body servants on the field of honour. It remained for Tottenham to think of it.

"We two shall have to carry you," he remarked, realizing the certainty of this objection.

"I have Tulip and the coachman."

"Tulip and your coachman have no business on the field. It could be argued that if a man were to bring his servants—"

"Damme," interrupted Sir Richard, "you're right. But, gentlemen, I never intended that such an imposition should be placed on you."

"There is no other way but to carry you on."

"You will not have the duty, should misfortune occur, of carrying me off!" And Sir Richard smiled grimly at the joke at his own expense.

Between them, his friends carried Sir Richard as expertly as porters carry a sedan chair. This accounted for the mysterious arrangement of the footprints that so puzzled Roche and Fosdyke as they approached the field.

"Stretcher bearers," Roche suggested, with so little awe in his voice that a cold shudder went along the spine of his principal.

"Somebody's been fighting here before us?" Fosdyke asked.

"If so," said Roche, "they have carried him off in the wrong direction."

Then they saw the group ahead of them on the sea shore. They passed Sir Dominick, who walked in the shelter of a sand bank. He was carrying a dark instrument case under his arm. They passed, but they did not hail him. It was the convention of the code that the surgeon be called in to render assistance if necessary after the fight. It was to be presumed that he knew nothing about it beforehand. He could not be a party to it.

With this observance, the formalities began. Apart from the Code of Clonmel there was an unwritten law pertaining to duelling. Everything must be conducted in the most leisurely manner. There must be the strict observance of punctilio. As they proceeded they passed Dr. MacDermot sitting on a huge chest. He had borrowed the outfit of a ship's surgeon. His own instruments, such as they were, were far away in County Mayo.

"You would think that he was attending an execution, waiting to draw and quarter," said Tiger Roche laughingly.

The group was closer now. Two figures leaning over a third were silhouetted against the rock, still in the shadow of the Hill of Howth's southwestern shoulder. These were Sir Richard, Tottenham, and his friend St. George. All the long expanse was vacant save for the lonely figure of a cockle-gatherer, in the distance, retreating with his creel from the wet sand which lined with a firm surface this side of the island.

"My friends, if you wish to rest, you can set me here. I see Fosdyke's second approaching." But Sir Richard's friends carried him on until his opponent's second signalled. It was not etiquette to bring principals within earshot of one another. St. George returned to Sir Richard, while Tottenham and Roche consulted alone. Fosdyke was left standing solitary, apart against the growing light, his armourer standing between him and his second.

After a few minutes' conference the seconds proceeded to pace out ten paces. The limits were then marked with white wooden pegs. When this was done Tottenham returned to Sir Richard and received his pistols. He brought them back to Roche. Roche consulted with his principal, but that he refused to accept either weapon was evident from the shake of his head before Roche had reached him. Roche ignored the armourer.

Fosdyke was satisfied with Roche's pistols. Let Sir Richard's second take his choice. Accordingly Tottenham selected a pistol, and tried the weapon, holding the hammer carefully and testing it past the half-cock, for at half-cock some of the pistols used in duelling were apt to jam. Satisfied with the weapon, he returned it to Roche, who proceeded to load it carefully from his powder horn. This metal flask was fitted with a nipple which measured as exactly as possible the charge of powder appropriate to the bore. This being done, Roche returned the weapons to their case before offering them to the opponents. The loading was done by Roche because when Trulock tried to load the pistols his hands shook too much.

Impatiently Fosdyke called out to Roche: "Cannot we get on with it?"

"Fair and softly, Sir," the Tiger replied. "This is a matter that must be conducted with the nicest propriety. I regard this duel almost as a sacred one. It differs from most duels in that it concerns a lady. It arises from no sordid dispute. We cannot rush the procedure."

"Damn it," Fosdyke said. "It's a shrewdly cold morning."

"Button your coat," his second replied.

Turning to Tottenham, he satisfied himself that it was impossible for Sir Richard to fight standing on one leg. The very lowering of his foot to the perpendicular caused a pain that might be calculated to upset his marksmanship. After this there was a long consultation between Fosdyke and Roche. Fosdyke argued that if he fought standing he presented a better target. At the same time he refused to accept a chair, because he would be unable to aim satisfactorily from a sitting posture, and also for a reason he did not profess—which was that he was unwilling to have it said that he had sought whatever little shelter there was by imitating his rival.

"Any delay now is solely due to your inability to make up your mind," his second informed him.

"I will stand up, then," Fosdyke said surlily. Roche seemed greatly relieved.

"There is no disadvantage at all, in my opinion," he said, "apart from a slight difference in level. In fact, a sitting man presents a far more vulnerable figure than a man who is standing because the vulnerable parts of his body are brought closer together. In addition, it is easier to aim from a position to which one is accustomed. The odds, if any, are against Sir Richard."

Tottenham conveyed this decision to Sir Richard.

"Give him a chair if he wants one; or let him kneel on one knee. It is my misfortune, not my wish, that I do not present a fuller target." Sir Richard was beginning to show heat. Fearing that this was the very thing on which Fosdyke was counting—a rage-shaken opponent—Tottenham did his best to keep his principal's temper from being ruffled.

"It has already been pointed out that the advantage is with him, and he has accepted it," he said.

Sir Richard nodded.

"May I pray you, Sir, to let nothing ruffle your temper," Tottenham continued. "Your opponent may attempt to exasperate you of set purpose."

"He will not exasperate me if he fights."

A sign from Roche drew Tottenham towards him: "We must toss for positions and the word."

Tottenham won the toss and chose the eastern end of the field, with the morning smoke of the city behind his man. Roche had the word—the privilege of giving the instructions as well as the word to fire.

"You will bring Sir Richard to his mark," he said.

Accordingly St. George and Tottenham lifted Sir Richard's chair and bore him to the mark. His right foot, swathed in bandages, they placed gently against the white wooden peg.

Roche brought Fosdyke up to his mark and said, "I must apologize to you, gentlemen, for reminding you—for I know that such an elemental rule is well known to you—that you must face each other with pistol muzzles pointing at the ground. The code insists that full instructions be given before every meeting, and it makes no exception, even in the case of experienced fighters. The word will be given as follows: First, I shall ask you, 'Are you ready?' On receiving from both principals a reply in the affirmative, I shall order you both to take aim and at the word 'Fire!' you may fire. I shall count 'One, two, three!' After, 'Three!' there must be no firing. I hope I have made myself clearly understood?"

Sir Richard grunted. He did not like the position of his foot. But Fosdyke requested that Roche rehearse the word before commencing.

"Are you ready?

"Take aim.

"Fire! One. Two. Three. Halt!"

The case was opened and each combatant took a pistol. The seconds of each gave a last look at the priming and set the weapons at full cock.

Roche stood back and took up a position between the combatants, but a few yards to the side.

"Are you ready?" he asked, in a clear voice, untroubled, as if he were starting a race amongst school children.

"Ready!" Sir Richard answered.

"No, wait!" Fosdyke called. "I must remove my fob. And this," he added, as he took a snuff-box from a pocket of his waistcoat. "I do not want any protection that might deflect a bullet. May I call for a search of my opponent?"

This was unheard of. Even his second was ruffled. Sir Richard fumed and drew up his foot. Tottenham went up to Roche. But the latter's attention was riveted on his man.

"Fosdyke," he said, "I have never heard of such a thing. I have no intention of searching Sir Richard or of permitting his second to search him. This is a meeting between gentlemen, not footpads. It is unlikely that Sir Richard is carrying flint or metal in his pockets in the hope of stopping a shot."

Livid, Sir Richard was struggling to his feet.

"Tottenham, take off my surtout, coat and waistcoat!" he shouted. "I will kill the scoundrel in my shirt!"

In vain Tottenham tried to dissuade him. The morning was chill, for the sun was only beginning to glint in silver upon the sea. However, he had to strip Sir Richard, leaving him to fight in his shirt, cravat and breeches.

"For God's sake, Sir," Tottenham whispered, "remember that this may be a trick designed to upset your aim."

"Leave him to me," Sir Richard said hoarsely, and stared at his man.

"Are you ready?"

This time: "Ready!" from both.

"Take aim!"

Sir Richard noticed that Fosdyke had his pistol levelled at his waistline. All hope that there would be no killing had to be abandoned. Not that Sir Richard had hope, but now he knew that his opponent's intentions were deadly and it relieved his mind.

"Fire!"

Two pistols blazed; but calmly the uninterrupted voice went on:

"One!

"Two!

"Three!

"Halt!"

In the midst of the report it seemed that a crash was audible from Sir Richard's end of the field. To Tottenham's horror he fancied that he saw Sir Richard roll over slowly, hidden in a cloud of smoke. St. George could hardly keep his place.

He could see Fosdyke holding his pistol in both hands and leaping up as if to get a view above the smoke his weapon had made. Fosdyke was not down but Sir Richard was—down with his arms folded, which was quite correct, for a man must not leave his mark without his second's permission. But Sir Richard was groaning.

"Are you hurt, Sir?" Tottenham asked anxiously.

St. George bethought him of MacDermot and looked in the doctor's direction. Suddenly Sir Richard said, in answer to Tottenham's inquiry, "I am not hurt by a bullet, but the fellow won't leave me a leg to sit on. He has blown the leg off my chair."

The crash heard was the leg of Sir Richard's chair and the pain came from the fact that in falling sideways, Sir Richard fell in such a position that he was seated on the ankle of his sore foot. After all, there was some advantage for a seated man against a standing adversary. Fosdyke had had to aim low, and bring his arm out of the horizontal position. Thus it came about that Sir Richard's bullet had torn through both forearm and upper arm, for the arm was bent.

Fosdyke was not jumping up and down in an endeavour to see the effect of his bullet but from the pain of his torn muscles.

And now, ironically, his second was removing Fosdyke's coat. A whistle brought Sir Dominick from the dunes. Dr. MacDermot followed, according to etiquette, the senior surgeon.

They were introduced to their respective patients. The doctor from Mayo bent over his patient and felt his heart. With considerable strength he lifted him from the ruins of his chair and placed him, sitting, on the sand. Then he turned and addressed his anxious companions with an assumed solemnity—which he thought was due to such an occasion—holding his sentences (he had been talking to Sir Dominick for half an hour) until they fermented in the minds of his anxious hearers.

"From a careful examination, a very careful examination, of the prominent features of the case, I incline to the opinion that the leg was broken by Fosdyke's bullet either because that gentleman, being younger, is possessed of more alert senses or because he had a pistol with a finer trigger. The deflection, the partial deflection of Sir Richard's aim, on the other hand, was undoubtedly due to his opponent getting his shot at the leg in first, and that, as I have endeavoured to explain, arose—"

"Is his leg broken?" Tottenham asked anxiously.

"I demand another shot," Sir Richard shouted from behind the speakers. Tottenham went to him.

Turning to Dr. MacDermot, St. George said, "Why cannot you speak like a rational being, doctor, and tell me if his leg is broken?" The doctor smiled enigmatically.

Sir Richard, after a word with Tottenham, shouted: "See here, doctor, I did not ask for your opinion on my shooting. I want you to do something to baffle this pain in my foot."

"I have seen an arm blown off in County Mayo, when they fired through a window at Crosbie seated in his chair after dinner. A chair is sometimes a protection," the doctor went on, unruffled, still addressing St. George.

"So it's the leg of his chair which was shot? Why the hell couldn't you say so?"

"See here, doctor," repeated Sir Richard, "I do not want a diagnosis of my shooting. I want you to baffle this pain in my foot."

The doctor opened his capacious salve box. He buried his head within it. When he arose he held a small boxwood bottle-cover in his hand.

"I cannot use this," he informed his patient, "it is marked 'laudanum.'"

"Damme, use something. My whole leg is throbbing like a drum."

The doctor had an idea.

"I will proceed to loosen the bandages," he said. "That will give you a little ease. You can have laudanum later on. If you got it now it would make you drowsy."

Accordingly the bandages were loosened on Sir Richard's right leg.

"Hurry, man, hurry. This throbbing is enough to distract anyone. Where the devil is my waistcoat? I will catch cold. Cruise always gives laudanum." That seemed to change Dr. MacDermot's decision. He opened the bottle and poured out a liberal draught.

Then St. George and the doctor carefully dressed the old warrior, who groaned when he tried to rise to facilitate the work.

Tottenham carried Sir Richard's demand for another shot to Roche, who received the request with the greatest sympathy, promising to use whatever influence he had with his principal to promote a continuance of the duel.

"We are in the hands of Aesculapius at the moment. We must await his report," he said, with some concern in his tone. He indicated Fosdyke, who was now sitting on the sand.

At last Sir Dominick rose. He approached Roche. Tottenham was about to withdraw. Roche held up his hand:

"It lies within my discretion whether the opponent's second hears our surgeon's report. I request you to wait until Sir Dominick gives his opinion."

"Gentlemen," Sir Dominick began, "the bullet entered the flexor aspect of the right forearm, as it was but partially extended. It traversed the entire length of the forearm, lacerating a portion of the lacertus fibrosis, being somewhat deflected by the epicondylus medialus of the humerus. It glanced off the seventh or eighth rib then, on its course inwards, passed through the serratus magnus and the muscles which go to form the posterior wall of the axilla. This it also traversed until it was at last arrested by the under surface of the scapula, against which bone I opine it lies at present, embedded in the subscapularis muscle. Its extraction should present no difficulty."

Roche's face brightened. He went to Fosdyke, whose seated figure formed an ironical counterpart to his rival's. Roche took off his own greatcoat and put it under the sitting man, whose breeches were beginning to seep in moisture from the sand.

"What about another blaze?" he inquired.

"Damn it, can't you see that my right arm is out of action? I cannot bend a finger, much less raise my arm to the firing position. It hurts to bend my trigger finger, which is rather weak. If I move my arm, it causes pain."

"I can hold your arm in position for you and take my chance of a shot. As for bending your trigger finger, those pistols of mine are fitted with hair triggers. That is how you were able to get in first. I will request that you be allowed to use one with a more delicate touch. Trulock can file the spring."

"I want to see no more of de Vesey," Fosdyke said sulkily.

"Tut, tut!" exclaimed the Tiger. "Surely not while you have a sound arm left?"

"I am neither left-handed nor ambidextrous," was all that Fosdyke would say.

"It seems to me that you are wasting a wonderful morning. Speaking for myself, I always favour that shadowless light," Roche said.

"Can't some of you bring that second chair? I see the fellow sitting up quite unconcerned," Sir Richard exclaimed from under his surtout, which was left hanging on his head like a shawl, for the effort to get him into it was judged to be an unnecessary infliction of discomfort.

His chair had sunken sideways and forward in the sand in spite of efforts to prop it up by its severed limb.

"A moment, Sir Richard. We must wait until we hear from Roche," Tottenham said. As he spoke the Tiger approached. A glance at his grave and mournful face was enough to tell Tottenham that there would be no concession to Sir Richard's request for a second shot.

"I have done my best. You behold in me the bearer of two apologies, one from myself—I have failed to impress upon my man that honour demands a continuance of the combat. He is fawning on his fate. He refuses. The second apology is from him—a full recantation of any insulting word he may have uttered in the Club. I have offered him all the assistance in my power. He declines it, urging as an excuse his wound, and the pain, which makes it impossible for him to shoot. He also refuses to shoot with his uninjured hand. Knowing Sir Richard's regard for honour, I took it upon myself to promise that Sir Richard, who is apparently in equal if not greater pain, will shoot with his left hand. It is all of no avail. Chivalry has fled from my end of the field. The glory of Ireland is on the wane. Fosdyke has even refused to nominate me as his substitute. I must therefore admit that we are defeated without the satisfaction of honour. I pray you to carry this message to your principal." Roche bowed ceremoniously. Tottenham bowed and turned to his friends.

Sir Richard sat in his chair, which was now held up by the doctor's medicine chest, his face still concealed by his surtout.

Tottenham had a word with St. George, whose services he requested to help him break the news to Sir Richard.

Denis listened and began to smile.

"This is no laughing matter!" Tottenham exclaimed, seeing his friend's face. Then, "What are you laughing at?" he asked roundly.

"I am thinking," said St. George, "of what Dashwood said the other night. 'Never choose an Irishman for your second.' "

"What the devil did he mean?"

"In England, he said, they consider it the first duty of a second to do all in his power to effect a reconciliation between principals so that a meeting may be prevented. Here, it seems that—"

"Nonsense!" Tottenham exclaimed, interrupting. "Did he tell you how they could ever have a duel if the seconds did all they could in their power to prevent it? That may be all very well for fops and beaux but it will not do over here, where we apologize only when we cannot fight on. That is what Fosdyke has done. And we must accept it."

But St. George was not listening. He was staring at the seated figure. Suddenly he asked: "Doctor, what is the matter with Sir Richard?"

The doctor's professional interest at the moment lay more in the opposing camp. So engaged was he in trying to estimate the condition of Fosdyke that his attention was diverted from his own patient.

He collected himself and went over to Sir Richard and removed the greatcoat that covered his head. Carefully he replaced it and returning on tiptoe to his companion:

"Begob, he's asleep!" he whispered. The friends looked at each other in consternation. Seeing their looks the doctor added: "He would take the laudanum."

Obviously it would never do to take the chance of such news leaking out, for fear it would be said that their man was drugged before, and not during the fight. Also, it would never do to have their efforts to arouse him observed. The only course open was to bear the victor from the field. But first, in order to register his victory, the apology of his opponent must be accepted, if possible without further parley. Tottenham had a good idea. He advanced half way towards the other group, stopped, raised his hat, and swept it down as he bowed deeply.

His gesture was answered by an equally ceremonious bow from Roche. Then they hastened to carry the slumbering fire-eater from the field. After a due interval another procession formed. Fosdyke's party began its retreat. Roche led the way. The gun-maker and Sir Dominick supported the wounded Fosdyke.

As Roche reached the position that the old knight had held so well he noticed that the white wooden mark had been forgotten and left behind. As he stooped to pick it up he found the shattered chair leg, examined it for a moment, and then flung it far out of sight among the sand dunes.

Silence settled on the party until they reached the gangway. Here they found Dr. MacDermot struggling with his sea-chest. The driver of his chaise ran to his aid, and they both returned to the lanes before they could collide with members of the opposing party.

As the doctor's chaise was whipping up, Roche arrived. He greeted the doctor formally. Then, suddenly, his eye fell upon his coachman's companion. "May I ask you to stop a moment, Sir?" he said.

He reached up and drew the companion downwards. From the breast-pocket of his coat, from which it was protruding, he extracted a strange object about sixteen inches long made of dark mahogany. It looked like the leg of a chair that had been roughly broken off from the seat.

"No souvenirs for sale, Toucher!" he said sternly, and placed the evidence of the fight in his own pocket where it bulged like another pistol.

"Off with you, now!" he said.

XXX. SIR RICHARD LEAVES TOWN

"DO NOT THINK I am ungrateful," Sir Richard remarked. "I dislike congratulations; and another thing I do not like is praise, on the rare occasions it comes my way. Damned embarrassing."

He was breakfasting in his town house with his nephew, several days after the duel. Hyacinth had got news of the result of the duel at Daly's almost as soon as it was over. But as it was all over and done with before the news leaked out, it obviously had been an admirably conducted affair.

True it was that Constable Crewcomb had ridden out furiously from Dublin Castle with a company of militia. He had met the parties just as they were turning towards town.

He had looked into one coach and seen Sir Richard fast asleep. In another he had found Fosdyke with his arm bandaged and in a sling. He had turned to Roche, who seemed to be the Master of Ceremonies, whatever they were.

"I am informed that a breach of the peace is about to take place, and I am here to prevent it," he had said.

"Nothing could be further from our thoughts," Roche had assured him. So he rode away.

The Toucher declared afterwards that he had overtaken the posse earlier in the morning as he himself was proceeding to pick cockles near the scene. From this it was evident that Crewcomb had deliberately delayed on the way, "To give the boys a chance to blaze first," a fact which exalted him in everyone's esteem. A remark of the Toucher testified to this:

"Crewcomb may not be a gentleman; but he is *after* a gentleman."

If Crewcomb had not enhanced his reputation by stopping duellists, he had at least captured a highwayman. His name was mentioned now.

"It was Crewcomb who caught the gang who tried to rob Tottenham's coach last week," said Sir Richard.

"Yes."

"Now that robbery—I cannot understand how the rogues got their information. Obviously it was known that Tottenham had won a considerable sum, enough gold to bulk largely in his pocket. Information of that sort could only come through the servants. It's impossible to get a staunch servant in these troubled times, with all the talk of Liberty flying about."

"Yes," Hyacinth agreed. "Liberty upsets servants. Lucky for Tottenham that he escaped with his gold."

"That is not quite the way it happened. A highwayman stopped his coach and demanded the thousand guineas 'one of you have won.' Tottenham and Dashwood were searched and an accomplice examined the coach with a dark lantern, but they found nothing of great value. They were so enraged that they even forgot to rob them of their rings and watches."

"That remark, 'one of you have won,' points to information received from within the Club. But how did Tottenham save his winnings?"

"By the very simple expedient of giving them to Tiger Roche to take to town for him."

"They never attack the Tiger?" asked Hyacinth.

"Not since he began to act as Judge, Jury, Gallows, and all. He has too much information. He can root them out and kill them at will. One night he walked single-handed into a den of thieves somewhere in the Liberties. Liberties!" Sir Richard repeated the name of the Dublin slums and laughed ironically. "He put two pistols on the table. 'Disgorge and get out,' was all he said."

"But what had they done?"

"He lost his fob, that elaborate and showy fob with the brown cameo he wears. And he wanted to get it back. It seems that if he, of all people, could be robbed with impunity, it would encourage crime. That is how he put it."

"Yet, for all his activities, there are more highwaymen abroad at the present moment than ever before in this country. His 'Society for Aiding Order,' as he calls it, is somewhat remiss."

"I suppose that the rogue who tried to rob Tottenham is still at large?" Sir Richard continued.

Hyacinth did not know. He reverted to the earlier part of the conversation. As he threw over a letter to Sir Richard, he said:

"If you wish to avoid notoriety you had better come with us to the West. It must be a long time since you have visited Lisadill."

Yes, Sir Richard had duties. He must not let a temporary disablement prevent him from visiting his estates. His sister and his niece, with Madame de Ronquerolles, would be returning there after the wedding of Ellice St. George and d'Estournelles. And from what General Lake said, things were simmering up to boil over in the country. The rebellion last spring was bad enough, but it was within a day or two's march of the city. It would be a far more serious affair if it broke out in the distant West—women unprotected, inadequate forces, and so on. Strangely enough, the stirring of Sir Richard's protective impulses raised in his mind a clear image of the pretty, defenseless Baronne.

"Whether it is the physic or not, or the starvation diet, this foot of mine is getting better more rapidly than it ever recovered before. Cruise says that I may be able to put it under me by the end of the week."

Hyacinth passed him another letter. Instead of reading it, he decided: "Damme, I'll be off with you. A good shaking and the country air will put the gout to flight. Not much gout in County Galway."

St. George was not returning with them. He had business which he had to transact at his lawyer's office, concerning his mother's approaching marriage. His coach would be at the disposal of some of the party. It would be easier travelling with additional room.

"We must stop at Lucan for the wedding," Sir Richard remarked. "After that, the sooner we are out of town, the sooner we shall have peace."

XXXI. THE NIGHT BEFORE LARRY WAS STRETCHED

THE TOUCHER STOOD before the Tiger in his den, or office, in Gloucester Street. His agitation was apparent. He kept his hat at arm's length in front of him and spoke nervously, hurriedly, without being spoken to. He was being put to the question.

"The doctor told me that wading was good for me corns, or I wouldn't have been wading for cockles that morning at all, Sir," he concluded.

The Tiger eyed him for a moment and bent his head over some crude papers on his desk. He spoke quietly, a fact that did not contribute to the Toucher's calm.

"Unpleasant as it must be for you, Mr. Plant, you will have to consent to understand me before I let you go. I am not interested any longer in why you thought fit to pry on gentlemen's affairs of a morning; but I am interested in your capacity for prying. Sit down."

The Tiger selected a crumpled piece of paper on which something was written. What it was the Toucher could not know, even had he been able to read, but his quick mind judged it to be—from the condition of the paper—an anonymous contribution of information from some member of the lawless world.

"Yes, I am interested, very much interested, in your capacity for prying. You will exercise that capacity, not in spying upon reputable but on disreputable people this time. You will proceed tonight to Newgate Gaol."

The Toucher gasped. What had he done to merit so severe a punishment from the Society for Aiding Order?

"You will ingratiate yourself with those who shall be waking a prisoner who is to be hanged in the morning." Greatly relieved, the Toucher volunteered information to show his sincerity.

"They are stretching Larry in the morning, Sir."

"You will, as I have said, ingratiate yourself with his friends, who will be consoling him on this his last night on earth."

"Yes, yer Honour, I'll do everything ye want."

"Well, then tell me what 'ingratiate yourself' means."

"Give them drinks they don't have to pay for," the Toucher answered glibly.

Faintly the Tiger smiled. Among such people as Larry's friends it would serve as well any other definition, he thought.

"You will therefore ingratiate yourself with those who will be in the cell with the highwayman, and find out who this Larry happens to be this time."

"Sure he is Larry Dooley, the highwayman, Sir."

The Tiger eyed him closely. Seeing no guile, he continued:

"I am surprised at you. That is where you are astray. Well you know, or should know, that when any robber is laid by the heels, he takes the name of the head of the gang. This he does, firstly, to call pursuit off from his chief; and, secondly, as he has to die in any case, he feels that he might as well die under an assumed name. You will return here tomorrow bringing me the real name of Larry and any plots or plans you may learn."

"The turnkey does be in the cell wid the prisoner all night."

"That is where you are to be, and come out with his friends after they have waked him, and go with them to the hanging. Then come here."

The Tiger produced two gold guineas and threw them in the direction of the Toucher, who gathered them rapidly and rose to go.

"Your manners?"

The Toucher turned and, bowing himself out backwards to the tune of "Thank you, Sir," was glad to escape.

Newgate Gaol, in spite of its stench, was tonight a clamorous, merry pit. It was a merry night for warders, from the head gaoler who accepted "passage money," and took sundry other bribes, won at cards and got as much as he could drink—and a little more for the morning—down to the lowest turnkey, who only got a small gratuity from the coffin-maker for recommending his wares to the man about to die. A coffin was a privilege, and it was rated as such. It cost money to make, so that it would "stand the lime," money to admit it into the prison, so that the would-be occupant could have the rueful satisfaction of knowing that he would be interred decently, and money to keep it in the large cell or "pantry" in which the condemned was accommodated and permitted to receive his final friends and to preside at what was nothing other than his own wake.

The session was in full swing when the Toucher was ushered in. Reluctantly he had to part with a crown. That would leave him only sixteen shillings for the night's entertainment, for he had resolved not to spend more than half of the money he had received from the Tiger. There would be lashings of drink without his contribution. It was after the hanging, when the mourning started, that he would be called upon to do his "standing," if he was to obtain any information worth knowing. There was, of course, the chance that he might win something at cards. In the guttering light of the dungeon, sleights-of-hand were not too easy to detect; besides, there was a certain abandon on the part of the prisoner, who had not to take thought beyond the morrow or acquire more goods in this world.

At first, it was hard for the Toucher to tell which was the condemned man. A certain deference on the part of the chief warden, as well as on the part of the dozen friends, indicated that it was a tall, dark, long-necked man who sat at the coffin's head—a man the Toucher was sure he had seen before, though he could not for the moment think where. He had a gypsy's pointed nose and chin.

"Ah, be Jaysus, it's the Toucher and no mistake!" the man said. "Sit down here and take a hand. But, eh, Chief, before I play with the Toucher, I'd like a new deck of cards. Can we have another pack?"

"Ah, me sound man, Larry, is it you?" the Toucher inquired.

"Larry it is and sound it is; but apt to die on a sudden all the same," Larry answered. And the sally brought forth applause.

The Toucher's face had weathered so many contingencies that all in it which might indicate surprise had long since been worn away. He looked cheerfully into the man's face, and recognized him as the guard of the Wicklow coach. It was no Dick Turpin or Larry Dooley that he saw—only the guard who used to leap down in the dark when the coach was traversing a winding road, meet it higher up or lower down by short-cutting through the fields, and hold the passengers to ransom. Then he would put on his livery and climb up again into his place. Of course this could only be done by collusion with the coachman, but that was almost natural between old comrades who had been entrusted with the care of the coaches for years.

The coach-guard's name, Plant recalled, was Billy Tabley, but it would not do to call him by other than the name he had assumed. Obviously its real owner, Larry Dooley the highwayman, was still at large.

A burly man was ushered in. He, too, greeted the prisoner first, calling him Larry. Evidently the boys were well posted. Or he may have read the name on the breast-plate of the coffin:

Larry Dooley
Aged 38
Obiit August 1798

No, no one with so little knowledge of the prisoner would have had any business in the place. What was Bumbeigh doing in it, then?

Larry did not know nor care. The more the merrier for him. And yet it was Bumbeigh who had "stood" the coffin to the man who was to die.

" 'Ere," Bumbeigh called, "wot about the company of a few ladies?" He spoke to the head-warden, who sat opposite half-way down the coffin, on which stood a black bottle of brandy uncorked and close to hand. The warden, whose face was like a walled-up doorway, muttered something and undid a large key from the ring chained to his belt.

"Will one of yez give that to Jaikes?" he asked.

"Where's that deck iv cards?" Larry shouted.

"Simmer, now, simmer," the warder requested. "All in good time."

"As I used to say to them gold watches," Larry interposed, and again won a laugh.

There was no doubt about it: Larry's last night on earth was proving that he could have had great success as a wit, had he confined himself solely to developing that side of his character.

Jaikes, the turnkey, a furtive, ill-visaged rat of a man, whose yellow face was red beneath from an old smallpox, came leading three women by the light of candle stuck in a bottle. Loud huzzas hailed the advent of the ladies.

Jaikes put down his candle and turned to go.

"Jayshus! Jayshus!" Larry called to him. "Don't ye know that three lights is unlucky? They's used to light a corpse." He made as if to quench the taper.

"Simmer, now. Simmer," said the warder. "Jaikes, bring us another light."

Two of the women who entered had been condemned to death for robbing visitors to the house the older woman had kept. They had "pleaded their bellies" and were respited pending the time that this claim would prove false or that they were brought to bed. The third was old and fat. Her flaked face, without eyebrows, was smeared over with a perpetual smile.

"Welcome to me family vault," Larry called.

"Aisy now, Larry, we want no sooners here. And them girls is delicate." Even the stone-faced warder smiled, encouraged by this rare jest.

"Christ! Look at the Toucher!" one of the girls said. "Eh, Toucher, where's me Valentine?"

"Is it brandy that's in it?" the old woman asked, looking at the bottle by his side. "Give us a sup and I'll light me pipe." She took from under her skirt a dudeen, a small clay pipe, the blackened bowl of which was broken off close to the stem.

A door closed heavily down one of the passages.

"Yer wanted, Mister," a turnkey said.

The warder couldn't get round the coffin.

"Ye are welcome to step over it and no disrespect," Larry invited, guessing that there was another visitor who had to buy his way in. He was right. But no visitor appeared. Instead the warder returned bearing a large hamper. "With the landlord's compliments." He either did not know or would not say from where it had come. Someone who did not wish to be identified too closely with the thief had not forgotten him.

Larry thought, and held his whist.

"Can't yez open it, ye whores?" the old hag called to the wenches. In a minute they had it ripped open. A brace of chickens, a large Limerick ham and two bottles of brandy were brought to light. Cheers greeted this abundance.

"Simmer, now," the warder said. "Tell Jaikes to bring us the plates. We can hardly eat on this."

"And what's wrong wid it?" Larry asked, assuming indignation. "It's the best wooden waistcoat in Cook Street. And hasn't it got a plate?"

Jaikes returned again and again. He had to collect the plates. At last he brought half a dozen stools, and this got him an invitation from the warder, who told him to simmer down.

Bumbeigh said automatically, " 'Ere's health!"

"Now if ye made it 'Long life!' " the Toucher suggested.

"Aisy now," Larry said: "this gentleman wants a word with me." After Bumbeigh had whispered, Larry nodded his head.

"I'll tell the Toucher. I can't talk to ye here."

"I was forgetting the pack," said Jaikes. "Who wants to take a hand?" Deferentially he handed the cards to the head warden who remarked that they seemed to be an old pack.

"I've a pack of me own here," the Toucher said meekly. Roars of laughter echoed off the groined roof of Larry's "family vault."

"He keeps them for telling fortunes," the old woman said, leering.

But the Toucher took no notice. He was interesting the warder and Larry with an account of the duel he had witnessed. By his account it seemed that, next to the principals', his had been the leading part.

"I had the leg of the very chair the auld chairman sat in, but just as I was coming away I gev it as a keepsake to a friend of mine."

"Blown off, was it?" the warder asked.

"You should have seen it. It leapt up in the air. That's when I caught it, when it was coming down."

"And what happened then?"

"The auld chairman—"

"That's a good wan," said Larry; "the auld chairman!"

Authoritative amongst the hurly, the great warder sat. His watchful eye had lost none of its alertness.

"That will do you now, Becky," he said, with a rumble. "Put that bottle back!"

"Jayshus, and I only warming it!" she exclaimed, as she took it from a pocket under her petticoat. "If ye think I was trying to scoop it, ye have only to say so," she added, aggrieved.

"Simmer now, all of yez," he said, speaking as if he were addressing his hand of cards.

Some diversion was caused at this point by an incursion from the outer prison of a motley crowd of wastrels of all ages and descriptions. Nearly all bore signs of smallpox. Some were half-witted and should have been beyond the law, yet they were held for what was equal to a life sentence. There was no hope for them ever to tread the righteous path, bereft of reason as they were. Gifts of whiskey only increased their degeneracy. The leering group settled down.

This relaxation was permitted by some grim kindness of the head warder, who knew that the roaring crowd would keep the condemned man from brooding, provide him with a gallery to which his vanity or his pride could appeal, and so keep him from dashing his head against the wall.

Experience had taught him that, given company, the prisoner's spirits would rise in the face of ruin with the strange exultant defiance peculiar to the men of Dublin who, wastrels though they were, bred true to the city the Danes had founded. But at the moment others were singing the equivalent of Larry's death song.

In the midst of the din and shouting the Toucher was assuring Larry, mouth to ear:

"There's a doctor friend of mine who says he will give you a snick in the jugular when they think ye're dead. It relieves congestion and has saved many a half-hanged man, he says." Larry was not drunk enough now to give this credence.

"You may ax him to snick me—"

"And make a Jewman of ye, is it?" Becky called out, leering.

The Toucher tried again:

"We might pay the sojers to cut you down soon, as they would be sure to do if there was anyone waiting to be stretched after ye. Bumbeigh has lots of coin. And, by the way, what did he want?"

"He axed me where the pocketbook was I took from him with his watch."

"Where is it?"

"Ye must ax Harris, the jeweller, who takes the swag he buys from us to London every month. There was nothing but names in it."

From out of the hurly the young whores, hysterical with drink, were starting up a bawdy old Dublin catch, when the granite hand of the warder seized one of them by the throat.

"In the name of Jayshus, cannot ye have common decency?"

Having silenced them, he withdrew his hand and picked up the cards on the coffin with short, quick, busy jerks.

"Yes, indeed," said Becky Cooper, "and him going to his God."

"And you shut your gue as well," the warder commanded.

"Here's a chance to win back yer watch." He addressed Larry, in front of whom was a little pile of money. The Toucher eyed it covetously. So did the head warder. But the gypsy-faced fellow had long acquaintance with cards and played with all the concentrated skill of the illiterate. Soon he took a few more shillings from the warder. Unperturbed, the warder played on. Who was to know what Larry had in his pockets before his execution?

A remark from Larry might well have caused a complication of the warder's designs.

"You will get my blue coat and flowered waistcoat, for ye were the first from outside to come in to see me, Toucher Plant. And, if they'll fit you, me buckled shoes."

A murmur went round the gaol and rose to articulate speech.

"The priest!" was the awed whisper.

"And be sure to get the boys to give me a good send-off!"

"Be sure I will," said the grateful Toucher. And turning to the warder:

"Ye heard that Larry has willed me his clothes?"

"Simmer, now. Simmer. He must go to the priest." He turned grimly to the condemned man.

"Come on now," he said. "You can't keep His Reverence waiting."

"Jayshus," said Larry, "and just as my luck was turning." The Toucher raised his glass from the coffin lid and as he was about to drain it said with a twinkle:

"In the midst of death we are in luck."

Resignedly Larry rose and pocketed his winnings.

"Just as me luck was turning!" he repeated regretfully.

On Larry's departure down the dark stone corridor, gloom settled on those in the vaulted cell. One or two of the crowd sniggered, oppressed by nervousness. Like a flicker from a burning heap of dank weeds, a rising snatch of bawdy song leapt up into the reeky air. It came from a far corner where two men sat in front of the two girls:

"I choose the wan wid the curly locks
Hey, ho! Me Randy O!
I went wid her but she gave me—"

Loudly the head warder banged on the coffin with the empty brandy flask.

"Shut it! Stop it, Baldy! If I hear another word out of ye, ye'll be on bread and water."

Baldy, a snout-faced, thick-set, leering bully, quickly withdrew his hand from the girl's hair.

"And what's more," the head warder continued, "if the priest hears yez, it's meself will be reported. Stop chawing that ham-bone, Poxy Cuffe, and listen."

A comrade nudged a one-eyed man who was chewing a bone. He was stone deaf. As he turned, his eyeless socket glistened momentarily as the light sunk in. His friend jerked his thumb in the head warder's direction. Poxy Cuffe pocketed the bone, and gazed attentively at the warder, who shouted:

"Out yez all go now, one be one. Jaikes!" he called to the turnkey.

"Think of singing dirty songs and a man making his sowl!" the old brothel-keeper exclaimed piously. She threw up her full eyes to the ceiling, crossed her arms on her breast and shook her head slowly. But her virtuous indignation was not sufficiently convincing to exempt her from the general order to leave.

"And you too, Becky. Out you go!"

Bumbeigh also rose to go.

"Wait awhile, Mr. Bumbeigh, till they're all out. Toucher, you can wait too."

"I'm vastly obleeged," said Toucher Plant.

Sternly the head warder watched the out-going of his scabby flock.

"Where's Sandy and the Greaser?" he inquired.

"D'ye think that they'd mix wid the likes of us?" Becky asked with a sneer.

Sandy was an attorney who had been convicted of blackmail. He and his accomplice, the Greaser, a plausible fellow who kept up an acquaintance with squireens or half gentlemen, had fallen out. The Greaser had been convicted of perjury. As intellectual rogues, they held themselves apart, far above the less privileged children of destitution.

"I thought that the brandy would have brought them in," the head warder commented.

"The Greaser is a great judge of auld brandy, be all accounts. Is there a drop in the bottle by any chance?" Becky asked as she lingered.

"There's some that never knows when they've had enough," the warder said sententiously. "Out with you now!"

He turned to adjust a candle that guttered in a bottle.

"Holy Cripes!" he exclaimed. "Where's me winnings? And I

hardly turned my back. Of all the bastards! That's the thanks I get for letting them in."

Becky's commiserations had only the effect of having her thrust out by the neck. When she came reeling into the corridor raucous yells greeted her. One of the girls let her indignation soar.

"I would like to see the big bowsey doing the like of that to me. Hitting a woman is all he's good for. I'm ashamed of ye, Becky, why in hell's blazes didn't you give him a clatter in the beak?" Then on her own account she hurled an insult at the head warder, "I'll meet ye in Mrs. Hayes's later on!" Mrs. Hayes's being a brothel near Gallows Green.

But Becky was turning sentimental and reminiscent. She cried softly.

"Is it me hit him?" she sobbed. "Yez don't know what yez are talking about. Is it me hit him? Reddin was once me nabs, me fancy man. There was once a time I thought that the sun of Heaven used to shine out of his brandy arse."

If the head warder remembered bygone days, he was in no mood to recall them. He was too concerned about his loss.

The Toucher was as surprised, even more concerned than the warder. He wondered who the thief could have been. Angrily the warder left the room.

"I'll be back in a minute," he said. "I must show His Reverence out."

"What did he say to you about my book?" Bumbeigh asked the Toucher. But the Toucher's mind had already been made up regarding the prospects the book offered.

"He said it would take a bit of travelling to come up with it."

Bumbeigh's face fell. He had presented a coffin to the condemned rogue, who had stolen what could be of no conceivable use to him—his private book with its lists of personal loans and moneys due by half the country's sportsmen. He had counted on learning at the last moment where it could be recovered. And now it was as inaccessible as ever, and, as if to add to his misfortune, a worse rogue, if possible, stood in his way.

But the Toucher foresaw a life of ease and pleasure, to be made possible by his selling at a discount to those concerned their names from the bookmaker's book of debts.

XXXII. THE BOYS

In the morning it was evident that the Toucher had not been unmindful of Larry's last request. Encouraging remarks and an odd cheer or two came from a safe distance at the back of the crowd as the bayonet-guarded cart lurched forward.

Doing his best to keep up a bold front, Larry stood upright, manacled on his "smalls," that is, on wrists and ankles. But his face was pale. It is hard to keep up your heart when you feel the felon's irons on hand and foot and see no human sympathy in a wall of faces, and derisive howls strike your ears; hard to die game when not nature but your fellow-men turn you out of life.

As the cart was drawn under the cross-bar, the hangman turned down Larry's collar.

"If ye hold yer chin up, it'll be aisier," he whispered in the condemned man's ear.

That was the last friendly word Larry heard on earth, for the shouts of his friends were dampened down by the grim spectacle.

The cart was drawn away. Larry swung to and fro for a moment till convulsions shook him and caused the swinging to cease. His chains shook tenaciously and sounded in the morning air. Then his body got longer and hung straight down. His whole frame twitched horribly once and shivered.

At last he hung limply with his head bowed at an angle, too abrupt for a penitent's, on his breast. Larry was "stretched."

But the Toucher's task was but half accomplished. True, he had ascertained that Larry was not the famous highwayman of that name; but he had not found out where that dangerous ruffian was, or where his next outrage was to take place.

There is a public house almost opposite the Brazen Head in Winetavern Street, just off the quays on the south side of the river, as the street slopes down from the High Street where Larry was hanged. Here at the Coach and Horses, if anywhere, accomplices of the real Larry Dooley would foregather to drink and mourn one of "the boys" who had recently departed. The sympathies of the Toucher and his attempts to rouse a friendly reception at the hands of the crowd when the cart appeared had been observed. The Toucher would be safe enough. He took the risk because there was worse behind him if he drew back, at the hands of the Tiger.

Another advantage of the Coach and Horses for the Toucher's purposes lay in the fact that, unlike most taverns, which belie their signs, the Coach and Horses was associated with those who drove and guarded coaches and those who had horses in their care.

"It was an aisier hanging than most," the landlord was saying to a customer, as the Toucher entered.

The landlord stood behind a bar with an open hearth at one end of it. Its fire was seldom out, for a kettle always hung over it with hot water for whiskey which, with the addition of sugar and a slip of lemon, became "punch."

The customer agreed. He was a short man in yellow-topped boots who, like many short men, wore a long-tailed coat to give him height.

"It was an easier hanging than that the soldiers gave Father Murphy on the bridge near Wexford (God rest him). They were so rough in turning him off that some say the rope broke his jaw."

"Glory be to God!" the landlord ejaculated, crossing himself, with a damp cloth still in his hand.

"They should have put the knot at the back of his neck," the short man explained.

The shrewd eyes of the landlord were on the Toucher. He grew cautious; for all he knew, the Toucher might be a Government spy, one of those *agents provocateurs*. His attempt to demonstrate his loyalty took a strange and somewhat crude form:

"What's wrong with hanging anyway?" he inquired sharply. He was answered, not by the Toucher, who was taken aback by the landlord's sudden about-face, but by the short man who had no suspicions and whose interest in hanging was impersonal, detached and free from any political significance.

"I'll tell you what's wrong with hanging," he said authoritatively. "When a man is killed, he falls down and leaves the measure of himself on the ground, which is right and proper and the natural thing to do; but to be strung up and you dead and can't fall to the ground, that's where the wrong comes in. That's the bloody disgrace. It isn't natural. That's what it isn't." His looks challenged landlord and visitor alike.

"There was a hanging," the Toucher said reminiscently, "where the hangman had to get down and hang on to the poor devil's legs."

"And where was that?" the short man asked, immediately interested.

"Let me see now," said the Toucher, playing his neighbour's taste for the gruesome. "Let me see, now, where's this it was?"

"Have a drink to aid the memory," the short man said.

The very mention of a drink seemed to have the desired effect. The Toucher had rapidly apprehended that the short man might know the Wexford area, so put the execution he was about to describe in Waterford, where they hanged the Irish rebels by the hundreds.

"It was at Waterford. But the hangman did not last long, if I know the Boys," he added. The mysterious suggestion to his two listeners of his familiarity with "the Boys" went home.

It did more.

It caused a door to open on the Toucher's right. It opened where you would not expect it to be in the wall. A swift whispering head appeared.

"Was you the last with Larry?" it inquired.

The Toucher was taken aback, it was so sudden. Just as he was getting along nicely in the bar. But above all, was it safe?

He nodded.

"Did he get the hamper?" the landlord asked hurriedly, on realizing whom he had for guest.

The Toucher nodded and a hand beckoned as he stared at the head.

"There's a few of 'the Boys' within there. They are asking for you," the landlord said.

The Toucher left the bar with trepidation. Who were "the Boys," he wondered.

He entered an inner room. One yellow window gave on a light shaft with a mouldering wall. At a table in front of a large fireplace four or five men were seated. Many glasses were on the table. They had been playing cards. It was not a place from which one could get out easily in a pinch.

A long-armed, high-shouldered man—a hunchback—rose and closed the door behind the Toucher.

"Ye can sit there," he said.

Before accepting the settee the Toucher bowed to the company. He wanted time to gather his wits.

There were no introductions. The Toucher was known. A dark-faced, sharp-featured, rat-eyed fellow stopped gesticulating to a man of bigger build beside him.

It was this man who spoke. He had a soft voice.

"You spent the last night with—with who?"

"Ye know well who I spent it with," said Toucher Plant. "With Billy Tabley, that's who." Now that he was alone with "the Boys," it would strengthen his hand to mention the forbidden name.

They looked at one another knowingly. The bigger man asked:

"And what did he tell you?"

"And how could he tell me anything with the guards in the room?" The Toucher was gaining their confidence by his very evasiveness.

"You're as safe as a house with us."

The hunchback rose to light a lamp, for the morning was darkening without.

"Maybe you can tell us how long you have known him?" the big man asked.

The Toucher was gaining confidence. These men depended on him for some information they thought was in his power to give. His apparent friendship with Billy, the stagecoach guard, could never be gainsaid by Billy now.

"Off and on these ten years, mebbe more," the Toucher answered.

"Did he leave anything with you?"

"He left me his waistcoat and his coat, and his shoes with the buckles. But God knows if I'll ever get them now. They took everything he had, watch and all."

They looked at one another.

"Mebbe it's in the lining, it is," the hunchback suggested.

"Small good that will do us," the sharp little man said. Then, pushing a bottle towards the Toucher, he remarked: "He's been up all night."

"Trying to comfort me poor friend," the Toucher added. " 'May your shrift be short,' I sez. 'Aye; but it'll be sharp,' sez he."

As the Toucher was drinking, there was a whispered talk between the members of the group.

"And why should he trust us?" he heard one ask.

At last the big man spoke:

"There was a lot of stuff, that Billy had. Some of it belongs to us. We can't be sure from what that old rogue Harris says whether he got it or not, and we are in no position to say that he did. There's a lot of stuff that's ours by right and we feel sure that if he only had the chance, Billy would have let us know its whereabouts."

"With the guard there all he said to me was that if he hadn't left Stony Batter he wouldn't be in the trouble he was in. He said he seen a spotter dodging about as he crossed over Bloody Bridge, and the guard got him then. Two more came and recognized him. He said he done it near the Rocky Valley when the light was too good."

"Stony Batter," the hunchback repeated. "Mebbe that's all we want to know."

"I could go blind-folded to his lodgings in Stony Batter this minute," the sharp little man said. "It's with the auld one where he lodged, if it's anywhere at all."

They agreed that this conjecture was correct. The condemned man could not have passed the information more openly than he had done without risking being overheard and having his lodgings searched.

"What the Hell possessed him to walk out in the light of day when he was safe enough?" the big man inquired. "Did he tell you that?"

"No," the Toucher admitted. "But he may have wanted to see Red Dander fight."

"The cock-fight—of course, it was that brought him out."

"It did not bring me out!" said one of the boys with a laugh. "Was you at it, Mr. Plant?"

"Wasn't I telling poor Billy about it? It cheered him half the night. Reddin let me stay in the cell as long as I liked because I had been at the main."

They huddled together with a new interest. They had not been about for nearly a week and to miss an event on which so much money was bet was a deprivation indeed. It was bad for trade too, to miss such an opportunity of mixing with the Quality and seeing what amounts they carried in cash.

They plied the Toucher with another drink.

"Tell us about it now."

The Toucher was a born story-teller, after the tradition of the Dublin teller of tales.

"Don't ask me about it!" he began, suggesting that no words of his could do justice to the scene. "Don't ask me about it! The pit was so full of feathers that I could hardly see. There was more than would have made a bed. Melia Murdher! Ye never seen such a fight! They didn't have to point the birds at all. The Dander nearly knocked Feeney down when he tried to take him out. That was after the first main. He won the three in succession. Jayshus, such a bird! They should cast him in gold for the top of Christ Church!

"They sucked the blood out of the third cock's head before he had time to put it down. They almost had to get a shovel to put him back in his cage. St. George is worth a mint from the result, and as for Feeney, who taught them how to train him, ye'd think it was himself had on the spurs."

The recitation was as good as a position at the side of the cock-pit. After a while the rat-like little fellow with Huguenot blood in him asked:

"Who is this St. George? Is he the same that owns Green Glint?"

"It's very likely," said Toucher Plant.

Yes. It was evident that this Toucher would be a useful acquisition to the Boys. He could go in and out of Newgate as the spirit moved him, and he could attend every race meeting and recognize every man of wealth in the land. The tip he had already given them, that the dead man's cache was at his lodgings in Stony Batter, was valuable.

If the Toucher felt that he had contributed to their needs without compromising himself, he was not quite right.

"But what possessed you to pay your way in to the jug to see him on his last night unless you had something on your mind?" the hunchback asked, with his little eyes fixed on the Toucher like gimlets.

"Weren't we children together?" And the Toucher winked.

To the Toucher the silence that ensued felt like the silence before the foreman of a jury spoke.

The hunchback tiptoed to the door, opened it silently, and peeped out.

"All right. Joe is still there," he said, and took his seat.

"Since you won't tell us your affairs, we will tell you some of ours," the big man began. "There is not one of us that can show his nose near Newgate. But you can. You have every reason to go there and gather your belongings. You may have to pay forfeit again to Reddin the head warder. That won't leave you out of pocket," he pointed to his breast. "And when you get the coat we can examine it with you. We know that you must be all right or Billy would never have trusted you. But it's the first time we suspected that you ever took the road."

The Toucher was elated. He was trusted. The danger, if there had been any outside his own imagination, was past. He could consider himself one of "the Boys." They thought that he had played the highwayman with the late lamented. But his elation was not to last long.

"We are far too well known to show our noses. That's why we

stayed here until Billy was stretched. We were undecided whether to strike at once now that the sojers think that they have got the real Larry, or to leave it alone, till they think a new man is working the road. But your coming and another man's going have forced our hand—it's not so bad as that—gives us a chance, would be more like it.

"Now we want you to listen to this. On Wednesday a rich old gent (never mind how we learnt it) is going down from here to Galway. He will be away maybe for months. With a face like yours, that never has been suspected, you'll stop the coach, and we'll do the rest. He can't stand up with the gout in his foot."

"But Holy Cripes!" the Toucher said.

"Hold yer whist," said the little rat-like man.

"I never stopped a coach in me life," the Toucher hastened to explain. Incredulous smiles were his answer.

"You may safely put yourself in our hands. We put ourselves in yours. This is Larry Dooley, for whom there is the hue and cry that took Billy Tabley to his grave this morning," the little sharp man added, with a sweep of his hand to the head of the table. Larry Dooley said nothing. The intelligent Toucher tried to be unconcerned.

Then in his deep voice Larry Dooley spoke.

"Ledoux here has not told you what we want. You don't have to hold a pistol to the driver's head. All you have to do is to ride up and warn him that there are highwaymen stationed on the Enfield Road. Gallop away—and come back next week for your share in the swag."

The Toucher thought.

"Isn't forewarned forearmed?" he asked.

"In this case, no. There won't be time either to turn for help or to go on. The old fellow within the coach will ask his man what it was you said. It's when he gets down to tell him that the traces will be cut. We won't ask you to carry a pistol. We will wait on the rise from Leixlip, and if you wish, you can gallop off down the lane to Celbridge, or go on and give the alarm to the Lucan guard-house. There's no one will suspect you. After this you may retire, for all we care."

"All they want is the loan of your face," the hunchback explained, thinking that the Toucher was vacillating. But he was only balancing two terrors in his mind: his present fear, and his indwelling fear of Tiger Roche. He was asking himself which was the better man.

"Where am I to meet you?" he asked.

"Before you come into Celbridge there is a turn down a hill to the river on the right. It's about two miles this side of Celbridge. It's the only road that leads off the main road to the right. There's a bridge there over the Liffey they call Newbridge. Be there under the trees on Wednesday night. It won't be dark enough then, but I want you there early, for fear they start sooner than we were told."

"I'll be there. But now I'm thinking of getting going, and asking Reddin for my blue coat. I hope it will cost me nothing to get it out. It cost me all I had to get meself in."

He left with five guineas more in his pocket, but it brought him small comfort. He tried to comfort himself by admiring Tiger Roche. At least he could be faithful to the Tiger. The Tiger would not desert him. He would never desert one who had got into such a predicament through obeying orders. And what a predicament it was! He had to send two or three men to the gallows in order to save his own neck, he that hated violent death, or death in any form. He had to go into the gap of danger and take a chance of being murdered if the Tiger failed to bring Larry Dooley to justice. Justice! That was the worst of all. The irony of it! He who had little enthusiasm for law and order found himself a most forceful agent of it now.

"Jayshus, Plant the hangman!" he said to himself.

XXXIII. TWO SURRENDERS

SIR RICHARD WAS in a merry mood. Everything had gone well. The surprise had been complete. The surprise was a marriage ceremony and a wedding feast at Lucan House. Constant d'Estournelles had been married to Ellice St. George.

"What gave me the idea was this," Sir Richard explained, in acknowledging the thanks of the guests. He did not keep his audiences long as a rule, but perhaps because of the champagne, his after-dinner speech was longer than his wont. "When I heard the glad tidings, I lost but little time having the arrangements, such as they are—thank you—made. Our very good and noble friend, the Chevalier, just lately has been forbidden by the military people here from living within four miles of the coast. These arrangements may have an important strategic value, but, damme, I can't see the meaning of them in our friend's case."

It was easy to speak to an audience with such appreciation. He stood straighter, and when silence reigned again, continued: "He is not likely to send signals to the sans-culottes."

If these cheers continued he would lose the thread of his speech.

"No. Hardly likely. Certainly not." There it was. It had gone. What the devil was he to say now? Oh, yes. Some little tribute to the French Abbé.

"Difficulties such as these beset the Chevalier. But just think of those which beset me. If his difficulties arose out of military regulations, mine arose out of religious regulations. I very nearly found myself turned into a Roman Catholic Bishop. Yes. What do you think of that? It came about from interfering in the affairs of the Church. And why? Because both parties agreed that a civil marriage would never do. They had seen too many civilities in France. Yes, they had. And they wanted to be married by a Churchman. And quite rightly.

"But where were my difficulties? Let me tell you where they were. There was difficulty about the diocese, place of birth, length of residence, the operator, no—that's not the word—the officiator, or the coadjutor—Monsieur l'Abbé will correct me if I'm wrong. Do not take it that I am an irreligious man, far from it, though perhaps I fall short this side of sainthood."

Cries of "Oh, no!" arose from the table.

"Perhaps not!" The cheering became more enthusiastic. "But Church discipline or procedure puzzles me. Then the Chevalier had a brilliant idea. He knew that a very good friend and a relation of his, an Abbé, had taken refuge in this country. How to find him was the problem. Well, Ladies and Gentlemen, I have a very good friend, though not a relation, and not in the Church but, of all places, in the Club. He found the Abbé for us. The Abbé got special permission to perform the ceremony which gladdened our hearts this morning.

"Yes. The Chevalier produced the idea, my friend produced the Abbé, but, not to be outdone, Ellice, now Madame d'Estournelles, produced the beautiful Madame de Ronquerolles. That's what I mean when I say that this morning gladdened our hearts."

The Chevalier was the first to see the disingenuity. He said something to his wife in French. What it was could only be heard by one other person besides the lady addressed, and that person blushed.

"He speaks like majesty," was what the Chevalier had whispered, but his smile turned on Clemente and the sequel was an apple-bright blush. She understood that d'Estournelles was referring to Sir Richard's use of the pronoun in the plural—"our hearts"— when he meant his own. She blinked her eyes prettily. She was confused. At long last the table caught the joke. The laughter and the sight of Madame's blushes confused Sir Richard.

"And if possible, she's looking better than ever now. In conclusion—"

"Hurrah!"

"Now the problem of the honeymoon arises. Dublin is on the sea. Lucan is ten miles from it. I propose that we all go off and leave them Lucan House."

"Hurrah!"

"I raise my glass to the bride and bridegroom, to the bridesmaid, to the Abbé who made this festival opportune, to the assembly, and to the best man!" He bowed and, putting his hand on his heart, drained his glass to the assembly and to himself, the best man.

Although Sir Richard and his guests did not start immediately on their journey, the coach he was to use did.

It started before there was time for any information to leak out. Feeney was not on the box, nor was Timsey on the leader. St. George's coachman was there.

A garbled account of the extraordinary departure soon ran through the servants' quarters.

"A bigger man than the master rode off in the coach," Tulip told the astonished servants, "and with the gout in his leg."

However they looked at it, there was no explaining it. There was no way of certifying the story of Tulip, who declared that, even as Sir Richard was making his after-dinner speech, according to the butler's timing, Sir Richard had driven off.

"It's a straight mile to Leixlip and you might be able to see the coach yet," Tulip said, as though the sight of it would corroborate his story.

Meanwhile on Newbridge, in a niche in the parapet of that ancient treble span, stood Toucher Plant. His friends of Winetavern Street had "borrowed" from him the horse he had himself borrowed. Horses were so easily recognized that a strange one was a godsend to Larry Dooley. Besides, it would be better for the Toucher to approach the coach on as sorry a nag or pony as could be procured. Men on coaches at nightfall are liable to be suspicious if they are approached by a man on a tall horse.

"Mount me on a jackass and be done wid it," the Toucher had fretfully complained.

He waited for his nag on the bridge instead of joining the two members of the gang who were hidden under the trees. He thought, "Mebbe it's because they want to keep an eye on me, or they don't want me to know who's in it with Larry himself."

Then another thought more disturbing than the last struck him:

"Mebbe it's that they don't want me to be able to gallop off. That's a fine roan Larry is on. I don't know what the others have. There's two of them, mebbe three. They wouldn't bring the fellow with the hump along. There cannot be more than three. The little rat of a fellow wouldn't be much good, except perhaps to run under and hamstring a horse. If he isn't here, that leaves two, one for each side of the road and Himself."

The Toucher had still more disturbing thoughts than these. A man who has witnessed a hanging is hardly fancy free—not for some time.

"If they kill the Tiger, I'll be taken as an accomplice and stretched. If they fail to kill the Tiger, one of them may put a parting shot into me to keep me mouth shut."

The clatter of approaching hooves ended his meditations. Dooley rode up, bringing with him a mount for Plant.

"This ought to do you. Up you get. And once more listen. Time yerself to meet the coach just before it gets to the quarry on the right-hand side of the road as you come from Enfield. The brakes will have to be on when they stop. There's a steep fall to the little river on your left. They can't turn. The brakes will be on to prevent its rolling back. All you have to do is to be ambling along quiet-like from Enfield. Throw up your hands in front of the coach. Shout, 'Thieves!' —or 'Rogues!'—or whatever you like; but you have got to stop that coach or we shall have to stop you. Forever," Larry added, as the Toucher took his seat.

One consolation came to the Toucher's mind. It almost made him smile when he thought of the gang's anxiety about his stopping the coach. "Jayshus," he said, "it will stop itself, very nearly, whether I'm there or not!" The farther he rode from the gang the more his courage mounted. He laughed: "If they only knew who's in it," was his amusing thought.

Meanwhile the great coach proceeded as some thought it would proceed, supposedly bringing Sir Richard westward on his long journey to Lisadill. Why it did not take the morning light to speed it on its way could only be explained by the wedding feast at which Sir Richard had presided. Even at this late hour, near nine of an August night, he could make Mullingar in four hours and stay with the Pakenhams on his way.

The Toucher knew how to sit on a horse. He could get as much out of it before he took it to the knacker's as any living man, short of a Red Injun.

It looked tired—the little pony that nobody with a heart for horseflesh would have ridden that far, for far it obviously had come. Even if it had only come from Enfield or Kilcock—and there was no town nearer—that was far enough, with such a weight on its back. If its rider had taken some of his weight from the middle of its back and used the stirrups more it might not have been so bad. But as it was the Toucher sat slumped and dejected, without spunk left in him to rise and fall as the poor creature padded along. And now here he was on the top of Leixlip Hill, with a grand yellow coach climbing up in its lordly strength and no effort at all on the four-in-hand.

Plant's little pony stepped carefully, feeling the ground with its forelegs out in front of it. It kept in the middle of the road, for it was hard enough set, even at that, to get out of anyone's way. Suddenly Plant saw the coach and let a shout out of him with his two hands raised high in the air.

"In the name of God, be on your guard, gentlemen! There's highway robbers down the road. I was robbed not an hour ago. They did not leave me a single groat."

"Go along out of that," said the coachman, and made at him as if he would strike him with his whip. Then the window opened and a gray head popped out.

"What is he saying? What is that fellow talking about?"

"Hold the reins," said the driver to his companion, and started to climb down.

The old gentleman in his excitement opened the door. The coachman was only half down when he was flung on his face and two blackguards raced out from each side of the road and cut the traces before you could say knife. Then off they went again before you could catch a glimpse of them. But that was not all. That's not half of it. Out from a cut in the hill comes a big lump of a man on a horse seventeen hands high if it is an inch. He is in no hurry either. He walks the horse round the back of the coach and he stoops to look into the door. That's where he makes the mistake of his life.

The old gentleman had his gouty foot half out of the open door. Sorra much gout there was in that same foot. He made one leap at the horseman or dived under his horse, so quick you could not tell which. Down he pulled Larry by the opposite foot and gave his leg a twist.

The action took place so swiftly as to baffle description and to invite exaggeration. As far as could be judged in the uncertain light, what had happened was as follows.

When Larry, from the quarry, saw that his accomplices had cut the traces, he took his time and came out without haste and rode round the back of the stranded vehicle on his high horse. As he came level with the coach door, which was on his left hand, he saw a bandaged foot appearing.

He made the mistake of his life: he thought the foot identified the man. He bent down, he rode so high, in order to level his pistol at the breast of the crippled owner of the gouty foot.

The next thing he knew, his mount was on the ground and he himself was pinned down with his right leg under the saddle.

His pistol had flown from his hand. A tall and somewhat burly gentleman in a dark velvet coat was sitting calmly on his horse's head. From one of his capacious pockets he was drawing a length of rope.

"Mr. Dooley, be pleased to maintain your aplomb. If you do not cease threshing about, I shall be compelled to break your arms."

In silence, like a brailed hawk, Larry glared at the stranger.

He was turned over on his face and his coat was pulled over his shoulders. His hands were pinioned insufferably tight behind his back.

The gentleman produced a pistol and began to spread the highwayman's coat under the horse's knees. His solicitude seemed inconsistent with the situation in which Larry found himself placed.

When the horse had risen, with the bridle on his arm, Tiger Roche bound Larry's ankles as securely as he had bound his wrists. Then he lifted him and laid him face downwards across the horse's withers. His hands were drawn towards his ankles under the horse's belly and foot and hand secured. His coat was thrown over his back.

His captor then led his mount to the quarry from which it had come some minutes before.

"Have you got them, Andy?" he called.

"One of them, yer Honour. I've trussed him up like a turkey. The other is dodging over there under the wall."

"Hold this horse a moment, if you please." He walked towards the dark wall, pistol in hand. A voice whined:

"Oh, for the love of Jayshus, Mr. Roche."

"Come out, Ledoux."

A rat-faced little man, with a head like that of a souteneur from the purlieus of Paris, came slowly forward with his hands raised over his head.

"Those hands of yours would be more trustworthy behind your back. Turn round."

"Can you manage to repair the traces, Andy?"

"Yes, yer Honour. I brought the chains."

"Then if you loop these heroes' necks and tie them arm to arm, I will proceed. Follow as soon as you can."

"Ah, yer Honour, ye may trust me!"

The Tiger mounted the great horse and adjusted his coat over the prostrated highwayman. Behind him he dragged the two who had cut the traces.

As the Tiger came from the quarry to instruct the outrider who was holding the horses, a broad-faced fellow dressed in a blue coat, the skirts of which nearly swept the ground on each side of the sorry pad on which he was riding, drew rein and came to a stand.

"Oh, dear, oh, dear! What has happened? Has there been a breakdown? Any assistance in my power I shall be delighted to give."

"What are you doing here, Plant? And who the devil dressed you in that coat?" So spoke the Tiger in order to save the Toucher from all suspicion of coöperation that might follow him and be reported to Larry's friends when they should visit him in gaol.

"I was going on to Maynooth, Sir. But if it will help you, I will turn back." Well Roche knew that the Toucher would turn back, for no man was more constrained by curiosity than Toucher Plant.

The Tiger did not reply but ambled back to Lucan House. He went slowly, for he waited for the coach.

He had just ridden the Irish mile which separates Leixlip from Lucan when he heard the sound of following wheels. He turned into the drive almost under the leaders' heads.

Hearing the sound of wheels, the ostlers ran to hold the heads of the horses of any visitors that might be arriving, for it was a festive house this night.

Tulip shouted, "Glory be to God!"

"Run in and tell your master that I would pay him my respects. I am incommoded, but ask him if he would grant me audience in the hall," the Tiger ordered.

"And who sooner? Of course I will, Mr. Roche." So, marvelling, Tulip ran and sent the message to the house.

Sir Richard's peroration was just concluding when the butler came behind him. Seeing him, Sir Richard turned. After a colloquy Sir Richard said:

"Ladies and Gentlemen, I promised you a surprise, but it is nothing to the one that awaits us at the door. It appears that while I was speaking to you I was on the Leixlip Road, capturing single-handed, Dooley, the highwayman, who lay there to rob or murder me. This extraordinary circumstance was made possible by our friend Roche, who in the interests of law and order impersonated me and my poor foot, which I am thankful to say is now nearly sound enough for dancing. Shall we go and inspect the Tiger's catch?"

Lighted by the many lanthorns and the August moon, Roche sat silently on the highwayman's horse. He awaited Sir Richard and his guests.

Sir Richard appeared, and twenty with him, the wedding guests.

"Well, really, Roche. You are a surprising fellow. Where did you get that wonderful horse? And where is Larry Dooley?"

Tulip, who was lengthening the stirrup leathers, was in the way.

The Tiger lifted the highwayman's coat and showed his shoulders and the back of his hanging head.

In the midst of a buzz of voices the voice of Dooley called out: "He is murdering me, Sir Richard. All I have in my waistcoat is pressing into me body and my leg is broken!"

The Tiger replaced the coat.

"We must be moving on," he said. "I have a little wager to collect at the Club. Take these heroes to the guard-house down the road." He threw the rope to Tulip and turned his mount.

"Damme, Roche," Sir Richard shouted as the Tiger turned to go. "There must be thirty stone on that horse."

"I will dismount and walk him up Mount Venus Hill. Good night!" He swept off his hat as he bent his head towards the ladies in the hall.

To the servants who, unsummoned, had crowded behind the guests, Sir Richard said:

"Run off and clear the tables. We will take wine in the drawing room." He led the way to the great drawing room to see to it that those of the party were being waited upon, for the event of the night had somewhat upset the household.

"I must pay my respects to the ladies. I will join you presently."

Going upstairs, he passed through one of the boudoirs. On a seat in front of the fire, Madame de Ronquerolles sat alone. Light from the pine logs and andirons lit her hair, turning its brown to glowing gold.

"By the way, I owe you some apology for drawing all that embarrassing attention to you this evening, I am afraid," Sir Richard said awkwardly.

Bending close to the fire Clemente shook her bonnie head. The embarrassment was Sir Richard's now.

"You must believe me when I say that I would be the last person in the world wilfully to make a lady the butt of my attempts at humour; but on a light and somewhat frolicsome occasion such as this, I may have said too much, and made my remarks rather personal. Believe me I never meant to cause pain to your charming self."

Clemente's graceful shoulders shook. She might be sobbing or laughing. How was Sir Richard to know when he could not see her face?

"Oh, dear, oh, dear," was all he said. He stepped back from the fire. He greatly wished to go but he feared to add rudeness to his thoughtlessness. He only took a step back and lingered in a most puzzled state of mind.

Madame de Ronquerolles turned a tearful face. She pressed a dainty handkerchief to an eye, rose and moved to a fireside ottoman, where she sat down closer to the cheerful hearth. The fire leapt. Sir Richard moved a log with his toe.

"What can I have done to give you such pain?" he inquired.

With her face lifted fully towards him, Clemente looked up and shook her curly head. She burst into tears and hid her face again.

"It is when people are so kind to me," she sobbed.

Sir Richard pondered this with doubtful relief. He moved to the ottoman and took his seat beside her.

"I am glad to hear it. I was afraid that you were not being treated with becoming deference in this wild country. You must be longing for France."

"Oh, no. Oh, no! It is not that," said Clemente rapidly, "but the very kindness I receive so far from my home and my friends—sometimes it nearly breaks my heart." She sobbed a little.

"Well, I am glad to hear that; not about your heart; but that it is nothing I said or did that made you weep. It upsets a man to see a woman weep, particularly when he doesn't know what for."

Gently he patted Madame de Ronquerolles' shapely arm. "There, there," he said. "Now, there."

Clemente looked at her folded hands and said in a low voice:

"I can be of so little use. I can give so little in return."

Sir Richard was well satisfied with his tact and the way he had managed things. He had thought when he saw Clemente weeping that he was "in for a scene." But it was as clear as day to him now. Here was a noble lady of France, a lonely émigrée from her native land, whose husband had been assassinated after the Revolution, and her estates seized. She had no prospects but to remain indefinitely in a strange and semi-savage country, but one in which, at all events, there were gentlemen who respected women. Sir Richard wished to avoid making her feel her position in any way.

"You have been of vast help to us," Sir Richard said. "My sister is devoted to you, and as for Mabs, what would she be without you? You are such a valuable example to her. Left alone with my sister she would be running wild. In fact I am not sure that she is not that way inclined, so to speak. And you have done all this for us spontaneously, when all we asked was your company and friendship."

Again Clemente burst into tears. She lowered her shoulders till the firelight made rosy the round of them near her neck.

"Damme, I don't want to be kind to you and make you cry, if that's what it does to you," Sir Richard exclaimed. "But when I think of your kindness, it almost makes me—well, what I mean is, I want to thank you—"

Clemente drew her lace cloak up over her shoulders.

"Mabs, Mabs!" she exclaimed despairingly. "Oh, I am such a failure! I have done my best with that girl. She is lovely and spirited but she has no idea of the proprieties, or of the demeanour that becomes a lady in her position. Some day she will grow up, and marry, and govern a stately house, but if she does not learn now what is required in noble society it will be too late, her manners will be formed. And I shall have failed. I *have* failed." Madame de Ronquerolles lifted her voice until it almost shrilled. She wrung her hands. "I have failed Mabs and—and you!"

"Oh, don't mind me," Sir Richard was about to say, but that was not what he wanted to say at all. So he did not say it. What he said was, "No one could be more grateful than my sister and I for all the loving care you give that girl. And she is responding. I will make sure that she is responding. You shall see if I don't. That is one of my reasons for leaving this and going on to Lisadill."

Clemente was filled with admiration for Sir Richard's solicitude for the education of his niece. Her hands lay palms upward on her lap. It was difficult to see her wedding ring. But it was easy to see the full fingers that tapered to such slender points and the coral ovals of her thumbs.

"We will take her in hand together when we get down there." There still was something oppressing in Clemente's mind. She turned to Sir Richard and solemnly and gently shook her head.

Her eyes were filling. "I will not cry," she said. "But I am a dreadful failure. I cannot influence that girl. Only this evening, this very evening, she told me of something that almost broke my heart and sent me into this room to be alone and away from the company. That is why you found me here. It was the result of my lack of will power. If I were strong-minded I could have made your niece more lady-like and things like this would not have come to this pass."

"But what the devil, that is to say, what did she tell you that almost broke your heart? Anything I should know?"

Clemente's fingers opened and came together once or twice in her lap. "You must forgive me if I weep again, I cannot help it. You will believe only too well how I have failed you when I tell you what Mabs told me."

Sir Richard's mind was in a whirl. He tried to imagine the worst offence Mabs might have committed.

"Card debts?" he asked.

"No, no. She does not play cards. I would not allow her even to play écarté."

"Betting or anything like that?"

There was a long silence. At last Clemente said in a far-away voice:

"She won two hundred guineas on some sort of fighting cock called Red Dander. I heard a servant telling her that she had won or that the cock had, and that her money was all right. It was not all right, as it turned out."

"What! You don't tell me that she lost. The cock won. What's this Plant reported? Oh, yes! He fought like a stallion."

"She was never paid. Some ruffian called Bumbeigh absconded."

Sir Richard was growing interested.

"But what did she put on?"

"On?" Madame de Ronquerolles asked. The lingo of betting was an alien tongue to her.

"What sum did she bet that the bird would win?"

"There was no sum. As far as I know if the fighting cock won Bumbeigh was to pay her two hundred guineas."

"But if he lost?" Sir Richard asked, gazing with approval at Clemente as she struggled with the fundamentals of Irish sport.

"If he lost, Bumbeigh was to get your coach and four!"

"What? Again?" Sir Richard almost shouted.

Then he pondered deeply. It would never do to give Madame any inkling of the enormity of the procedure of which his niece had been guilty. True, it might be said that the family was supporting the fighting cock; but it would seem too ridiculous to pretend that he had given permission to Mabs to lay his coach and team of horses on the cock. When she had shown him the two hundred guineas she had won on Deaf Burke, he had asked her what odds she had got and where she had got the money with which to bet:

"Never mind, Uncle," she had said, "you can still drive us down to Lisadill."

Denis St. Gorge had been unable to stop laughing when he told Sir Richard what the magic words were that revived Deaf Burke.

"She told him she had laid your coach and four," he had said. And Sir Richard had treated the affair in the spirit in which it was represented to him—as a joke. But it was really no joke, this gambling habit in one so young—and with his own coach and horses. Had she lost, what a fool and laughing stock he would have looked. He would have had to pay out the equivalent of his horses and his coach.

But this time Mabs had no money to flourish. That could only mean one thing: she had not been paid. If she had been, she would have counted on success to obtain his forgiveness. This time there was a win; but where was the cash? Its absence could mean only one thing. Bumbeigh had not paid up. Better appear to treat the matter lightly. To let it pass. Wait. There was one thing which he could not let pass and that was Bumbeigh's default. He would have to go himself to Bumbeigh, even though it would put him in an absurd position, and pretend that Mabs had had his full permission to lay his coach and four. Was Bumbeigh not counting on the fact that he had the girl in a difficulty, that she could not reveal to her uncle what she had done? But when her uncle came to claim— Wait again. He would refer the whole transaction to Roche.

Yes, the Tiger would smooth out matters. It was the kind of affair in which that strange being revelled.

That settled that in Sir Richard's mind. But the sooner Mabs went home the better. He would start away in the morning.

To the Baronne he said: "Oh, a little bet like that is merely playful. But first thing in the morning, bright and early, we'll get out of this." He rose as if to start there and then.

"I cannot go," she said. As though to emphasize her firm resolve not to travel, she removed her frail lace cape from her shapely shoulders with a resigned gesture.

Sir Richard was taken aback. He had not realized how much the thought of the divertissement of the Baronne's company was reconciling him to the prospect of long evenings with his sister at Lisadill. And yet he was in no position to make plans for her, much less to interfere with any she might have made for herself.

The way she had said, "I cannot go," coming as it did from the midst of a storm of nerves, gave him to think that he might, with a little exercise of his delicate tact, alter the situation.

"If it is only the obstreperous conduct of that sprightly girl that makes Lisadill obnoxious—" he began.

A spark flew from the pine logs and ignited the hem of Clemente's voluminous muslin dress.

With a little cry of alarm she caught her skirts up to her lap, beating out the spark with her helpless little hands. Sir Richard came bravely to the rescue. He, too, caught up the burning garment, and soon extinguished the flame. Clemente pushed down her dress and blushed with the fresh apple blush of an embarrassed child.

"Don't, don't, my dear," Sir Richard said. "Don't give way to alarm. All is well. I hope you are not burned?"

Clemente gazed at her scorched dress. She gazed at the palms of her hands. Sir Richard caught one and examined it.

"I hope it is not paining you," he said. "One never sees what a burn can be until the place blisters."

Madame rose, without withdrawing her hand from Sir Richard's.

"May I hold this little hand, my dear?" Sir Richard said. "I would like to hold it forever."

Madame bent down her head. She left her hand limply in Sir Richard's. She did not shake her comely head.

Sir Richard was a courageous man, but this was a position which called for more than the courage required to deal with a man.

"Damme, she is a tender, helpless little thing," he thought. His compassion overcame him.

He put a protecting arm around her jimp waist.

"My dear, my dear," he said. "Let me bring you as my wife to Lisadill. I am old, I know—that is to say, I am getting on. But—"

Madame de Ronquerolles began to cry, but with a mighty effort she suppressed her tears so that she was able to turn dewy eyes to the gallant gentleman.

"You are not old," she whispered, as her head fell upon his breast. "You are the only one I have ever known who understands me."

"But have I your promise, Clemente?"

She did not reply at once. She gathered her ruined skirt about her, covering the rent the fire had made, which exposed her petticoat.

"You have, my dear, brave man," she said. "You must not think that you are old. You are only in your early maturity. But I must seek my chamber."

Sir Richard kissed her as she stood.

"Damme, I'll tell the company this very night, so that it will be too late for you to change your mind."

Clemente fled daintily from the room before Sir Richard could reach the door to open it for her.

Down in the servants' hall, Toucher Plant was describing the scene he had witnessed on the road. His account seemed to contradict the rôle he should have performed. One would think to hear him that he had been an eye-witness from some clump above the quarry and not a chance passerby on his way to "Maynooth and Kilcock."

"It was Andy Byrne, Sir Richard's valet, that cotch the other two. You couldn't tell if he wasn't worse than the Tiger himself. He ran after the bigger blackguard and gave him a clatter on the head with the butt end of a pistol as big as a blunderbuss."

"And why shouldn't he? He's an ould sojer and fought with Sir Richard," the cook asserted.

"And they had plenty of rope between them. They trussed them all up. Wherever the Tiger was going, he wasn't taken by surprise."

"Tulip said that the Tiger was going nowhere but to catch Larry Dooley by himself. Wasn't the coach and all ready for a drive through the night when Tulip goes out to the stables only to see it moving away with Andy on the box?"

Loudly a bell rang, and kept ringing, swinging by itself alone, in a line of bells under the kitchen ceiling.

"And all was ready to go across to the West this very night," the butler said. He rose and left the servants' hall.

So rapt were all with the Toucher's story that no one noticed the butler's return. His face was as expressionless as a blacksmith's apron.

"Wonders will never cease," he said. "We have another wedding on our hands. And it must take place before the Abbé goes."

"Glory be to God! Wouldn't you have thought that one wedding would have satisfied them?" the cook asked the spellbound household.

"Whose is it this time?" the Toucher asked. "No matter whose it is, it suits me," he added. "It's all fair as far as I am concerned. Devil a lie in it."

"Ye will never guess," the butler said, enjoying the interest he had aroused and pausing to increase the suspense. "It's the Master and that lady from France that came up for the races with Miss Penelope."

"Ye don't mean it!" said the cook.

"Oh, don't I, begob? 'If I may crave one further service of you, Father Abbé,' Sir Richard says, 'I will be forever obliged. I want you to join a very charming lady and myself in holy matrimony, just as soon as such things are permitted by your Church—the sooner the better. I want to get away from Lucan and leave it to lovers who are, I hope, as happy as I shall be!' "

"Jayshus, that sounds like business," the Toucher affirmed. "He's a grand ould codger anyway."

"And he never asked if the cellar could stand it," the butler added, aggrieved.

"We'll have them on our hands for the rest of our born days, at this rate," the cook suggested.

"Where's your 'bright and early' now?" Tulip inquired, with affected complaint.

"Them was my orders. 'We leave this bright and early in the morning,' himself said. I yoked up that coach twice. The first time it was taken by the Tiger. I had it hardly brushed out and dusted down but I had to span them again. And here I am now, not knowing if he wants it at all."

But it was "bright and early," three days afterwards, when Sir Richard left his guests and bowled along, going westward with his bride in his own coach and followed by his immediate friends.

The Toucher remained on for a week.

"It took a week to get the last of the guests out of the laurels in the woods," he explained later. "The first popping cost five hundred pounds. It was the properest wedding I was ever at, though I only seen the most of it from outside."

Yes, it was quite true, such a wedding as Sir Richard's was rarely seen even in Ireland, that most liberal of lands.

Sir Richard had taken heed of a remark his fiancée had made. Not only was he far from being old, but he was only in his "early maturity," and what was the good of maturity if you did not use it to show your character? That is the moment, or never at all. To wait a little would mark the decline. So in his full ripeness, Sir Richard ordered that all the villagers be admitted to share his liberality. What did it matter how they trampled his lawns and stole his flowers? They would revive again. But would he? Whether he would or not, now was the time to show what a liberal hand he had. He would give a wedding feast that would continue long after he had left it, and the memory of it would be remembered throughout the county long after he had gone away.

All was as merry as a wedding bell. The little steeple of the village church rocked with its jocund carillon. Madame looked as innocent as a bewildered child, with her apple cheeks bright behind her veil. And Sir Richard realized that what he had thought were age and gout were in truth nothing but results of the sinister life of celibacy which he had been leading.

And the Toucher's remark was, for a wonder, no exaggeration. It was a week, and Sir Richard had reached Lisadill, before the last guest was discovered snoring in the laurels by the Liffey's stream.

BOOK V

XXXIV. ANOTHER LANDING FROM FRANCE

HYACINTH WAS TRANQUILLY boating with Ninon at sundown, on an enchanted length of living golden water that glanced with the laughing sparkle of yellow wine. He would pull the oars, and then let the skiff drift when it emerged into the long sunlight from the shadow of an island's trees. Half a mile away the rich green fields sloped gently upwards, unburned by the August suns. Standing in gray dignity, the great house could be seen in the centre of its wooded crescent as it reigned over the rising land. Its tall windows flashed, diamonding the air.

The water hardly rippled beside the gliding boat, the air was so still. The cool serenity of the moment passed into Martyn's mind. Balanced as he was between two elements, that of the palpable and mysterious water and the invisible immortal air, he had the feeling of being disembodied and a part of the living scene.

On lake, sky and land a divine silence was outpoured.

"Oh, the beauty of it!" Ninon said, almost sighing.

"I was just wondering if happiness is anything more than perfect peace," Hyacinth remarked.

But Ninon did not answer. She bent her head to her knitting and plied the long ivory-topped needles to make a woolen buskin for a tiny foot.

As he regarded Ninon, Hyacinth felt that he had reached the summit of all happiness—the realization that he possessed God's greatest gift to man, an intelligent, lovely and devoted wife. And that before long his happiness was to be crowned by the birth of a child.

For a while no word was spoken. The afternoon was enough. Nature could offer human minds no greater measure of contentment.

To the southwest a long cloud floated, sailing towards the sun. Low down on the horizon the light-hidden hills began to appear.

"I wonder how they are getting on at Lisadill?" said Ninon, gazing at the distant hills. "I consider myself gifted with a good constitution, but another wedding like that and I would have been an invalid for life."

Hyacinth laughed.

"Uncle Dick took good care to get away long before the feast was over."

The first faint coolness of the evening came on. Martyn turned the boat. Ninon chatted as he rowed.

"How long do you think Uncle Dick will remain at Lisadill?" she asked.

"You mean how long will he be detained there? A year at least," Hyacinth replied. "You have heard of Clemente's library plan? All rising intellects in the neighbourhood are to be given free access to the library. A course of reading is marked out for them and when they have read the prescribed books and Clemente is satisfied that they are worth a University education, Sir Richard is to send them up to a crammer in town."

"And then?" Ninon asked, smiling.

"Then they will live unhappily ever after." Hyacinth laughed.

As they landed, Hyacinth whistled for the boatman.

"So long as they are happy, what does it matter?" he added. Again he whistled. But no boatman came. He took the cushions on which his wife had been resting and, jumping ashore, helped her by the hand.

He had to kneel down to get the chain that moored the boat.

"What the devil has become of Patsy?" he wondered aloud.

Together they walked slowly, sheltered by translucent trees, up the long slope to the house.

The hall door was open, for in the country there was no fear of theft. The peasants, so far as larceny went, were an honest race. Robbery was town bred.

Hyacinth rang the bell as he entered a room to wash.

No one came.

Presently he heard Ninon's bell ringing from above. There was a strange sense of emptiness through the great house. He tore at the bell-pull. He could hear the sound of Ninon's bell crossing the sound of his own.

He ascended the stairs and called to his wife.

"Dearest, is there no one up with you?"

On seeing Ninon's face at the stairhead he added: "There is no cause for alarm."

"There is not a servant in the house," Ninon said as she came downstairs. "Let us go into the basement."

Through the basement they went, through the kitchen, sculleries and the servants' quarters. The servants' hall was empty. Even Biddy could not be found. What had caused a flight such as this? When had it taken place? Surely they would have heard a call over the lake if there had been a raid or panic of any kind. And yet stained carpets, scratched walls and chipped banisters pointed to the rough passage of men from the fields. Apparently a mob had stormed the house in their absence.

"There must be something in the air to clear every servant out of the house," Martyn said. "Revolution?"

"More likely the long-threatened landing," Ninon answered.

"Wait till I go through the stables, dear."

"I will go with you," Ninon said. "Put on your riding coat."

Together they went through the stables. There were only two horses in the stalls. "Feeney will not desert us," Martyn assured her, and they went to Feeney's room. But it was empty. In a loose box under it, where tightly packed hay was stored, Ninon noticed that the hay was torn and tossed about half-way up the bale. She guessed what that meant and pointed out the breach.

"They've been hiding arms here. It must be revolution in dead earnest." There was nothing for it but to saddle the horses and go to the village for news of whatever was toward.

"They have left us two horses," Ninon said. "Yours and mine. Feeney must have left them for us."

"Yes, darling, but if there is revolution, the first thing that will be done is to have every possible cavalry charger and every horse of any kind that could be used to draw cannon, or supplies, seized by the authorities. It looks as if Crabbe had sent some of his men to clear the place, and that Feeney—faithful fellow that he is—succeeded in having two horses left for our use. Evidently that is what has happened here. The military may have acted on that report of Crosbie's that I took from the highwayman Collier and gave to Sir Richard for delivery to General Lake, naming the supposed rebels at Martyn Hall."

Hyacinth brought round the horses.

"Step on my hand," he bade Ninon, and lifted her on to her saddle. He sprang on his own mount and together they rode from the yard.

At the gate Ninon said, "We have left the place wide open." She looked back. Then she saw it.

High from the central chimney stack, where a green branch had been placed when the house was completed, a green flag lay limp against its staff. A ripple in the wavering evening air stirred it and almost opened it. Listlessly it fell back against the flag-staff.

Her husband's gaze followed hers. The flag lay dark against the golden azure of the zenith, which was turning to the colour of night.

"It could not have been Major Crabbe after all. If he saw that, he would occupy the house. What the devil do these rogues mean, going up through my house, sticking their flag in my chimney and stealing my horses? Come along."

As he rode along by the beechen lane, Hyacinth searched the fields with his eyes. There was not a horse to be seen. It was too dim beyond the woods to see if the cattle had followed in the wake of the horses.

"The brood mare has gone and she was carrying a valuable foal. This damned pretence at a campaign will cost us dearly. It started with amazing suddenness. I'm surprised at Feeney."

"Maybe they would have killed him for refusing to join the movement."

"They are all in it, every one of them. Yet Crosbie should have told me that he was reporting to the authorities; they should have acted on it sooner and forestalled this uprising. Revolution raises the hand of every servant against his master. We are no exceptions. They do not recognize ties of gratitude, unless as ties to bind servitude."

A dark mood settled on the master of Martyn Hall as he rode slowly with his wife towards the village, but a mood in which resolution had replaced indecision. Crosbie's report had placed Hyacinth in a dilemma, and his hesitation to dismiss Crosbie for treachery was characteristic of his attempt to take neither side in the struggle. Now his reference to Crosbie signified a vindication of himself.

He saw a gate from a field left open.

"The scoundrels!" he exclaimed. "I wonder who is the local ruffian responsible?"

Ninon said, "Hark! Do you hear that?"

A heavy, chant-like cheer rose for a moment and fell away. It rose again, intermittent and uncertain. As they rode nearer to the village, there it was again! Unmistakable this time, it was not a cheer but a slogan that sounded as a crowd's voice sounds when it encompasses the house of a popular leader and bids him show himself. It was almost articulate now.

As they turned into the main road they could see frieze-clad men crossing the fences from fields, the way they did on Sundays when they took a short-cut to Mass. All were going towards a dark crowd of people whose gathering closed the village street.

Half a dozen young men rushed past their horses, causing Ninon's to throw up his head, taking fright at the sudden glint of steel. The young men carried long poles fitted with axe heads, behind which there was a short, sickle-like hook turned downwards. These were pikes and they were designed for cut-and-thrust and axe work, also for severing the reins of cavalry horses.

As Hyacinth came beside his wife he cursed the heedless louts.

The shouts that sounded like "Fee, faugh, fum" changed into clearer sounds.

"Here!" Martyn-Lynch called out to a barefoot boy scampering past. "What's the meaning of all this?"

The gossoon turned his head without stopping:

"The French are at Killala!" he shouted.

That was what the rumbling roar farther on was saying:

"The French are at Killala!"

"My God!" thought Hyacinth, "we shall be in the centre of the battle." He gazed anxiously at his wife.

As each unit joined, the crowd roared to encourage it, "The French are at Killala!"

Hyacinth halted and listened. Deep-throated the roar continued. This was humanity's primal cry, the deep rumble of the world's discontent; the voice of Man as it was raised first against the Looser of the Avalanche that blocked the cave, or Him who smote the forest with fire from the sky. It was the voice of darkness and of suffering men, the voice of Patience, turned and at bay. It was the voice of all the slaves that ever suffered uncomplainingly on Earth. It was the terrible voice, delayed through the centuries, that had called to God for Justice, and had only brought down worse evils on its head. It was the voice of a people, kind-hearted and faithful, who long had looked to Heaven for some respite from the lot that condemned them to be slaves and see their famished children grow hollow-eyed and die while extravagance was sated and wealth abounded above their lowly roofs. It was the voice now raised in vengeance that took the place of long unanswered prayers. It was the voice of downtrodden Ireland, the immemorial utterance of the green earth that compassed all languages in its universal moan. Darkly it rose, and it was ominous now. Martyn-Lynch knew that that growl held a menace for him and his wife, as for the English. It was the roaring threat of the rabble, hollow-hoarse from famishing years.

Hyacinth turned to Ninon and said: "I wish you would ride back. I must go up to them and look for Feeney."

"I will stay here," Ninon answered.

Ten or twelve more men came driving in, hilariously singing. The crowd opened and enclosed them.

"The French are at Killala!" rose again in rhythmic beats.

A strong farmer trotted along on his bare-backed nag. He was leading a bony horse. Was he presenting it to the invading forces? More likely secret money had paid for it in gold, the possession of which might soon be punishable by death.

They were beginning to light flares now. From the far side of the dark mass, men who appeared to be in some kind of uniform were moving away with a hundred horses or more.

How many of Martyn's horses were in that regiment?

As they returned to Martyn Hall, they saw a lanthorn swung down the lane. There was the sound of a horse walking and soon its silhouette and that of its rider could be seen.

"I have a presentiment that there goes Feeney. There is something familiar about the way he sits a horse." Martyn started forward but, remembering Ninon, drew rein again.

"We will soon overtake him." A moment later they did.

"Feeney, is that you?"

"Indeed, Master Hyacinth, it's meself surely. And I have the mare with me back again."

"But what has happened? Why did you leave the house?"

"And why wouldn't I, and the horses gone? The rebels come and took them. 'Lave the mare where she is,' I asked the boys. Not a bit of them would. 'The Frinch is at Killala,' was all they would say. They took the guns, too."

"Guns?"

"They didn't leave a gun in the gun-room. All your pistols is gone."

Martyn-Lynch felt his pocket to reassure himself; but with one small flask of powder and half a dozen balls, there was little reassurance in the one pistol in his riding coat.

Feeney explained that after the rebels had gone with the guns and horses, he had not wanted to lose any time in trying to get the mare back, but had stayed to guard the house.

"But even at that I didn't stir out of it until Mr. Crosbie took charge of the house. 'Lave it to me,' he says."

Hyacinth reached out and pressed Ninon's arm in the darkness.

"Crosbie!" he said significantly, then, "Tell me, Feeney," he said aloud. "Who hung out the green flag from the chimney?"

"There I lave you, yer Honour. After the boys was gone, Mr. Crosbie took charge of the house. 'Lave it to me,' he says.

"Seeing Crosbie was there to look after things, I went to ask His

Reverence to use his influence about the mare. 'A mare in foal can't be much use to the Frinch,' I says. 'Not that I wouldn't put out a hand to help them if need be.'

" 'In the name of God, Feeney,' he says. 'Cut, shuffle or deal, have nothing to do with them. General Lake is on his way with twenty thousand sojers, Hessians and all.' He put on his hat and took the mare from a young ijit who was bringing her to Myles. 'Lave her go,' he says; and the gossoon released her. That, yer Honour, is why I left the house."

They were now out of the range of the roaring crowd. The horses plodded in the crisp leaves. He walked his horse to keep pace with Feeney.

"I had better not turn her out again," Feeney remarked. "I will keep her in a loose box. It did her little good to be chased round the paddock."

The night was brightening, with the moon coming up through the trees.

The back door was locked when they tried to enter the house from the yard. Hyacinth banged on it again.

"I seen a light in one of the windows," Feeney told him.

"Where?"

"It's gone again," Feeney whispered from the yard.

Ninon was growing cold and fretful. Her house locked against her, unknown people hiding in it, and the vanishing light—all the terror in the air filled her with foreboding.

"Let us go round by the drive," she prayed.

"In a little while, my dear."

Hyacinth dismounted and took Feeney's lanthorn. He walked with it to one of the stalls. He did not wish to alarm Ninon by looking to the priming of his pistol before her. When he assured himself that it was loaded and the flint screwed firm he put it in his pocket and mounted his horse.

"Let us try the front door. Put up the mare, Feeney, and come with us."

Feeney took the lantern and went to stable the mare. Some instinct concerning the stables made him delay. He may have heard the champing, but he felt that new horse-flesh was already housed. He opened the half-doors of two boxes. He turned as if to rejoin his master and then, bethinking himself, he examined all the boxes in the yard.

"What is he doing?" Ninon asked anxiously.

Feeney came over to them.

"There's two horses saddled and one of them is Mr. Crosbie's," he whispered. "The other one is strange. It has been ridden hard."

Though Hyacinth distrusted him, it was something of a relief to know that Crosbie was in the house. The identity of the other, whose tired mount was in the stall, would soon be known.

As he rode to the front door the moon was rising. Seen from the drive the house rose hollow in the ghostly light. In the charged stillness it had an empty and ownerless look that aroused presentiments too unwelcome to entertain.

Ninon was the first to sense something repellent in the air. Her great house warmed to her no longer. Only two windows flickered, as if from a death light held within. Walls hospitable in the sun were cold now in the moonlight. The great house was an enemy of the low roofs around it. Would the great house sink down and become deserted as the small ones grew high? Had the end of all great houses come? Had grandeur and magnificence no longer a place in the land? Had the day dawned when there would be no room in Ireland for nobility?

She thought of Clemente and the Chevalier, and wondered whether she and Hyacinch were to become émigrés as these two members of the élite of France had become. If so, in what land would they find sanctuary? Even in her self-pity, she pitied Clemente and Constant more, overtaken and surrounded once again as they were by revolution.

Hyacinth banged upon the hall door.

"There's a light coming down the stairs," Feeney reported from the gravel. Martyn-Lynch heard the footsteps on the stairs, an ominous sound in a house unnaturally stilled.

"Who is there?"

It was Crosbie's voice.

"It is I, Martyn-Lynch. Let me in, Crosbie. Open the door at once."

"There are others with you. Who are they?"

"What the devil does it matter? Open the door at once. My wife and I are here."

"I must refuse unless you say who else is there."

Speechless with rage, Hyacinth refused to reply, whereupon Feeney called out:

"Open the door, Mr. Crosbie. The Missus is out here in the night."

Martyn-Lynch thundered on the door. Abruptly his opinion of Crosbie had taken a turn for the worse. Now he was certain that Sir Richard's forebodings had been correct, and that Crosbie's messages to General Lake were evidence, not of loyalty to his master, but of a plot to blacken Martyn's name and have his property seized. Hyacinth cursed himself for the vacillation that had caused him to keep the agent on even after the clear evidence of treachery that the packet had contained.

"Patience, patience, Hyacinth," Ninon prayed. "You do not know but that he has reason to be afraid. He may think that you and I are being held as hostages by the rebels so as to force an entry to your house."

After she had spoken, Hyacinth could hear the great door slowly being unbarred. He heard the catch-chain loosed from the lock. The fanlight shone. Someone within was lighting the lamps in the hall. The door opened. Instead of allowing his wife to precede him, Martyn-Lynch entered first. Crosbie and Weld stood back in the hall, their pistols levelled. As Ninon entered, Hyacinth turned and closed the door.

"I want an explanation of this," he commanded.

Crosbie turned to Weld as if for corroboration before he spoke.

"We thought you were a prisoner and were being forced to give the rebels an entry to your house. They were here in your absence. We feared that they might return again."

"Yes," Hyacinth sneered, "that is why you decorated my chimney with their flag, to invite a raid on a friendly house after they had gone."

"I repeat, there was every likelihood that they would return again."

"There was far greater likelihood," Martyn answered angrily, "that Major Crabbe's men would see the flag, occupy my home and have me sent to Dublin Castle, if not hanged on the spot."

"I repeat that I did it to prevent your house being burnt to the ground as Weld's house was burned this afternoon."

"You knew that this afternoon? At what time, pray?"

Weld intervened:

"Everyone with a sense of loyalty and responsibility knows that every gentleman's house in the country will be looted and burned to the ground by the local insurrectionists if this invasion succeeds. The French have already landed one thousand men at Killala. There are thousands more on the high seas, about to descend on our defenceless coasts. It may be a week before General Lake arrives from Dublin. Until then it is obviously our duty to prevent the rebels from establishing themselves in such buildings as could be turned into redoubts by the enemy. This is a house from which they could only with difficulty be dislodged. Martial law has been declared."

After a while Martyn-Lynch asked:

"On whose invitation came you to seek asylum in my house? There were nearer places than this."

"It is the duty of every loyal man—"

"Sir, I ask you to give me no admonition about my duty. I will have none of it. The country may be under martial law but even a magistrate cannot invite himself, much less housebreak, into a citizen's house. Go about your business, Sir!"

A little sigh from Ninon brought Hyacinth to her side. As he led her to the stairs he said, "I will deal with both of you if you are not gone when I come down." He took a taper from a marble bracket and ascended.

Crosbie secured the door Martyn-Lynch had closed. Weld replaced his pistol in his pocket. They returned to the drawing-room from which they had come. Crosbie lit the chandelier and stirred the fire.

He put a decanter of brandy out of sight on the floor behind a tall Chinese screen. Weld made slits of his eyes in his yellow face as he watched.

"You need not conceal it for my sake," he said.

Hyacinth entered. He saw the lighted candles and the blazing logs.

"So, Crosbie, you are master here?"

"I came to protect your house in your absence. In times like these—"

"In times like these you hoisted an invitation to the troops to seize my house, or, failing that, to identify me with Rebellion. You sent to General Lake a list of my tenants whom you accused of being disaffected. If that is an account of your stewardship, you are no longer sufferable here. Take your ill-will and cunning out of my house."

He pointed to the door.

"And as for you, you ill-omened visitant," he said to Weld, "out you go with him."

Weld remained motionless with his back to the fire. He spoke in an unperturbed voice.

"Is this the moment a man who pretends to be a loyal subject should choose to expose the only two Kingsmen in the county to the resentment and fury of a blood-drunken peasantry? My house has been burned over my head. . . ."

"This house will be burned over my head if it holds you a moment longer."

"So you would turn me over to the sans-culottes?"

Martyn-Lynch held his anger. It was clouding his head. As collectedly as he could he said:

"You have sought me out to put me in this enigmatical position. Go to Crosbie's house, which I have yet to learn has been burned. But get out of this. I regard you as nothing other than an officer of the law who has established himself without warrant in an honest man's house in order to bring him into disrepute and to get for yourself the estates you would have attainted or outlawed. It would not be the first time in our island's history that the unwelcome guest ousted the native honest man." He handled his pistol.

"Speaking of warrant," Weld said coldly, "you are aware, of course, that if you have no written permission for that pistol of yours, I could commit you to prison. Illegal possession of firearms is punishable with death."

Deliberately Martyn-Lynch cocked the pistol. He held himself well in control. He smiled wryly and spoke slowly.

"Punishable with death, you say? I give you time to arm yourself."

His eye caught a motion of Crosbie's hand.

"No treachery, Crosbie! Put up your hands." He advanced. "Turn to the wall."

He took a pistol from Crosbie's coat and turned to Weld.

"A pistol with a permit, I presume?" he said, as he held out Crosbie's pistol. His eye caught sight of Ninon standing in the doorway, her face tense.

"There is somebody moving about upstairs," she said. "I am frightened."

Despair of searching the great attics satisfactorily without help flashed across Hyacinth's mind. He thought that Weld had posted men in the house.

Frowning on him: "Is this your doing, Sir?" he asked.

"I escaped alone."

Just at that moment Feeney appeared, carrying over his shoulder a green bedraggled flag.

"I thought, begob, if General Lake seen this, it's the Hessians we'd be housing."

Hyacinth drew Ninon to one side of the door. Turning to Weld and Crosby:

"End this intrusion," he said. Then to Feeney:

"Feeney, show these gentlemen to their horses. They must leave by the yard door."

Bowing stiffly to Ninon, Weld and Crosbie followed Feeney down the stairs. Martyn-Lynch went after them with a candle.

When they left the house, Hyacinth stood in the doorway for a moment before securing the strong back door. From the stables he heard exclamations of dismay.

"Our horses!" came Crosbie's voice. "They're gone!"

Hyacinth slid the key in the great lock. Just before the door closed he could hear Feeney sympathizing with Crosbie and Weld.

"Can you beat it! The pair of them gone. And me back barely turned."

XXXV. LAW AND ORDER

HYACINTH RETURNED TO the front drawing room, where Ninon awaited him by the open hearth.

If it were possible for a man to be over-solicitous towards a young expectant mother, Martyn-Lynch was. He was of two minds whether to congratulate her on her brave bearing through the alarming scenes with Weld and Crosbie, or to treat it nonchalantly. If he were to give her credit for courage she might think all the more that the occasion called for courage and remain under a strain. On the other hand, if he treated the incident carelessly its effect on her would be diminished. Adopting the second course, he said cheerfully:

"Good riddance to bad rubbish! I have locked them out to fend for themselves. And their horses have gone the way ours went. I could hear Feeney sympathizing. His sympathy could hardly conceal his satisfaction." Hyacinth laughed for the first time that evening, and Ninon laughed in her turn.

Greatly curious, Hyacinth said:

"Let us stand on the back lobby in the dark and open the window ever so little and listen to the sympathy and the chagrin in the yard." Ninon forgot the tension of the moment in her interest in this espionage. They could hear Weld in the yard, saying in magisterial tones:

"Feeney, I don't trust you or believe a word out of your mouth. You, too, are in this conspiracy as deeply as your master. You have permitted our horses to be stolen under your nose."

"And I suppose that it was I stole his Honour's horses and sent them to Killala to the Frinch?" Feeney asked sarcastically.

"It concerns me little what you have done with Mr. Martyn-Lynch's horses. I must have the use of the two I see saddled in those stalls. Wherever their destination is this night, it must be changed. I am a magistrate and I order you to provide a loyal subject—"

"Include me," Crosbie begged.

"—With mounts which either are not needed immediately or, if they are, can be used for no good purpose at a time when every true man should be at home."

"Is it rob the master, ye would have me, and you a judge?" Feeney whined.

"Those horses are saddled."

"Yer Honour had me so moidered that I had not time to unsaddle them. You never know what's wanted these days."

"Crosbie, speak to this wretch," Weld commanded.

As Crosbie was about to remonstrate, a yellow glare at the yard gate caught his eye. Feeney saw it too.

"In the name of God, yer Honour, don't have yer death on me hands. The boys is mustering, and if they find you here horse-thieving, I don't know what'll be the end of yez. Slip out at once by the wicket and not another word out of you."

"I will hold Martyn-Lynch responsible for any breach of the peace on his premises," Weld said, as he went up to the back door and knocked on it.

"It's not the least use," Feeney said. "The master has had as many visitors as he cares to entertain this night, and, besides, he's in the front of the house where yer Honours were entertaining yerselves before he came home. He's not receiving this evening—as the saying is—be the back door."

Whoever held the torch at the yard gate must have extinguished it. No light could be seen now.

Weld and Crosbie started to go to the front of the house when the dead torch came to life again and showed them plainly as they left the yard. Loud whoops came from all the undergrowth. A shot rang out. Crosbie took to his heels, followed by Weld. They reached the front of the house and hastened up the great steps. Frantically Crosbie thundered on the door.

"Let us in! Let us in! The rebels are here! Open at once. At once!" Hyacinth had followed their flight from the back to the front of the house. He was in no mood to open again to the malicious pair. Instead of that he played a mocking, fatal game. He repeated the questioning that Crosbie had put him to before opening the great hall-door.

"Who is there?"

"It is I, Crosbie. Let me in or it will be too late."

"There are others with you. Who are they?"

"Weld is here. Our horses have been stolen and there are armed men coming out of the woods on every side."

But Martyn-Lynch was in no mood to be forgiving or lenient.

"I must refuse unless you say who else is there."

He had carried the play too far. He heard a rush of feet on the gravel, and a fury-hoarsened voice.

"It's Weld, land-grabber, and Crosbie the informer. Let them have it with the pike!"

He heard the door take several sickening thuds. He shouted to the men without, and dragged open the encumbered door. Weld was pinned against it. One pike had gone through his throat and another lunge had transfixed him to the door. Crosbie's bleeding body fell into the hall.

"What the devil is the meaning of this, you murderous dogs?" shouted Hyacinth.

Men stampeded past him.

"Not up those stairs," he called. In the torch-light he saw his drink-maddened peasants make for the drawing-room floor in a staggering rush.

He rushed after the leader and flung him through the banisters. The graceful balustrade turned outwards and broke as the body fell in a heap on the black-and-white tiled pavement of the hall.

"Shure, it's the Master, Mr. Martyn-Lynch," one tipsy ruffian muttered. Martyn turned in despair. They were pouring into his house over the bleeding body of Crosbie. Sparks flew from their torches. The hall filled with smoke. To close the door was impossible without help. And for what help could he hope?

Two men came up the steps to the front door where Hyacinth stood. One of them was Myles the blacksmith.

"What is the meaning of this outrage?" Martyn cried. "Call these ruffians out of my house immediately."

A small, dark, rat-eyed little Dubliner, who accompanied Myles, said brusquely:

"Your time for giving orders is over, Mr. Martyn-Lynch. Though you may not know it, this house is taken over by the Irish Republic. By orders of the Central Executive the houses of those who resist must be burned!"

Hyacinth repeated: "I ask you, Myles, what is the meaning of this murderous outrage on a friendly Irishman's home?"

Myles for a moment was awed by the commanding accents of the landlord. But gathering arrogance from the presence of the deputy leader from the city, he said: "All differences of station is gone now, Mr. Lynch. He who is not with us is against us in this struggle. We intend no violence. Your house must not fall into the tyrant's hands, and you must not call the members of the Irish Republican Army murderers."

"Damn you and them," said Hyacinth with heat. "If a set of drink-sodden ruffians who burst into my house after killing my steward and a neighbour and frighten my wife be the Irish Republican Army, I warn you now that I will shoot the pair of you if you don't call your scoundrels out of my house at once."

The jackeen from Dublin blew a whistle. Half a dozen men hidden in the night set matches to the torches and began to advance on the house.

"Forward, soldiers of the Irish Republic!" the small dark man commanded.

Hyacinth fired and shot him through the head. The men with torches turned and disappeared into the darkness. Only Myles the Slasher was left face-to-face with his master. He eyed Martyn-Lynch cautiously. He seemed quite sober. Martyn took a second pistol out of his pocket, the one he had taken from Crosbie.

"Mind you, Sir," said Myles the Slasher, "I am armed too."

"My wife is alone in this house. Will you call your ruffians out?" he asked, as he aimed deliberately at the Slasher's head.

"I am under orders to leave no position of strength unoccupied for the English to garrison. General Humbert is on his way and will be here in the morning from Killala with a thousand men."

"Will you call your ruffians out?"

Myles the Slasher shook his head. Suddenly a window was opened and Ninon leant out above the door where Martyn stood.

"Hyacinth, my darling, I have locked myself into the drawing-room. They are hammering at the door and I cannot find the key to the boudoir door."

Hyacinth called to her in French. She was to make her way with what rugs she could gather and try to find Feeney and get him to take her through the night to Lisadill.

"But I cannot leave you."

"For God's sake, and all our sakes, do as I implore you, love." The window was closed. A pike-man who had appeared from inside and stood behind Martyn-Lynch lowered his pike when his master turned. He awaited orders from Myles. None were forthcoming, for out of the dark a wild, red-haired horseman came galloping. It was Roddy.

"What the hell are you all up to? What are ye doing to Mr. Martyn-Lynch? He never evicted any man. The French are coming on through Castlebar. Major Crabbe and his men have run from the barracks. They are burning all before them. Mulcahy's is on fire and all the village is in flames. They'll be here in a minute. If you want to fight, fall back and join the French by the Westport road."

Myles the Slasher went up to him and took his horse by the bridle.

"Is it a lie ye are telling me to save a landlord?" he asked.

"If ye want to wait to find out, then the devil take you. I've given ye the warning and off I go."

"You will wait here and don't move," Myles commanded.

A glow in the eastern sky proved that Roddy had spoken the truth. Soon the crunch of military wagons and of field guns could be heard under the trees. Lights appeared in the distance on every side. Save to the southwest, the place was surrounded. Major Crabbe had "fallen back" from his barracks. The "Castlebar Races" had begun.

Myles called to his men. Only one responded. The man with the pike came from the house. Where were the rest, a full score or so? They must have gone out by the back door. If so, they could only have walked straight into the hands of the soldiers.

Martyn retreated into his house. He rushed up the great stairway to the drawing-room. As Ninon had said, the door was locked, but there was no sign of the men who had tried to force it. Up another flight he ran to where the landing gave on to the servants' staircase. Down this he went and entered by the door of the boudoir. There was no sign of Ninon. The white sheepskin rug had gone from the fire-place. Her escritoire was open and the little drawers unlocked. She had gone and taken her treasures with her: his letters. He hoped that her jewels had not been left behind. He noticed that her knitting, dearer to her than her jewels, was gone. A great wave of tenderness melted his heart.

Shouts came from the basement. They were answered by voices on the bedroom floors. He smelt smoke. Torches? Or was the house on fire?

Reassured by not finding Ninon, he ran to a back window. There was no sign of life in the yard. He rushed down the stairs. The back door stood open. His wife had made her escape.

"Feeney!" he shouted into the darkness. Not an answering voice. He could trust Feeney. Pray God, he had taken her safely through the ring of bayonets that were closing in from Castlebar.

Up from the cellar staggered a dozen men, bearing between them unopened cases of wine. The unmistakable crackle of burning timber assailed his ears. Hyacinth rushed into the yard and looked up to where the menacing sound came from. The upper stories were aflame. Even without "the General Executive," his own people had set his home on fire in their drunken raid through his house.

He went back to the hall. He dared not open the front door for fear of the draught it would cause. Down the stairs rushed four or five fright-sobered men. Finding the door locked, they frantically undid the fastening. They held it open too wide to slacken the lock-chain.

By brute force they burst the links and fled into the night. A cry came from the woods—was it Roddy's voice?—"Save yourselves, boys, the soldiers!"

On they came in close formation, driving a score of men before them at the bayonet's point. In command was Major Crabbe.

Those who rushed from the house were added to the captives. Lieutenant Cole advanced with half a company.

"In the name of the King!"

"What the devil do you want?" asked Martyn-Lynch.

"I have come to take over this house in the name of the King to save it from enemies of His Majesty. If you are loyal to His Majesty you will assist. If you offer any resistance I shall be compelled to put you under arrest."

Excitable and eager natures, such as Martyn-Lynch's, often take on in times of great excitement an extraordinary and sardonic calm.

"There's a pretty medley here of friends and enemies. Take your choice," he said.

As he spoke, yellow flames burst through the upper windows and licked the stone work over them. With pistol cocked the lieutenant made his way past Martyn into the house. His pistol cracked in the hall. Some drunken straggler had come to his senses only to meet death.

Cole called a number of his men into the house. Through the opened windows furniture was hurled to the lawn. Martyn's desk broke open as it fell down.

"Save those papers," the lieutenant commanded.

The house was an inferno now. Through the windows flames and smoke shot into the night. And yet the stout roof held.

Seen by gleams, white and red under their tall shakos, the Hessians made a wall in front of the flaming pile. The dark group of what remained of the Irish Republican Army was being tamely bound, hands behind backs and foot to the next man's foot. The voice of Major Crabbe could be heard above the flaming roar.

"Take the prisoners to the coach-house and keep them strictly under guard. None must escape. The court-martial will be at dawn."

More than a score of men hobbled away as best they could, guarded by a double file of troopers with bayonets on each side. Tall in their midst, with unbowed head, Father Colyer moved along.

"This," said Lieutenant Cole, "is Martyn-Lynch, in whose house I took the French émigré. This is the man who left so unceremoniously from the barracks. His house has been reported by Mr. Weld the magistrate as a meeting-ground for rebels and a breeding-ground for sedition."

Pushing the lieutenant aside and striding forward: "I can speak for myself," said Martyn-Lynch. "Major Crabbe, the Frenchman this lieutenant refers to is a French aristocrat, exonerated by yourself. My house is no haunt of sedition. It was my newly-built home. This evening I came from the lake with my wife to find my horses stolen and my house ransacked. I was barely permitted to enter by my agent and the late magistrate Weld. At last my wife and I gained admission only to have it raided by some ruffians who called themselves Republicans."

"He had a green flag flying from one of the chimneys when it was taken over, doubtless in the King's name, by Mr. Weld," Cole interposed.

"What have you to say to that?" asked Major Crabbe.

"My man removed it when it was discovered. I did not put it there."

"And yet you admit that when you returned the house was occupied only by such loyal subjects as Mr. Weld, and—what is your agent's name?"

"Crosbie."

"And where is this Crosbie?"

"Dead in my hall."

"And Weld is impaled with a pair of pikes against the hall door," said Lieutenant Cole.

"From reports and from the evidence before us, I must hold you as a suspect under arrest. Your house has harboured enemies of the King."

"Was I likely to burn it?" Martyn-Lynch inquired hotly.

Major Crabbe thought awhile. He was trying, like many a man before him, to solve an Irish problem. He ended by being, like the problem, two-sided.

"Hold yourself under open arrest until I deal with the rebels."

"Without parole," said Martyn-Lynch quietly. If he did not give his word of honour to hold himself under arrest, his compulsion to do so would be lighter. The Major had turned away.

In the coach-house at dawn Major Crabbe held his court. Like many Englishmen, though in a desperate position, he remained unyielding and cool. His ferocity was terrible because of its sang-froid. Ceremony was not absent from the trial. A tucket of drums opened the proceedings. Father Colyer was the first to be tried. The lieutenant and three troopers testified that a highly seditious pamphlet printed in France was found on the person of the priest.

"Is that admitted?" asked Major Crabbe.

Father Colyer bowed his head in acquiescence and raised his hand. He was about to speak. "Enough, Sir," said Major Crabbe. Troopers took the priest aside.

Myles the Slasher came next before the drumhead tribunal. Major Crabbe read out a report.

"For the last twelve months your forge has been the centre of conspiracy. You yourself have forged weapons for enemies of the King. Last night or early this morning you were taken at the head of a group with arms in your possession. Preparatory to joining hands with the French invaders you were prepared to occupy and to fortify against the King's troops the house known as Martyn Hall. Is that admitted?"

"Up the Republic!" Myles the Slasher shouted. He, too, was led aside.

The group of twenty men were tried en masse. They looked frightened and dishevelled. All they saw now, like so many of their countrymen before them, was the gallows, in place of Freedom's bright hope. Some were fathers of young children, some were grown "boys," or unmarried men, and some gossoons, or boys still in their teens. They stood bound, hands behind their backs, like the men who had preceded them.

Misery did not reconcile these men to death. They felt that they were victims of bad luck. Their undoing had actually arisen from an English defeat. The French were at Killala. There was no doubt of that. They had already taken possession of the town. Major Crabbe's flight from Killala had been the cause of this rebel group's defeat and arrest. The flight had lent Crabbe the swiftness of movement that enabled him to encompass them. Would there ever be hope for Freedom when even the landing of the French was of no avail; when an English defeat spelt victory?

Cold in the morning air, without food, and sickened for the most part by the effect of too much drink, they stood, man and boy, before the deadly formality of a lawful court. Lawful by whose laws? That mattered little now. It was an English court answerable only to England and its King.

Pat McDonough Oge—that is, junior, to distinguish him from his father, who still lived beside the hearth of his two-acre farm—was gaunt and gray-faced. His thoughts had gone beyond the gallows, and were upon his widow and his three little children, who must be wondering when their daddy would cross the door again. One son, a lad of sixteen, was beside him. Warned repeatedly by His Reverence, Father Colyer, to have nothing to do with godless Frenchmen, he had been unable to resist the flame that swept the land. Who could? It was the immemorial breath of the earth of Ireland. And His Reverence was caught too. What sort of law was it that took every man into its toils?

There was tall McDade and his two fine sons. He was taken while he was actually trying to disarm his boys. "Taken with arms," as in fact he was, the law provided for no exceptional case such as his. He stood dulled by despair. In his long neck his Adam's apple moved up and down as if it sensed the approach of strangulation.

"And they shall be hanged in groups of three. The priest shall not be disembowelled; but the blacksmith, who is the prime mover of this conspiracy, shall be."

Another tucket of the drums, cynically cheerful in the morning air, marked the rising of the court. Terrible is the ferocity of the English for its coldness, but when it is formal it is more terrifying still.

The troopers passed a rope through the arch of the little belfry that held the yard bell. Under it they held a double ladder on which two men stood. Father Colyer was about to be led, but he shook his head and walked unaided. A trooper helped him up the ladder, for his hands were tied. For decency's sake, or because it was in the King's Regulations governing executions, his feet were quickly tied. The noose was passed over his head, down over the quivering eyelids and muttering mouth from which the prayers for the dying were being intoned: *"De profundis clamavi ad te, Domine."*

A sudden shove from a soldier on the opposite side of the ladder flung the priest off into the air. His body fell as his weight took the slack, then jerked up until he seemed to be standing at the head of his flock. Reverently the men he had tried to save closed their eyes. When they opened them, all vibration from the rope had gone. The soldier who shoved him so roughly off was a man who had been forced by his captain into marriage as a result of representations made by the priest.

The soldiers raised the corpse, opened the noose and hitched the rope higher. It was ready for another neck. They laid the priest, with protruding tongue and purple face uncovered, beside the gallows under the arch.

The cockney sergeant, consulting a paper, called, "Myles, the blacksmith, next!"

All of a sudden an amazing interruption took place. A wild, red-haired figure on a galloping horse spurred up and drew rein. His horse sent sparks flying from the cobbles. It was Roddy. He glanced at the corpse, leapt from the saddle, and flung his pistols to either side.

Briskly he ran up the ladder before he could be stopped.

"Who the hell wants to live in slavery under all these cowardly scuts?" he shouted. "I am going where the brave are gone before me. Erin go braw!" he shouted, louder still. He put his head in the noose and flung himself off backwards from the ladder.

Dumfounded, the soldiers awaited orders. None came. Both officers were gone. The sergeant who was on execution duty ordered Roddy's body to be taken down. The thin neck had been broken by the violence of the fling.

Roddy did not die in vain. The old heroic surge of the immemorial warrior land, the Land of Conn the Hundred Fighter, that had possessed him, passed with his untamable spirit into the sorry, half-starved group who awaited strangulation at the hands of their country's oppressors. They had seen their priest go before them. Deprived of his consolation, they were about to die in dumb despair.

Now a cheer broke from them one and all. What did they care? Like Roddy, they would die defiantly, heroically.

Martyn had watched it all. He had seen enough. Conflicting emotions passed through him. He drew consolation from the thought that for years he had never drawn rent or added to his peasants' misery. He was all sympathy with these wretches now, despite the fact that his house still smouldered and down one of the inner walls his silver ran like solder. All his worldly goods were gone. But he had treasure stowed away in safety, as he hoped, afar. While the executioners with steaming knife were doing their gruesome duty on the naked body of a man who had neither the influence nor the money to pay them to kill him outright with the rope, Hyacinth slipped round his smouldering mansion. He caught Roddy's mount upon the lawn.

The soft turf made no sound as he jumped a little stream. Roddy's was a sturdy horse. The Devil's in the dice if they caught Martyn now. He's away to Lisadill.

XXXVI. ST. GEORGE'S "LEP"

HALF A DOZEN men anxiously awaited their master, Denis St. George—half a dozen men who lay three on each side of the lane that led from the stables along the garden wall. At the end was a little door that gave on the fields, and thence to the brook that bounded the southern end of the demesne of Attymon House. The men were armed with a heterogeneous collection of guns and pistols. One, the leader, had a musket, purchased from a Hessian for ten shillings.

What happened to the Hessian who sold it was not ascertainable; but everyone knew that the Hessians had no heart for a fight that brought their master, the Duke of Brunswick, eleven shillings for each of them when wounded, two pounds a head when killed. He had received over two and a half million pounds for the farm lads he sold off his estates to the English to prosecute the American wars. How much he was getting for the wounds and deaths of these serfs who fought as English mercenaries, only Mr. Pitt, who sympathized so much with Ireland could tell, but he "dare not avow."

Anyway, it was no harm in one simple Hessian lad's eyes to take ten shillings for his long-bayoneted musket and to say that he had been waylaid. Waylaying was sufficiently common if a soldier was fool enough to trust himself to the village taverns unaccompanied. One drawback there was: the captain commanding the company had begun to suspect these waylayings that brought little injury to those waylaid and much drink in the succeeding days.

Of the half-dozen men who waited anxiously for St. George, the leader, as stated, had a Hessian musket and a bayonet too. But he was not mounting the bayonet on this occasion. It caught the light and he was unaccustomed to anything between him and his quarry.

Their anxiety for St. George was not wholly solicitous. They could not be said to be anxious for his health or welfare. They were lying in ambush to shoot St. George in cold blood. He had had warnings enough. He must either stand in with the Republicans or give them all the help he could. If not, he would be judged no better than his neighbour Weld, who was transporting the real owners of the soil to Virginia or Van Dieman's Land; or Crosbie beyond, at Martyn Hall, who sent lists of suspects as often as he could to the barracks at Castlebar or—worse even—by the kind offices of certain citizens of Athlone, to Dublin Castle itself.

They were giving St. George a last chance. They wanted his horses. They had received orders from the Dublin Deputy to occupy or burn his house. On no account must it, or its stores and livestock, be permitted to fall into British hands.

He ought to be passing here now. There was to be no galloping away for him if he refused them his horses. They would know in a minute. They would have him in a cul-de-sac between the sides of the lane and the six-foot wall at the end. He would have no time to dismount and open the wicket gate. It was too small, for one thing, to let out a horse and, for another, the key had been removed.

A shot rang out. The boys on each side of the lane grew tense. One said a prayer, half audibly, for God to direct his aim and steady his hand, for he had never raised it against one of the Quality up to this.

"Here he is!"

St. George on his dappled gray was galloping down the lane.

"Hold yer fire for a minute! We have him now!"

St. George leant over Grayling's neck. Lightly the horse rose to the six-foot rough-topped wall. The six men watched in amazement. Man and horse were gone!

"In the name of God, why didn't ye quench him, Shamus, when ye had the chance?" But Shamus was still gazing at the incredible leap.

"And who the hell would want to quench a man who can lep like that?" Apparently there was still room for sportsmanship among the new Republicans on the old sod. Shamus, as an assistant in the forge, was an admirer of men who rode upon horses.

With his house on fire behind him, St. George sped away from his embattled tenants. He was going full gallop across country to Martyn Hall.

The flames from Weld's house flaked the air above the trees as he passed the estate. If he, St. George, were despoiled, what could have been the fate of Weld? Thank heaven, his mother was still on her honeymoon at Lucan House.

He rode on. Every cottage seemed to be deserted. Would he take the road and risk again the loss of his horse? The road was easier going than the fields. He must make Martyn Hall before nightfall and he was surer on the road of good going. It is not easy to find the gates after dark in the fields.

He met a farmer riding bareback and leading a horse.

"Good evening, Curtin," he said. But Curtin never answered. Perhaps he resented being discovered red-handed in his dearth of patriotism. Curtin was hiding his horses from the Frenchmen at Killala in spite of the good times they were to bring. What did an old bachelor like him want of foreigners and changes?

Denis rode on. Would he be in time to warn Hyacinth? He was coming near the village now. There on the left was Myles's forge. How acrid the smoke smelt! That was never blown by bellows. But the Republicans would not be likely to burn Myles's forge, ringleader as he was, if all that was said were true. And yet you never knew. He might have been suspected. One thing that the Revolution brought, in unbounded quantity, was suspicion. Myles may have been suspected of seeking a post in the English Army. There were men who had tried to sell themselves in Ireland before. There! You could see the evening light through the rafters. The forge had, for some reason or other, been burned out.

And here came another farmer saving his horses, riding straight towards Denis; or would he take the turn to Killala at the junction of the road? A nice bunch of them he had—three or maybe more.

Now what farmer had that team? No man in Mayo. No man had more land than could be dug up with the spade.

Four horses! A change for the mail coach, maybe; but what would they be doing here?

The horseman approached, a conical red cap on his curls. He reached the turn of the road. What Denis saw then startled him almost out of his saddle.

"Mabs!" he yelled.

Mabs pointed to the northeast and said something in a tired voice from which the silver bells were gone. What it was could not be heard, but her tone carried more meaning to Denis than words could have. He rode up on his strong gray and putting an arm around her waist drew the exhausted enthusiast onto his saddle. Mabs was too tired to protest.

"Are you coming to Killala too?" she asked.

"That is the last place I want to see. I am going to warn Hyacinth and your sister that there is a strong and murderous gang of insurrectionists at large. They have burned my house and seized my horses."

"You did not give your horses to the Republic?" Mabs asked, as one who already knew the answer.

"I gave the contents of a horse pistol instead, and here I am homeless, with nothing left me in all the world but my clothes and my horse."

Something in the way he said it aroused Mabs. She struggled, but St. George held on. "Let me down, let me down! They will take your horse at the village. They let me through because they knew that I was bringing mounts to General Humbert."

"Now, Mabs, do not be a silly little fool. What is to be gained by encouraging men to murder their masters? They will murder you in your turn because you belong to the master class. That is the unforgivable sin to them—to be a man and not a menial. I must save your sister, and I am going to save you whether you want to be saved or not. I could never forgive myself if I allowed anything to happen to you." Denis, surprised at his own impassioned tone, said more quietly, "Surely your Uncle Dick never gave you his horses?"

"They belong to Ireland and not to Uncle Dick."

"To whom did they belong when you laid them on Deaf Burke with the coach included?"

Mabs was contritely silent. Whether because of something in Denis's tone and look, or because of her fatigue, all rebellion seemed to have left her.

"Mister, Mister!" an urchin called from behind a hedge. "Don't let the sojers catch you with the horses. They're all over Martyn Hall and in the stables and the house is on fire."

"Good God!" Denis exclaimed. "Who burned it? Here, come out of that!"

But in a flash the boy was gone.

Mabs's slim figure shook with sobs.

"Poor Ninon!" she cried.

"I don't like the way that boy ran off when I asked him who burned Martyn Hall," Denis said. "It was not the military who burned my house, but my own people. It may be the same way with Martyn Hall."

The leading rein of the four horses fell to the ground. The horses turned with pointed ears. "Let me down! Let me down!" Mabs cried.

"Mabs, you know I will never let you go." Denis tightened his arm about her waist.

Something was startling the horses. They would have to be held. A man came out from the field on their left. It was Mulcahy, the inn-keeper.

"In the name of God, Mr. Denis, don't go near Martyn Hall. The sojers is in it. The house is blazing and they have taken twenty men prisoners and hanged every mother's son. Mrs. Martyn-Lynch got away with Feeney."

"Is Mr. Hyacinth taken?"

"There's no word of it, Sir."

Mabs said eagerly, "She is gone to Lisadill!"

"Whoa, there! Whoa, my beauties," Mulcahy said to steady the horses as he handed up their leading rein.

"There's no good can come out of it now that Crabbe and his men are mad," Mulcahy added.

"Denis, let me down. I will ride with you wherever you are going," Mabs said. She slid down. Mulcahy helped her to mount. Though his back was turned to Denis, he kept on with his story.

"And they run from Castlebar and cotch the man from Dublin that was ordering the houses to be destroyed. They burned the village, every roof in it, and my house, slates and all. I have nothing but the stars for a roof from this out. There's not a house, horse or a stack of hay in the parish."

"You tell me," St. George asked, "that Major Crabbe left Castlebar?"

"They say he had gone to meet the French at Killala, and is now in retreat."

Denis understood the situation. Hyacinth must have suffered as he himself had. Inflamed by the worst intoxication in the world, revolution, the ravenous conspirators were glad of any excuse to vent their vengeance on everything they felt stood for oppression.

If they had burned the house of a popular man like Martyn-Lynch, whose rentals had never been fully collected, but left to voluntary payments since Aiken was dismissed, how could St. George have expected better treatment? However, he was not filled with solicitude for Hyacinth. If Ninon had got away safely, Martyn was well able to look after himself; and Major Crabbe could hold nothing against one who had sustained such a loss as a victim of the rage of the insurgents.

Denis felt confident that Hyacinth was safe as surely as Ninon, and Ninon was on her way to Lisadill. What was he to do with Mabs? Who could be sure of her if she were confronted by the soldiery in her present mood? And how could he explain the presence of the horses and still save them—the only means of communication between Lisadill and the outside world? Bad indeed would be their plight at Lisadill if they were left without any means of escaping to Dublin should the need arise.

"Mulcahy, is there a stable left in the village?"

"Keep out of it, Sir, for the love of God. The sojers is all around it. They cotch a lot of the boys that was cheering for General Humbert. And what would ye be doing with a stable and no hay? Put them on the grass and we'll catch them in the morning and away with ye round by the lake where there are no sojers. It's tired they look and they'd do with a bite of grass."

It was true. The beasts were far spent. Mabs was kept from fainting with fatigue only by the excitement of the hour. When that was passed, where could he find help and attention for her?

Night was falling. Mulcahy opened a gate and drove the horses into a field of sparse grass. It was well sheltered by the gorse which was left standing on a quarter of the field, thanks to some fatuous idea of the unimprovable race of farmers that the gorse "helped the grass."

If we had even a glass of milk, St. George thought. So did Mulcahy, with all the native courtesy that the presence of a lady evokes in a countryman. And a lady as tired as this one required more than the usual hospitality of a glass of milk.

"I'll go over to the forge and look for a can or a tumbler. They may have smashed everything but there will be a cup or a can about the place. Then if we can find a cow that has not gone off with the sojers . . ."

"Surely the militia have not seized the cattle as well as the horses?" St. George asked.

Mulcahy answered: "King's Regulations, yer Honour. 'Leave nothing that would be of the least use to the enemy.' They read that out when they were digging up the potatoes in me own bit of a field."

"The people will starve this winter," Denis said.

Mabs required his immediate attention. Her horse was turned sideways to the field. She made no attempt to urge him into it. She was bowed with sleep.

Between them they helped her down and carried her to a clump of furze. Mulcahy was for putting his *coatie mor* under her to protect her from the thorns that lay on the withered patch beneath the gorse bush. But Denis would not have it. "You will want it yourself," he said.

He took off his blue riding coat, removed his pistols from it, and wrapped Mabs in it. As he leant over her she swung an arm with a sleepy gesture round his neck. Gently, almost reluctantly he disengaged it and stood up. Mulcahy was halfway across the field on his search for food and milk.

To pass the time till his return Denis scraped with his boot a clear space for himself in the dry dust and withered sprays of furze. He took the saddles off the horses. There would be a pillow for Mabs if she woke. There were worse pillows than a saddle turned upside down, and it was hard for one unaccustomed to the open to sleep without any support for the head.

Ah, there were horse cloths on two of Sir Richard's horses. That was a piece of luck. The horse clothes would shelter Mulcahy and himself for the night. He went to where the horses were grazing, rejoicing in the dank grass. He unsaddled his own and that on which Mabs had ridden and removed the bridles. He found that he would have to wait for Mulcahy's help to catch the unbridled horses. When he went back to the gorse clump Mulcahy was there, holding a jug covered with wet muslin.

"The buttermilk was all I could find. And a stone of oats. They have not left even the flitch of bacon that was hung on a chain in the kitchen chimney. The chimney didn't burn, yet the bacon was gone. They'll be famine in the land before Christmas. If they are fighting the French with starvation, they intend to starve out all that crosses them, plain or gentle; and sorra word of a lie in it."

He placed the milk carefully in a hollow of the ground. "Missy will be glad of it in the morning, I'm thinking. Here's carrots and a drop of the creature, yer Honour, for yourself."

A light wind rose. It made the air heavy for a moment with the smell of wet wood ashes. "That was surely a terrible fire up at the House," Mulcahy added. Denis sat down in silence. His own and Weld's and Martyn's houses were gone, friend's and foe's alike. Was there no discrimination? Was general destruction all that Revolution meant?

Mulcahy was digging into the ground with a knife. "It's here I'll bury me watch and the few guineas I have," he said. "They can't take off me what I haven't got." As he wrapped his purse in his neck-cloth, a sound of deep breathing disturbed St. George. He looked out from under the furze. The horses stood watching them, looming in the misty night. It was an easy task to get the horse cloths.

Mulcahy refused a cloth.

"It's to Castlebar I'll be going," he said. "Where there is a crowd it will be safer than where there is not."

Denis had difficulty in persuading him to remain. He finally agreed to wait, but said he must put a distance between him and the occupied site of the village before there was strong light.

St. George wrapped himself in a horse cloth and with his head on a saddle lay down to a restless sleep.

He was awakened in the early morning by Mulcahy's hand on his shoulder.

"I'm for Castlebar now. If you want to get safely away with the horses, go south by the lake keeping west of the forge. Maybe the sojers will come to rake the ashes for money now that the floors is down. There's not even a ruin from which they don't look for toll. If ye're finished with them saddles ye ought to be mounted and off. Ye'll catch the mounts better if I lend ye a hand."

When the steeds were saddled and the coach horses collected, Mabs was sitting up. Her little pointed cap reminded Denis of the quaint little hood Clemente had worn the first time he saw her. Clemente, an exile, was in better case now than the masters of the land in which she dwelt.

"Take this, Missy." Mulcahy held out the jug of buttermilk. "It's all ye'll get until ye reach yer home."

It took some persuasion to make her drink it. She acted as if she were being offered a cup of gall.

She took some sips with a wry face and handed the jug to Denis.

"Drink some yourself," she said. There was no trace of rebellion left in her voice. Gratitude and contrition were in her expression.

XXXVII. "YOUR HOUSE, TOO?"

MULCAHY HAD BEEN right. It was well that they took his advice and avoided the forge. Sparks rose from it and were borne by the freshening wind. Troopers on patrol duty were searching for the gold that they were convinced every Irish farmer hoarded.

As they rode southwest the breeze increased. Charred fragments came floating from the higher air, upborne by the warm currents that arose from conflagrations in the distance.

An hour later, from where they forded an inlet of the lake, the great hollow eyes of Martyn Hall could be seen staring from smoke-blackened sockets across the inscrutable land.

Mabs turned away her face. From her bosom she took a folded paper and handed it to Denis with an air so dejected that it might have been that of an unshriven penitent.

"AN ADDRESS TO THE PEOPLE OF IRELAND ON THE PRESENT IMPORTANT CRISIS," he read.

With one hand he unfolded it and looked through it.

"Where did you get this?" he inquired, keeping all criticism out of his tone.

"Roddy gave it to me. He gave me lots of them. I was to give one to—no, leave one where Uncle Dick would be sure to find it. 'When read, destroy' was written on his copy. Roddy said that they would hang anyone found with a copy, man or woman. That's why I kept it."

Denis did not know what to answer. He felt a surge of fury against Roddy. With the rein on his arm he tore the page to fragments. Finding that Mabs made no comment, he refrained from speech. He would know soon enough what effect the ruin of her sister's house had on Mabs's susceptible mind. Even if she did not think of the ruin of his own house, as he found himself wishing she would, the sight of Martyn Hall given over to the crows must have deeply moved the impulsive girl. Was that why she gave up the pamphlet and why, when he destroyed it, she said no word?

Mabs was disturbed by his silence. "Are you angry with me?" she asked contritely.

"No, but I am angry with the fellow Roddy, who was cowardly enough to give a girl such a suicidal thing."

She spoke with returning spirit, or perhaps only the vehemence of childish pique.

"I asked him for them for Uncle Dick. We wanted to get him to join General Humbert. Uncle Dick was a general or something in the army himself. He would be given the command and be made Governor of Connaught if he joined in. He never got a copy, though I laid them on his plate. I suspect Madame Clemente of spoiling the plan. So I took the horses. Roddy is not a coward. He is always risking his life. That is why I have engaged myself to him."

"Engaged to him?" Denis exclaimed.

"Yes," Mabs said demurely. "But he doesn't know it yet. He is wilful and noble. You would understand me if you could only meet him," she added, as if to appease him.

"Never want to see the fellow," said Denis gloomily, fighting down an impulse to speak more strongly. Through his mind went the long pageant of the scions of the old county families who had married beneath them. Where were the Fants, the Lahiffes, the Morrises, the Nugents, the Skerrits? And old Atty Persse who, when his wife—the daughter of his groom—was pregnant, had intercalary bastards by her sister? Maybe the woman was not even his wife. And as for the Dalys, they were all more or less daft, and Mabs was related to the Dalys. Yes, the old families had raised up their own blood against them by marrying into the soil. Was this very revolution an outcome of generations of decadence? An act of Nemesis? Who could tell? And now this fellow and Mabs.

As though sensing what was in his mind, she said, pouting:

"He may not be of an old family but he is a nephew of Father Colyer who speaks French, and that is the language of culture according to Uncle Dick's Madame, that is, his wife. And she ought to know, being French herself."

Denis felt that he might as well humour her. She must be feeling remorse, and, woman-like, was becoming defiant on an unconnected theme.

After some hours they came in sight of a cottage, the thatch of which was intact. The retreating campaign of Major Crabbe had not reached it yet. Denis looked again as they came nearer. The top of the half door, which had certainly been open when he saw it first, was shut now. The owner doubtless distrusted any mounted men.

He knocked. His conjecture was right. Whoever owned the shieling thought it better to put what protection he could between himself and marauding troopers.

"St. George of the Galway Blazers, from Attymon House!" he called out, to reassure the peasant by announcing himself as a member of the famous hunt. How cynical the title sounded with his Galway house ablaze! He might have called himself Major Crabbe for all the welcome he got. He could not see through the single window when he stooped from the saddle. He rode round the cabin. A few chickens scurried off. The patch of potatoes had been recently turned up. Mabs called: "There's somebody within. I saw a puff of fresh smoke."

By the time he came to it the door was open. A tall man put his head out as he leant over the lower part of the door, undoing the bolt.

"I was afeard, yer Honour, till I heard the lady's voice. It's yer Honour that is welcome and the lady herself."

He came out, and stood as high as his cottage as he awaited the entry of his guests. They dismounted, and were about to tie their horses to the post, when the farmer said:

"They'd be better out of sight. There's terrible doings up at the House. It blazed all through the night. I don't know what's coming to the country." He looked in the direction of Martyn Hall.

Inside, when their eyes grew accustomed to the smoke, St. George could see an old woman seated by the fire, which she had just stirred.

St. George told his story. The farmer was all sympathy; at least so it appeared. Anything that might have been abject in his servility was lost. He had genuine solicitude for his guests. There were potatoes on the rekindled fire—he had buried his crop of them in a trench where they were unlikely to be discovered even by the most experienced forager. He had a few chickens, which nobody could catch without a fistful of meal, and where would you get the likes of that? One of these St. George refused, knowing that payment for their hospitality would not be accepted, and would be taken unkindly if pressed.

"Potatoes and milk and new-laid eggs—many a better man has had a worse breakfast," Denis said cheerfully.

"Begging yer Honour's pardon, you couldn't say as much for the lady," the farmer ventured, with the politeness inherent in the race. Denis began to think that the farmer knew of his misfortune and took a certain satisfaction in patronizing the victim of it. But such a suspicion was unjustified.

"Terrible times indeed!" the old crone echoed from her seat beside the fire, as if it had taken all the time for the idea to sink in. "Terrible times indeed!" And she seemed to get a certain satisfaction in the thought, as near neighbours to misery sometimes do.

"I seen the Master spurring away this morning, going west."

"He saw Hyacinth," Mabs exclaimed. "I was right: he has gone to Lisadill."

Although he knew that "going west" might indicate any direction, when used in peasant speech, Denis wondered what had detained Martyn overnight and how it came that he had permitted Ninon to go with no better escort than Feeney.

Were there troopers on the road to Lisadill? The farmer could not say, but by all appearances they would make a barracks out of the stables of Martyn Hall, unless the General came along, by which he meant Humbert and his thousand Frenchmen. The farmer was not afraid of the Hessians and Major Crabbe. He had sent his daughter over to Loughrea and there was nothing in the house but what you saw. Right enough it was treasonable to hide food, that he knew; but there was half a drill of praties in the ground and they would hardly search beyond that. The cow he did not expect to save, but the sojers didn't mind the goats. If left alone after the expected visitation, they would get through the winter with the help of God.

Mabs and Denis rode away through country that was purple and brown. The lush fields of the limestone round Martyn Hall had given place to seeping bogs at the foothills of the long, low range that looked, when seen from the upper stories of Martyn Hall, as if it was built of faint and evanescent turquoise. The dull colour of burnt umber was in keeping with Denis's mood.

It was tiresome going for the horses. Bearing the words of the farmer in mind, Denis thought that they might take the high road without risk of being challenged and deprived of their valuable steeds.

"It will make our journey hours shorter," Mabs agreed.

"And that's what we want," her companion answered.

Where to take the road was a problem. It had been built without much regard for drainage. Like all roads that rose to ascend the hills, it had been made by following the path of a cow, the easiest ascent, or so it seemed to the countrymen. Inevitably they would come across it soon in one of its windings. It was hard to guess your directions through rolling moors where no hunt goes after the fox. Stone wall after stone wall gave only on more sodden fields, but the sun was due south, and by keeping it on the left they knew they were going west.

At last came the tang of seaweed on the air!

"Straight on for Lisadill!" Denis sang out.

They must have been two hours away from the cottage where they had breakfasted when they were hailed by Martyn-Lynch. He was coming down from a long flat hill. His horse had its belly wet with black mud.

"These damned bogholes," said Hyacinth, and greeted them with his eyebrows raised in delighted surprise.

Neither knew who should question the other first. Finally, Hyacinth asked: "Your house, too?"

Denis nodded gravely. They were brothers in adversity. Hyacinth turned to Mabs and her horses. He could guess how she had come there, but this was no time, Hyacinth realized, to question his impulsive sister-in-law or to take her to task. From the look of her, she had already suffered enough. He was prayerfully thankful that Denis had been able to deflect her from her rebellious "mission."

When their experiences had been related, their thoughts flew forward to the only house left to the three—Lisadill.

The road crossed their path.

"The road at last!" Martyn cried. "I have been lost for hours in the bog."

Martyn removed the few stones, without any binding save weeds and moss, which made the wall that bounded the road. When the riders had passed through, he asked for one of the led horses that belonged to Sir Richard. His own animal was exhausted and had been for many hours without food. He saddled it and took his late mount in tow.

When they came to discuss Mabs's escapade, Martyn agreed with St. George that it would be best if they were to keep silence. Sir Richard's anger never lasted long, and her political impulsiveness would be largely compensated by the presence of the horses safely restored.

As the two homeless men and Mabs approached Lisadill, Denis, seeing that Mabs was turning off the drive in the direction of the stables, ventured to whisper to her a reminder of a happier prank, when she had returned uncriticized from her attendance at the fight:

"It's not the first time, Mabbie."

She trotted off, pouting and fanning her curls with her red cap. That will not appear again, Denis thought. It seemed to him a good omen that she no longer wore it on her head.

It took days for the reunited friends to discuss the tragedy of the destruction of their houses, and to lighten their hearts with winged words. Hyacinth kept for private ears when talking to Sir Richard, the scenes he had witnessed and the death of the priest.

One night at dinner when Sir Richard unguardedly asked to be told how Martyn accounted for the death of Roddy, Denis, watching closely, could not see that Mabs was greatly concerned. And yet it must have come as a shock. Women were inscrutable, anyway, Denis thought, and those rising to womanhood more so. Perhaps the return to her own luxurious home, in contrast to what she had experienced, had wrought a change, had brought about a conversion. Who could tell? But better not take any reaction for granted. To do so might bring on another. So Denis bided his time. He would cheerfully wait as long as might be necessary to see again the light that had been in her eyes as she sipped the buttermilk he gave her that morning in the field.

XXXVIII. LOVE AT LISADILL

THREE FURTIVE MEN visited the library daily. Ostensibly they were taking advantage of Lady Clemente de Vesey's plan whereby promising persons in the neighbourhood were given free access to the library and encouraged to follow reading courses. Sir Richard, impressed with Clemente's argument that enlightenment was the most effective foe of insurrection, had agreed to act as patron to those who proved worthy of a University education.

The three daily visitors did not reveal the fact that their conversion to learning had been started by the fright they got when Martyn-Lynch shot the deputy from Dublin. They were three of the six men who had thrown down their torches and stampeded into the night. Of the others, two were the sons of Coyne, the farmer at whose cottage Denis and Mabs had breakfasted. The third they did not know. For all they knew, he had saved himself from hanging by offering to enlist. If the Republicans won, that action, if known, would give him no hope of a share when the property of the Quality came to be divided. They had either to be victors or martyrs or join the other side. There were martyrs enough already and there was little likelihood of victory, for their fathers had not much belief in the Revolution and preferred to keep what little land they had got than to risk taking leave of it all.

Actually, the three men sought an audience with Sir Richard, to crave a recommendation to Major Crabbe with the intention of enlisting among either his regulars or his mercenaries. Whether because the baronet knew what was needed in a soldier (loyalty, for one thing), or because he had learned from his agent that the men were needed on the estate, he refused shortly, and sent them about their business, which happened to be rebellion when they were at any business. Though their attempts to enlist did not meet with success, they would not have been there at all were it not for the library, as Madame explained.

Yes; Sir Richard conceded the point.

With so many new interests in the house, was it any wonder that Mabs's delinquency was, if not overlooked, uncorrected and the culprit unscolded? There was neither complaint nor punishment. Perhaps this showed that since her marriage to Sir Richard, Clemente had become less exacting and less prone to discipline his niece. So Mabs got off. She had run away once before and had not returned with her cousins. Now she had returned, and their misfortunes so closely related them that it was neither the time nor the place to single her out for a lecture.

As for the offence of running away with the horses, that was passed over because the story of their disappearance never reached Uncle Dick's ears. Had it been told to him, now that they were back, he would have been inclined to discount it as a tale told by the Toucher, full of hyperbole.

And the reason the tale never reached Sir Richard's ears was that Feeney had said to Tulip, when Mabs went off:

"We'll give her a day or two. Mebbe she'll get sick and tired of the Frinch. Hasn't she got Frinch enough in the house? And the sojers may be here shortly and mebbe himself will think she run away to save his cattle from Major Crabbe and his men."

Tulip had heartily concurred. He was countryman enough to know what to do when in the country. According to Feeney, even the horses were discreet. As he said later:

"There they were with their heads out of their loose boxes and not a wink out of them when Sir Richard come round the yard."

The Revolution was crushed at last by sending Cornwallis over from England with real soldiers. Those who suffered, purged from the dross of mortality, were added to the hierarchy of the martyrs who died for Ireland's cause. Ballads were composed in their honour.

They took their place beside the men of Wexford. Their defeat had endeared them to the hearts of a nation, whose badge was sufferance. Their punishment redeemed their past.

"Shaun O'Dwyer a Glanna, we're worsted in the game."

The nation sustained itself on grief. Woe betide any man who was not loyal to the memory of those who rose to right an immemorial wrong.

One morning Sir Richard, in a serious tone, said to Hyacinth:

"Come along into the smoking room, and we'll call Denis. I want to talk over this affair of the burnings with you two."

St. George was not in the house. He might be with Miss Mabs in the garden, a servant said.

Sir Richard discussed with Martyn the compensation which the Government proposed to give its loyal subjects who had suffered from the outrages of the miscreants, who had taken the law into their hands and had presumed to act for the nation against the better part of the nation's interests.

"I don't know whether I'm loyal or not," Hyacinth said, somewhat gloomily. He remembered the scenes in his own yard.

"That's all very fine, my boy," said Sir Richard. "But are you in a position to refuse money due to you by a Government that failed to give you the slightest protection from the Revolutionaries, though it was well aware of the condition of things in the country? Wexford was an example to them, which they failed to take into account. Are you bent upon making your child an heir to nothing? No, my boy, I must not talk to you like that. But leave the matter of compensation to me."

In the garden there was another member of the family who was of two minds like her cousin.

Denis had caught and cornered her in the greenhouse. She had been looking at the clusters which were still half-green on the vine. Against her breast she pressed a little stick no longer than a sulphur match, one of those used to keep blossoms supported. As if springing from some substance endowed with spontaneous expansion, it sprang out elastically and struck Denis in the eye. Cupid never so strangely nor so cunningly shot such an intimate dart.

Covered with confusion, Mabs did not know whether to run away or to attend to his eye. Who, without a mirror, can treat his own eye? Had she blinded him?

She was lost in solicitude. She came so near, he might never get her nearer. Suddenly he grasped her and held her fast. Gasping, but ignoring her position, she asked: "Have I blinded you?"

"Of course you have. Is not Love blind?"

"It was one of those little sticks for holding roses."

"Darling!"

"Oh, let me go!"

"Never, as I told you when I took you from your horse."

"You are squeezing me. I cannot see your eye."

"Don't mind my eye. It is all right. Let us be married, my darling, and I shall see the whole world coloured like a rose."

"I was engaged to Roddy," she said.

"Engaged to Roddy! You never wore an engagement ring. How was one to know?"

"He did not know it himself."

Dumfounded, he relaxed his grasp.

"But we would have been engaged all the same if he did."

Oh, amazing Mabs!

"Do you love me, darling, even the least little bit?" He pressed her again.

"I do not know whom I love," she said. And it was true, as true as Martyn's uncertainty as to where his loyalty lay.

"You are very young. But be engaged to me now."

"If you really want me."

And then the servant, acting without orders, came upon them to say that Sir Richard was inquiring as to his Honour's whereabouts. If you wanted the fellow to take a message in a hurry, he could never be found.

Aunt Penelope was invited to the family conference. There was no doubt that the Government was prepared to indemnify all who lost their property through action of the insurgents. There was much of it that was irreplaceable, such as the furniture, pictures, and tapestries of Attymon House and the silver and china of Martyn Hall. But a cash compensation would go some way towards enabling the sufferers to collect fine things again and, if they were so minded, to rebuild their mansions. About this rebuilding the discussion circled. It was rumoured that there would be no grant of money except on the condition that the house destroyed should be built in the district in which it had originally stood. This was to enable taxes to be levied, because, were there no great houses, there would be no people who could pay the taxes. The supposition was that these taxes went to the relief of the very poor.

Hyacinth was unwilling to build again. How could he collect rents from people not only impoverished but filled with hatred for the man whose house had been responsible for all their woes; for so facilely would run their reasoning. Denis, now that his mother was married to Constant d'Estournelles and still living at Lucan, was uncertain about planning for the future.

"There is someone I will have to consult before I will be in a position to decide," Denis said.

"Congratulations!" said Aunt Penelope, jumping to conclusions. "I hope that it will make her settle down."

"What's this I hear?" Sir Richard asked. "Wedding bells again?"

"Oh, tell me, tell me!" Clemente asked in her sweetest and demurest voice. No longer distrait, her temperament was as gentle as her intonation.

"This rogue," answered Sir Richard, "and that tomboy, my niece." He slapped Denis on the back with a thunderous, hearty blow. "Young limbs, my lad, young limbs!" he shouted. "And why the devil not?"

Though this gave St. George the assurance that her uncle would "place no obstacle," he foresaw a stormy interview with Mabs herself, who would hate to be taken for granted. But he also saw that this would be offset by the way her family had accepted him for her. Sir Richard's congratulations were as joyous and as binding as wedding bells. Mabs's mind would be made up for her by all that went before her—her family and its traditions.

He left the assembly, taking care to avoid a tête-a-tête with his lady. His precautions were unnecessary. Mabs was in no position for a tête-a-tête with anybody. As he went through the low woods, as distraught with joy as a man can be with desperation, he caught sight of the object of his hopes standing naked on a little rock at the base of which was the only deep pool that could give water enough to let a diver off unscathed, provided always that the diver could curve back and straighten up in time before cutting too deeply into the shallows. Her body was glistening. She had risked one dive and brought it off safely. She was sideways when he saw her. Then she disappeared. He heard her cut the water and awaited the gleam of her head. To his astonishment there was no sign of it. She was swimming under water, of course. Slowly he scouted to the margin of the wood, that wood that dipped its front ranks in the sea. No sign! Anxiety seized him, then terror. He ran the twenty yards that separated him from the sand and the rock. On the rock he stood. Through three feet of water he saw her lying still. Unhesitatingly he jumped in and lifted the limp and slippery body up. He carried her into the cover of the boskage. Her head lolled back insensible. He bethought him quickly. That was the wrong way. MacDermot had once said, "Get the water out of them first—water's enough to kill anyone anyway." He turned her over. Water gushed from her mouth. He laid her on her side and pressed her ribs. He turned her on her face again.

Although the action was not rhythmical, by good hap it synchronized with the time of natural respiration. Mabs opened her eyes. He risked another pressure on the ribs. Faint inarticulate sounds escaped. If they were of his making, for God's sake press again. And now she awakens. What is he to do? Her clothes are nowhere. Off with his coat, cover her up and run before she fully recovers consciousness.

When he dared to peer through the trees she was sitting up and looking about. He heard the farmyard bell calling all hands to their midday meal. Sir Richard was right. Sometimes we anticipate things which are near actualities. Wedding bells!

Later that evening: "I don't know what has come over that girl. I can only attribute the improvement to your influence, Clemente. I am sure your patience and consideration are well rewarded now," Aunt Penelope said when she found that Mabs was too shy even to appear at dinner "with all those men."

XXXIX. THE WOODS OF ARCADY ARE DEAD

No wood is lovelier than a wood of Irish ash trees. But where is one to be found? Nowhere now.

There were by the lake at Martyn Hall forty acres of an ash wood, the silver-gray boles of which made pillars for the rising and setting sun to aisle with light.

When Hyacinth rode over to thank the cotter who had given him and his party breakfast on the memorable morning of their escape, he saw only the stumps of the trees sticking up like headstones in some barbarous cemetery. The peasants had not been able to resist the destruction of his "ornamental woods." And yet those woods were not ornamental only. They had been planted by Martyn's grandfather so that shelter might be provided for the cows in the winter and the springtime, when the winds of March dried the udders and deprived children of milk. The peasants, their own worst enemies, had cut down his sheltering ash grove for firewood.

Over the white and broken stumps, chopped off at half the height of a man and left to be a scar on the land for many a day, he gazed at the charred skeleton of his house. The lake had lost nothing of its loveliness. It laughed in the light, for its immortal water was reckless of the hatred of peasant and the love of lord alike. The beauty of this gleaming, unsubstantial lake made the destruction of the less lasting trees seem, in some strange way, all the more criminal. No matter what side won, ruin always remained the victor in the end.

Regardless of all expressed ideals—love of country, liberty, elegance and civilization—no matter what device was borne upon the banners of those who owned the land, these things in time came to an end, but the inexorable law of ruin worked in favour of the peasant, because he allied himself to ruin. To realize this was disheartening, but it was maddening to remember the natural beauty that was destroyed when the wood of ash trees was cut down. Beauty that would take seventy years to restore. Seventy years! He had redress from neither Time nor Man. Dumb would be their expression and heavy and mute their attitude were he to expostulate with the tenants who had razed his estate. Their plea would be the perpetual plea, the plea of poverty, the peasants' stock in trade.

The bogs were too wet for cutting the turf, they would say, so they had to lay by a store of fuel for the winter, and what else had they but the wood? The truth was that they wanted (oh, that cursed word!) grazing land. For this the wood was ruined, for this the only shelter save the woods about the Hall was destroyed, and as a result of the want of shelter the cattle that were sent to the new "grazing" would be milkless until next spring. The children in the hovels would be milkless too, and subjected to all the ills of under-nourished childhood. As a more distant but equally sure result, when they grew up they would be nerve-starved from the stewed tea used in the place of milk, and many would become imbeciles or madmen. The imbeciles would remain, while the landlord had to yield.

Gone was that ash wood with its grassy floor so clean and free from undergrowth. The soft small grass that had carpeted their feet when he and Ninon first explored the great demesne had enriched the clean boles of the silver trees closely and trimly. When you turned you could see far through many bright groves, for the trees stood apart from each other, each keeping its distance and respecting the presence of its neighbour—aristocrats among trees, now fallen and destroyed, never to rise again and winnow the tremulous tides of light.

The leaves came late, for an ash wood does not suffer itself to be hustled like the hedgerows in the spring. In the autumn, when they fell, the leaves did not encumber the earth but faded or blew away, leaving the grassy smoothness clean. How much life there had been in his lovely wood! Hyacinth remembered how it never shuddered, but held calm boughs aloft like a living and sheltering presence when he wandered aimlessly in tempered light along its clear arcades. And now look at it! Not even cut properly, but left with half-torn stumps to stand hideous and repulsive for years to come.

It was strange how the loss of his wood went deeper into his heart than the loss of his home. The dull, obstinate, persistent peasant hatred was never manifested worse than here. You would think that these infesters of the land had seen into your mind with demoniacal cunning and destroyed all that you held dear and appreciated for its beauty. If the beauty and grandeur that were a part of him were reft, Hyacinth thought, was it not a sign that he too should go?

He would leave the land to the maggots who could thrive on decay and hideousness. Let it be forever the refuge of meanness, hate, suspicion and stultifying ignorance. Leave the country to its fate; and what worse fate could there be for any country than to be left to its peasantry?

He would not be the first Martyn or Lynch to go over the seas. Dublin would be too small for him. Deep in his soul was the sentiment of land. He would go where there was land and fenceless leagues of it to be had for the possessing. He would never rebuild Martyn Hall. What it stood for was undermined and its grandeur out of date, part of a past when the few were stronger than the many. The money the Government would grant might build a madhouse, a barrack, a lazar house or a gaol. Let the Government build some such structure and pay him for it at a valuation. Sir Richard was right. He must not leave his child an "heir to nothing." But what future for a gentleman was here?

He could not deny that a stigma was attached to emigration. But why was there a stigma? Because hitherto few but the persecuted and the outcast had gone to America. Even England had despised its colony, and had never encouraged any of its best to go to that recalcitrant and ungrateful land.

With him it would be different. His people were there before him. How many Irish had fought with Washington—an Englishman snubbed into resentment by Englishmen—no one could say. What mattered more was that he was great enough to recognize failure when he saw it confronting him, and to save his child from that heritage.

Goodbye to Martyn Hall! There was a land, greater than any of its inhabitants, that offered a large and unlimited life to all who had the courage and the foresight to wrench themselves out of the slough of custom and make a newer thoroughfare. In America even the climate helped in prolonging life. There were more lovely and liveable days in the dry bright air in a year, than five years could provide to a dweller in County Mayo. He would bring his blood stock to the wide meadows of Virginia or the rolling fields of Maryland and with it the tradition of horsemanship. It would be hard on Ninon, but if he could persuade Denis to come with him and bring his bride, Ninon would have her sister by her. And St. George had grand-aunts and grand-uncles in Virginia. Mabs was the lever now. The wild prospect would be sure to invite her, and once she was enlisted she would run to the first ship. Uncle Dick he would not expect, no; he would not even suggest it to the baronet. He would go on living with his Baroness in Dublin and Lisadill. Her nimble mind would keep him from vegetating and growing old. And Aunt Penelope would doubtless stay with her brother.

Hyacinth rode slowly back to Lisadill. As Feeney took his horse he noticed a few gloomy figures lurking, appearing not to move, along one of the sides of the yard.

"What are those men doing over there?"

"They came to see your Honour."

"Tell them to go to hell."

In the bitter mood that obsessed him he wanted to shut out forever the ominous sight of his slow-moving, lowering countrymen. They always hung about yards and back doors. Never did they come straight forward on any errand. They worked sideways like conspirators, and drew one's servants into every action, innocent or otherwise, that they devised.

In a change of mind, but chiefly in order to get rid of them, for well he knew that time to them meant nothing, and that they could wear him down by their patient, pathetic, ill-omened haunting of the yard, he asked:

"Feeney, what do they want?"

"They come on behalf of the servants that was at the Big House."

"Those blackguards who ran away?"

"They say that their wages was not paid."

"Wages? For what? For arrant cowardice and desertion?"

"They say that they have never been given notice and so was never dismissed."

His temper blazed. He walked up to the group.

"Off with you!" he said.

But you could not get rid of countrymen by merely telling them to clear out. You might as well without faculties try to lay a ghost. Hatred grew like a dank fungus in their inert souls.

Hyacinth turned his back on them and entered the house.

Dinner was at three o'clock. It was the fashion in the provinces of France, and Uncle Dick was being introduced to it now. Supper was the correct designation for the later feasts and claret routs to which he had been accustomed.

"Some scoundrels had the audacity to come here collecting for what they call 'a month's mind.' I told them to go to hell and sent them a crown," Sir Richard remarked as he seated himself at the head of the table.

Aunt Penelope asked:

"What is a month's mind?"

Clemente was able to answer her: "We have them in France. A month's mind is a religious celebration in honour of those who have been dead a month."

Sir Richard snorted.

"It will turn into an annuity if it is to be continued every year."

"I hardly think it will," Martyn said. "I would not object to it. It is a proof that the country people, instead of planning another rising, have resigned themselves to celebrating the victims of military severity." He was thinking of the scenes he had witnessed at the hanging of Father Colyer.

"But what I do object to," he continued, "is an attempt on the part of my servants to collect wages for abandoning me at Martyn Hall and leaving it to be entered and set on fire by their relatives and friends."

"I'd be damned before I paid them," Sir Richard said.

"I have no intention of paying them."

"Then why complain?" Penelope asked.

"Because I see in it an attempt to put me in the wrong. Mark you, none of my servants came in person. They stirred up sympathy, real or feigned, in your tenants here, and it was they who hulked about your yard looking for 'wages due.' This is a sinister sign of deep resentment which is directed now against this house, since they have none other on which to wreak their hate. It is this kind of conspiracy of hate that has determined me to take myself and family to America, and leave this country to its fate."

He looked to see what the effect of this would be on Ninon. Though she said nothing, he took her silence for acquiescence in his plans. She too had had her fill of insurrection. Far more than he did she regret the loss of her stately hall. A house is part of a woman's personality; she felt as if she had suffered some bodily hurt when the home she loved went up in flames. She was prepared to leave her country, not because it had left her homeless—that loss could be remedied—but because she wanted to take Hyacinth away from his bitter mood and the exasperating reminders of his lost happiness.

Sir Richard allowed himself one glass of port. He nursed his glass and said, when he had recovered from his surprise at Martyn's announcement:

"Why go from one revolution into another? Why, man, there is nothing but Puritans, Presbyterians and Red Indians over there. Don't forget that this state of things here cannot go on forever. Cornwallis is cleaning up effectively. Were it not for that, damme, I'd take myself out of the country once and for all."

Martyn said: "A revolution that succeeds is acceptable. What Cornwallis can never clean up is the feeling I have for what are, after all, I suppose, my own people. Why should I be made to entertain so much hate? It divides a man against himself."

This was serious talk for dinner, thought Sir Richard. He turned to Mabs. He would rally her.

"Do you think you would have room enough to exercise my horses in America?" he asked.

His remark was badly put. He had confused the girl. He had only meant to imply that he would give her a handsome present for her American farm if she were in the mind to go. Denis came to the rescue.

"We have both thought of going. My mother can rebuild Attymon House if she and Constant care to live again in Galway. But he is expecting reinstatement in France any day now. It has done him no harm in the minds of the authorities in Paris to be associated with Ireland. Paris is full of Irish émigrés from British rule. General Buonaparte is at heart an aristocrat, and the sympathy extended to émigrés overflows in favour of the Chevalier."

"I hope the same thing applies to you, my dear," said Sir Richard to his wife. He knew that she had often pined for her château in the south and though she had valiantly kept back her tears, her sorrow, suppressed, had turned bitter in her heart and made her more shrewish than nature meant her to be.

"We could spend the winters there," she said wistfully.

"Anywhere to get away from the damp!" Sir Richard exclaimed and shifted his leg. It had been agreed that since Sir Richard allowed himself only one glass, it was not wine but the weather that was responsible for the occasional swelling and pain in his foot. Provençal wines may have begun to ripen in his imagination. In France at least he could do as the French did; and they drank nothing but wine.

"There is one thing about America; it is easier to return from it than to reach it," Aunt Penelope contributed.

Her remark mitigated the apprehension that all of them felt for the parting that they knew had to come soon. It left a prospect open and seemed to make departure less final.

One day Kelly rode over from Attymon with a picture under his arm. He had saved it from the fire, by claiming it as a keepsake for himself. It was the Leonardo da Vinci. Madame was convinced of its genuineness.

Kelly reported the visit of one Skator, a picture fancier or dealer, who was visiting all the great mansions of the west intent on acquiring masterpieces at the depreciated prices that ruin brought in its train. He was a fat and plausible fellow full of the commercial tenderness of a dealer who assumed the social airs of those he was despoiling. With him went a tall, flashy woman, "just like one of the Quality, but her feet were too big." So Kelly assessed the dealer's companion.

The pleasure Denis felt at having the chief treasure of his mother's house restored to him was dampened by the remark Hyacinth made bitterly:

"A dealer and his drab! The vulture and the banshee! The Choosers of the Slain! The terrible harpy and the grinning wolf who only appear when a country is disintegrating, and its grandeur is going. Money-lenders and traders in beauty. They represent the unluckiest sight a man could see. God keep them from Lisadill."

But Clemente was unmoved by Hyacinth's diatribe. She was thinking only of the Old Master.

"I have the very place for it," she said, "over the mantel-piece."

The thought of the fungoid dealer and his "mort," like jackals over the graves of great houses, confirmed Hyacinth and comforted him in his resolve to leave the land. The undertakers of grandeur were arrogant in its halls.

Clemente herself had relatives in Virginia—or was it Maryland?—near the new territory of Kentucky that had been opened up. Denis' mother, Ellice d'Estournelles, had kinsfolk there. Martyn and he would fall amongst friends. With what remained of his winnings Martyn would buy an extensive farm for his bloodstock where the best limestone formed the foundation. Thank Heaven Feeney had saved the mare and foal on the night of August the twenty-second. The son of Green Glint would prance in another and more spacious clime.

Looking through the window at the rain-swept landscape, gray and desolate without the leaf, Sir Richard remarked:

"You have chosen the worst time of the year."

"It may be months before we can sail," Hyacinth said. "To say nothing of the season of storm, it is the worst time to put to sea because of the high cost of passage in wartime. But that must not postpone our preparations. Now that my mind is made up to go, any delay will be irksome."

Then, thinking that his words might sound ungracious to Sir Richard, he was about to qualify them when the baronet asked:

"Who have you got to keep you informed? How will you know when the ship, whether British or French, by which you intend to run what is little less than a blockade—with all these ships of the line, frigates and razees about—is to be found and where? Why, man, it seems to be impossible to leave the island."

"I have left it already," said Martyn-Lynch.

XL. TOMORROW TO FRESH WOODS

It was some weeks later that news came in the person of Toucher Plant. He who had helped in the landing of la Baronne and the Chevalier from France was now to arrange for the embarkation of Martyn-Lynch and his household from Ireland. The Toucher had apparelled himself in "sub-fusc" clothing and now looked like a parody of Dr. MacDermot. The circumspection of his manner, too, would have deceived anyone who had not met him before the assumption of such grave airs. When he was ushered into Martyn's presence he bowed with assurance. Hyacinth guessed by his confident manner that he had satisfactorily performed his mission, to find out when and where a suitable ship would sail.

"Have you found a ship?" he asked.

"Your Honour," said the Toucher proudly, "I have found two."

"Two?"

"One for Feeney and the horses. The other for your lady and yourself."

This was most satisfactory. At least it sounded so. The next thing to do was to ascertain where the crab would be. But on questioning Plant, Hyacinth could find no fault. Perkins had chartered a ship to take some bloodstock to America. He had not enough to fill it. There was ample space aboard for fifty horses. Whether he filled the space or not, he had to pay for the freight and the risk. He would be glad of a partner who would share his expenses.

"I wouldn't give a rogue like that more than fifty guineas, your Honour," the Toucher said. "The ship sails whether he fills it or not. He bought the space. If he hadn't, I would have dealt with the captain, meself."

"Who is the captain?"

"Captain Fayolles."

"A Frenchman. Why should Perkins, who is English, employ a Frenchman for business?"

"The very words I asked him, yer Honour! 'For business,' he says."

So Perkins was sending horses to America? With the detachment of an Englishman, permitting nothing to interfere with business, he must have realized that there was nothing but ruin in store for him if he remained in the land. If it cost an Englishman no pang to go abroad and take what America had to offer, why could Martyn not do likewise? If Perkins was sending his bloodstock to America, it meant that country was already prospering and that there were gentry there who took their delight in horses—a comforting thought.

As though sensing the trend of Martyn's thoughts, the Toucher said, "There's nothing doing on the race-courses now. All the Quality are removing their studs."

"Are there no English ships?" Hyacinth asked, not diverted by the last remark.

"They are all gone after General Buonaparte to Toulon, and that puts the price up for any that can remain and do a bit of private trade, while the seas round here are left open."

Martyn-Lynch thought that the Toucher's information was undoubtedly well founded, probably obtained from the Tyrrells, the fishermen of Arklow who had seen Clemente and Constant safely ashore. Hyacinth knew that he would never get at Plant's source, so forbore to question further. But Perkins's known sagacity and caution were assurance enough that the passage to America would be unobstructed.

"Why cannot I and my household go on that ship?"

"It is a French ship. Leave that to Perkins. I have an English ship for her Ladyship and yourself, with three masts in it and a room near the captain's. A room for boxes and a hold for furniture—saving your presence, I didn't mean to mention that," added the Toucher, remembering the end of the treasures of Martyn Hall.

"Well, between the horses on a French and the family on an English ship you have made tolerably certain that some remnant of Martyn Hall will reach America. I am obliged to you, Plant. I will meet you in Dublin as soon as you have got my animals from the Curragh safely aboard, wherever the French ship lies."

"She's coming into Waterford the first week in March. That's one reason Perkins chose her. You have to row out to meet the British ship and that would never do for horses that have to walk on board."

The realization that he was about to take an irretrievable step gave Martyn a pang. But after questioning the Toucher further and reassuring himself of the country's dismal outlook, he realized that he should take comfort from the thought that he was leaving a sinking ship.

"What makes you think that there is nothing doing, as you say, on the race-course?" he asked.

"Ah, yer Honour, and how could there be? All the gallus fellows who loved horses and to have a bit of a bet on are gone away. There is nothing left now but horse-jobbers and race-touts." Plant spoke contemptuously of the latter. "Mr. Wentworth is gone, and Mr. Bagshot; Mr. Luttrel is ruined and even Mr. Fosdyke. And the Buck, Sir—begging your pardon, I mean Mr. Jerusalem Whaley, him that done the twenty-foot jump on horse-back from his lobby window in St. Stephan's Green—they say he is reformed in the Isle o' Man. The big houses round Wexford is burned and even them that's left are not lit up window-for-window with dancing every night. There's nothing but suppressions going on and ye would never hear a laugh or music coming down from the drawing rooms where the ladies with the yellow dresses used to be leppin' in the good old days. No. Not if ye were to listen for a week. No. There's nothing doing on the turf."

At the end of this sad recital the Toucher smacked his lips, not because he relished his speech but because it had made him dry.

Hyacinth pulled a bell rope. Before he addressed the servant he turned to the Toucher and inquired, "Whiskey, I suppose?"

The Toucher sighed. "Begging yer Honour's pardon, I'd be vastly obleeged wid a glass of wine."

Outside in the stable yard, Feeney was becoming anxious. He missed Sir Richard from the field in which he had been exercising his horse. He could see the field and the smaller ones that lay between it and the gardens, but there was no sign of Sir Richard. It was getting late. Sir Richard could not have gone from the fields unless he took the boreen which lay sunken between the fields and the wood, and if he was riding up the boreen he should be coming into view now. If he were anywhere at all, it was in the hollow he would be, opposite to a little bridle-path from the wood. Look as he would there was no sign of Sir Richard.

Fear seized Feeney. He called Tulip. They saddled two of the farm horses and cantered down to the opening of the lane. A half-mile ride brought them right into a company of dragoons. The officer was talking to Sir Richard. Their horses were together. The troopers, half of whom had not emerged from the wood, held three men prisoners. They had been surprised as they lay in ambush on each side of the lane. These were the three who had obtained an interview with Sir Richard and had their requests for his help in joining the English Army peremptorily refused.

"Burn the country first," Sir Richard had said at the time, "and now you try to slip away from your rascality when the troopers are running you scoundrels to earth. If you were in earnest you should have joined long ago. No officer would trust the like of you."

Their application to Sir Richard, since he had rejected it, had been too great a secret to leave with him. He might tell it as a good story before the servants in the dining room and out it would leak. They would look like a trio of traitors to their country. With the month's mind for the martyrs who had given their lives for Ireland only just over, and everyone filled with sympathy for the heroic dead, their lives would not be safe for a moment. They and their families would be eternally disgraced. If it were known that they had asked

Sir Richard for a recommendation to the ranks of the Sassenach, they could hear the neighbours mocking their parents, "How are yer sojer sons?"

There were one or two agents still about in the country guarding against treachery and the survival of any who might know the secrets of the United Irishmen and could not be trusted to keep them. It came to this: It was Sir Richard's life or theirs. They had only two guns, but the three of them must be in on this quenching. It would never do to have one of their number, the one who did not fire, turning King's Evidence and getting off at the expense of the two who actually fired the fatal shots. No; Mihaul would aim the second gun and Paudeen would pull a cord attached to its trigger. They would get Sir Richard as he cantered back up the boreen. They would reload the gun and shoot his horse so that it could not gallop away and raise the alarm before they had time to bury their weapons and make good their escape. Fearlessly then, with honour unscathed, they could merge into the great company of patriots, until after a decade or two of patient hatred they could rise again and strike a blow for their native land against all such men as Sir Richard.

But the hoof-beats they heard were not those of Sir Richard's mount. They listened from their hiding places and were prepared to raise their heads and to peep out to make sure when to their consternation they heard the hooves not of one but of many horses. Too late! Troopers jumped down while others kept them covered. They were caught.

While the officer was interrogating them, up rode Sir Richard. The three men swore that they were on their way to the barracks with the only weapons they could find, to hand them in and to offer themselves for enlistment, and they appealed to Sir Richard to bear them out. Had they not petitioned the baronet weeks before to get them into the English ranks?

"Damme, it occurs to me that they did. That is, if these are the same fellows. I remember that they asked to see me and I said if they were in earnest they should have joined long before."

The officer smiled grimly.

"It will interest you to learn, Sir, that we caught these men lying on either side of this path with guns pointing into the lane. They had the obvious intention of murdering you as you walked your horse back from the lower field."

Sir Richard started in astonishment, causing his mount to rear. "Steady!" he cried. When he had controlled the horse, he said: "Shoot me? The ruffians! What the devil do they want to shoot me for? And with a blunderbuss!" he added as his eye caught sight of the short-range, murderous little cannon that had been taken from one of the prisoners.

"Send them to the devil out of this," he said to the officer, "and join us at supper."

The officer smiled and gave a short command. The company began to file away with the three men they had captured. As they moved off a last appeal could be heard like a wail:

"Ah, for the love of God, Sir Richard. And your own men too!"

Meanwhile, upstairs, Martyn was the prey of many conflicting and obstinate emotions. Was he alone, of all his friends, destined to go in new directions? Why had he not a few brothers, as Atty Persse had, so that he might curb his enemies by the only curb that held them—that of fear? Why could he not be like Sir Richard, whose means made him independent of Irish vicissitudes? Would the stigma of leaving his own country not be inherited by his child? Why should he be like the mandrake and shriek when torn up by the roots?

Since his night ride and his swim across the Shannon, Martyn had realized ruefully his proneness to precipitation. Was this sudden desire to be out of the country and to be done with it but another example of that nervous and exaggerated haste? What was troubling him was vacillation. Anything was to be preferred to that state of mind. Rather than betray such a state he had foreborne to ask Denis St. George if he could recall more of his grand-uncle's letters that had, when they did not directly praise Virginia, at least left it to be inferred that it was a country whose advantages needed no demonstration. The stately homes were there, a challenge to all returning visitors to disparage or to match. And the long recitals of those who had returned were witness enough that the land was more than a nine days' wonder. Life there, according to their comparisons, had many advantages over the life left open to men here. It was true that there were slaves, but the slaves were happy and part of the household, which was more than could be said of the serfs at home.

In what, he asked in self-depreciation, did his case differ, except in the advantage of birth and its privileges, from the case of his lower self, Toucher Plant? Were they not both living on the community? The Toucher's quarry had gone, the same men on whom he depended, if not for livelihood, at least for friendship and companionship. The gay companions had gone to England, whence they or their forebears had come.

Perhaps at the bottom of all his troubles was the fact that he was a remnant and a freak. His ancestors should have left their land in the Flight of the Earls or have spread a wing with the Wild Geese after Aughrim's fatal field. His friends originated from a different stock: Cromwellians and Williamites, whom the ruinous genius of the Old Lands had caught and infected with its out-of-date and heroic virtues —liberality, prodigality and mad grandeur. Their vigorous souls were spent. They were gone, all gone, the gay companions, the men who lived carelessly, the men of wit and worth, of gallantry and figure— all gone in a blaze of glory, like the young chivalry of Homer, and their vigorous souls were spent.

When Hyacinth had reduced his mind to the lowest depths of despondency, he began to recoil, by virtue of the Irish blood in his veins, from misery to exultation.

"Pluck up thy heart!" he adjured himself. Virginia! There were men of honour there. For one thing, it was the home of the descendants of the Cavaliers who had fought against that sour-faced and savage Cromwell, the man who murdered his King. And had he not read of a duel lately? There must be worthy men and gallants there. Not to mention the sturdy yeomen who had starved and stood by Washington in as dark days as these. And there were Lynches there too. If not exactly in Virginia, then somewhere close by. Was not Lynchburg in Virginia? The clan was everywhere in Freedom's van. He would not be too far from home.

Perhaps he was too closely concerned with his surroundings to take a longer and more liberal view. What Roman scented the Fall of Rome until he stood amid its ruins? For all he knew it was the end of an era, a short flaring-up of glory in Ireland; of a splendour and magnificence the land might never see again. Grandeur had gone mad and was being destroyed, and the tendency of the time pointed towards a levelling. Signs were not far to seek on the Continent, whence all that was new arose, and where changes took place more quickly than in this cul-de-sac of Western Europe, this shelf over an ocean far removed from all factors that made for change. Virginia! He had read of the fenceless fields of that land.

As if sent to dispel his doubting mood, Denis St. George came in exultant. He, though his mind was neither deep nor contemplative, had seized the situation more rapidly, and it appeared to present no qualms to him.

"She says that she'll marry me in Virginia," he blurted out.

"Excellent, excellent," Hyacinth answered, not yet fully extricated from his own thoughts.

Not noticing his friend's preoccupation, Denis went rapturously on:

"There are parsons enough in that country, if we are to believe my mother's uncle, who writes occasionally. One thing she remarked to me about his letters was this: that they never spoke with much concern about Europe. He seems self-contained and quite contented with his life in the Old Dominion. He finds it more spacious and inexhaustible, if you see what I mean. You might gallop for days without coming within sight of a boundary to his estate. That's the place!"

It was just the right note finally to dispel Hyacinth's gloom. If this youth, he thought, with all life before him, can look forward with such enthusiasm to leaving Ireland, why not I? What holds me here? My ancestors? By Gad, that's the family churchyard!

"What does he do?" Hyacinth asked.

"Apples and bees, and he raises cows and blood stock somewhere on the Shenandoah River, a land flowing with milk and honey . . . and everything."

Hyacinth said, releasing his mind from his bitter mood:

"I suppose he crossed a cow with one of the Toucher's 'stallion bees'!" It was not like Martyn; Denis was taken aback, but he entered into the jest.

"That probably is the reason why the cow jumped over the moon. Anything is possible in America. But grand-uncle spoke of a place called the Blue Ridge, where there is limestone in the soil, and where they can raise horses as well-boned as any in Meath or Tipperary. We will bring our studs out there and show the Americans what a blood horse is. All I am waiting for is spring and a good east wind."

Martyn, who had given much thought to the voyage, said:

"The prevailing wind is west. That makes it hard to sail out, but all the more easy to come back."

"Come back to what?" asked Denis St. George.